KU-002-811

The Shivering Sands

Born Eleanor Alice Burford, Victoria Holt was one of Britain's most prolific writers of historical romance, writing 183 books over the course of her career. Always determined to keep her birth date and private life a closely guarded secret Holt wrote under many pseudonyms – Jean Plaidy was one of her most popular, and was created when she lived near Plaidy Beach in Cornwall. She decided to be a novelist at an early age but did not publish her first book, *Beyond the Blue Mountains*, until 1947. Having written over ninety historical romances, she then began a new series of Gothic romances, the first of which, *Mistress of Mellyn*, appeared in 1961. *The Shivering Sands* was first published in 1969 as part of the same series. She died at sea in January 1993, somewhere between Greece and Port Said, Egypt.

Visit www.AuthorTracker.co.uk for exclusive updates on your favourite HarperCollins authors.

BY THE SAME AUTHOR

Mistress of Mellyn
Kirkland Revels
Bride of Pendorric
The Legend of the Seventh Virgin
Menfreya
The King of the Castle
The Queen's Confession
The Secret Woman
The Shadow of the Lynx
On the Night of the Seventh Moon
The Curse of the Kings
The House of a Thousand Lanterns
Lord of the Far Island
The Pride of the Peacock
The Devil on Horseback
My Enemy the Queen
The Spring of the Tiger
The Mask of the Enchantress
The Judas Kiss
The Demon Lover
The Time of the Hunter's Moon
The Landower Legacy
The Captive
Secret for a Nightingale
The Silk Vendetta
Snare of Serpents
The India Fan
Daughter of Deceit

VICTORIA HOLT

The Shivering Sands

HARPER

This novel is entirely a work of fiction.
The names, characters and incidents portrayed in it are
the work of the author's imagination. Any resemblance to
actual persons, living or dead, events or localities is
entirely coincidental.

Harper
An imprint of HarperCollinsPublishers
77–85 Fulham Palace Road,
Hammersmith, London W6 8JB

www.harpercollins.co.uk

This paperback edition 2006
1

First published in Great Britain by
William Collins 1969

Copyright © Victoria Holt 1969

Victoria Holt asserts the moral right to
be identified as the author of this work

ISBN-13 978 0 00 723554 4
ISBN-10 0 00 723554 2

Typeset in Sabon by Palimpsest Book Production Limited,
Kemfine, Earls Road, Grangemouth, Stirlingshire FK3 8XG
Printed and bound in Great Britain by
Clays Ltd, St Ives plc

All rights reserved. No part of this publication may be
reproduced, stored in a retrieval system, or transmitted,
in any form or by any means, electronic, mechanical,
photocopying, recording or otherwise, without the prior
permission of the publishers.

This book is sold subject to the condition that it shall not,
by way of trade or otherwise, be lent, re-sold, hired out or
otherwise circulated without the publisher's prior consent
in any form of binding or cover other than that in which it
is published and without a similar condition including this
condition being imposed on the subsequent purchaser.

Chapter One

I am wondering where I should begin my story. Should it be on the day when I saw Napier and Edith being married in the little church at Lovat Mill? Or when I was sitting in the train starting out on my journey to discover the truth behind the disappearance of my sister Roma? So much of importance happened before either of these significant events; yet perhaps I should choose the second alternative because it was then that I became inescapably involved.

Roma – my practical, reliable sister – had disappeared. There had been inquiries; there had been theories; but no indication of where she had gone had been revealed. I believed the solution to the mystery was to be found where she had last been seen; and I was determined to discover what had happened to her. My concern for Roma was helping me over a difficult period of my life, for sitting in that train was a lonely and bereaved woman – broken hearted, I should have said had I been a sentimentalist, which I was not. Indeed, I was a cynic – so I assured myself. Life with Pietro had made me so. Now here I was without Pietro, like a piece of driftwood – lost and aimless – and with only the smallest of incomes which it was imperative to augment by some means, when this opportunity was offered to me by what appeared to be the benign hand of fate.

When it had been clear to me that I must do something if I wanted to eat adequately and keep a water-tight roof over my head, I had tried taking pupils and I had a few but the money this brought in was not enough. I had believed that in time I should build up a clientele and perhaps discover a young genius which would have made my life worth while; but so far my ears had been in constant rebellion against halting renderings of *The Blue Bells o Scotland* and no budding Beethoven ever sat on my piano stool.

I was a woman who had tasted life and found it bitter – no, bitter-sweet, as all life is; but the sweetness was gone and the bitterness remained. Poised, yes, and experienced; the thick gold band on the third finger of my left hand bore evidence of that. Young to be so bitter? I was all of twenty-eight, but that would generally be agreed to be young to have become a widow.

The train had travelled through the Kent countryside, that 'Garden of England' which would shortly be pink and white with blossoming cherry, plum and apple, past hopfields and cowled oast houses, and was plunging into a tunnel to emerge a few moments later into the uncertain sunshine of a March afternoon. The coastline from Folkestone to Dover was startlingly white against the grey green sea and a few grey clouds were being scurried across the sky by a tetchy east wind. It was sending the water hurtling against the cliffs so that the spray shone like silver.

Perhaps, like the train, I was emerging from my dark tunnel and coming into sunshine.

It was the sort of remark which would have made Pietro laugh. He would have pointed out what a romantic I was under that entirely false facade of worldliness.

Such uncertain sunshine, I noticed at once, with a hint of cruelty in the wind – and the ever unpredictable sea.

Then I suffered the familiar grief, the longing, the frustration, and Pietro's face rose up from the past as though to say: A new life? You mean a life without me. Do you think you will ever escape from me?

No, was the answer to that. Never. You will always be there, Pietro. There is no escape . . . not even the grave.

Tomb, I told myself flippantly, would sound so much better. Much more Grand Opera. That was what Pietro would have said – Pietro my lover and rival, the one who charmed and soothed, the one who taunted, who inspired and destroyed. There was no escape. He would always be there in the shadows – the man with and without whom it was impossible to be happy.

But I had not come on this journey to think of Pietro. The object was to forget him. I must think of Roma.

Now I should say something about the events which led up to this moment, how Roma came to be at Lovat Mill and how I met Pietro.

Roma was two years my senior and we were the only children. Both our mother and father had been dedicated archæologists to whom the discovery of ancient relics was of far greater importance than being parents. They constantly disappeared on 'digs' and their attitude towards us was one of vague benevolence which was at least unobtrusive and therefore not unwelcome. Mother had been something of a phenomenon for it was unusual in those days for a woman to take a part in archæological exploration and it was through her interest in the subject that she met Father. They married, no doubt expecting a life of exploration and discovery; this they started to enjoy until it was interrupted first by the arrival of Roma and then by myself. Our appearances could not exactly have been welcomed but they were determined to do their duty by us and at early ages we were shown pictures of flint and bronze weapons discovered in Britain and were expected to show the interest most young children would have felt for a jigsaw puzzle. It soon became apparent that Roma did feel this interest. My father made excuses for my youth. 'It'll come,' he said. 'After all, Roma's two years older. Look, Caroline, an entire Roman bath. Almost intact. What do you think of that, eh?'

Roma was already their favourite. Not that she set out to be. This overwhelming passion had been born in her; she did not have to pretend. Perhaps rather cynically for one so young, I would try to assess my own value in my parents' eyes. As much as a pieced-together necklace of the Bronze Age? Not quite. Not to be compared with a Roman mosaic floor. A flint from the Stone Age? Perhaps, for they were fairly common.

'I wish,' I used to say to Roma, 'we had more *ordinary* parents. I'd like them to be angry sometimes . . . perhaps they could beat us – for our own good of course, which is how all parents excuse themselves. That would be rather fun.'

Roma, in her matter-of-fact way, retorted: 'Don't be silly. You'd be furious if they beat you. You'd kick and scream. I know you. You only want what you haven't got. When I'm a little older Papa will take me on a dig.'

Her eyes shone. She could scarcely wait for the day.

'They're always telling us we must grow up to do *useful* work.'

'Well, so we should.'

'But it only means one thing. We have to grow up to be archæologists.'

'We're lucky,' stated Roma. She always made statements; she was so sure that what she said was right; in

4

fact she wouldn't have said it until she was sure. That was Roma.

I was the odd one, the frivolous one, who liked to juggle with words, rather than relics of the past, who saw something amusing when she should have been serious. I didn't really fit into my own family.

Roma and I were often at the British Museum, with which my father was connected. We would be told we might amuse ourselves there with the implication that we had been given the entry into some holy place. I remember walking on the sacred stones and pausing, my nose pressed against cold glass, to examine weapons, pottery and jewellery. Roma would be entranced; and later she always wore odd beads, usually of rough hewn turquoise matrix or chunks of amber and badly drilled cornelian – her ornaments always looked prehistoric as though they had been dug up from some long ago cave. I suppose that was why they appealed to her.

Then I discovered an interest of my very own. From my earliest memories I was interested in sounds. I loved that of trickling water, the sounds of fountains playing, the clop-clop of horses' hoofs on the road, the call of the street traders; the wind in the pear tree in our tiny walled garden in the house near the Museum, the shouts of children, the birds in springtime, the sudden bark of a dog. I could even hear music in the dripping of a tap which exasperated others. When I was five years old I could pick out a tune on the piano, and would spend hours perched on the stool, my hands, scarcely emerged from their bracelets of baby fat, exploiting the miracle of sound. 'If it keeps her quiet . . .' shrugged the nannies.

When my parents noticed my passion they were mildly pleased. It was not archæology of course but it was a worthy substitute; and in view of what happened I am ashamed to say that I was given every opportunity.

5

Roma had pleased them; even her school holidays were spent with my parents on 'digs'. I had my music lessons, and stayed at home in the charge of our housekeeper to practise the piano. I improved steadily and the best teachers were found for me although we were not well off. Father's salary was just about adequate, for he spent a great deal of his personal income on his excavations. Roma was studying archæology and our parents used to say that she would go much further than they had been able to, for discovery added to the knowledge not only of the past but of working methods.

I used to hear them all talking sometimes. It sounded like gibberish to me, but I was no longer an outsider because everyone said that I was going to succeed with my music. My lessons were a joy to me and my teachers. Whenever I see stumbling fingers on the piano I remember those days of discovery – the first gratification, the sheer abandonment to pleasure. I became tolerant towards my family. I understood how they felt about their flints and bronzes. Life had something to offer me. It gave me Beethoven, Mozart and Chopin.

When I was eighteen I went to Paris to study. Roma was at the University and as her vacations were spent on the 'digs' I saw little of her. We had always been good, though never close, friends, our interests being so wide apart.

It was in Paris that I met Pietro, fiery Latin, half French half Italian. Our music master owned a big house not far from the Rue de Rivoli and there we students lived. Madame, his wife, ran the place as a *pension* which meant that we were all gathered together under one roof.

What happy days when we wandered in the Bois and sat outside the cafés all talking about the future. Everyone of us believed that we were the chosen and that our fame would one day resound round the world. Pietro and I were two of the most promising pupils, both ambitious and determined. Our emotions were first stirred by rivalry but we were soon completely fascinated by each other. We were young. Paris in the spring is the perfect background for lovers and I felt that I had never really lived until this time. The ecstasy and the despair I experienced were the true stuff of life, I told myself. I was sorry for everyone who was not studying music in Paris and in love with a fellow student.

Pietro was the complete and dedicated musician. I knew in my heart that he surpassed me and this made him all the more important to me. He was different from me. I feigned a detachment which I did not feel and although he knew that in the beginning I was as involved, as determined as he, it exasperated while it fascinated him that I could disguise this. He was absolutely serious in his dedication; I could pretend to be flippant about mine. I was rarely ruffled; he was rarely anything else and my serenity was a constant challenge to him, for his moods changed with every hour. He could be inspired to great joy which had its roots in his belief in his own genius; and in no time he could be plunged into despair because he doubted his complete and unassailable gifts. Like so many artists he was completely ruthless and unable to conquer his envy. When I was praised he was, deep down in himself, angry and would seek to say something wounding; but when I did badly and was in need of comfort, he was the most sympathetic of companions. Nobody could have been kinder at such times and it was this absolute understanding, this complete sympathy which made me love him. If only I could have seen him then as clearly as I saw this ghost who was constantly appearing beside me!

We began to bicker. 'Excellent, Franz Liszt,' I would cry when he played one of the Hungarian Rhapsodies, pounding the piano, flinging back his leonine head in a good imitation of the master.

'Envy is the bane of all artists, Caro.'

'And one with which you are on familiar terms.'

He admitted it. 'After all,' he pointed out, 'excuses must be made for the greatest artist of us all. You will discover that in time.'

He was right. I did.

He said I was an excellent interpreter. I could perform gymnastics on the piano, but an artist was a creator.

I would retort, 'Was it you, then, who composed the piece you have just played?'

'If the composer could have heard my rendering he would know he had not lived in vain.'

'Conceit,' I mocked.

'Rather the assurance of the artist, dear Caro.'

It was only half in jest. Pietro believed in himself. He lived for music. I was continually teasing; I clung to our rivalry but this may have been because subconsciously I knew that it was that rivalry which had attracted him in the first place. It was not that, loving him, I did not wish him all the success in the world. I was, in fact, ready to give up my ambition for his sake – as I was to prove. But our bickering was a form of love-making; and it sometimes seemed that his desire to show me that he was my superior was an essential part of his love for me.

It is no use making excuses. All Pietro said of me was true. I was an interpreter, a performer of gymnastics on the piano. I was not an artist, for artists do not allow other desires and impulses to divert them. I did not work; at a vital stage of my career I faltered, I failed, and my promise was one of those which were never redeemed; and while I dreamed of Pietro, Pietro was dreaming of success.

My life was suddenly disorganised. Later I blamed what

I called ill luck for what happened. My parents had gone to Greece on a dig. Roma was to have gone with them for she was a fully-fledged archæologist by this time, but she wrote to me that she had a commission to go up to the Wall – Hadrian's of course – and that she would be unable to go with our parents. Had she gone I might not have been travelling up to Lovat Mill; for I should never have thought there was anything significant about the place. My parents were both killed in a railway accident on their way to Greece. I went home to the memorial service, and Roma and I were together for a few days in the old house near the British Museum. I was shocked, but poor Roma had been close to our parents and was going to miss them bitterly. She was as ever philosophical. They had died together, she said, and it would have been more tragic if one of them had been left; they had had a happy life. In spite of her sorrow she would make what arrangements had to be made and then go back to work at the Wall. She was practical, precise, she would never become emotionally involved as I was fast becoming. She said we would sell the house and furniture and the proceeds would be divided between us. There was not much but my share would enable me to complete my musical education, and I should be grateful for that.

Death is always disturbing and I went back to Paris feeling dazed and uneasy. I thought a great deal of my parents and was grateful for so much that I had casually accepted. Afterwards I said it was due to my loss that I behaved as I did. Pietro was waiting for me; he was in control now; he was surpassing all the rest of us; he was beginning to put that great gap between us and himself that always divides the real artist from those who are merely talented.

He asked me to marry him. He loved me, he said; he had realised how much while I had been away, and when he had seen me so deeply shocked by my parents' death his great desire was to protect me, to make me happy again. To marry Pietro! To spend my whole life with him! It filled me with elation even while I sadly mourned my parents.

Our music master was aware of what was happening for he watched us all carefully. He had made up his mind at this stage that while I could doubtless go a long way in my musical career, Pietro was going to be one of the blazing stars in the musical sky; and I realise now that he had asked himself whether this marriage was going to help or hinder Pietro in his career. And mine? Naturally a talented player must take second place to a genius.

Madame, his wife, was more romantic. She took an opportunity of talking to me alone.

'So you love him?' she said. 'You love him enough to marry him?'

I said fervently that I loved him completely.

'Wait a while. You have suffered a great shock. You should have time to think. Do you understand what this could mean to your career?'

'What should it mean? It will be good for it. Two musicians together.'

'Such a musician,' she reminded me. 'He is like all artists. Greedy. I know him well. He is a very great artist. Maestro believes it is a genius we have there. Your career, my dear, would have to take second place to his, and it is dangerous for an artist to settle for second place. If you marry him you may well be just a good pianist . . . a very good one without doubt. But perhaps it is good-bye to dreams of the big success, to fame and fortune. Have you thought of this?'

I didn't believe her. I was young and in love. It might be difficult for two ambitious people to live together in harmony; but we would succeed where others had failed.

Pietro laughed when I told him of Madame's warning and I laughed with him. Life was going to be wonderful, he assured me. 'We'll work together, Caro, for the rest of our lives.'

So I married Pietro and quickly learned that Madame's advice should not have been dismissed so lightly. I didn't care. My ambition had changed. I no longer felt the deep urge to succeed. All I wanted was for Pietro to do so; and for a few months I was certain that I had achieved my purpose in life which was to be with Pietro, to work with Pietro, to live for Pietro. But how could I have been so foolish as to imagine life could be so simply docketed, like papers that were safely filed away under the heading 'Married and lived happily ever after'?

Pietro's first concert decided his future; he was acclaimed; and those were wonderful days of achievement, when he went from success to success, but he did not become easier to live with because of this. He demanded service; he was the artist, and I was musician enough to be told of his plans, to listen to his renderings. He had success beyond even his grandiose dreams. I can see now that he was too young to cope with the attention which came his way. It was inevitable that there should be those who smothered him with adulation . . . women, beautiful and rich. But he always wanted me there in the background, the one to whom he could always return, the one who was a near artist herself, who understood the constant demands of the artistic ego. No one could be as close to him as I was. Besides, in his way he loved me.

Had I been of a different temperament we might have managed. But meekness was a quality I had never possessed. I was not slave material, I pointed out to him, and I was soon bitterly regretting my folly in jettisoning my own career. I was practising again. Pietro laughed at me. Did I think one could dismiss the Muse and then summon her back when one felt like seeing her again? How right he was. I had had my chance, thrown it away and now would never be anything but a competent pianist.

We quarrelled constantly. I told him I would not stay with him. I contemplated leaving him, all the time knowing I never would; and maddeningly so did he. I was anxious for his health because he was squandering it recklessly and I had discovered that he was not strong. I had noticed a certain breathlessness which alarmed me, but when I mentioned this he shrugged it aside.

Pietro was giving concerts in Vienna and Rome as well as in London and Paris and was beginning to be spoken of as one of the greatest pianists of the day. He took all the praise as natural and inevitable; he grew more arrogant; he gloated over everything that was written of him. He liked to see me pasting the cuttings into a book. This was my rightful place in his life – his devoted minion who had thrown aside her own career to further his. But like everything else the book was a mixed blessing, for the mildest criticism could throw him into a fury which would make the veins stand out at his temples and take his breath away.

He was working hard and celebrating the success of his concerts far into the night, and then he would be up early for his hours of practice. He was surrounded by sycophants. It was as though he needed them to keep alive his belief in himself. I was critical, not realising then how young he was and that it is often more of a tragedy than a blessing when success of this magnitude comes too early. It was an unnatural life . . . an uneasy life; and during it I learned that I could never be happy with Pietro, yet could not face a life without him.

We came to London for a series of concerts and I had an opportunity of seeing Roma. She had taken rooms near the British Museum where she now worked in between digs.

She was her old self, sturdy, full of common sense, jangling her weird prehistoric bracelets, a chain of uneven rather cloudy looking cornelians about her neck. She referred to our parents in a sad though rather brisk way, and asked after my own affairs, but of course I did not tell her very much. I could see that she thought it was rather strange of me to have given up a career after having spent so much time and energy on it – and all for the sake of marriage. But Roma had never been one to criticise. She was one of the most sane and tolerant people I had ever known.

'I'm glad I was here when you came. A week later I should have been away. Going to a place called Lovat Mill.'

'A mill?'

'That's merely the name of the place. On the Kent coast . . . not all that far from Cæsar's Camp, so it's not surprising really. We discovered the amphitheatre and I'm certain that there's more to be found because as you know these amphitheatres were invariably found outside the cities.'

I didn't know but I refrained from remarking on this.

Roma went on. 'It means excavating on the local Nabob's land. It was quite a bit of trouble getting his permission.'

'Really?'

'This Sir William Stacy owns most of the land round about . . . a difficult gentleman, I do assure you. He made a fuss about his pheasants and his trees. I saw him personally. "You cannot think your pheasants and trees are more important than history?" I demanded. And in the end I wore him down. He's given his consent for us to excavate on his land. It's a really ancient house . . . more like a castle. He has plenty of land to spare. So he can allow us this little bit.'

I wasn't paying much attention because I was hearing the second movement of the Beethoven No. 4 Piano Concerto, which was what Pietro would be playing that night, and I was asking myself whether or not I should go to the concert.

I suffered agonies when he was on a platform, playing each note with him in my mind, terrified that he would stumble. As if he ever would. His only fear would be that he would give something less than his best performance.

'Interesting old place,' Roma was saying. 'I think Sir William is secretly hoping we may find something of importance on his estate.'

She went on talking about the site and what she hoped to do there, now and then throwing in an observation about the people in the big house nearby; and I didn't listen. How was I to know that this was to be Roma's last dig, and that it was imperative to learn all I could about the place.

Death! How it hovers over us when we least suspect it. I have noticed how it will strike in the same direction in quick succession. My parents had died unexpectedly and before that I never gave a thought to death.

Pietro and I left London for Paris. Nothing unusual happened that day; there was no premonition to warn me. Pietro was to play some Hungarian dances and the Rhapsody No. 2. He was strung up – but he always was before a performance. I sat in the front row of the stalls and he was very much aware of me there. I sometimes had the impression that he played for me, as though to say, 'You see, you could never have reached this standard. You were only the performer of gymnastics on the piano.' And that was how it was that night.

Then he went to his dressing-room and collapsed with a heart attack. He did not die immediately, but there were only two days left to us. I was with him every minute and I believe he was conscious of me there for now and then his dark soulful eyes would look into mine, half mocking, half loving as though to say he had scored over me yet again. Then he died and I was free from bondage to mourn forever and long for those beloved chains.

Roma, like the good sister she was, left her dig and came to Paris for the funeral, which was a grand affair. Musicians from all over the world sent tributes; and many came to pay personal homage. Pietro had never been so famous alive as he was dead. And how he would have revelled in it!

But the shouting and the tumult was over and I was left in an abyss so dark and so desolate that I was in greater despair than I thought possible.

Dear Roma! What a solace she was at that time! She showed so clearly that she would have done anything for me, and I was deeply touched. I had sometimes felt shut out when I had heard her and my parents discussing their work together; I no longer felt that. It was a wonderful comfort to belong, to feel these family ties; and I was grateful to Roma.

She offered me the greatest consolation that she could imagine. 'Come to England,' she said. 'Come down to the dig. Our finds were beyond expectations – one of the best Roman villas outside Verulamium.'

I smiled at her and wanted to tell her how I appreciated her. 'I shouldn't be of any use,' I protested. 'Only a hindrance.'

'What nonsense!' She was the elder sister again and going to take care of me whether I liked it or not. 'In any case, you're coming.'

So I went to Lovat Stacy and found comfort in the company of my sister. I was proud of her when she introduced me to friends on the dig, for it was clear what respect they had for her. She would talk to me with that enthusiasm of hers, and because I was so glad of her company and that affection which she had always tried not to show but which was so obviously there, I became mildly interested in the work. These people were so fervent that it was impossible to be unaffected. There was a small cottage, not far from the Roman villa, which Sir William Stacy allowed Roma to use and I shared this with her. It was primitive and had a couple of beds and a table and a few chairs and little else. The lower room was cluttered with archæological tools – shovels and forks and picks, trowels and bellows. Roma was delighted with the place because as she said, it was so close to the dig and the others were scattered about the place lodging in cottages and at the local inn.

She took me over the finds and showed me the mosaic pavement, which was the delight of her life; she pointed out the geometrical patterns of white chalk and red sandstone; she insisted on my examining the three baths they had discovered which showed, she informed me, that the house had belonged to a nobleman of some wealth. There was the tepidarium, the calidarium and the frigidarium. The Roman terms rolled off her tongue in a kind of ecstasy and I felt alive again as I listened to her enthusiasm.

We went for walks together and I grew closer to my sister than I had ever been before. She took me to Folkestone to show me Cæsar's Camp; and I walked with her to Sugar Loaf Hill and St Thomas's Well at which the pilgrims on their way to the shrine of St Thomas à Becket had paused to drink. Together we climbed the four hundred feet or so to the summit of Cæsar's Camp and I shall never forget her standing there with the wind ruffling her fine hair, her eyes brilliant with delight as she indicated the earthworks and entrenchments. It was a clear day and as I looked across that twenty miles or so of calm translucent sea I could clearly make out the land which was Cæsar's Gaul and it was not difficult to imagine the legions on the march.

On another occasion we went to Richborough Castle – one of the most remarkable relics of Roman Britain, Roma told me. 'Rutupiae,' she called it.

'Claudius made it the principal landing place for his legions crossing from Boulogne. These walls give you a good idea of what a formidable fortress it must have been.'

She took great delight in showing me the wine cellars, the granaries and the remains of the temples, and it was impossible not to share in her excitement as she pointed out these wonders to me – the remains of massive walls of Portland stone, the bastion and its postern gate, the subterranean passage.

'You should take up archæology as a hobby,' she told me half wistfully, half hopefully. She really believed that if I would I could not fail to find the compensation in life which I so badly needed. I wanted to tell her that she herself was a compensation; I wanted her to know that her care of me and her affection had helped me so much because she had made me feel that I was not alone.

One could not, however, talk of such things to Roma; she would have cried: 'Nonsense!' if I had tried to thank her. But I promised myself that in the future I would see more of her; I would interest myself in her work; I would let her know how glad I was that I had a sister.

And trying to lure me to forgetfulness she set me to help in restoring a mosaic plaque which had been found on the spot. It was specialised work and my task was merely confined to fetching the brushes and solutions which were needed. It was a yellowish disc on which was some sort of picture and the object was to restore that picture to something like it had originally been. It was too delicate a job for the pieces to be moved, Roma told me, but when it was completed it would have a place in the British Museum. I was fascinated by the care and minute attention which went into the restoration and again I was catching some of the excitement as the pieces were fitted together.

And then I discovered Lovat Stacy itself – the big house which dominated the neighbourhood and by the grace of whose owner Roma and her friends had been allowed to excavate.

I came upon it suddenly and caught my breath with wonder. The great Gate Tower stood dominating the landscape. This consisted of a central tower flanked on either side by two higher and projecting octagonal towers. As I looked up at these battlements I was impressed by the aggressive aspect of power and strength. Tall narrow windows looked out from the tower. I could see through the gate the high stone walls beyond. Leading to the gateway was a road flanked on both sides by stone walls on which grew moss and lichen. I was enchanted and for the first time since Pietro's death I ceased to think of him for some few minutes and experienced an almost irresistible urge to walk up that road and pass under the gateway to see what was on the other side. I even began to but as I started up the road I saw the carved gargoyles over the gateway – venomous, cruel looking creatures – and I hesitated. It was almost as though they were warning me to keep out, and I stopped myself in time. One simply did not go walking into people's houses merely because they excited one.

I went back to the cottage full of what I had seen.

'Oh, that's Lovat Stacy,' explained Roma. 'Thank goodness they didn't build the house over the villa.'

'What about these Stacys,' I asked. 'Is there a family?'

'Oh yes.'

'I'd like to know about people who live in a house like that.'

'My concern was with Sir William – the old man. He's the lord and master, so he was the one who could give the permission we wanted.'

Dear Roma. I would get nothing from her. She saw life only in the terms of archæology.

But I found Essie Elgin.

When I was starting on my musical career I had been sent to a music school and Miss Elgin had been one of my teachers. Taking a walk in the little town of Lovat Mill a mile or so from the dig I met Essie in the High Street. We looked at each other in bewilderment for some seconds and then she said in that Scots accent of hers, 'Well, I do believe, it's wee Caroline.'

'No longer so wee,' I told her. 'And of course . . . Miss Elgin.'

'And what would ye be doing here?' she wanted to know.

I told her. She nodded gravely when I mentioned Pietro. 'A terrible tragedy,' she said. 'I heard him in London when he was last there. I went up specially for the concert. What a master!'

She looked at me sadly. I knew that she was thinking of me in that regretful way in which teachers think of pupils who have not fulfilled their promises.

'Come into my little house,' she said. She pronounced it hoose. 'I'll put the kettle on and we'll have a chitter-chatter together.'

So I went and she told me how she had come to Lovat Mill because she wanted to be near the sea and was not yet ready to give up her independence. She had a younger sister three or four miles out of Edinburgh who wanted her to go up there and live and she reckoned she would come to it in time; but here she was enjoying what she called her last years of freedom.

'Teaching?' I asked.

She grimaced. 'What some of us come to, my dear. I have my little house here and pleasant it is. I give a few lessons to the young ladies of Lovat Mill. It's not much of a living, but it's improved since I have the young ladies of the big house.'

'The big house? Do you mean Lovat Stacy?'

'What else? It's our big house and by the grace of God there are the three young ladies to be taught their music.'

Essie Elgin was a born gossip and she did not need to be prompted very much. She realised that my own career was a painful subject so she happily chatted away about her pupils from the big house.

'What a place! Always some drama going on up there, I can tell you. And now we'll soon be having the wedding. It's what Sir William wants. He wants to see those two man and wife. Then he'll be happy.'

'Which two?' I asked.

'Mr Napier and young Edith . . . though she's not old enough I'd say. Seventeen, I believe. Of course some people at seventeen . . . but not Edith . . . oh no, not Edith.'

'Edith is the daughter of the house?'

'Well, you could call it that in a manner of speaking. She's not Sir William's daughter. Oh, it's a complicated household with none of the young ladies being related. Edith is Sir William's ward. She's been with the family for the last five years . . . since she lost her father. Her mother died when she was quite a baby and she was brought up by house-keepers and servants. Her father was a great friend of Sir William's. He had a big estate over Maidstone way . . . but it was all sold when he died and everything went to Edith. She's an heiress in a big way and that's why . . . Well, her father made Sir William her guardian and she came to Lovat Stacy when he died and lived there as though she were Sir William's daughter. Now of course he's brought Napier home to marry her.'

'Napier would be . . . ?'

'Sir William's son. Banished! Ah, there's a story for you. Then there's Allegra. Some connection of Sir William's, I've heard. She speaks of him as her grandfather. Proper little tartar and gives herself airs. Mrs Lincroft, the housekeeper, runs the place and she is Alice's mother. There are my three young ladies: Edith, Allegra, and Alice. For although Alice is only the housekeeper's daughter, she is allowed to join in their lessons – and so she comes to me, too. She's being educated as a proper little lady.'

'And this . . . Napier?' I said. 'What a strange name!'

'Oh, some family name. They're rare ones for family names . . . families who have been joined with theirs in marriage, so I heard. His is an odd story. I've never quite learned the wrongs and rights of it, but his brother Beaumont died . . . and Beaumont's another family name. He was killed, and Napier was blamed. He went away and now he has come back to marry Edith. It's a condition, so I gather.'

'How was he to blame?'

'People don't talk much round here about the Stacys,' she said regretfully. 'They're frightened of Sir William. He's a bit of a tartar too and most of them are his tenants. Hard as nails, they say. Must have been, to have sent Napier away. I'd like to know the ins and outs of that story but I can't speak to the young ladies about it.'

'I was very attracted by the house. There was something menacing about it. It looked so beautiful from a distance and when I was close to that great gateway . . . ugh . . .'

Essie laughed. 'You're letting your imagination run away with you,' she said. Then she asked me to play something for her and I sat down at the piano and it was like old times when I was young, before I had gone abroad to study, before I had met Pietro, before I threw away my chance.

'Aye,' she said, 'ye've a pretty touch. What do you plan?'

I shook my head at her.

'Oh come, lassie,' she said. 'That's nae the way. You go back to that Paris school and see whether you can take up where you left off.'

'Where I left off . . . before my marriage?'

She didn't answer. Perhaps she knew that although I was a competent pianist, although I could be a good teacher, I lacked the divine spark. Pietro had taken it from me; no, if I had had it I should never have chosen marriage instead of a career.

Then finally she said: 'Think about it . . . and come again soon.'

I walked back to our little cottage and thought about Essie and the old days and the future; but every now and then I would see the big house in my mind's eye, populated by vague and shadowy figures who were only names to me, and yet seem to have some life of their own.

I remember those days vividly; sitting in the cottage watching the mosaic emerge from under the skilful fingers of the restorers and sometimes strolling over to Essie's house for a cup of tea and an hour or so at the piano. I think Essie wanted to warn me to make an effort to pick up the threads; she was telling me that I did not want to find myself in a position such as hers.

One day she said to me: 'The wedding's on Saturday. Would you like to see it?'

So I went to the church and saw Napier and Edith married. They came down the aisle together – she fair and fragile, he lean and dark, though I noticed his blue eyes which were startling in his brown face. I was seated at the back of the church with Essie as they went by and the organ was playing Mendelssohn's wedding march. I felt a strange emotion as they passed – almost a premonition I might have said. But it was not that. Perhaps it was because I sensed the incongruity of the match; they did not belong together, those two, and it was obvious. The girl looked so young, so delicate and could I really have seen the apprehension in her face? I thought: She is afraid of him. And I remembered the day Pietro and I had married; how we had laughed together, how we had teased each other, and how we had loved. Poor child, I thought. And he had not looked too happy either. What was his expression. One of resignation, boredom . . . cynicism?

'Edith makes a pretty bride,' said Essie. 'And she'll continue with her lessons after the honeymoon. Sir William wants her to.'

'Really?'

'Oh yes. Sir William's all for music . . . now. Although there was a time when he wouldn't have it in the house. And Edith's got a pretty talent. Oh nothing great, but she plays well and it's a shame to drop it.'

I went back with Essie for a cup of tea and she talked about the young ladies at Lovat Stacy and their music . . . how Edith was good, Allegra lazy and Alice painstaking.

'Poor little Alice, she feels she has to be. You see, having so much given to her, she has to take advantage of it.'

Roma agreed with Essie that I should go back to Paris and carry on with my music. 'I can see,' she said, 'that it's the right thing for you to finish your studies. Though I'm not entirely sure of Paris. After all it was there . . .' She fingered her turquoises almost impatiently and decided not to mention my marriage. 'If you feel it's impossible . . . we could work out something else.'

'Oh Roma,' I cried, 'you are so good. I don't know how to tell you what a help you've been.'

'Nonsense!' she retorted gruffly.

'I'm realising how good it is to have a sister.'

'But naturally we stick together in times like these. You must come here more often.'

I smiled and kissed her. Then I went back to Paris. It was a foolish thing to have done. I should have known that I could not endure to be in a place which was so full of memories of Pietro. It only showed how different Paris was without him, and that it was stupid of me to think that I could start all over again. Nothing could be the same again because the foundations on which I must build my future would be the past.

How right Pietro was when he had said that one did not beckon the Muse and expect her to return after one had deserted her.

I had been in Paris some three months when news came that Roma had disappeared.

It was extraordinary. The dig was finished. They were preparing to pack up and leave within a few days. Roma had been superintending the departure in the morning and it was evening before she was missed. There was no sign of her. It was as though she had just walked out into nowhere.

It was a great mystery. She had left no note but had simply disappeared. I came back to England feeling bewildered, melancholy and deeply depressed. I kept remembering how good she had been to me, how she had tried to help me over my grief. I had been telling myself during those difficult weeks in Paris that I would always have Roma and that, through my sorrow, I had discovered a new relationship with my sister.

I was interviewed by the police. It was thought that Roma had lost her memory and might be wandering about the country; then it was suggested that she might have taken a swim and been drowned, for the coast was dangerous at that point. I clung to the first suggestion because it was more comforting, though I could not imagine Roma in a state of amnesia. Each day I waited for news. None came.

Some of her friends volunteered the suggestion that she might have had sudden news of a secret project and gone off to Egypt or somewhere like that. I tried to force myself to accept this comforting theory, but I knew it was not like precise and practical Roma. Something had prevented her from letting me know what had happened. Something? What could have prevented her but death?

I told myself that I was obsessed by death because I had lost my parents and Pietro in such a short time. I could not lose Roma too.

I was wretchedly unhappy and after a while I went back to Paris to settle up there because I knew I couldn't stay any longer. I returned to London, took rooms in a house in Kensington and advertised that I was a teacher of the pianoforte.

Perhaps I was not a good teacher; perhaps I was impatient with the mediocre. After all I had had dreams for myself, and had been Pietro Verlaine's wife. I was not earning my keep. My money was dwindling in an alarming way. Each day I hoped for news of Roma. I felt helpless because I did not know how to set about finding my sister. And then came my opportunity.

Essie wrote that she was coming to London and would like to see me.

I saw that she was excited as soon as she arrived; she was a born schemer for other people; I never remembered her scheming very much for herself.

'I'm leaving Lovat Mill,' she said. 'I haven't been so well lately and I think it's time I went to my sister in Scotland.'

'That's a long way,' I replied.

'Oh aye, a long way; but what I've come to tell you is this. How would you like to go down there?'

'To go . . .' I stammered.

'To Lovat Stacy. To teach the girls. Now listen. I've had a talk with Sir William. He was a wee bit put out when I told him of my plans. You see he wants Edith to continue with her lessons . . . and the others too. And then they used to have musical evenings years ago, by all accounts and he would like to revive them now that there's a young bride in the house. It was his idea that he should have a resident teacher who would play for his benefit and that of his guests, as well as teach the girls now and then. He broached this subject with me when I told him I was going and I thought at once of you and said that I knew the widow of Pietro Verlaine who was a clever musician herself. Now if you're agreeable he would like you to write to him and some arrangement could be made.'

I felt breathless. 'Wait a moment!' I said.

'Now you're going to be a coy young lady and say "This is too sudden." Some of the best things in life are; and you have to make up your mind suddenly or lose them. If you say no, Sir William will be advertising for a resident teacher for the girls, because once I'd put the idea to him that you might come he was eager.'

I was seeing it so clearly: the dig; the little cottage; the big house and those two coming down the aisle together. And Roma of course . . . Roma urging me not to forget her.

I said abruptly: 'Do you believe that Roma is alive?'

Her face puckered. She turned her head away and said: 'I . . . I don't believe she would have gone away without telling someone she was going.'

'Then she was spirited away . . . or she's somewhere where she can't let us know. I want to find out . . . I must.'

Miss Elgin nodded.

'I didn't tell Sir William that you are her sister. He's annoyed about the whole affair. There was too much publicity. I've heard it said that he declares he should never have allowed them to excavate there. That brought enough limelight and when your sister disappeared . . .' She shrugged her shoulders. 'So I didn't say you were the sister of Roma Brandon, I merely told him you were Caroline Verlaine, widow of the great pianist.'

'So I should go there . . . *incognito* as far as my connection with Roma was concerned?'

'I honestly don't believe he'd want you if he knew. He'd think you might have some reason for going there other than teaching.'

'If I went,' I said, 'he'd be right.'

I wanted to think about it and Essie and I walked together in Kensington Gardens where Roma and I used to sail our boats when we were children. That night I dreamed of Roma; she was standing in the Round Pond holding out her hands to me and the water kept rising higher and higher. She called 'Do something, Caro.'

It may have been this dream which made me definitely decide that I would go to Lovat Stacy.

I sold the few pieces of furniture I possessed to the landlady in whose house I rented my two rooms. I put my piano in store and packed my bags.

I had at last found a purpose in life. Pietro was lost to me forever; but I would try to find Roma.

Chapter Two

The train had stopped at Dover Priory and quite a number of people had alighted. There was a halt of five minutes here while the mail was put on and as the last of those who had left the train passed through the barrier I was aware of a woman hurrying along the platform, a young girl of about twelve or thirteen beside her. She saw me for my head was out of the window as she passed; then, halting, she turned and came back, opened the door, and the two came into the carriage.

She glanced at me covertly, and so did the girl, as they seated themselves opposite me. The woman sighed and said: 'Oh, dear, shopping always makes me so tired.'

The girl said nothing but I knew they were both studying me with curiosity. Why? I wondered. Did I look so odd? Then it occurred to me that the train served smaller stations after Dover Priory and it might well be that the people who travelled on this train after that were local people who were known to each other. In which case I would be picked out immediately as a stranger.

The woman put a few small packages on the seat beside her and when one of these fell to the floor right at my feet and I retrieved it, the opening for conversation was at hand.

'So tiring these trains,' said the woman. 'And one gets so dirty. Are you going as far as Ramsgate?'

'No, I'm getting off at Lovat Mill.'

'Oh really. So are we. Thank Heaven it's not far now . . . another twenty minutes and we'll be there . . . providing we're on time. How strange that you should be going there. But of course we've had a lot of activity lately. These people, you know, who found the Roman remains.'

'Oh yes?' I said non-committally.

'You're not connected with them, I suppose?'

'Oh no. I'm going to a house called Lovat Stacy.'

'Dear me. Then you must be the young lady who is going to teach the girls music.'

'Yes.'

She was delighted. 'Well, when I saw you, it did occur to me. There are so few strangers you see and we had heard that you were coming to-day.'

'You belong to the household?'

'No . . . no. We're at Lovat Mill . . . just outside, of course. The vicarage. My husband is the vicar. We're friends of the Stacys. In fact the girls come over to my husband for lessons. We're only a mile or so from the House. Sylvia takes lessons with them, don't you, Sylvia?'

Sylvia said 'Yes, Mamma,' in a very quiet voice. And I thought it not unlikely that Mamma ruled the household – including the vicar.

Sylvia seemed meek enough but there was something about the line of her jaw and the set of her lips that belied her meekness, and I imagined her humility might evaporate with the departure of Mamma.

'I daresay the vicar will ask you if you will take on Sylvia at the same time as the Stacy girls.'

'Is Sylvia interested in music?' I was smiling at Sylvia who looked at her mother.

'She is going to be,' said that lady firmly.

Sylvia smiled rather faintly and threw back the plait which hung over her right shoulder. I noticed the rather spatulate fingers which did not look to me like those of a pianist. I could already hear Sylvia's painful performance at the piano.

'I am so pleased that you are not one of those archæologist people. I was very much against letting them invade Lovat Stacy.'

'You don't approve of this sort of discovery?'

'Discovery!' she retorted. 'Of what use are their discoveries? If we had been meant to know these things were there, they would not have been covered up, would they?'

This amazing logic was all against my upbringing, but this forceful woman was clearly expecting a reply, and as I did not want to antagonise her because I guessed she could probably tell me it good deal about Lovat Stacy, I smiled non-committally, murmuring an inner apology to my parents and Roma.

'They came down here . . . disturbing *everything*. Goodness gracious me, one could not move without coming across them. Pails, spades . . . digging up the earth, completely *ruining* several acres of the park . . . And to what purpose? To uncover these Roman remains! 'There are plenty of them all over the country,' I said to the vicar. 'We don't want them here.' One of these people came to a strange end . . . or perhaps it wasn't an end. Who's to say. She disappeared.'

I felt a prickling down my spine. I felt that I might betray my relationship with the one who had disappeared; and that was something which I was determined not to do. I said quickly: 'Disappeared?'

'Oh yes. It was all very strange. She was there in the morning . . . and no one saw her after that. She disappeared during the day.'

'Where did she go?'

'That's what a lot of people would like to know. Her name was . . . what was her name, Sylvia?'

Sylvia's spatulate fingers with the bitten nails clenched themselves, betraying her tension, and for a moment I thought she was disturbed because she knew something about Roma's disappearance; then I realised that she was in awe of her mother, particularly when she asked a question to which she might not be able to find the answer.

But she had this one. 'It was Miss Brandon . . . Miss Roma Brandon.'

The woman nodded. 'That was it. One of these *un-womanly* women . . .' She shivered. 'Digging! Climbing about! Most unnatural, I call it. It was very likely a punishment for meddling. Some people say it was due to that. There's quite a superstition about it. This . . . whatever it was that happened to her . . . took place because she had *meddled*. A sort of curse. I think it ought to be a lesson to these people.'

'But they've all left now?' I asked.

'Oh yes, yes. They were about to leave when this happened. Of course, when the fuss started it delayed them. It's my belief she was taking a bathe and was caught by the currents. A most immodest habit, bathing. It's the easiest thing to get carried out to sea. A sort of judgment. People should be more careful. But the local people will tell you that it was some sort of revenge. One of these Roman gods or someone who didn't like his house being disturbed saying: Take that for meddling. The vicar and I try to tell them this is nonsense but at the same time it does seem a rough sort of justice.'

'Did you ever meet this . . . woman who disappeared?'

'Meet her. Oh no. We didn't meet those people, although they were rather friendly with some of them up at the House. Then Sir William is a little odd. Mind you, they are a very great family and of course we are friends. People of our sort do tend to stand together in a small community; and because of the girls we are constantly seeing one another. By the way, I don't think I asked you your name.'

'It is Caroline Verlaine. Mrs Verlaine.'

I watched her anxiously, wondering whether she would connect me with Roma. Although Essie had assured me that Sir William did not know I was Roma's sister, there had been a great deal of publicity at the time of her disappearance. Roma was after all Pietro's sister-in-law; he was famous; and this might have been mentioned. I felt ridiculously dismayed. But I need not have worried. It was clear that my name meant nothing to the vicar's lady.

'Yes, I heard you were a widow,' she said. 'Frankly I had expected someone much older.'

'I have been a widow for a year now.'

'Ah, sad, sad.' She allowed a little pause as an expression of her compassion. 'I am Mrs Rendall . . . and this is of course Miss Rendall.'

I bowed my head in acknowledgment of the introduction.

'I heard that you hold many diplomas and such like.'

'I have some diplomas.'

'That must be very nice.'

I lowered my head to hide my smile.

'You will find Allegra a handful, I don't doubt. The vicar says her mind never stays on one subject for more than a few seconds at a time. A mistake to educate her. A servant's child even though . . . But it's disgraceful. Such a complicated household . . . and none of them related. It's so odd of Sir William to allow that little Alice Lincroft to share. But she's such a quiet girl. One can't really take exception. She is treated like the others . . . Sylvia is allowed to be their companion.' She shrugged her shoulders. 'It's *very* difficult, but since Sir William accepts them what can we do?'

Sylvia seemed alert as though she were listening intently. Poor Sylvia! She would be one of those children who spoke only when spoken to. Again I felt grateful to my own parents.

'And who is Alice Lincroft exactly?'

'The housekeeper's daughter, if you please. Mind you Mrs Lincroft is a very *superior* housekeeper. And she was with the family before her marriage. She was companion to Lady Stacy, then she left and came back after she was widowed . . . came back with Alice. The child was only about two years old then . . . so she has lived most of her life at Lovat Stacy. It would be intolerable of course if she were not such a *quiet* child. But she gives no trouble – unlike Allegra. But that was a flagrant mistake. There'll be trouble with that girl one day. I have often said so to the vicar and he agrees with me.'

'And Lady Stacy?'

'She died quite a long time ago . . . before Mrs Lincroft came back as housekeeper.'

'And there is another young lady whom I am to teach.'

Mrs Rendall smirked. 'Edith Cowan . . . or rather Edith Stacy now. I must say it is all very odd. A married woman . . . poor thing.'

'Because she is married?' I prompted.

'Married!' snorted Mrs Rendall. 'I must say that was a very odd arrangement. I said so to the vicar and I shall continue to say so. Of course it is clear to me why Sir William arranged it.'

'Sir William?' I put in. 'Didn't the young couple have anything to say about it?'

'My dear young lady, when you have been at Lovat Stacy for a day you will learn that there is only one person who has any say in affairs there and that is Sir William. Sir William took Edith in and made her his ward and then he decided to bring Napier back and marry them off.' She lowered her voice. 'Of course,' she excused her indiscretion, 'you will soon be one of the household so you will discover these things sooner or later. It was only the Cowan money which could have induced Sir William to have Napier back.'

'Oh?' I was prompting her to go on but I think she realised she had been a little too communicative and she sat back in her seat, her lips pursed, her hands clasped in her lap, looking like an avenging goddess.

The train rocked in silence while I was trying to think of an opening gambit which would lure the loquacious woman to further indiscretions when Sylvia said timidly: 'We are almost there, Mamma.'

'So we are,' cried Mrs Rendall, getting to her feet and scattering parcels. 'Oh dear, I wonder if this wool is the right ply for the vicar's socks.'

'I am sure it is, Mamma. *You* chose it.'

I studied the girl sharply. Was that a little irony? However Mamma did not appear to have noticed. 'Here,' she said to the girl, 'take this.'

I too had risen and took down my bags from the rack. I was aware of Mrs Rendall's eyes on them, assessing them as she had assessed me.

'I daresay you'll be met,' she said and gave Sylvia a little push after which she followed her daughter on to the platform and turning to me continued: 'Ah yes, there is Mrs Lincroft.' She called in her somewhat shrill and penetrating voice: 'Mrs Lincroft. Here is the young person you are looking for.'

I had alighted and stood with my two large bags beside me. The vicar's wife gave me a brief nod and another to the approaching woman and went off with Sylvia at her heels.

'You are Mrs Verlaine?' She was a tall, slender woman in her mid-thirties, I guessed. There was an air of faded beauty about her and I was immediately reminded of the flowers I used to press among the pages of books. A large straw hat was tied under her chin with light coloured veiling; her large eyes were a faded blue; her face a little gaunt for she was very slender. She was dressed in grey but her blouse was a cornflower blue, which I suspected gave a deeper blue to her eyes. There was certainly nothing formidable about her.

I told her who I was.

'I'm Amy Lincroft,' she replied, 'housekeeper at Lovat Stacy. I have the trap outside. Your bags can be sent up to the house.'

She signed to a porter and gave him instructions and in a few minutes she was taking me through the barrier to the station yard.

'I see you have already made the acquaintance of the vicar's wife.'

'Yes, oddly enough she guessed who I was.'

Mrs Lincroft smiled. 'It could have been by design. She knew you'd be on that train and wanted to meet you before the rest of us did.'

'I feel flattered to have inspired her to do so.'

We had reached the trap. I got in and she took the reins.

'We're a good two miles from the station,' she told me, 'nearer three.' I noticed her delicate wrists and long thin fingers. 'I hope you like the country, Mrs Verlaine.'

I told her I had been used to living in towns so that it was something I should have to discover.

'Big towns?' she asked.

'I was brought up in London. I lived abroad with my husband and when he died I came back to London.'

She was silent and as she too was a widow I wondered whether she was thinking of her husband. I tried to imagine what he would have been like and whether she had been happy. I thought not.

How different from the vicar's wife who rarely stopped

talking and had told me so much in such a short time. Mrs Lincroft would be, I imagined, almost secretive.

She talked vaguely of London where she once lived briefly; and then she mentioned the east winds which were a feature of this coast. 'We get the full force of them. I hope you don't feel the cold, Mrs Verlaine? But then the spring is almost here and the spring is quite lovely. So is the summer.'

I asked her about my pupils and she confirmed that I should be teaching her own daughter Alice, as well as Allegra, and Edith: Mrs Stacy.

'You will find Mrs Stacy and Alice good pupils. Allegra is not really bad – just high spirited and perhaps a little prone to get into mischief. I think you will like them all.'

'I am looking forward to meeting them.'

'That you will do very shortly for they are all eager to meet you.'

The wind was keen and I fancied I could smell the sea, and now we had come to the Roman remains.

Mrs Lincroft said: 'This was discovered quite recently. We had archæologists down here and Sir William gave them leave to excavate. He wished afterwards that he hadn't. It has brought crowds here to see the remains and there was an unfortunate affair. You may have heard of it. There was a great fuss at the time. One of the archæologists disappeared and . . . I fancy . . . hasn't been heard of since.'

'Mrs Rendall mentioned it.'

'There was talk of nothing else at the time. We had people prying . . . It was very upsetting. I saw the young woman once. She came to see Sir William.'

'So she disappeared,' I said. 'Do you have any ideas as to how it happened?'

She shook her head.

'Such a forthright young woman. One can't imagine how she could have done such a thing.'

'What . . . thing?'

'Just walked off and told no one where she was going. That must have been what happened.'

'But she wouldn't have done such a thing, surely. She would have told her sister.'

'Oh . . . did she have a sister?'

I flushed slightly. How foolish I was. If I were not careful I should betray myself.

'Or her brother or parents,' I continued.

'Yes,' conceded Mrs Lincroft. 'Surely she would have done that. It's very mysterious.'

I fancied I had shown too much interest, so I quickly changed the subject.

'I can smell the sea.'

'Oh yes, you'll see it in a moment. And you'll see the house too.'

I caught my breath in wonder, for there it was, just as I had been remembering it – that impressive gate house with its mouldings, its mullions and arched transoms.

'It's magnificent,' I said.

She looked pleased. 'The gardens are quite lovely. I do a little gardening myself. I find it so . . . soothing.'

I was scarcely listening. A great excitement had come to me. This house thrilled, yet repelled me. The machicolated towers with their crenellations seemed to give a warning to those who would carelessly enter through the gate below. I imagined arrows and boiling pitch being thrown from the heights of those towers on to the enemies of the great house.

Mrs Lincroft was aware of the effect the house was having on me and she smiled. 'I suppose we who live here are inclined to take it all for granted,' she said.

'I was wondering how it felt to live in such a house.'

'You will soon find out.'

We were on the gravel path, bounded on both sides by

the moss-covered wall, which led directly to the gate house. It was an impressive moment as we passed under the arch and I saw the door of the gatekeeper's lodge with the peephole through which visitors to the mansion must have been scrutinised. I wondered whether anyone was watching there now.

Mrs Lincroft brought the trap to a standstill in a cobbled courtyard. 'There are two courtyards,' she told me, 'the lower and the upper.' She waved a hand at the four high walls which enclosed it. 'These are mostly the servants' quarters,' she went on. She nodded towards an archway through which I caught a glimpse of stone steps going up. 'The nurseries are over that gateway; and in the upper courtyard are the family's rooms.'

'It's vast,' I said.

She laughed. 'You will discover how vast. The stables are here. So if you will alight I will call one of the grooms and then take you into the house and introduce you. Your bags will be here shortly . . . by the time I have given you tea, I imagine. I'll take you to the schoolroom and there you can meet the girls.'

She drove the trap into the stables, leaving me standing there in the courtyard There was a hushed silence and now that I was alone I felt I had stepped right back into the past. I calculated the age of those walls which closed me in. Four hundred . . . five hundred? I looked up; two hideous gargoyles projected from the walls, seeming to scowl at me. The Gothic tracery on the lead-work of the water spouts was exquisitely delicate in odd contrast to those grotesque figures. The doors – four of them were of oak, studded with massive nails. I looked at the windows with their leaden panes and I wondered about the people who lived behind them.

As I stood there, though completely fascinated, I was again

conscious of that feeling of revulsion. I could not understand it, but I felt I wanted to run away, to go back to
London, to write to my music master in Paris and beg for
another chance. Perhaps it was the evil expression on the
faces of those stone images jutting out from the walls. Perhaps
it was the silence; that overwhelming atmosphere of the past
which made me fancy that I was being lured from this present
century into an earlier age. I had a vivid picture of Roma
coming through that gate into this courtyard, demanding to
see Sir William, asking him if he thought his park and trees
were more important than history. Poor Roma. If he had
refused his permission, would she be alive to-day?

It seemed that the house was alive, that those grotesques
were not merely stone figures. Was that a shadow at the
window over the second gateway? The nurseries, Mrs
Lincroft had said. Perhaps. But what more natural than that
my pupils should be interested enough in their new music
teacher to take a preview of her, when they believed her to
be unaware of them?

I had never been inside a house of such antiquity before,
I reminded myself. It was the circumstances of my coming
which made me feel as I did. 'Roma,' I whispered to myself,
'Where are you, Roma?'

I could imagine that the gargoyles behind my back were
laughing at me. I felt as though something was telling me
that I should not stay here, that if I did I should be hurt in
some mysterious way. And with this feeling came the certainty
that the riddle of Roma's disappearance was hidden somewhere in this house.

This is absurdly whimsical, I admonished myself in a voice
which was just like Roma's. How she would have laughed
at such an idea. The romantic, Pietro would have commented,
forever in me, peeping out from behind the poise, the air of
worldliness.

Mrs Lincroft appeared and she looked so comforting that the illusion vanished.

In fact, I continued to tell myself, I had not come here so much to solve the mystery of Roma's disappearance as to earn an adequate living, to make sure of a roof over my head. Once I admitted that this was an end of my grand ambitions and looked at this venture as a practical and most sensible move, the more reasonably I should view my situation.

Mrs Lincroft led the way under the second gateway over which were the schoolroom windows. I paused to read the inscription.

'You can scarcely make it out,' she said. 'It's in medieval English. "Fear God and honour the King."'

'A noble sentiment,' I remarked.

She smiled and said: 'Be careful of the steps. They're steep and worn in places.'

There were twelve of them leading to the upper courtyard; this was larger and bounded by tall grey walls. I noticed the similar windows with their leaded panes, the gargoyles and the intricate designs on the head of the water spouts.

'This way,' said Mrs Lincroft and pushed open a heavy door.

We were in an enormous hall about sixty feet long with a vaulted ceiling and four window embrasures. Although the windows were large the panes were small and leaded which meant that there were dark shadows although it was only afternoon. At one end was a dais on which stood a grand piano, at the other a minstrels' gallery. There was a staircase close to the gallery and two arched openings through which I caught sight of a dark passage. On the lime-washed walls were weapons, and a suit of armour stood at the foot of the staircase.

'The hall is rarely used nowadays,' said Mrs Lincroft. 'Once balls were held there . . . and there were musical occasions. But since Lady Stacy's death and since er . . . Well, since then, Sir William has done little entertaining. An occasional dinner party . . . but of course we shall be using the hall now there is a young mistress of the house. I daresay we shall have some musical entertainments too.'

'Shall I be expected to –?'

'I daresay.'

I tried to imagine myself seated at the grand piano on the dais. I could hear Pietro's laugh. 'A concert pianist at last. Through the back door, one might say . . . No, through the castle gates.'

As Mrs Lincroft led the way to the staircase, I laid my hand on the carved banister and saw the dragons and the fierce looking creatures engraved there.

'I'm sure,' I said, 'that no animals ever looked quite like these.' Mrs Lincroft again smiled her quiet smile, and I went on: 'I wonder why they always wanted to frighten people away. People who want to frighten others are very often frightened themselves. That's the answer. They must have been really afraid . . . hence these fierce looking creatures.'

'Calculated, as they say, to strike terror into the hearts of the invaders.'

'They would do it most successfully, I'm sure. It's the long shadows . . . just as much as those carvings, which are really too fantastic to be true, that give this feeling of . . . menace.'

'You are sensitive to atmosphere, Mrs Verlaine. You will be hoping that there are no ghosts in the house. Are you superstitious?'

'That's something we all deny until we are put to the test. Then most of us prove we are.'

'You mustn't be here, you know. In a place like this where people have lived for centuries within the same walls stories circulate. A servant sees her own shadow and swears it is a ghost in grey. Easily done, Mrs Verlaine, in a house like this.'

'I don't think I am going to be afraid of my own shadow.'

'I know how I felt when I first came here. I remember arriving in this hall and standing here terrified.' She shivered at the recollection.

'And all turned out well, I suppose.'

'I found . . . a place in this house . . . in time.' She shook herself slightly as though shaking off past memories. 'Now, I think first to the schoolroom. I will have tea sent up there. I am sure you're ready for it.'

We had reached a gallery in which hung several portraits and I noticed some fine tapestries which I intended to examine later, for their subjects seemed most intriguing.

She opened a door and said: 'Mrs Verlaine is here.'

I followed her into a lofty room and there were the three girls. They made a charming picture, one of them on the window seat, another seated at a table and a third standing with her back to the fireplace on either side of which stood two great firedogs.

The one in the window seat came towards me and I recognised her at once, because I had seen her coming down the aisle on the arm of her bridegroom. She looked so shy – she was uncertain as yet, I guessed, of her new dignity as mistress of the house; and indeed it was incongruous to think of her as such. She looked like a child.

'How do you do, Mrs Verlaine?' The words were spoken as though she had rehearsed them many times. She held out her hand and I took it. As it lay for those few seconds limply in mine I felt sorry for her and knew I wanted to protect her. 'We are glad you have come,' she continued in that stilted way.

Her hair was certainly her crowning glory. It was the colour of corn in August, and little tendrils escaped to nestle on her low white forehead and at the nape of her neck. It was the only vital thing about her.

I told her I was glad to be here, and was looking forward to my work.

'I am looking forward to working with you,' she said, and her smile was sweet. 'Allegra! Alice!'

Allegra left the fireplace and came towards me. Her thick dark curly hair was tied back with a red ribbon; her eyes were black and bold, her skin inclined to be sallow.

'So you've come to teach us music, Mrs Verlaine,' she said.

'I hope you're eager to learn,' I replied, not without asperity, for my association with pupils as well as Mrs Rendall's warning, told me to expect trouble with this one.

'Should I be?' Oh yes, she was going to be difficult.

'If you want to learn to play the piano, yes.'

'I don't think I want to learn anything . . . at least things which teachers teach.'

'Perhaps when you are older and wiser you will change your mind.' Oh dear, I thought, engaging in verbal battles so soon was a very bad sign.

I turned from her to look at the third girl, who had been sitting at the table.

'Come, Alice,' said Mrs Lincroft.

Alice stood before me and made a demure curtsey. I guessed her to be of the same age as Allegra – about twelve or thirteen – although being smaller she looked younger. She radiated neatness and wore a white frilled apron over her grey gaberdine dress; her long light brown hair was held back from her rather severe little face by a blue velvet band.

'Alice will be a good pupil,' said her mother tenderly.

'I'll try to be,' replied Alice with a shy smile. 'But Edith . . . er Mrs Stacy . . . is very good.'

I smiled at Edith, who flushed a little and said: 'I hope Mrs Verlaine will think so.'

Mrs Lincroft said to Edith: 'I asked for tea to be brought up here. I wonder if you will wish to stay and . . .'

'Why yes,' said Edith. 'I shall want to talk to Mrs Verlaine.'

I gathered that everyone was a little embarrassed by the new status Edith had acquired in the household since her marriage.

When the tea arrived I saw it was of the kind we used to have in the schoolroom at home – big brown earthenware pot and the milk in a china Toby jug. A cloth was put on the table and bread and butter and cakes laid out.

'Perhaps you will be able to tell Mrs Verlaine how far you have progressed with your studies,' suggested Mrs Lincroft.

'I'm eager to hear.'

'Miss Elgin recommended you, didn't she?' said Allegra.

'That's so.'

'So *you* used to be a pupil.'

'I did.'

She nodded laughing, as though the idea of my being a pupil was incongruous. I was beginning to understand that Allegra liked to take the stage. But it was Edith who interested me – not only because I was so curious about her life and because she, a young girl, was mistress of this big house, but because she was clearly something of a musician. I could sense it by the manner in which her personality changed when she talked of music. She glowed, and became almost confident.

While we talked a servant came to say that Sir William was asking for Mrs Lincroft.

'Thank you, Jane,' she said. 'Pray tell him that I will be with him in a few moments. Alice, as soon as tea is over, you can show Mrs Verlaine her room.'

'Yes, Mamma,' said Alice.

As soon as Mrs Lincroft had gone the atmosphere changed subtly. I wondered what this meant, for the housekeeper had given me the impression of being an extremely gentle woman; there was a certain firmness about her, but I did not think she was one who would impose her personality on a young girl – particularly one as high spirited as Allegra appeared to be.

Allegra said: 'We expected someone older than you. You aren't all that old to be a widow.'

Three pairs of eyes were studying me intently. I said: 'Yes, I was widowed after a very few years of marriage.'

'Why did your husband die?' pursued Allegra.

'Perhaps Mrs Verlaine would rather not speak of it,' suggested Edith quietly.

'What nonsense!' retorted Allegra. 'Everyone likes talking about death.'

I raised my eyebrows. 'It's true,' went on the irrepressible Allegra. 'Look at Cook. She'll go into the gruesome details of her late lamented (her name for him) whenever you ask her . . . and you don't even have to ask. She revels in them. So it's nonsense to say people don't like talking about death, because they do.'

'Perhaps Mrs Verlaine is different from Cook,' put in Alice in a quiet little voice which was scarcely audible. Poor little Alice, I thought, as the housekeeper's daughter she is not exactly accepted as one of them, although she is allowed to share their lessons.

I turned to her and said: 'My husband died of a heart attack. It's something that can happen at any time.'

Allegra looked towards her two companions as though she were expecting to see them collapse.

'Of course,' I went on, 'there are sometimes signs that an attack is imminent. People work too hard, worry . . .'

Edith said timidly: 'Perhaps we should change the subject. Do you like teaching, Mrs Verlaine, and have you taught many people?'

'I like teaching when my pupils respond . . . not otherwise; and I have taught a number of people.'

'How does one respond?' asked Allegra.

'By loving the piano?' suggested Edith.

'That is exactly so,' I said. 'If you love music, if you want to give the pleasure to others which music gives to you, you will play well and enjoy your playing.'

'Even if you have no talent?' asked Alice almost eagerly.

'If you have no talent to begin with, you can work hard and acquire skill at least. But I do believe that the gift of music is something you are born with. I propose that we start our lessons tomorrow. I shall take you all in turn and we will see who has this talent.'

'Why did you come here?' pursued Allegra. 'What were you doing before?'

'Teaching.'

'What of your old pupils? Won't they be missing you?'

'There were not many of them.'

'Well, there are only three of us. This is not a very lucky place for people.'

'What do you mean?'

Allegra looked conspiratorially at the others. 'There were some people who came to dig up our park. They were . . .'

'Archæologists,' supplied Alice.

'That's right. People said it was wrong to disturb the dead. They're gone and they're in peace and they don't want other people digging up their graves and their homes. They say they leave a curse that if someone disturbs them they will have their revenge. Do you believe that, Mrs Verlaine?'

'No, it's a superstition. If the Romans built beautiful

46

houses I believe they would want us to know how clever they had been, how advanced.'

'Did you know,' said Alice quickly, 'that they kept their houses warm by means of pipes full of hot water. The young lady who died told us. She was pleased if we asked questions about the remains.'

'Alice always tries to please everyone,' said Allegra. 'It's because she's the housekeeper's daughter and feels she has to.'

I raised my eyebrows at this rudeness and looked at Alice in a manner which I hope conveyed to her that I meant to make no distinctions.

'So to please this . . . archæologist, you pretended to be interested?' I suggested.

'But we *were* interested,' said Alice, 'and Miss Brandon told us a great deal about the Romans who used to live here. But when she heard about the curse she was frightened and then it overtook her.'

'Did she tell you she was frightened?'

'I think that's what she meant. She said: "We are after all meddling with the dead. So it's not surprising there is this curse."'

'She meant that it was not surprising there was a *rumour* about the curse.'

'Perhaps she believed it,' suggested Allegra. 'It's like having faith. People in the Bible were cured because they had faith. So perhaps it works the other way and Miss Brandon disappeared because she had faith.'

'So you think that if she hadn't believed in the curse she would not have disappeared?' I asked.

There was silence in the schoolroom. Then Alice said: 'Perhaps I thought afterwards that she was frightened. It's easy to imagine things like that when something's happened.'

Alice was evidently a wise young girl in spite of her humility – or perhaps because of it. I could well imagine how Allegra treated her when they were alone. I expected that hers was a life of countless humiliations – the poor relation who is given a roof over her head and outwardly similar privileges in return for doing light but menial tasks and accepting slights from those who believed themselves to be her superiors. I warmed towards Alice and imagined she did towards me.

'Alice is full of imagination,' scoffed Allegra. 'Parson Rendall says so every time she writes an essay.'

Alice blushed and I said: 'That's very creditable.' I smiled at the young girl. 'I am really looking forward to teaching you the piano.'

The footman came to announce that my bags had arrived and were in the yellow room which had been made ready for me.

I thanked him and Alice said at once: 'Would you like me to take you there now, Mrs Verlaine?'

I admitted that would be pleasant.

She rose and the others watched her and I decided that showing people to their rooms was a task for the higher servants, the class to which Alice belonged.

She said politely: 'Allow me to lead the way, Mrs Verlaine,' and began to mount the staircase.

'This place has been your home for a long time,' I said conversationally.

'I have never really known another home. Mother came back here when I was about two.'

'It's certainly impressive.'

Alice laid her hand on the banister and looked down at the carved figures there. 'It's a lovely old house, isn't it, Mrs Verlaine. I should never want to go away from it.'

'Perhaps you will change your mind when you get older. Perhaps you will marry someone and that will be more important to you than staying here.'

She turned to look down at me in a startled way. 'I expect I shall stay here and be a sort of companion to Edith.'

She sighed and turning proceeded up the stairs. There was an air of resignation about her and I pictured her first as a young woman, then as a middle-aged one and an old one – not of the family and not belonging to the servants' hall, called upon in moments of crisis in the family. Little Alice at everyone's beck and call, of no account except when some unpleasant task had to be performed.

She turned suddenly and smiled at me. 'It is after all what I want.' She lifted her shoulders. 'I love this house. There are so many interesting things in it.'

'I'm sure there are.'

'Yes,' she said almost breathlessly. 'There is a room where a King is supposed to have lodged. I think it was Charles I during the Civil War. I suppose he was afraid to go to Dover Castle, so he came here. It's the bridal suite now. It's supposed to be haunted, but Mr Napier doesn't care about that. Most people would. Edith does. Edith's *terrified* . . . but then she's often terrified. But Napier believes that it's all for her own good to face up to what she's frightened of. She has to learn to be brave.'

'Tell me about it,' I said, hoping to hear more of Napier and his bride, but she merely went on to describe the room.

'It's one of the largest in the house. They would give the largest to the King, wouldn't they? There's a brick fireplace which the vicar says has a chambered arch and jambs. The vicar is very keen on anything that's old . . . old houses, old furniture . . . old anything.'

We had walked along a gallery similar to the one below and here Alice paused to open a door.

'This is the room my mother selected for you. It's called the yellow room because of the yellow curtains and the rugs. The counterpane is yellow too. Look.'

She threw open the door. I saw my bags standing on the parquet floor and was immediately aware of the yellow curtains at the big window and the rugs and the counterpane on the fourposter bed. The ceiling was high and a chandelier hung from it, but there were dark shadows in the room for like most windows in the house, this one had leaded panes which shut out a good deal of the light. It was very grand, I thought, for someone who had merely come to teach music; and I wondered what the room was like which was occupied by Napier – the one which had once sheltered a King.

'There's a powder closet – only a little one. But it will be your dressing-room. Would you like me to help you unpack?'

I thanked her and said that I could manage by myself.

'Your view is lovely,' she said. She went to the window. I crossed the room and stood beside her. I looked over the lawns to a copse of fir trees and beyond that the sea was breaking about the white cliffs.

'There!' she stood back watching me. 'Do you like it, Mrs Verlaine?'

'I think it is enchanting.'

'It is beautiful – all of it. But they do say hereabouts that this is an unlucky house.'

'Why? Because a young woman mysteriously disappeared when . . . ?'

'You mean the woman at the excavations. She wasn't really anything to do with the house.'

'But you knew her and she had been working on the estate close to this house.'

'I wasn't thinking of her.'

'Then there is something else?'

Alice nodded. 'When Sir William's eldest son died everyone said it was . . . unlucky.'

'But there is Napier.'

50

'Napier was his brother. This was Beaumont. They called him Beau. It suited him, you see, because he was so beautiful. Then he died . . . and Napier was sent away and he stayed away until he came back to marry Edith. Sir William never got over it nor did Lady Stacy.'

'How did he die? Was it an accident?'

'It could have been an accident. But then it might not have been.' She put her fingers to her lips. 'Mother says I am never to speak of it.'

I could not prompt her then, but she added: 'I suppose that's why they call it an unhappy house. It's haunted they say . . . by Beau. But whether they mean he's a real ghost who glides about at night or whether they just mean you can't get away from the memory of him, I don't know. But it's a sort of haunting which ever way, isn't it? But Mother would be angry if she knew I'd mentioned him. Please don't tell her, Mrs Verlaine, and forget it, will you?'

She looked so pathetic, pleading with me in this way, that I said I would not mention it and immediately dropped the subject.

Then she said: 'It's clear to-day. Not clear enough to see the coast of France, but you can see the Goodwin Sands if your eyes are good enough. Well, you can't exactly see the Sands themselves but you can see the wrecks sticking up.' She pointed and I followed the direction which she indicated.

'I can see something that looks like sticks.'

'That's it . . . that's all you can see. It's the masts of boats which long ago were caught on the Sands. You've heard about the Sands, Mrs Verlaine. Quicksands . . . shivering sands . . . Boats are caught in them and they can't get off. They feel themselves held in a grip so fierce that nothing will release them . . . and slowly they begin to sink into the shivering sands.' She looked at me.

'Horrible!' I said.

51

'Yes, isn't it? And the masts are always there to remind us. You can see them very easily on a clear day. There's a lightship out there to warn shipping. You'll see it flashing at night. But some of them still get caught on the shivering sands.'

I turned away from the window and Alice said: 'You'll want to unpack now. I expect you will be dining with Mother and me. I'll ask Mother what the arrangements will be. Then I suppose Sir William will send for you. I'll be back in an hour.'

Quietly she slipped out of the room. I started to unpack, my thoughts flitting from Mrs Lincroft to her daughter, to Allegra who was very likely going to give me trouble, to pale Edith who was Napier's bride and of the ghost of Beau who had had an accident and who was believed by some to haunt the place . . . in one way or another.

I listened to the water being tossed against the cliffs and in my mind's eye I saw those masts protruding from the treacherous sands.

In fifteen minutes, having washed in the powder room and unpacked my belongings, I was ready for the summons; I walked about my room examining the details. The cloth which lined the walls was of yellow brocade and must have been there for years for it was a little faded in places; the arched alcove, the rugs on the parquet floor, the sconces in the wall in which stood candles. Then I went to the window and looked out across the gardens to the copse and the sea. I looked for the masts of those sunken ships and could not see them.

I had nearly three quarters of an hour to wait so I decided I would have a look at the gardens. I was sure to be back in my room within the hour.

I put on a coat and found my way down to the hall and out into the upper courtyard. Passing under an archway I descended a flight of stone steps and before me was a terrace leading to lawns bordered with flowers which I guessed would be glorious in the late spring and summer. Rock plants grew in the stone—clumps of white arabis and blue aubrietia. The effect was charming.

There were no trees except stubby yews which looked as though they had stood where they did for centuries; but the shrubs were numerous. At the moment the only blooms were the yellow forsythia flowers, the colour of sunshine, I thought – but this was because it was early spring, and again I imagined the riot of colour there would be later.

I made my way through the shrubs and came to a stone archway over which a green plant was creeping. I passed under the arch and was in a walled garden – a quadrangle – cobbled, with two wooden seats facing each other across a water lily pond. It was charming and I pictured myself coming here during the hot summer weather in between lessons. I imagined I should have some spare time for I was beginning to plan a curriculum for the girls and although I intended to have each one at the piano every day, it seemed I should still have time to spare. But there was that suggestion that I was to play for Sir William. What could that entail? All sorts of possibilities presented themselves. I saw myself in that hall, playing on the dais . . . to a large assembly.

I wandered out of the walled garden and made my way back across a terrace, past the powerful buttresses; and as I looked up at those grey walls at the corbelled oriels and more of those hideous gargoyles, I thought how easy it would be to lose my way.

Trying to find my way back to the courtyards, I came to the stables. As I was passing by the mounting block, which must have been used by the ladies of the house for centuries because the stone was very worn, Napier Stacy came out of the stables leading a horse. I felt embarrassed to be caught wandering about and would have liked to avoid him, but I was too late, he had seen me.

He stood still, looking at me in a puzzled manner, wondering, it seemed, who dared trespass on his domain. Tall, lean, legs apart, bellicose, arrogant. I immediately thought of fragile Edith married to such a man. Poor child, I thought. Poor, *poor* child. I disliked him. The heavy dark brows were frowning above those startling blue eyes. They had no right to be blue, I thought illogically, in such a dark face. His nose was long, slightly prominent; his mouth too thin, as though he were sneering at the world. Oh, certainly I disliked him.

'Good afternoon,' I said defiantly – it was a natural attitude with which to face such a man.

'I don't think I have the pleasure . . .' He spoke the last word cynically to imply that he meant the opposite – or perhaps that was my imagination.

'I'm the music teacher. I've just arrived.'

'Music teacher?' He raised those black eyebrows. 'Oh, I remember now. I've heard some talk of this. So . . . you have come to inspect the stables?'

I felt annoyed. 'I had no fixed intention of doing so,' I said sharply. 'I came here unintentionally.'

He rocked a little on his heels and his attitude had changed. I was not quite sure whether for the worse or the better.

I added: 'I saw no harm in walking through the grounds.'

'Did anyone suggest there might be harm in such an innocent action?'

'I thought perhaps you . . .' I floundered. He was waiting expectantly, enjoying – yes, enjoying my discomfiture. I went on boldly: 'I thought perhaps *you* objected.'

'I don't remember *saying* so.'

'Well, since you don't object I'll continue with my walk.'

I moved away; as I did so I passed the back of the horse. In a second Napier Stacy was beside me; he had roughly caught my arm and dragged me violently to one side as the horse kicked out. His blue eyes blazed hotly; his face was tight with contempt. 'Good God, don't you know better than that?'

I looked at him indignantly; he was still gripping my arm and his face was so close to mine that I could see the clear whites of his eyes, the flash of his large white teeth.

'What are you . . .' I began.

But he silenced me curtly. 'My good woman, don't you know that you should never walk close behind a horse. You could have been kicked to death . . . or at least badly injured . . . in a second.'

'I . . . I had no idea . . .'

He released his grip on my arm and patted the horse's head. His expression changed. How gentle he was! How much more attractive he found a horse than an inquisitive music teacher!

Then he turned to me again: 'I shouldn't come to the stables alone if I were you, Miss er . . .'

'Mrs,' I said with dignity. 'Mrs Verlaine.' I waited to see the effect my married status would have on him; it was, however, perfectly clear that the fact was of no significance to him whatsoever.

'Well, don't come to the stables if you're going to be such a fool, for God's sake. A horse hears a movement behind him, naturally he kicks out in self preservation. Never do such a thing again.'

'I suppose,' I said coolly, 'you are reminding me that I should thank you.'

'I'm reminding you to show a little common sense in future.'

'You are most kind. Thank you for preserving my life . . . however ungraciously.'

A slow smile spread across his features but I did not wait for more. I started to walk away, horrified that I was trembling.

I could still feel his grip on my arm and I guessed I should have bruises for days to come to remind me of him. It was most disturbing. How was I to have known his wretched horse was going to kick out. Common sense, he would say. Well there were some of us who were more interested in our fellow human beings than in horses. The expression on the man's face when he had turned to the horse – and how it had changed for me! I didn't like him. I kept thinking of Edith at the wedding, coming down the aisle on his arm. She was frightened of him. What sort of man was he to frighten a young girl? I could guess and I hoped I should not have to see very much of Mr Napier Stacy. I would put him out of my mind. Pietro would have despised him on sight. That complete . . . what was it . . . virility, masculinity . . . would have irritated him. A Philistine, would have been Pietro's comment – a creature with no music in his soul.

I could not banish him from my mind, however.

I found my way back to my room and there I sat on the window seat looking out, not seeing the grey green water but the contempt in those startlingly blue eyes.

And then Mrs Lincroft came to my room and told me that Sir William would see me.

As soon as I was presented to Sir William I saw the resemblance between him and Napier. The same blue penetrating eyes, the long nose somewhat hawk-like, the thin lips and – something more subtle – that look of defiance against the world which was built up on arrogance.

Mrs Lincroft had explained to me on the way that Sir William was half paralysed due to a stroke he had suffered a year before. This meant that he could not move without great difficulty. I was beginning to fit things into some sort of shape and I realised that the stroke was probably another reason why Napier had been called home.

He sat in his chair, within his reach a stick with a handle inlaid with what I believed to be lapis lazuli; and he wore a dressing-gown of cloth with dark blue velvet collars and cuffs; he was obviously very tall and it seemed to me infinitely pathetic that such a man should be incapacitated, for he had clearly once been as strong and virile as his son. Heavy velour curtains were half drawn across the windows and he sat with his back to the light as though he were determined to avoid what little there was. The carpet was thick and it deadened the sound of my footsteps as I approached. The furniture – the great ormolu clock, the Buhl bureau, the tables and chairs, everything was heavy, and the effect was oppressive.

Mrs Lincroft said in her quiet but authoritative voice: 'Sir William, this is Mrs Verlaine.'

'Ah, Mrs Verlaine.' There was a slight slurring and hesitancy in the speech which I found moving. I suppose I was conscious – perhaps because of my recent encounter with his son – of the great change that illness had brought about in this man. 'Pray be seated.'

Mrs Lincroft put a chair immediately in front of Sir William, so close that I gathered his eyesight was failing too.

I sat down and he said: 'You have good qualifications, Mrs Verlaine. I am glad. I think Mrs Stacy has some talent. I should like it to be developed. You have not yet had time to discover, I suppose . . .'

'No,' I answered. 'But I have talked with the young ladies.'

He nodded. 'When I realised who you were I was immediately interested.'

My heartbeats quickened. If he knew that I was Roma's sister he might guess why I had come.

'I never had the pleasure of hearing your husband perform,' he went on, 'but I have read of his great talent.'

Of course, he was referring to Pietro. How nervous I was! I should have known.

'He was a great musician,' I said, trying to hide the emotion I felt when speaking of him.

'You will find Mrs Stacy something less.'

'There are very few people living who can be compared with him,' I said with dignity; and he inclined his head in a brief respect to Pietro.

'I shall require you to play for me from time to time,' he went on. 'It will be part of your duties. And perhaps on occasions for our guests.'

'I see.'

'I should like to hear you play now.' Mrs Lincroft was suddenly beside me.

'There's a piano in the next room,' she said. 'You will find the piece which Sir William wishes you to play there.'

Mrs Lincroft drew back a heavy curtain behind which was a door. This she opened and I followed her into the room. The first thing I noticed was the grand piano. It was open and a piece of music was set up on it. The room was furnished in the same colours as the one I had just left; and there was the same indication that the owner wished to shut out the light.

I went to the piano and glanced at the music. I knew every note by heart. It was Beethoven's *Für Elise*, in my mind one of the most beautiful pieces ever written.

Mrs Lincroft nodded to me and I sat down at the piano

and played. I was deeply moved, for the piece brought back memories of the house in Paris and of Pietro. He had said of this piece: 'Romantic . . . haunting . . . mysterious. *You* couldn't go wrong with a piece like that. With that you can hypnotise yourself into thinking you're a great pianist.'

So I played and I was soothed and I forgot the sad old man in the next room and the discourteous younger one whom I had met in the stables. Music has this effect on me. I am two people – the musician and the woman. The latter is practical, a little gauche in her defiance of the world because she has been hurt and doesn't intend to be again, muzzling her emotions and her feelings, pretending they don't exist because she is afraid of them.

But the musician is all emotion, all feeling; when I play I can imagine that I am carried away from the world, that I have a special sense, that I am in possession of some subtle understanding which is denied to ordinary people. And I felt as I played that this room which had been dark and sad for a long time was suddenly alive again; that I had brought back something for which it had long yearned. Fanciful yes. But music is not of this mundane world. Great musicians draw their inspiration from the divine influence . . . and although I am not great, I am at least a musician.

I finished playing and the room returned to normal, for the magic had disappeared. I felt I had never done better justice to *Elise*, and that had the master overcome his deafness and heard my rendering he would not have been displeased.

There was silence. I sat at the piano waiting. Then as nothing happened I rose and went through the door holding aside the curtain which was not completely drawn over it. Sir William was lying back in his chair, his eyes closed. Mrs Lincroft, who had been standing by him, came swiftly to my side.

'It was very good,' she whispered. 'He was greatly touched by it. Can you find your way back to your room alone, do you think?'

I said I could and I went out wondering whether the music had so moved Sir William that it had made him ill. At least Mrs Lincroft felt she must stay with him. What comfort she must be to him – far more than an ordinary housekeeper! No wonder he wanted to repay her by giving her daughter Alice every advantage of education and upbringing.

Thinking of Sir William, Mrs Lincroft, and of course the encounter with Napier Stacy, I did not find my way back to my room as easily as I had imagined I would. The house was enormous; there were so many corridors and pairs of stairs which looked so much alike; therefore it was quite understandable that I should take the wrong turning.

I came to a door and wondering whether it would lead me back to that part of the house in which I had my room, I opened it. The first thing I noticed about this room was the bellrope and it occurred to me that I should ring this and ask a servant to conduct me to my own room.

As soon as I stepped into this room I was aware that there was something strange about it. It had what I can only call an air of studied naturalness, the impression being that its occupier had a moment before left it. A book was open on a table. I went over and saw that it was a stamp collection; a riding whip lay on a chair, and on the wall were pictures of soldiers in various uniforms. Over the fire-place hung a painting of a young man. I went to it and stood looking at it for it was a fascinating study. His hair was chestnut brown, his eyes vivid blue; the nose was long and slightly hawk-like and the mouth was curved into a smile. It was one of the most handsome faces I had ever seen. I knew of course who it was. It was the beautiful brother who had died and I had come into the room which had once been his. I was startled for I knew I had no right to be in this holy of holies; yet I found it difficult to take my attention from that face on the canvas up there. The picture was painted so that the eyes seemed to follow you no matter where you were; and as I stepped backwards keeping my gaze on the picture the blue eyes watched me, seeming sad one moment, smiling the next.

'Ha. Ha.' I heard a high-pitched titter which sent a shiver down my spine. 'Are you looking for Beau?'

I turned round and for a moment I thought it was a little girl standing behind me. Then I saw that she was by no means young. She must have been in her seventies. But she was wearing a pale blue dress of cambric and about her waist was a blue satin sash. Her hair was white but in it she wore two little blue bows, one on either side of her head, the same colour as the sash; the frilled skirt would have been more suited to Edith than to this woman.

'Yes,' she said almost coyly, 'you *are* looking for Beau. I know you are . . . so don't deny it.'

'I am the new music teacher,' I said.

'I know it. I know everything that goes on in this house. But that doesn't prove, does it, that you weren't looking for Beau.'

I studied her closely; she had a small heart-shaped face and in her youth must have been extremely pretty. She was certainly very feminine and determined to retain that quality; the dress and the bows gave evidence of that. She had light blue eyes that sparkled from her wrinkles with a kind of mischief, and a flat little nose like a kitten's.

'I have only just arrived,' I explained. 'I was trying to . . .'

'Look for Beau,' she finished. 'I know you have only just arrived and I wanted to meet you. But you'd heard of Beau, of course. Everybody has heard of Beau.'

'I wonder whether you would be good enough to introduce yourself.'

'Of course, of course. How remiss of me.' She giggled. 'I thought you might have heard of me . . . as you'd heard of Beau. I'm Miss Sybil Stacy – William's sister, and I've lived in this house all my life so I've seen it all and I know exactly what it's all about.'

'That must be very gratifying for you.'

She looked at me sharply. 'You're a widow,' she said. 'So you're a woman of experience. You were married to that famous man, weren't you? And he died. That was sad. Death is sad. We have had deaths in this house . . .'

Her lips quivered and I thought she was going to weep. She brightened suddenly, as a child will. 'But now Napier is back; he is married to Edith; there will be little children. Then it will begin to be better. The children will put everything right.' She looked up at the picture. 'Perhaps Beau will go away then.'

Her face puckered.

'He's dead, isn't he?' I said gently.

'The dead don't always go, do they. Sometimes they decide to stay. They can't tear themselves from those they've lived with. Sometimes it's love that keeps them . . . sometimes it's hate. Beau's still here. He can't rest, poor Beau. It was so lovely for him, you see. He had everything. He had beauty, charm, and he was brilliantly clever; he used to play the piano to make the tears run down your cheeks. Beau had everything. So he wouldn't want to leave a life which was perfect, would he?'

'Perhaps he found greater perfection.'

She shook her head and stamped her foot in a childish gesture. 'It wasn't possible,' she said angrily. 'Beau couldn't have been happier anywhere . . . neither on Earth nor in Heaven. Why did Beau have to die, do you think?'

'Because his time had come,' I suggested. 'It happens so . . . now and then. Young people die.' Pietro, Roma, I thought. I felt my lips quiver.

'Oh, he was beautiful,' she said. She raised her eyes to the picture as though she were before some god. 'That was him . . . to the life. That picture seems to speak to you. And I'll never forget the day. The blood . . . the blood . . .'

Her face puckered, and I said: 'Please don't think of it. It must be very distressing even now.'

She came closer to me and all the sorrow had left her blue eyes; they sparkled with that mischief which was more alarming than her grief.

'They took his dying depositions. The doctor insisted. He said it was not Napier's fault. They were playing with the guns . . . as boys will. "Hands up or I'll fire!" said Napier. And Beau replied: "I'll get you first." At least that's what Napier told us. But no one was there to see. They were in the gun-room. Then Beau reached for his gun and Napier fired his. Napier said they both thought the guns weren't loaded. But you see they were.'

'What a terrible accident.'

'Nothing has ever been the same again.'

'But it was an accident.'

'You are a very sure person, Mrs . . . Mrs . . .'

'Verlaine.'

'I shall remember it. I never forget a name. I never forget a face. You are a very sure person, Mrs Verlaine. And you have not been here a day yet. So you must be very sure indeed.'

'I can't know anything, of course,' I said, 'but I can quite see how two boys playing together could have an accident. It's not the first time it's happened.'

She whispered conspiratorially: 'Napier was jealous of Beau. Everybody knew it. How could it have been otherwise?

Beau was so handsome; he could do everything well. He used to challenge Napier in lots of ways.'

'Then he couldn't have been so wonderful,' I said sharply and wondered why I wanted to protect Napier. It was the boy I was eager should have justice, not that arrogant man in the stables.

'Just in a boyish way. He was so boyish . . . And Napier, well, he was quite different.'

'In what way?'

'Difficult. He'd go off on his own. He was always going off on his own. Wouldn't practise the piano.'

'They have always been fond of music in this house?'

'Their mother played the piano beautifully. As well as you do. Oh yes, I heard you just now. I could have believed it was Isabella come back. Isabella could have been a very great pianist, I've heard it said. But she didn't go on studying when she married. William didn't wish it. He wanted her to play for him only. Can you understand that, Mrs Verlaine?'

'No,' I said vehemently. 'I think she should have been allowed to go on with her studies. If we have talent we should not hide it away.'

'The parable of the talents,' she cried, her eyes alight with pleasure. 'It's what Isabella thought too. She was . . . resentful.'

I felt a sympathy with Isabella. She had thrown away a career no doubt for marriage . . . somewhat as I had.

I felt those childish yet penetrating eyes on me.

Then she turned once more to the picture. 'I'll tell you a secret, Mrs Verlaine. That is my work.'

'Then you're an artist.'

She put her hands behind her back and nodded slowly.

'How interesting!'

'Oh yes. I painted that picture.'

'How long before he died did he sit for it?'

'Sit for it. He never would sit for anything. Imagine getting Beau to sit down! And why should I want him to? I knew him. I could see him clearly then . . . just as I see him now. I didn't need him to *sit*, Mrs Verlaine. I only paint the people I know.'

'It's very clever of you.'

'Would you like to see some more of my pictures?'

'I'd be most interested.'

'Isabella was a clever musician, but she wasn't the only clever one. Come to my rooms now. I have my own little suite. I've had it all my life. There was a time when I might have left here. I was going to be married . . .' Her face puckered and I thought she was going to burst into tears. 'But I didn't . . . and so I stayed here where I had been all my life. I had my home and my pictures . . .'

'I'm sorry,' I said.

She smiled. 'Perhaps I'll paint you one day, Mrs Verlaine. It'll be when I've learned to know you. Then I'll see how I'll paint you. Come with me now.'

I was fascinated by this strange little woman. She sprang round daintily and I saw her black satin slippers peeping out from beneath her blue skirt. There was mischief in her smile; as I have said she was like a high spirited little girl and the manner coupled with that wrinkled face was intriguing and yet, I fancied, a little sinister. I wondered what I was going to see in her room, and if she really was responsible for the picture over the fireplace in Beau's room.

Upstairs and through corridors we went. She looked over her shoulder at me and said: 'Now, Mrs Verlaine, you are lost, are you not?' in the manner of a teasing child.

I admitted I was but added that I supposed I should be able to find my way about in time.

'In time . . .' she whispered. 'Perhaps. But time does not

teach everything, does it. Time heals they say, but everything they say is not true, is it?'

I did not want to enter into a discussion at this point so I did not attempt to disagree with her; and smiling she went on.

Eventually we came to what she called her suite. We were in one of the turrets and gleefully she showed me the apartment. There were three rooms in the great tower. 'It's a circle,' she pointed out – 'you can go all round – one room leading to another and you come back to where you started from. Isn't that unusual, Mrs Verlaine? But I want to show you my studio. It faces north, you know. The light is so important to an artist. Come along in and I'll show you some of my work.'

I went in. The windows were bigger in this room than in the others and the north light was strong. Her look of youth was harshly denied in this room; the little bows, the blue gown with its satin sash, the little black slippers, were not enough to combat the wrinkles, the brown smudges on the thin claw-like hands; but she had lost none of her animation. The room was simply furnished; there was a door at each end which I knew opened on to the next room; on the walls were several pictures, and canvases were stacked up in a corner. On a table lay a pallet, and an easel was set up; on this was a half finished picture of three girls; and I knew at once that they were Edith, Allegra and Alice. She followed my gaze.

'Ah,' she said conspiratorially. 'Come and look.'

I went closer beside her. She was watching me eagerly for my reactions. I studied the picture; Edith with her golden hair; Allegra with her thick black curls and Alice neat with a white band holding back her long straight light brown hair.

'You recognise them?'

66

'Of course. It's a good likeness.'

'They're young,' she said. 'Their faces tell nothing, do they.'

'Youth . . . innocence . . . inexperience . . .'

'They tell nothing,' she said. 'But if you know them you can see beneath the face they show the world. That is the artist's gift, don't you think? To see what they are trying to hide.'

'It makes the artist rather alarming.'

'A person to be avoided.' Her laughter was pitched and girlish. She was looking at me with those childlike eyes and I felt uneasy. Was she trying to probe my secrets? Was she seeing my stormy life with Pietro? Would she attempt to probe into my motives? What if she discovered that I was Roma's sister.

'It would all depend,' I said, 'whether one had something to hide.'

'All people have something to hide, don't they, Mrs Verlaine? It could be only one little thing . . . but it's something so very much one's own. Older people are more interesting than the young. Nature is an artist. Nature draws all sorts of things on people's faces which they would prefer to hide.'

'Nature also draws the pleasanter things.'

'You're an optimist, Mrs Verlaine. I can see that. You're like the young woman who came here . . . digging.'

My uneasiness increased. 'Like . . .' I began.

She went on: 'William didn't want the place disturbed, but she was so persistent. She wouldn't let him rest so he said yes. And they came down looking for Roman remains. It hasn't been the same since.'

'You met this young woman?'

'Oh yes. I like to know what's going on.'

'She would be the one who disappeared?'

She nodded delightedly, her eyes almost lost among the wrinkles.

'You know why?' she said.

'No.'

'Meddling. They didn't like it.'

'Who didn't?'

'Those who are dead and gone. They don't go . . . altogether, you know. They come back.'

'You mean the . . . Romans?'

'The dead,' she said. 'You can sense them all round you.' She came closer to me and whispered: 'I don't think Beau will like Napier's coming back. In fact I know he doesn't. He's told me.'

'Beau . . . has told you!'

'In dreams. We were close . . . He was my little boy. The one I might have had. I'd pictured him . . . just like Beau. It was all right when Napier wasn't here. It was right and proper that he should be sent away. Why should Beau be gone and Napier stay. It wasn't fair. It wasn't right. But now he's back and that's bad, I tell you. Just a moment.' She went to the stack of canvases and brought out a picture. She set it against the wall and I gasped with horror. It was a full length picture of a man. The face was wicked . . . the hawknose was accentuated; the eyes were narrowed, the mouth was curved into a repulsive snarl. I recognised it as Napier.

'You recognise it?' she asked.

'It's not really like him,' I said.

'I painted it after he'd murdered his brother.'

I felt indignant. For the boy, I told myself fiercely once more. She was watching my face and she laughed.

'I see you are going to take his side. You don't know him. He's wicked. He was jealous of his brother, of beautiful Beau. He wanted what Beau had . . . so he killed him. He's like that. I know it. Others know it.'

'I am sure there are some who . . .'

She interrupted me. 'How can you be sure, Mrs Verlaine? What do you know? You think because William brought him back and married him to Edith . . . William is a hard man too, Mrs Verlaine. The men of this house are all hard . . . except Beau. Beau was beautiful. Beau was good. And he had to die.' She turned away. 'Forgive me. I feel it still. I shall never forget.'

'I understand.' I turned my back on that portrait of the young Napier. 'It is very kind of you to show me your pictures. I was trying to find my way to my room. I think I may be wanted.'

She nodded. 'I hope that one day you will see more of my pictures.'

'I should like to,' I said.

'Soon?' she pleaded like a child.

'If you will be so good as to invite me.'

She nodded happily and pulled a bellrope. A servant came and she asked the girl to conduct me to my apartments.

When I reached my room Alice was there.

She said: 'I came to tell you that you will be having dinner with Mother and me to-night, and that I will come and take you to her rooms at seven o'clock.'

'Thank you,' I replied.

'You look startled. Was Sir William kind to you?'

'Yes. I played for him. I think he liked my playing. But I lost my way and met Miss Stacy.'

Alice smiled understandingly. 'She is a little . . . strange. I trust she did not embarrass you.'

'She took me to her studio.'

Alice was surprised. 'You must have aroused her interest. Did she show you her pictures?'

I nodded. 'I saw one of you with Mrs Stacy and Allegra.'

'Did you? She didn't tell us she was painting us. Is it good?'

'It seems a perfect likeness.'

'I should like to see it.'

'She will surely show it to you.'

'She's a little odd at times. It's because she was crossed in love. By the way did you notice anything strange about our names, Mrs Verlaine?'

'Your names?'

'The three of us . . . your pupils?'

'Alice, Edith, Allegra. Allegra is unusual.'

'Oh yes, but the three of us together. They come into a poem. I like poetry. Do you?'

'I like some,' I answered. 'To which poem are you referring?'

'It's by Mr Longfellow. Shall I say the bit I like? I know it by heart.'

'Please do.'

She stood beside me, her arms folded behind her back, her eyes lowered as she quoted:

'From my study I see in the lamplight,
Descending the broad hall stair,
Grave Alice, and laughing Allegra,
And Edith with golden hair.

A whisper and then a silence:
Yet I know by their merry eyes
They are plotting and planning together
To take me by surprise.'

She lifted her eyes to my face and they were shining. She said: 'You see, *laughing* Allegra, Edith with *golden hair*, and I am *grave*, am I not? You see it *is* us.'

70

'And you are planning to take someone by surprise?'
She smiled her quiet little smile.

Then she said with undoubted gravity: 'I expect all of us
surprise each other at some time, Mrs Verlaine.'

Chapter Three

I dined that night with Mrs Lincroft and Alice – Mrs Lincroft herself doing the cooking for she had a small kitchen attached to her little suite of sitting-room and bedroom. 'I found it made it easier,' she explained, 'when the family was entertaining, and now I often do it. It saves the servants trouble and I rather enjoy it. I think now that you have come, Mrs Verlaine, you might take your meals here with me. Alice will join us when she does not dine with the family. Sir William very kindly invites her now and then. He may suggest you join them occasionally.'

It was a pleasant meal and very well cooked. Alice sat quietly with us. I should always think of her as Grave Alice in future.

Mrs Lincroft spoke of Sir William's illness and how he had changed since he had had his stroke a little less than a year ago.

'His wife used to play the piano to him. When Mr Napier came home I suppose he was reminded of the old days and that is why he thought of bringing music into the house again.'

I was silent thinking how much Sir William must have

loved his wife since he had banished music from the house after her death.

'There are changes now,' went on Mrs Lincroft. 'And of course now that Mr Napier and Edith are married there will be more.' She smiled. The one maid who was waiting on us had gone to the kitchen. She added: 'It will be more like a normal household. And it is a relief to know that Mr Napier has taken over the management of the estate since his return. He is very active; a first-class horseman; in fact he rides everywhere. He is taking care of everything . . . magnificently. Even Sir William must agree to that.'

I waited, but she seemed to realise that she had said too much. 'Would you care for some more of this pie?'

I thanked her and declined while complimenting her on its excellence.

'Do you ride, Mrs Verlaine?' she asked then.

'My sister and I went to a riding school, and we rode occasionally in the Row. Living in London didn't give us the opportunities for riding that the country would have offered and we both had other great interests which absorbed us.'

'Is your sister a musician too?'

'Oh no . . . no . . .' There was an expectant pause and I saw how easily I could betray my identity and I wondered how they would react if they knew that I was the sister of the woman who had disappeared so mysteriously.

I added lamely: 'My father was a professor. My sister helped him in his work.'

'You must be a very clever family,' she said.

'My parents had advanced ideas on education and although we were girls we were educated as though we were boys. You see there were no boys in the family. Perhaps if there had been it would have been different.'

Alice spoke then. She said: 'I should like to be educated

in that way, Mrs Verlaine ... like you and your sister. I expect you wish you were with her instead of with us.'

'She's dead,' I replied shortly.

I thought Alice was about to ask more questions but Mrs Lincroft silenced her with a look. She herself said: 'Oh, I am sorry. That is sad.' And there was a short sympathetic pause which I broke by asking if the girls were good horsewomen.

'Mr Napier is determined that Edith shall be. He takes her riding every morning. I expect she has improved a great deal.'

'She hasn't,' put in Alice. 'She's worse. Because now she's frightened.'

'Frightened!' I echoed.

'Edith is timid and Mr Napier is trying to make her bold,' explained Alice. 'I really believe Edith would rather jog along on poor old Silver than ride the fine horse Mr Napier arranges for her.'

Mrs Lincroft again glanced at her daughter and I wondered whether Alice's demure manner meant that she was suppressed.

When the meal was over I stayed for an hour or so talking to Mrs Lincroft and then, for as she suggested I was very tired, I went to bed, but I slept only fitfully. My confused thoughts of the day's experience kept me awake but I told myself that once I had worked out a routine for the days I should settle down.

Breakfast was brought to my room on a tray and when I had eaten it Edith knocked and asked if she might come in.

She looked very pretty in a midnight blue riding habit and black bowler type hat.

'You are going out to ride?' I asked.

She shuddered so faintly that it was scarcely perceptible. She was, I discovered, unable to hide her feelings. 'Not yet,' she said, 'that will be later, but I may not have time to change. I wanted to talk to you about my tuition.'

'Of course.'

'And then I will take you to the vicarage where the girls are having their lessons. You'll want to fit yours in with those they get from the vicar, won't you? I hope I'm not going to disappoint you, Mrs Verlaine.'

'I don't think you will. I can see you feel strongly about the piano.'

'I love playing. It . . . it helps me when I'm . . .' I waited and she finished lamely, 'When I'm a little downcast.'

'I'm so glad. Shall we start right away?'

She took me to the schoolroom adjoining which was a smaller apartment to which she referred as the music-room. In it was an upright piano.

There she played for me and we talked of her progress and I quickly got an idea of how advanced she was. I realised that she would be a good pupil – hardworking and eager – that her talent was frail but definitely there. Edith would get a great deal of pleasure from her music but she would never be a great musician. It was what I had expected and I should know how to work with her.

She became animated, talking of music.

'You see,' she said in a rush of confidence, 'it's the only thing I've ever really been any good at.'

'And I think you'll be very good if you work hard.'

She was pleased; and suggested we leave for the vicarage.

'It's only fifteen minutes walk, Mrs Verlaine. Would you care to walk or would you like the trap?'

I said the walk would be delightful and we set out.

'Mr Jeremy Brown will be teaching the girls this morning,

I daresay. He often does.' She had flushed slightly, which she did often. 'He's the curate,' she added.

'Was he your teacher too?'

She nodded and smiled. Then she was suddenly grave. 'Of course since ... my marriage I have not been having lessons. Mr Brown is a very good teacher.' She sighed. 'I think you will like him, and the vicar.'

We reached the vicarage, a lovely old grey stone house beside the church with its tall grey tower.

Mrs Rendall greeted me like an old friend and said she would take me to the vicar's study. She looked at Edith questioningly. I noticed that people were unsure how to treat Edith; because, I presumed, she seemed neither a young girl nor a married woman.

Edith said: 'Don't worry about me, Mrs Rendall. I'll go to the schoolroom and join the scholars for a while.'

Mrs Rendall lifted her shoulders in a manner which suggested she thought Edith's behaviour a little odd. Then she said she would take me to see the vicar.

The vicar's study was a charming room with tall windows looking on to a well-kept lawn sloping down to the churchyard. In the distance I could see the gravestones and I thought it would look a little eerie by moonlight. But I had little time for such contemplation for the vicar was rising from his chair, his spectacles pushed up to his forehead and precariously balanced there, his thinning grey hair combed across the top to hide his baldness; an air of unworldliness about him which I found rather charming and in great contrast to his energetic wife.

'This is the Reverend Arthur Rendall,' announced Mrs Rendall ceremoniously. 'And Arthur, Mrs Verlaine.'

'Delighted ... delighted!' murmured the vicar; he was looking not at me but at the table and I realised why when Mrs Rendall barked out: 'On your forehead, Arthur.'

'Thank you, my dear, thank you.' He reached for the glasses, set them in their rightful place and looked at me.

'It is a great pleasure to welcome you here,' he said. 'I am very pleased that Sir William has decided to proceed with the girls' musical education.'

'I must discover when it will be convenient for them to have their lessons. There must not be any overlapping.'

'Oh, we will work that out together,' said the vicar smiling happily.

'Pray take a seat, Mrs Verlaine,' put in Mrs Rendall. 'Really, Arthur . . . keeping Mrs Verlaine standing like this. I'm sure the Reverend will want to talk to you about Sylvia. I am anxious that she too shall continue with her music.'

'I am sure that can easily be arranged,' I said.

The vicar then began to explain to me the times of the lessons and we decided that I should give the lessons at the vicarage where there was a good piano, one which the girls had used previously. Edith, Allegra and Alice could also practise at Lovat Stacy and Sylvia at the vicarage. It could all be very satisfactorily fitted in.

Mrs Rendall left us while we were planning this and when she had gone the vicar said: 'I do not know how I should get along without my dear wife. *Such* a clever manager . . .' as though excusing his subservience to her. And when we had made our arrangements he began talking to me about the antiquities of the neighbourhood and how excited he had been by the discoveries of the Roman remains recently.

'I often went along to the excavations,' he told me, 'and I was always welcome there.' He looked uneasily at the door and I remembered his wife's observations and pictured the vicar paying secret visits there. 'Indeed, I had always believed that something of interest would be discovered here. The amphitheatre was found quite a long time ago and as you know amphitheatres were usually built outside the city . . . so it seemed reasonable that there would be other remains not far off.'

I was reminded vividly of Roma and my heart began to beat faster as I said: 'Did you meet the archæologist who disappeared so mysteriously?'

'Oh dear me, what a terrible affair . . . and so extraordinary! Do you know it would not surprise me if she had gone off somewhere far away . . . abroad . . . Some project . . .'

'But if there had been another project wouldn't it have been known? She wouldn't have gone alone. There would have been a party. These things are often organised by the British Museum and . . .'

I floundered and he said: 'I see you are very well informed on these matters, Mrs Verlaine. Far better so than I.'

'I am sure that is not so. But I did wonder about this . . . disappearance.'

'Such a practical young lady,' mused the vicar. 'That was what made it seem so strange.'

'You must have talked to her a great deal because of your common interest in those remains. Did you think she was the sort of woman who . . . ?'

'Who would take her own life?' The vicar looked shocked. 'That was suggested. An accident? It must have been. But she was not the type to have an accident . . . like that. I am baffled. And I come back to my opinion that she has gone off somewhere. An urgent call . . . No time to explain . . .'

I could see that he did not wish me to disturb his pleasant solution of the mystery and, as I guessed he could tell me nothing new about Roma, I gladly accepted his invitation to show me round the church.

We left the house and crossed the garden, taking a path between the gravestones to the church, through the porch with the notices attached to boards hanging there. The habitual hushed cool atmosphere greeted us. The vicar was clearly proud of his stained glass windows, which, he informed me, had been given to the church by members of the Stacy family. The Stacys were the squires of the neighbourhood, the benefactors on whom so many depended.

He took me to the altar that I might admire the beautiful carvings there.

'They are really unique,' he told me beaming with pride.

I noticed a memorial tablet in the wall, set in a niche above which was a statue of a youth in long robes, hands folded together.

Beneath it said:

> 'Gone from us but not forgotten
> Beaumont Stacy.
> Departed this life . . .'

While I tried to work out the date in Roman figures the vicar said: 'Ah, yes. Sad, very sad.'

'He died very young,' I said.

'In his nineteenth year. A tragedy.'

The vicar's eyes were misted. 'He was shot . . . accidentally, by his brother. He was a handsome boy. We were all so fond of him. Ah, it is long ago and now that Napier is home again all will be well.'

I was already accustomed to the vicar's optimism, so I wondered whether this was really so. I had only been in the house a day and I was conscious of some brooding melancholy, some remaining aura of a past tragedy.

'How terrible for the brother.'

'A great mistake . . . to blame him. To send him away like that.' The vicar shook his head and looked sad. Then he brightened: 'However, he's back now.'

'How old was . . . Napier when this happened?'

'About seventeen, I should say. I think he was the younger by two years. He was quite different from Beaumont. Beaumont had the charm. He was brilliant; everyone loved him. And so . . . Well, boys should never be allowed to play with guns. It can so easily happen. Poor Napier, I was sorry for him. I said to Sir William that it could have a very ill effect to blame him in this way. But he wouldn't listen. He simply could not bear to look at Napier after it happened. So Napier went away.'

'What a dreadful tragedy! I should have thought that having lost one son he would have felt the remaining one to be doubly precious.'

'Sir William is an unusual man. He doted on Beaumont, and Napier reminded him of the tragedy.'

'Very very strange,' I said. And I could not take my eyes from the statue of that youth, palms together in prayer, eyes raised to heaven.

'I was delighted when I heard that Napier was to come back. And now he is married to Edith Cowan all will be happily settled. At one time it seemed likely that Sir William would make Edith his heiress. There would have been an outcry if he had. But he was very fond of Edith's parents and he had made her his ward. However, this is the happiest of solutions. Edith *will* inherit . . . through her marriage with Napier.'

The vicar was beaming like the good fairy who has waved a wand and made everything as it should be.

At that moment a maid appeared at the church door to say that the churchwarden had called to see the vicar on a matter of some urgency and was waiting in the drawing-room. I told the vicar I should like to look round the church by myself and he left me.

'You will find your way back to the house, Mrs Verlaine.

Mrs Rendall will be delighted to give you some refreshment . . . and then you will be able to meet my curate, Jeremy Brown, and talk of the young ladies' lessons with him.'

Left alone I went back to that statue in the wall and thought about the young man who in his nineteenth year had been shot by his brother. But chiefly I thought of the brother who at the age of seventeen had been sent away because of the accident. How could parents have behaved so to a son however much they had loved his brother, unless . . . Oh, no, it most certainly would have been an accident.

I turned away and wandered into the graveyard. The silence all about me moved me deeply. There I stood among those memorials to the dead and I saw from the inscription on some that they had stood there for over a hundred and fifty years – some even longer; they looked as though they were so old they could no longer stand up straight and some of the names and writing on them was half obliterated by time.

I wondered if that boy was buried here. It was almost certain that he would be; and I was sure I should have no difficulty in finding his grave for surely the Stacys would have the most magnificent of vaults or mausoleums.

I looked about me and sure enough there was a vault grander than all others. Wrought iron surrounded it and when I saw the name Stacy, I knew this was the family vault. Marble statues of angels with drawn swords had been placed at the four corners as though to guard it from intruders; and there was a gate, padlocked, which led down to the vault. Inside the iron railings was a great tablet on which the names of those buried there had been inscribed with the dates of their births and death. The last on the list was Beaumont Stacy.

As I was turning away I thought of Isabella Stacy in whose room I had sat and played the piano, the mother of Beaumont and Napier. She was dead, but where was her name. It was not on the scroll. Surely she would have been buried here?

I studied the scroll once more; I walked round the vault; I looked about me as though I could find the answer to this mystery here in the graveyard. I was filled with a burning desire to know where she had been buried and why not here.

And as I retraced my steps to the vicarage I was reminded once more that the strangeness of this new world into which I had been suddenly launched was occupying my mind as much as the mystery of Roma's disappearance.

Mrs Rendall was waiting for me in the vicarage hall.

'I wondered what had become of you,' she announced. 'I told the Reverend to look after you.'

I said quickly: 'I asked to be allowed to look round the church alone.'

'Alone!' Mrs Rendall was surprised, but mollified. 'I hope you liked our windows, Mrs Verlaine. They are some of the best in the country.'

I hastily said that I was sure they were, and added that I had walked through the graveyard and seen the Stacy vault. Was Lady Stacy not buried there? I had seen no mention of her.

Mrs Rendall looked startled, which was a strange position for her to find herself in, I was sure.

'My word, Mrs Verlaine,' she said with a touch of asperity, 'you are a regular detective.'

I was sure in that moment that she suspected my motives for coming to this place were not solely to teach music.

'I was interested naturally to see anything connected with the family,' I said coolly.

'And I am sure it does you credit,' she replied. 'I'll tell you this: Lady Stacy was not buried in the vault. You probably know that suicides are buried in *un*consecrated ground.'

'Suicides!' I cried.

She nodded gravely; then her lips formed into lines of disapproval. 'Just after Beaumont's death, she killed herself. It was most unfortunate. She took a gun into the woods . . . and died in the same way . . . only in her case the wound was self-inflicted.'

'What a terrible tragedy.'

'She couldn't bear life without Beaumont. She doted on the boy. I think the affair turned her brain.'

'So it was a double tragedy.'

'It changed everything up at the house. Beaumont and Lady Stacy dead and Napier sent away. Everything was blamed on to Napier.'

'But it was an accident.'

Mrs Rendall nodded mournfully. 'He was always up to something. A bad boy . . . so different from his brother. It was almost as though they believed it wasn't an accident after all. But blood's thicker than water and Sir William didn't want everything to go out of the family after all. Though at one time we thought he might disinherit Napier. However, he's back now and married to Edith, which is what Sir William wanted, so it seemed Napier was ready to please his father at last . . . for the sake of the inheritance, of course.'

'Well, I hope he'll be happy,' I said. 'He must have suffered a great deal. Whatever he did, he was only seventeen and to banish him in that way seems a terrible punishment.'

Mrs Rendall sniffed. 'Of course if Beau had lived Napier wouldn't have inherited. It's a consideration.'

I felt rather indignant on behalf of Napier – though I couldn't think why I should feel so for someone whom I had disliked on sight, except for my sense of justice. I decided that Sir William was an unnatural father whom I was very ready to dislike as much as I already disliked his son.

I said nothing however and Mrs Rendall remarked that I might care to come to the schoolroom and meet Mr Jeremy Brown.

The vicarage schoolroom was a long room, rather low ceilinged. As in the big house, the windows had the leaden panes which, while they looked charming, let in little light.

It was a delightful scene which met my eyes as Mrs Rendall threw open the door without knocking. I imagined she rarely warned people of her approach. There were the girls at the big table – Edith among them, bent over their work; there was a fourth member of the party: Sylvia. And seated at the head of the table a very fair, delicate looking young man.

'I have brought Mrs Verlaine to meet you,' boomed Mrs Rendall and the young man rose and came towards us.

'This is our curate, Mr Jeremy Brown,' went on Mrs Rendall.

I shook hands with Mr Brown, whose manner was almost apologetic. Another, I thought, who stood in awe of this formidable lady.

'And what is it this morning, Mr Brown?' asked Mrs Rendall.

'Latin and geography.'

I saw the maps spread out on the table and the girls' notebooks beside them. Edith looked happier than I had so far seen her.

Mrs Rendall grunted and said: 'Mrs Verlaine wants to take the girls through their music. One by one, I suppose, Mrs Verlaine?'

'I think that would be an excellent idea.' I smiled at the curate. 'If you are agreeable.'

'Oh yes . . . yes . . . indeed,' he said. Then I noticed the rapt expression in Edith's eyes.

How the young betray themselves! I knew that there was some romantic attachment – however slight – between Edith and this Jeremy Brown.

As Mrs Rendall had said, I was a detective.

In the next day or so I slipped into a routine. There were meals with Mrs Lincroft when often Alice was present; there were the piano lessons for the girls and some of these were taken at the vicarage where it was often more convenient, as I was able to take the girls one by one while the others were at their lessons with the vicar or Jeremy Brown. There was also Sylvia to be considered. She was a very indifferent pupil but tried hard – I imagined because she feared her mother's reaction to miserable failure.

The four girls interested me because they were all so different; and I couldn't help sensing when they were all together that there was something exceptional about them. I was not sure whether it was in themselves or in their relationship towards one another. And I told myself that it was because of their unusual backgrounds – in fact the only ordinary one was Sylvia's, and her overwhelmingly domineering mother could have an effect on a child.

Allegra and Alice left each morning at half past eight for the vicarage to start lessons at nine o'clock; on some days I followed an hour later. Sometimes Edith walked over with me just, she said, for the walk, but I felt it was something more than the walk which attracted her. This gave me an opportunity of getting to know the young Mrs Stacy.

She had a gentle and unsubtle nature and I often had the notion that she was longing to confide in me. I wished she would, but somehow she always seemed to draw back just as I thought I was going to hear something of importance.

I suspected that she was afraid of her husband; but at the

vicarage with Jeremy Brown her manner underwent a change and she seemed happy in a furtive way, like a child who is snatching some forbidden yet irresistible treat. Perhaps I was too curious about the affairs of others; I made excuses for myself. I was here to discover what had become of Roma and I must therefore find out everything about the people around me. But what had the relationship between Edith and her husband and the young curate to do with Roma? No, it was plain curiosity, I warned myself, and no concern of mine and yet . . .

I can only say that the desire to know was too deep to be dismissed and I felt that Edith would be my best source of information for the reason that she was guileless and easy to read.

When she offered to take me into Walmer and Deal, the twin towns a few miles along the coast, I was delighted and we set out one morning as the girls were leaving for the vicarage.

It was a lovely April day with an opalesque sea and the lightest of breezes blowing off it. The gorse bushes were clumps of golden glory; and under hedges I caught glimpses of wild violets and wood sorrel. And because it was spring and I smelt the good scent of the earth and felt the gentle warmth of the sun I was elated. I didn't quite know why, except that the budding shrubs and bushes and the birdsong and the gentle sunshine all seemed to offer some promise and I experienced that springtime fever which made me believe that there was something symbolic in all nature's awakening to a new life. Every now and then the song of a bird was on the air – whitethroats and swallows, sedge warblers and martins. There was no sign of the gulls whose melancholy cries I had already noticed in gloomy weather.

'They come inland when it's stormy,' Edith remarked. 'So perhaps their absence means it'll be a lovely day.'

I said that I had never before seen such a magnificent display of gorse, at which Edith asked if I knew the old saying that when the gorse was out that meant it was kissing time.

She smiled rather charmingly and went on: 'It's a joke, Mrs Verlaine. It's because the gorse blooms all the year round somewhere in England.'

She had become animated and clearly enjoyed introducing me to the country. I realised more than ever that I was a town woman. The parks of London, the Tuileries and the Bois de Boulogne had been my countryside. But this was different and I was revelling in it.

She brought the trap to a standstill and told me that if I looked round I should see the battlements of Walmer Castle. 'There were three castles,' she told me, 'all within a few miles of each other, but only two of them remain. Sandown is a ruin. It was the encroaching sea which has taken it. But Deal and Walmer Castles are in perfect condition. If you could look down on them you would see that they are built in the shape of Tudor roses. They're only small castles . . . fortifications really to protect the coast and shipping in the Downs which is the four miles between the coast and the Goodwins.'

I looked at the grey stone battlements of the castle – the home of the Warden of the Cinque Ports – and then back to the sea.

'You're looking for the wrecks on the Goodwins,' said Edith. 'You should be able to see them to-day. Ah yes . . .' She pointed, and I saw them – those pathetic masts no more than sticks at this distance.

'They call the Sands the Ships Swallower,' said Edith and she shivered. 'I saw them once. My . . . my husband took me out to see them. He thought I ought to . . . to overcome my fear of things.' She added half apologetically: 'He's right, of course.'

'So you've actually been out there!'

'Yes, he . . . he said it was safe enough . . . at the right time.'

'What was it like?'

She half closed her eyes. 'Desolate,' she said. She went on hurriedly: 'At high water the whole of the Sands are covered with the sea . . . even the highest point when submerged is eight feet or so under the water. You simply would not know they were there. That is why they are so dangerous. Imagine in the past the sailors not suspecting that only eight feet under water were those terrible sands waiting to swallow them.'

'And when you saw them?' I prompted.

'It was at low water,' she said, and I sensed that she did not want to talk of this but could not stop herself. 'That would be the only time to see them, wouldn't it, because if they were covered you wouldn't *see* anything, you'd only *know* they were there. It would have been more horrible, don't you think, Mrs Verlaine. Things you can't see are more frightening than things you can.'

'Yes,' I agreed, 'that's true.'

'But . . . it was low water and I saw the Sands . . . lovely looking clean golden sand, all rippled. There were deep holes and these were filled with water; and the sand moves as you watch and forms itself into strange shapes, like monsters some of them . . . with claws . . . waiting to catch anyone who wandered there and pull them down. There were gulls circling overhead. Their cries were so mournful, Mrs Verlaine. Oh, it was frightening, so lonely, so desolate. They say the Sands are haunted. I've talked to one of the men from the North Goodwins Lightship and he says that when he's on watch he sometimes hears wild heart-rending cries from the Sands. They used to say it was the gulls, but he wasn't so sure. Terrible things have happened there, so it seems likely . . .'

'I suppose at a place like that one would have the oddest fancies.'

'Yes, but there is something so cruel about the Sands. My husband told me about them. He said the more you try to extricate yourself the deeper you go. Long long ago there was no lightship. Now it's there, and they say that the Goodwins lightship is the greatest benefit to sailors ever set on the seas. If you could see those Sands, Mrs Verlaine, you would believe that.'

'I believe it now.'

She pulled gently on the reins and the horse trotted on. I was thinking of Napier taking her out to see the Goodwins. I imagined her reluctance. He would laugh at her cowardice, and tell himself that he must teach her to be brave when all the time it was to satisfy some sadistic desire to hurt her.

She changed the subject and told me how when she was very young her father used to bring her to Lovat Stacy. In those days, it seemed, it had been a kind of El Dorado.

'Everything at Lovat Stacy seemed exciting,' she told me. 'Of course Beau was alive then.'

'You remember him well?'

'Oh yes, you'd never forget Beau. He was like a knight . . . a knight in shining armour. There was a picture of one in a book I had and he really looked just like Beau. I was only about four years old and he used to put me on a pony and hold me there.' Her face hardened a little . . . 'so that I shouldn't be afraid. Sometimes he put me on his horse and held me. "Nothing to be afraid of, Edith," he used to say. "Not while I'm here."'

Poor Edith, she could not have said more clearly that she was comparing the two brothers.

'So . . . you were fond of Beau,' I pursued relentlessly.

'Everybody was. He was so charming . . . never cross.'

Again her face puckered. So Napier was often cross, impatient with her simplicity and inexperience.

'Beau was always laughing,' she went on. 'He laughed at everything. He seemed about ten feet tall and I was so little. Then suddenly I didn't visit Lovat Stacy and I was very miserable. After that, when I did come here it was all changed.'

'But when you used to come here your husband was here too.'

'Oh yes, he was here. But he never took any notice of me. I don't remember him very much. Then a long time after – it seemed a very long time after – my father brought me back and neither of them was here. It was all different. But Alice and Allegra were here and there were the three of us – although they seemed so much younger.'

'At least you had someone to play with.'

'Yes.' She looked dubious. 'I think my Papa was worried about me. He knew that he wouldn't live long because he had consumption, so he arranged with Sir William that he should be my guardian and I came to Lovat Stacy when he died.'

Poor Edith, who had had no hand in forming her own life!

'Well, now that you are mistress of the house that must make you very proud.'

'I always loved the house,' she agreed.

'You should be happy now everything is settled.'

A trite and foolish remark, because clearly she was not happy and everything was far from settled.

We had come down to the sea, which was gently rising and falling on the shingle.

'This is where Julius Cæsar landed,' said Edith. And she pulled up the trap for a few moments so that I could savour this.

'It didn't look very much different then,' she went on. 'It couldn't, could it. Of course the castles weren't there. I wonder what he thought when he first saw Britain.'

'One thing we can be certain of – he wouldn't have had much time for admiring the scenery.'

Before us lay the town of Deal with its rows of houses almost down on the shingle, and lying on that shingle were many boats so close to the houses that their mizzen booms seemed as though they were running into them.

Edith told me that the yellow 'cats', the smaller luggers, were used for fueling big ships which lay at anchor in the Downs.

We drove past Deal Castle – circular in shape with its four-bastions, its pierced portholes, its drawbridge, its battlemented gateway and thickly studded door – set deep down in its grassy moat, and on into the town.

It was a busy sight on that lovely spring morning. Several fishing boats had just come in and were selling their catch. One fisherman was bringing in the lobster pots – another was mending his nets. I caught a sight of Dover soles and cat and dog fish, and the smell of fish and seaweed mingled in the salt sea air.

Edith had come to shop and she drove me away from the coast to an inn where she said she would leave the trap and perhaps I would care to explore the town a little while she visited the shops.

Because I sensed that she wished to be alone I agreed to this and I spent a pleasant hour wending my way through a maze of narrow streets with enchanting names – Golden Street, Silver Street, Dolphin Street. I wandered along by the sea, as far as the ruins of Sandown Castle, that one which had not stood up to time and sea, and I sat for a while on a seat which had been put in a convenient spot where the crumbling rocks made a natural alcove. From there I looked across that benign sea and my eyes sought the masts on those ship swallowing sands – a reminder of how quickly change could come.

When I returned to the inn where I was to meet Edith she was not there, so I sat outside on one of the wicker seats to wait for her. In my anxiety not to be late I had arrived ten minutes early, but it had been a pleasant morning and I felt very contented.

Then I saw Edith. She was not alone. Jeremy Brown was with her, and I wondered whether they had met by appointment. The thought flashed into my mind that I may have been asked to accompany her to divert any suspicion that she was meeting the curate, if suspicion there was.

I think they had been about to say good-bye to each other when Edith caught sight of me. There was no doubt that she was a little embarrassed.

I rose and went over to them. 'I'm a little early,' I said. 'I was afraid of misjudging the distance.'

Jeremy Brown explained with his frank and disarming smile: 'The vicar is taking the girls for their lessons this morning. He feels he should now and then. I had one or two calls to make . . . so here I am.'

I wondered why he felt he had to explain to me.

'We – ran into each other,' said Edith in the rather painful, breathless way of someone who is not accustomed to telling untruths.

'That must have been very pleasant.' I noticed that she carried no packages, but perhaps whatever she had bought was already in the trap.

'Mrs Verlaine,' said Edith, 'you should try our local cider. It's very good.'

She looked appealingly at the curate who said: 'Yes, I'm thirsty too. Let's all have a tankard.' He smiled at me. 'It's not very potent and I expect you're thirsty, too.'

I said that I should like to try the cider and as the sun was shining and we were sheltered from the breeze we decided that we would sit outside and drink it.

As Jeremy Brown went into the inn Edith smiled at me almost apologetically, but I avoided her eyes. I did not want her to think that I was putting any special construction on her meeting with the curate. In fact, it was only her manner which suggested that there might be something to be suspicious about.

The curate rejoined us and in a very short time three pewter tankards were brought out to us. I found it very pleasant sitting in the sun. I did most of the talking. I explained where I had been and how enchanting I found the town and I asked all sorts of questions about the boats which were lying on the shingle. The curate knew a great deal about local history, which is so often the case with people who are not natives. He talked of the smuggling that went on and how many of the boats were forty feet long and hollow; that they had enormous sails which helped them to escape the revenue ships and so bring in safely their contraband brandy, silks, and tobacco. Many of the old inns had secret underground cellars and in these the goods were stored until there was no longer danger from the excise men.

Such activities were by no means rare along this coast.

I found it all very stimulating, sitting there idly in the sunshine while Edith glowed with pleasure, chatting and laughing so that it seemed to me a new personality emerged.

Why could she not always be like this? That very morning I discovered the answer, for as we sat light-heartedly chatting there was the sound of horses' hoofs in the cobbled yard close by and a voice said: 'I'll be an hour or so.' A well-known voice which made Edith turn pale and my own heartbeats quicken.

Edith had half risen in her seat when Napier came into sight.

He saw us immediately.

'Well,' he said, and his eyes were cold as they swept over Edith. 'This is an unexpected pleasure.' Then he saw me: 'And Mrs Verlaine too . . .'

I remained seated and said coolly: 'Mrs Stacy and I came together. We met Mr Brown.' Then I wondered why I had felt I had to explain.

'I hope I'm not intruding on a merry party.'

I did not speak and Edith said in a flustered voice: 'It's – it's not exactly a party. We just happened . . .'

'Mrs Verlaine has just told me. I hope you will not object to my joining you for a tankard of that cider.' He looked at me. 'It *is* excellent, Mrs Verlaine. But I am repeating what you already know, I am sure.' He signed to one of the waiters who were dressed like monks in long dark robes tied about the middle with cords, and said he would have some cider.

As he sat down opposite me with Edith on one side and the curate on the other, I knew he was conscious of the embarrassment of those two, and I wondered whether he guessed at the cause of it.

'I'm surprised to see *you* here,' he said to the curate. 'I always imagined you were so overworked. But sitting outside an inn sipping cider . . . well, it's quite a pleasant way of working, don't you agree, Mrs Verlaine?'

'We all have to have our leisure moments and I imagine work all the better for them.'

'Right . . . as I'm sure you always are. Still, I must confess that I'm pleased to see you all *at leisure*. What do you think of the neighbourhood?'

'Fascinating,' I said.

'Mrs Verlaine has been exploring as far as Sandown,' said the curate.

'What . . . alone?'

The curate flushed; Edith cast down her eyes.

'I had some shopping to do . . .'

'But of course. And Mrs Verlaine had no wish to visit our shops. Why should she? I believe you live in London, Mrs Verlaine, therefore you will find our little shops scarcely worthy of your attention. With Edith it is different. She is constantly driving around to see . . .' he paused and smiled from Edith to the curate '. . . the shops. What have you been buying this morning?'

Edith looked as though she was going to burst into tears. 'I really couldn't find what I wanted.'

'Did you not?' he looked surprised and again his glance took in the curate.

'N . . . no. I wanted to match some . . . some ribbon.'

'Ah,' he said. 'I see.'

I put in: 'Colours are so difficult to match.'

'In these little towns, of course,' he said. And I thought: He knows that she has come to meet Jeremy and he is angry about it. Or is he angry? Doesn't he care? Does he just want to make them uncomfortable. And for myself, why is he harping on my coming from London. Why should he be angry with *me*?

'Well, Mrs Verlaine,' he said, 'what do you think of our cider?'

'It's very good.'

'Great praise.'

He finished his and setting his tankard on the table, stood up. 'I know you will excuse me if I hurry away. I have business. You didn't ride in?'

Edith shook her head. 'We came in the trap.'

'Ah yes, of course. You wanted to take all those purchases back with you. And you?' He had turned his contemptuous gaze on the curate.

'I came in the vicarage trap.'

He nodded. 'Thoughtful of you. You were going to help with the purchases. Oh, but of course, the meeting was accidental, wasn't it?'

For a few moments his eyes lingered on me.

'*Au revoir*,' he said.

And he left us.

We sat silently at the table. There was nothing to say.

Edith was very nervous during the drive back and once or twice I thought we were going into the ditch.

What an explosive situation, I thought; and I felt very sorry for the young girl beside me – scarcely out of the schoolroom. How would she cope with the kind of disaster to which she could be heading? I wanted to protect her, but I could not see how.

I sat in the vicarage drawing-room, Allegra beside me, while I listened with some pain to her performance of scales.

Allegra made no attempt to learn. At least Edith had a little talent, Sylvia was in fear of her parents and Alice was by nature painstaking. But Allegra possessed none of these incentives; and she was not going to bestir herself for anyone.

She brought her hands down on the keys with an abandoned finale and turned to grin at me.

'Are you going to report to Sir William that I'm quite hopeless and you refuse to go on with me?'

'But I don't consider you hopeless. Neither do I refuse to go on with you.'

'I suppose you're afraid there won't be enough work for you here if you let one of your pupils go.'

'That had not occurred to me.'

'Then why did you say you didn't consider me hopeless?'

'Because no case is hopeless. Yours is a bad one admittedly – largely due to yourself – but not hopeless.'

She regarded me with interest. 'You're not a bit like Miss Elgin,' she said.

'And why should I be?'

'You both teach music.'

I shrugged my shoulders impatiently and picking up a piece of music set it on the stand. 'Now!' I said.

She smiled at me. She had beauty of a provocative sort. Although her hair was dark, almost black, her eyes were a slatey colour, most arresting under dark brows, and fringed with abundant dark lashes. She was undoubtedly the beauty of the household, but it was sultry beauty, a beauty of which to beware. And she was conscious of it too; she wore a bright red string of coral beads about her neck – long narrow ones strung tightly so that they looked like spikes.

She laughed and said: 'It's no use your trying to be like Miss Elgin, because you're not. You've *lived*.'

'Well,' I said lightly, 'so has she.'

'You know what I mean by living. *I* intend to live. I shall be like my father, I suppose.'

'Your father?'

She laughed again. It was a low mocking laugh which I had already come to associate with her.

'Hasn't anyone told you of my shocking birth? You've met my father. Mr Napier Stacy.'

'You mean he . . .'

She nodded mischievously, enjoying my vague discomfiture.

'That's why I'm here. Sir William could hardly turn away his own granddaughter, could he?' The mockery went out of her face, and fear showed itself. 'He wouldn't. No matter what I did. I mean I am his granddaughter, am I not?'

'If Mr Napier Stacy was really your father that is certainly true.'

'You say it as if you doubt it, Mrs Verlaine. You must not do so because Napier himself acknowledges me as his.'

'In that case,' I said, 'we must accept the fact.'

'I'm ill-e-git-i-mate.' She spoke the word slowly as though relishing each syllable. 'And my mother . . . you want to hear about her? She was half gipsy and came here to work . . . in the kitchen it was. I believe I look very like her, only she was darker than I . . . more of a gipsy. She went away after I was born. She couldn't live in a house.' She began to sing in a pleasant, rather husky voice:

'She went off with the raggle taggle gipsies oh.'

She looked at me to see the effect of her words, and was delighted, because I must have shown that I was taken aback by this further revelation of Napier's character.

'I've some gipsy in me but I'm a Stacy too. I'd never give up my goosefeather bed nor pluck off my high heeled shoes – not that I'm allowed to wear them yet. But I'll have them, and I'll have jewels in my hair and I'll go to balls and I'll never, never . . . never leave Lovat Stacy.'

'I am glad,' I said coolly, 'that you appreciate your home. Now let us try this piece. It's very simple. Take it slowly at first and try to feel what the music is saying.'

She grimaced and turned to the piano. But she was not attending; her thoughts were far away; so were mine. I was thinking of Napier, the bad boy who had brought such disaster to his home that he had had to be sent away.

'I often wonder,' said Allegra, apropos of nothing, 'what became of that woman who disappeared.'

We were having tea in the schoolroom – the four girls and myself, for Sylvia was with us.

I almost dropped my teacup. I had tried to make people talk of Roma and yet it was a shock when they did without prompting.

'Which woman?' I asked – I hoped guilelessly.

'Why, the woman who came down here and dug up things,' said Allegra. 'People don't talk about it much now.'

'At one time,' put in Sylvia, 'they talked of nothing else.'

'Well, people don't disappear every day.' I spoke casually. 'What do you think happened?'

Sylvia said: 'My mother says they arranged it all just to make a lot of talk. Some people are like that.'

'For what purpose?' I demanded.

'To be important.'

'But she wouldn't have stayed hidden. How could that make her important?'

'It's what my mother says,' insisted Sylvia.

'Alice wrote a story about it,' said Edith quietly.

Alice blushed and lowered her eyes.

'It was very good,' added Allegra. 'It made our hair stand on end . . . at least it would if hair ever did stand on end. Has yours ever, Mrs Verlaine?'

I said I could not recall its having done so.

'Mrs Verlaine reminds me of Miss Brandon,' said Alice.

My heart began to beat fast in dismay.

'How?' I asked. 'In what way?'

'Being *accurate*, as so few other people are,' explained Alice. 'Most people would say "No, my hair hasn't stood on end" or "Yes, it has" and then tell some story very exaggeratedly. You say you can't recall its having done so, which is very accurate. Miss Brandon was very accurate. She said she had to be in her kind of work.'

'You seem to have talked to her quite frequently.'

'We all talked to her at times,' said Alice. 'Mr Napier did

too. He was very interested. She was always showing him things.'

'Yes,' said Sylvia. 'I remember my mother's noticing it.'

'Your mother notices everything . . . especially things that are not very nice,' put in Allegra.

'What wasn't nice about Mr Napier's being interested in the Roman remains?' I asked.

The girls were all silent although Allegra had opened her mouth to say something.

Alice said suddenly: 'It's a very good thing to be interested in the Roman remains. They had catacombs, Mrs Verlaine, did you know?'

'Yes.'

'Of course she knew!' scolded Allegra, 'Mrs Verlaine knows a geat deal.'

'A labyrinth of passages,' said Alice, her eyes dreamy. 'Christians used to hide in them and their enemies couldn't find them.'

'She'll be writing a story about that,' commented Allegra.

'I have never seen them, so how could I?'

'But you wrote about the disappearance of Miss Brandon,' Edith pointed out. 'It was a wonderful story. You should read it too, Mrs Verlaine.'

'It's about the gods being angry and turning her into something else,' explained Sylvia.

'They did, you know,' put in Alice eagerly. 'They turned people into stars and trees and bulls and bushes when they were offended, so it seems natural that they should turn Miss Brandon into something.'

'What did they turn her into in your story?' I asked.

'That's the odd thing about it,' said Edith. 'We don't know. Alice doesn't tell us. In the story the gods take their revenge and they turn her into something, but Alice just doesn't tell what.'

'It has to be left to the reader's imagination,' Alice explained. '*You* can turn Miss Brandon into anything you want.'

'It gives me a funny feeling,' cried Allegra. 'Imagine Miss Brandon being turned into something, and we don't know what it is.'

'Oh . . . exciting!' squealed Sylvia.

'Even your mother doesn't know what,' teased Allegra. Then she cried out: 'What if it's Mrs Verlaine?'

Four pairs of eyes studied me intently.

'Come to think of it,' said Allegra, mocking and mischievous, 'she has got a look of her.'

'How do you mean?' I demanded.

'It's the way you talk perhaps. But something . . .'

'I think,' said Edith, 'that we are embarrassing Mrs Verlaine.'

I was touched when Edith seemed to find some comfort in my company. It seemed to me reasonable that she should turn to me. Although she was nearer in years to the girls, I had been married and that must draw us together. She seemed to me a pathetic creature and I longed to help her.

One afternoon she asked me if I rode and when I explained that I had done a little riding but was far from proficient in the art she asked me if I would ride with her.

'But I haven't the necessary clothes.'

'I could lend you something. We aren't so very different in shape, are we?'

I was taller than she and not so slender but she insisted that one of her habits would fit me very well.

She was pathetically eager. Why? I knew of course. She was a nervous rider; she wanted to improve and she could do so by practise. Why should she not practise with me, so that when she went out with her husband she would be more accustomed to being in the saddle.

I gave in – with some misgivings – and she took me along to her room and I was soon fitted out in a riding habit – a long skirt, a tailored jacket in olive green, and a black riding hat.

'You look elegant,' she cried with pleasure, and I was not displeased with what I saw. 'I'm so glad.' Her eyes were anxious. 'We can ride often together, can't we?'

'Well, I have come here to teach music, you know.'

'But not all the time surely. You must have some exercise.' She twisted her hands together. 'Oh, Mrs Verlaine. I'm so glad you've come.'

I was puzzled that she should feel so strongly. It was not, I was sure, because of any great affection she felt for me. She had sensed my interest in people; she had a faith in my knowledge of the world; she wanted to confide. Poor Edith, she was a very worried young bride.

We went down to the stables together, and one of the grooms selected horses for us.

I explained that I was something of a novice. 'My riding has been confined to a London riding school though I've ridden occasionally in the Row.'

'Well, you take Honey. She's as mild as her name. And Mrs Stacy, Madam. I suppose it'll be Venus.'

Edith said nervously: No, she thought not. She would like a mount as mild as Honey.

As we rode out of the stables Edith said: 'My husband likes me to ride Venus. He says that Sugar-Plum . . .' she tapped her mount gently as she said her name '. . . is for children to practise on. The girls learned on her. Her mouth is quite insensitive. But I feel very comfortable on her.'

'Then you can enjoy your ride.'

'I am enjoying this with you, Mrs Verlaine. Sometimes I

think I shall never make a rider. I'm afraid I'm a great disappointment to my husband.'

'Well, riding is not the whole meaning of life, is it?'

'No . . . no. I suppose not.'

'You lead the way. You know it better than I.'

'I'll take you towards Dover. I think the scenery's magnificent. The castle on the skyline, and then that drop down to the harbour.'

'I'd like that,' I said.

It was a wonderful day; I saw things about the country which I had never noticed before. I was enchanted by the rich purple of nettles in a field and yellow cowslips in meadows.

'You can see the Roman remains from here,' Edith told me. 'If you look back.'

I did, thinking of Roma.

'I suppose we should have heard if they ever found out what happened to that woman,' said Edith. 'It's horrible, isn't it . . . to think of someone . . . just disappearing like that. I wonder if there was someone who . . . who wanted her out of the way.'

'There couldn't have been,' I said too fiercely.

I turned away from the remains and we went forward, keeping to the coast road.

The sea was a pellucid green and there was scarcely a cloud in the sky; the air was so clear that I could see the outline of the French coast.

'It's beautiful,' I said. As we came within a short distance of Dover, she pointed out a haunted house on the road. 'A lady in grey comes out when she hears the sound of horses' hoofs. They say she was running away and came out to stop the coach as it passed. The driver didn't see her and ran her down . . . and killed her. She was running away from a husband who was trying to poison her.'

'Do you think she will come out when she hears our horses?'

'It has to be by night. Most horrible things happen at night, don't they? Although they say that woman archæologist walked out in broad daylight.'

I did not answer. I was remembering standing with Roma not far from this very spot looking at that magnificent castle – the key and stronghold of all England, as it has been called. There it had stood for eight hundred years defying time and the elements, a grim warning to any unwelcome invader. Set proudly on the grassy slope it was a masterpiece in grey stone dominated by the Keep – holding watch over that narrow strip of Channel. The rectangular Keep, the Constable's Tower defended by the drawbridge and portcullis, the medieval semi-circular towers, the deep tree-lined moat, the mighty buttresses, the solid walls – all were so impressive that I could not take my eyes from them.

'It's so strong, is it not?' said Edith, almost timidly. 'So formidable.'

'Magnificent,' I replied.

'That's Peverel's Tower with the arched gateway, and over there on the north east wall is the Avranches Tower. There's a platform there on which the archers used to stand to shoot out their arrows. There are trapdoors in St John's Tower and platforms on which there are all sorts of appliances for pouring down molten lead and boiling oil.' She shivered. 'It's rather horrible – but fascinating.'

I was able to point something out to Edith – the remains of the Roman lighthouse which was older than the castle itself. Pharos, I remembered Roma's calling it.

'Oh yes,' said Edith, 'this is indeed Roman country.'

'Isn't the whole of Britain?'

'Yes, but this is where they came first. Imagine! That lighthouse used to guide them across the sea.' She laughed, a little nervously. 'I didn't think about Romans until those people came. It's because all that was discovered in our own park.'

And as we looked a horseman came up the hill towards us. I recognised him a second or so before Edith did. She was short-sighted, I learned – so I was able to witness the change in her.

She grew perceptibly paler and then flushed deeply.

Napier swept off his hat and called: 'An unexpected pleasure!'

'Oh!' said Edith. It was an exclamation of dismay; he was aware of this, I sensed, and his reply was to give her a sardonic look. 'What have they given you to ride?' he demanded. 'Old Dobbin from the nursery?'

'It's . . . it's Sugar-Plum.'

'And Mrs Verlaine? Oh, why didn't you tell me you wished to ride. I should have seen you had a worthy mount.'

'And one of which I should have been far from worthy. I am no rider, Mr Stacy. This mount suits me perfectly. I am assured she is mild as her name and that's what I need.'

'Oh no. You are quite wrong. I shall insist you ride a real horse.'

'I don't think you understand. I have been so rarely on horse-back.'

'An omission you must rectify. Riding is a pleasure you should indulge in frequently. It's superb exercise and most enjoyable.'

'In your opinion. Perhaps others might find different pursuits more to their taste.'

Edith looked uneasy; she had immediately lost confidence.

'Were you returning to the house?' he said. 'Then let us go back together.'

The journey back was not the pleasant meandering one it had been coming, for he was not content to walk his horse quietly through the lanes. He took us across country; he cantered and we did likewise. When his horse broke into a gallop mine followed and I was not sure whether I could have stopped him had I wished to. I was aware of Edith clinging white-faced to her reins and a great resentment rose up in me against this man who was making her miserable.

We had come out close to the haunted house of the grey lady and Napier looked at Edith to see what effect this had on her. I was conscious that she had kept close to me and I knew how nervous she was. I was angry. He knew too and he deliberately taunted her. He took her out for rides on a horse she feared. I could well imagine his breaking into gallops suddenly which she would have to follow.

A horrible thought occurred to me. It may have been the sight of the derelict house – half a ruin now – from which it was said the grey lady walked. Her husband had tried to poison her. What if Napier wanted to be rid of Edith. What if he brought her for these rides; what if he – skilful horseman that he was – could lead her to places which were dangerous for such a nervous rider. What if he should spur his horse to a gallop suddenly in some dangerous spot and hers should follow . . . and she be unable to control it . . .

What a fearful thought and yet . . .

I had ridden on and he was close beside me. He said: 'You would make a good horsewoman, Mrs Verlaine, with practise. But I daresay you would be good at anything you undertook.'

'I am flattered that you have such a high opinion of me.'

Edith was calling out: 'Please . . . Wait for me . . .'

Sugar-Plum had bent his head to the hedge and was gripping a piece of foliage with his teeth. Edith was pulling at her reins but the horse would not budge. It was as though some spirit of mischief had got into him and he was as eager to discomfit Edith as her husband was.

Napier turned and smiled.

Poor Edith. She was scarlet with mortification. I hated the man beside me.

Then he said: 'Sugar-Plum. Come along.'

And meekly Sugar-Plum released the foliage and began to trot in the direction of the voice, as though to say, you see how amenable I am.

'You shouldn't ride that practise mount,' said Napier. 'You should keep to Venus.'

Edith looked as though she were near tears.

I hate him, I thought. He is a sadist. He enjoys hurting her.

He seemed to sense my feelings for he said to me: 'I shall find a better mount for you too, Mrs Verlaine, no matter what you say. You'll find Honey only too ready to play the same tricks on you. She's been plagued too much by children.'

The pleasure had gone out of the morning. I was glad when Lovat Stacy came into sight.

Strangely enough my antagonism towards Napier Stacy made me conscious of my appearance – something in which I had taken little interest since the death of Pietro. I found myself wondering how I appeared to this man. A woman past her first youth – a woman who had had some experience of life, being a widow. Tall, slender with a pale though healthy complexion which Pietro had once likened to a magnolia flower – a description which had delighted me so that I treasured the memory. I had a short, rather pert nose, slightly retroussé, at odds with my big dark eyes which could grow almost black when I was moved to anger or carried away by music. I had thick straight brown hair. I was no beauty but on the other hand by no means unattractive. I was rather pleased about this; and the right colours and the right clothes worked wonders for me. As Essie Elgin once said to me, I 'paid for dressing.'

I was thinking of this as I smoothed down a pale mauve dress – one of the colours which became me most – and put on my grey coat. I was going for a walk. There was a great deal about which I wanted to think.

My position here for one thing. I had not played again for Sir William, nor had there been any suggestion of my doing so for his guests; the girls' lessons did not really occupy me fully. I wondered whether they would decide I wasn't worth my salt. Mrs Lincroft had told me that Sir William had plans but that he had not been very well since my arrival, but when he recovered a little I should find myself busier.

I did not want to think too much about Napier Stacy. The subject, I told myself, is unpleasant; but I did wonder a great deal about his relationship with Edith. Roma was constantly in my mind. I longed to press on with my inquiries, but I was afraid that if I did so I should immediately arouse suspicion. Even so, I feared I had made my interest in her too obvious.

Thoughts of her took me to the ruins that day. I wandered about, my memories of her so vivid that it almost seemed that she was there beside me. The place was deserted. I suppose Roma's discoveries were minor ones compared with many in the country; and after the first excitement few people came to see them. I looked at the baths and the remains of the hypocausts with which they were heated and I could hear Roma's voice and the pride in it as she had shown me these things.

'Roma,' I whispered. 'Where are you, Roma?'

I could picture her so clearly – her eyes alight with enthusiasm, the chunky necklace rising and falling on her sombrely clad bosom.

As if she would have gone away without telling me where she was going. She could only be dead.

'Dead!' I whispered; and a hundred scenes from our childhood came to my mind. Dear solid Roma with never a spark of malice, her only fault a certain pitying tolerance towards those who failed to appreciate the joys of archæology.

I walked to the cottage where she had lived during those days of the excavation and which I had shared with her. During that time I had never seen any of the people who were becoming so familiar to me now; and they had been unaware of me . . . at least I hoped so. If anyone had seen me then and recognised me now, I should have discovered it surely. When I had last been here there had been many strangers walking about the 'dig'. Why should one of them have been singled out?

The cottage looked more derelict than ever. I pushed open the door for it was not locked. It creaked uneasily on its hinges. Why should I be surprised that it was unlocked? There was nothing to protect here.

There was the familiar room . . . the table at which I had sat watching the restoration of the mosaic. A few brushes lay about and a pick and a shovel with a pail. An old oil stove on which Roma had done her casual cooking – and a big drum in which she had kept the paraffin. Just enough to show that the archæologists had passed this way.

And out of this cottage Roma had walked one day and never returned.

Where, Roma, *where*?

I tried to visualise where she would go. Would she have gone for a walk? She never walked for the sake of walking . . . only to get from one place to another. Had she gone for a swim? She swam very little; in fact she never had time for it.

What had happened on that day when she had finished her packing and walked out of the cottage?

The answer was somewhere; and I was more likely to find it here than anywhere.

I started up the stairs which led from the room. They twisted round and at the top of them was a heavy door. Opening this one stepped straight into a small box room and in this room was a door which opened on to a bedroom – which was in fact only a little larger than the box room. It had one tiny window with leaded panes and I remembered how dark it had been even at midday. I had slept in a camp bed in that bedroom and Roma had had her camp bed in the box room.

I pushed open the heavy door and looked inside. The beds had been removed. Roma would have had them ready to be taken away no doubt when she walked out of this cottage.

I shivered. The stone walls were thick and it was cold.

Yet here in the cottage I felt close to Roma. I kept murmuring her name: 'Roma! Roma, what happened on that day?'

I thought of her standing at the little window looking out towards the dig. She had been completely absorbed by her work here. She had talked of it while she hastily washed in the water which had been heated on the old paraffin stove downstairs. On that last day, of what had she been thinking? Of her departure. Of new plans?

And then she would put her plain coat over her plain skirt and blouse and her only adornment would be a string of cornelian beads or odd shaped turquoises . . . and have gone out into the fresh air to which she was addicted. She would have walked across the dig and beyond into . . . limbo.

I shut my eyes. I could see her so clearly. Where? Why?

The answer could be in the cottage.

Then I heard a sound below. I felt suddenly colder and

there was a prickly sensation at the back of my spine. I thought of Allegra's words: 'Has your hair ever stood on end?' And I was immediately aware of the isolated position of the cottage; and the thought entered my head: You came to find out what happened to Roma. Perhaps you could learn if the same thing happened to you.

A footstep in the silence. The creak of a board. Someone was in the cottage.

I looked at the window. I knew from the past how small it was. There was no escape that way. But why should I feel this sense of doom simply because someone else had decided to look at an empty disused cottage?

I was too fanciful perhaps; but it seemed to me that Roma was in this place . . . warning me.

I crouched against the wall listening. My sudden fear was the result of an over-fevered imagination. It was because Roma had been here, because her spirit still seemed to linger as those who have been violently hurried from life are said to linger. Yes, it was the spirit of Roma warning: Danger.

And then I heard the creak of a board, a step on the stair. Someone was coming up to the bedroom. I decided I would go boldly to meet whoever it was, so I thrust my trembling hands into the pockets of my coat and stepped through the bedroom and the box room.

As I did so the heavy door was cautiously pushed open. Napier stood before me. He seemed to loom over me; he seemed so big in this little place; and my heart began to beat too fast. He smiled, fully aware of my fear, I knew.

'I saw you come into the cottage,' he said. 'I wondered what you could find of interest here.' As I did not answer he went on: 'You look surprised to see me.'

'I am.' I was struggling for my self control, angrily demanding of myself why I was being so stupid – and more foolish still to betray it. The man was a bully, I thought;

and what he enjoyed doing was frightening people. That was why he had come quietly into the cottage, had crept stealthily up the stairs.

'Did you think you were the only one interested in our Treasures of the Past?' He spoke those words as though they had capitals – as though he knew the ghost of Roma was in this place, and mocked it.

'Far from it. I know that many people are interested.'

'But not the Stacys. Did you know that in the first place my father tried to prevent the work being carried out?'

'And couldn't he?'

'He was over-persuaded. And so . . . in the name of culture . . . the Philistines gave way.'

'How fortunate for posterity that he was persuaded.'

His eyes glinted a little. 'The triumph of knowledge over ignorance,' he said.

'Precisely.'

I made as though to step past him towards that heavy door; and although he did not exactly bar my way he did not move, so that I should have had to brush past him to reach it. So I hesitated, not wishing to betray my desire to escape.

'What made you come here?' he asked.

'Curiosity, I suppose.'

'Are you a very inquisitive person, Mrs Verlaine?'

'As inquisitive as most people, I daresay.'

'I often think,' he went on, 'that the inquisitive are a little maligned. After all, it is really a virtue to be interested in one's fellow men. Do you agree?'

'Virtues if carried to excess can become vices.'

'I am sure you are right. Did you know that one of the archæologists lived in this cottage?'

'Oh?' I said.

'The one who disappeared.'

'What happened to her?'

'I don't accept the view that some Roman god rose in his fury and wiped her off the face of the earth. Do you?'

He moved a step nearer to me. 'You remind me of that archæologist.'

He kept his eyes on my face, and for one moment I thought: He knows. He knows why I have come here. It would be easy to have discovered that I was Roma's sister, Pietro Verlaine's wife . . . It could even have been mentioned in the press. Perhaps he knew that I had come to discover what lay behind Roma's disappearance. Perhaps . . .

The wild thoughts that come to one in a lonely cottage when alone with a man . . . a man who killed his brother . . .

I said feebly: 'I remind you . . . of her?'

'You don't look like her. She was not a beautiful woman.' I flushed. 'I did not mean, of course . . .' He lifted his hands feigning embarrassment. He was telling me that I had jumped to the conclusion of thinking he was telling me I was beautiful. How he liked to humiliate! 'She had a look of dedication. So sure that she was right.'

'I see, and I too have this look?'

'I did not say that, Mrs Verlaine. I merely said that you reminded me of the poor unfortunate lady.'

'You knew her well?'

'The dedication was obvious. One did not need to be on familiar terms with her to be aware of it.'

I said recklessly: 'What happened to her?'

'You are asking for my theory?'

'If you have nothing better to offer.'

'But why should you imagine I should have more than a theory to offer?'

'You have met her. You saw her. Perhaps you have some notion of the sort of woman she was . . .'

'Or is,' he said. 'No need to speak of her in the past tense. We cannot be sure that she is dead. I'm inclined to think she went off on some project. But it is a mystery. Perhaps it will always be a mystery. There are many unsolved mysteries in the world, Mrs Verlaine. And this one . . . perhaps it's a warning to let the past alone.'

'One which every archæologist will, I am sure, ignore.'

'I can tell by your tone that you thoroughly approve. So you think it is good to probe into the past?'

'Surely you admit that archæologists are doing valuable work?'

He smiled at me, that slow maddening smile which I was beginning to hate.

'So you don't,' I said heatedly.

'I did not say so. I was not in fact thinking of archæologists. You have become obsessed by this young woman. I merely said do you think it is good to probe the past? Pasts are something we all have. They are not the prerogative of these scrabblers in the dust.'

'Our personal pasts are our own concern, I think. It is only the historical past which should be revealed.'

'A fine distinction – for who made the historic past but the individuals? I was being impertinent – a not unusual habit of mine – and was suggesting that you, like myself, would doubtless prefer to forget the past. Ah, you find me . . . indelicate. I should not have said that. One does not say such things in polite society. It is "What a fine day to-day, Mrs Verlaine? The wind is not so cold as it was yesterday." Then we discuss the weather of the last few weeks and pass on pleasantly unruffled, and we might just as well never have spoken. So you object to bluntness.'

'You leap to conclusions, do you not? As for bluntness I find that those who pride themselves on being frank usually apply the term to their own plain speaking. They often have another for other people's – rudeness.'

He laughed – little lights shooting up in his eyes. 'I will prove to you that that is not the case with me. I will speak plainly about myself. What have you heard of me, Mrs Verlaine? I know. I murdered my brother. That's what you have heard.'

'I have heard there was an accident.'

'That is what is commonly known as being couched in diplomatic terms.'

'I was not attempting to be diplomatic. I was merely speaking frankly. I had heard that there was a fatal accident. I know that these occur.'

He lifted his shoulders and put his head on one side.

'And,' I said, 'although they are deeply deplored, they should be forgotten.'

'This was no ordinary accident, Mrs Verlaine. The death of the heir of the house – handsome, charming, well beloved. Shot dead by his brother – who became the heir to the house and was neither handsome, charming, nor well beloved.'

'Perhaps he could have become so . . . had he tried.'

He laughed and I heard the terrible bitterness in the laughter, and my opinion of him changed a little in that moment. He was cruel, he was sadistic, because he was taking his revenge on a world which had treated him so badly. I was actually sorry for the man.

I said, rather gently I supposed: 'No one should be blamed for what was done accidentally.'

He came closer to me – those eyes, so brilliantly blue, so startling in the bronzed face, looked into mine 'But how can you be sure that it was done accidentally? How could they?'

'But of course it was,' I said.

'Such sentiments expressed so forcibly by a sensible young woman are very flattering.'

I opened my coat to look at the watch pinned to my dress.

'I see it is nearly half past three.'

I moved towards the door, but he remained in his position between me and it.

'You,' he said, 'know so much about our family. Yet I know so little about you.'

'I cannot believe that you would wish to. As to what I have learned – I know very little beyond what you have just told me. I am here in the capacity of music teacher, not family historian and biographer.'

'But how interesting it would be if you were here in that latter capacity. Perhaps I should suggest this to my father. What a chronicle you would be able to produce. The shooting of my brother . . . why, even the disappearance of our archæologist. It all happened hereabouts.'

'Music is my profession.'

'But you have such a vital interest in everything concerning us all. You are fascinated by the disappearing lady . . . simply because she disappeared here.'

'No . . .'

'No? You would have been equally interested if she had gone somewhere else to disappear?'

'Mysteries are always intriguing.'

'Far more so, I agree, than a straightforward shooting. There can be little doubts about the motive behind that.'

'Accidents are without motive. They just . . . happen.'

'So you have very kindly convinced yourself that it was an accident. Perhaps later you will change your mind, when you have listened to what certain people have to tell you.'

He puzzled me. I wondered why my opinion should be of importance to him. My desire to get away had completely left me. I wanted to stay and talk to him. In a strange way he reminded me of Pietro, who would sometimes lash himself into a state of nervous despair over some critical judgment of his work which he declared he didn't believe.

I must have softened, thinking of Pietro, for Napier went on: 'I've been away for a long time, Mrs Verlaine. I've been on a cousin's property in the outback of Australia. So you must forgive me if I lack your English diplomacy. I would like to tell you my version of the . . . accident. Will you listen to me?'

I nodded.

'Imagine two boys . . . well, hardly boys. Beaumont was almost nineteen, I was nearly seventeen. Everything Beaumont did was perfect; everything I did was suspect. Quite rightly so. He was the white sheep; I was the black one. Black sheep become resentful – they grow as black as people believe them to be . . . so this black sheep grew blacker and blacker until one day he picked up a gun and shot his brother.'

If he had shown some emotion I should have felt happier; but he spoke in a calm, cold-blooded way and the thought came into my mind: It was *not* an accident.

'It happened a long time ago . . .' I began uneasily.

'There are events in life which will never be forgotten. Your husband died. He was very famous. I am, as you so kindly pointed out, a Philistine, with no drawing-room accomplishments, yet even I have heard your late husband's name. And you are also talented.' His eyes scanned my face lightly and he said mockingly: 'That must have been idyllic.'

And as he spoke I saw Pietro, his eyes full of rage because of some slight to his genius; I heard his voice taunting me . . . And I thought: This man knows what my marriage was like and he is trying to spoil my memories. He is cruel after all. He likes to destroy. He wants to mutilate my dream . . . and he wants to hurt Edith. He would hurt me if he could, but I am beyond him except when he sneers at my marriage.

'I shouldn't have said that,' he remarked, and he implied

117

that he understood what I was feeling. It was as though he were peering into my past, that he heard Pietro's mocking laughing. 'I have reminded you of what you would prefer to forget.'

The quietness of his voice was somehow more cutting than his sneers would have been because I was aware of the cynical undercurrents.

I said: 'I really must go. I have lessons to prepare.'

'I will accompany you back to the house,' he told me.

'Oh . . . there is no need.'

'I am walking that way, unless, of course, you would prefer that I did not walk with you?'

'I see no reason why I should.'

'Thank you, Mrs Verlaine.' He gave a little ironic bow. 'My heartfelt gratitude.'

He opened the door and stood aside for me to pass down the stairs. The foolish uneasy feeling remained with me. I did not like to think of his walking close behind me. He had unnerved me by his near confession that he had killed his brother. He seemed to glory in it. Or did he? I was not sure. The man was an enigma. But that was no concern of mine. But was it? He had been here when Roma had been here. He had known her, spoken to her. 'You remind me of her, Mrs Verlaine,' he had said.

I breathed more easily when we had left the cottage.

As we passed close to the excavations he said quite suddenly: 'We didn't hear much about the family. The parents I believed had been killed in the service of archæology.'

'What?'

'Our mysterious lady, of course. Would it surprise you if she turned up one day . . . in an absentminded way? It drew attention to her discoveries, you know. People came to see the place where the lady disappeared, not the remains of Roman occupation.'

I said warmly: 'You should not credit her with such intention. I am sure she did not deserve them.'

'But how can you be so sure?'

'I . . . I don't think those people are like that.'

'You have a kind heart and believe the best of everyone. What a comforting person to have around.'

He began to talk about the discoveries and I gathered that he was well acquainted with them. He mentioned particularly the mosaic pavement. The colours he believed were as bright as anything that had been found in Britain.

I said unthinkingly: 'An application of linseed oil and exposure to the sun helps a great deal.' I was unconsciously quoting Roma. 'Although, of course, the colours would be brighter still if they had been exposed to a tropical sun.'

'How knowledgeable you are!' Another false step. This man unnerved me in a strange way. He was smiling and I caught the gleam of his teeth – as startling in their whiteness as his blue eyes in that brown face. 'You're not a secret archæologist, are you?'

I laughed . . . but uneasily.

'You are not down here on a secret mission, are you?' he pursued the point. 'You won't creep out in the night and begin delving under the foundations of our house?'

I thought: Does he know? And if so what will he do about it? He killed his brother. What does he know about Roma's disappearance?

I said as calmly as I could: 'If you had the slightest knowledge of archæology you would quickly discover that I know practically nothing. It's common knowledge that the sun and linseed oil restore colour.'

'Not all that common. I was unaware of it. But perhaps I am unusually ill-informed.'

The house loomed before us, magnificent against the background of blue sea.

'One thing my family shared with the Romans,' he said. 'They knew how to choose a good building site.'

'It's wonderful,' I said, softened by the sight.

'I am glad you approve of our dwelling.'

'You must be proud to belong to such a house.'

'I would prefer to say that the house belongs to us. You are thinking of the stories those bricks could tell if they could talk. You are a romantic, Mrs Verlaine.' Pietro again. The romantic under the façade of worldliness . . . Did it show so clearly then in spite of all I had done to suppress it since I lost Pietro? 'But in fact,' he went on, 'it's a mercy the bricks don't talk. What they say might be very shocking. But you believe the best of people don't you, Mrs Verlaine?'

'I try to . . . until the worst is proved.'

'A philosopher as well as a musician. What a combination!'

'You are laughing at me.'

'Sometimes it is very pleasant to laugh. But I cannot hope that your beneficent attitude extends to me. When the mark of the beast is as clearly defined, the most kindly philosophers must accept it.'

'The mark of the beast . . .' I echoed.

'Oh yes, it was put on me when I killed my brother.' He put his hand to his forehead. 'It's there, you know . . . No one fails to see it. You will if you look, Mrs Verlaine. And if you do not see it there will be plenty to point it out.'

I said: 'You should not talk in that way. You sound . . . bitter.'

'I?' He opened his eyes wide and laughed. 'No . . . only realistic. You will see. And once the mark of the beast is set upon a man . . . or woman . . . only a miracle can remove it.'

The sun was shining on the water and it was as though a giant hand had scattered diamonds over it. Across that dazzling strip of water I could just make out the masts on the Goodwins. I looked down on the towns in the distance and from this spot it seemed as though the houses were falling into the sea.

Neither of us spoke.

He left me in the courtyard and I went up to my room feeling very disturbed by the encounter.

Later that afternoon, having half an hour to spare, I went into the gardens. I had had an opportunity of exploring them and although I admired the terraces and the parterres my favourite spot was the little enclosed garden which I had discovered on my first day. A luscious green Virginia creeper covered one wall and I imagined the splash of scarlet it would be with the coming of the autumn. Inside these four walls there was peace and I felt I needed to be alone to think, for Napier Stacy had disturbed me more than I cared to admit.

I had been sitting on the seat looking into the lily pond for some seconds when I was suddenly aware that I was not alone.

Miss Stacy had been standing by the green shrubs at the far end of the garden, so still, that I had not noticed her; she was wearing a green dress which had seemed like part of the bush. It was an uncanny feeling when I realised that she must have been watching me through those silent seconds.

'Good afternoon, Mrs Verlaine,' she cried gaily. 'This is a favourite spot of yours. I know.' She tripped towards me lifting her finger and coyly shaking it at me. I saw the little green bows in her hair – the colour of her dress.

She must have noticed my gaze for she touched them lightly. 'Whenever I have a new dress I have my bows made at the same time. I have bows for every dress that way.' A look of satisfaction spread across her face as though she were inviting me to comment on her cleverness. Her movements and her voice were so youthful that it was such a shock when she came so close that I could see the smudges of brown on her neck and hands and the wrinkles round the blue eyes. In fact then she seemed older than she actually was.

'You've changed since you came here,' she announced.

'Oh? Is that possible? In such a short time?'

She sat beside me. 'It's peaceful here. It's a lovely little garden, don't you think? But of course you do. You wouldn't come here if you didn't, would you? One gets the impression that one is shut away from the world. But one isn't, you know.'

'Of course not.'

'*You* would realise that. I think you are very clever, Mrs Verlaine. I think you know about a lot of things as well as music.'

'Thank you.'

'And . . . I'm glad you came. I have definitely made up my mind to paint your portriat.'

'That's very kind of you.'

'Oh, but it might be unkind.' She laughed. 'Some artists *are* unkind. At least their subjects think they are . . . because they paint what they see and it could be something the subject might not want seen.'

'At least I should be interested to discover what you see in me.'

She nodded. 'Not yet though . . . I have to wait a while.'

'We have only met once.'

She began to laugh. 'But I've seen you many times, Mrs Verlaine. I'm very interested in you.'

'How good of you.'

'Then again it might not be good. It all depends.'

She clasped her hands like a young girl who is hugging a secret to herself. Here was another member of this household who made me feel uncomfortable.

'I saw you come in to-day,' she said. And she nodded several times like a mandarin. 'With Napier,' she added.

I was glad that my skin did not flush and so betray my embarrassment.

'We met by accident . . . at the Roman remains,' I said rather hotly and then realised I was foolish to more or less offer an excuse.

She did her three or four little nods which I gathered were to denote wisdom.

'You are very interested in these remains, Mrs Verlaine.'

'Who wouldn't be. They are of national interest.'

She turned to me and regarded me coyly from under those shrivelled lids. 'But some people in the nation are more interested than others. You will agree with that.'

'Inevitably.'

She stood up and clasped her hands together. 'I could show you some remains . . . closer at hand. Would you like to see them?'

'Remains?' I said.

She pressed her lips together and nodded.

'Come.' She held out a hand and I could do nothing but take it. Hers was cold and very soft. I dropped it as soon as I could.

'Yes,' she said, 'we have some remains here. You must see them now that you are becoming so interested in us all.'

She tripped to the wrought iron gate and opening it stood there poised like an ancient fairy, her expression conspiratorial. I caught her excitement and asked myself why nothing seemed to be ordinary in this house.

'Remains,' she murmured as though to herself. 'Yes, you could call them remains. Not Roman though, this time. Still, there's no reason why the Stacys shouldn't have remains if the Romans had them.' She gave her high-pitched titter.

I passed through the gate; she shut it and was beside me, then she tripped past leading the way and turning to smile at me in her little girl manner.

She took me through a shrubbery to a part of the garden in which I had never been before. We followed a path and came to a little copse of fir trees – thick, bushy evergreens.

There was a path through the trees and as she tripped along this and I followed I wondered whether she was more than slightly mad.

But at last I saw the object of this visit. It looked like a white circular tower; she ran on ahead.

'Come on, Mrs Verlaine,' she called. 'This is the remains.'

I hurried after her and I saw that the tower was a shell and that the inside walls were blackened by fire. It was not large – just a circular wall; the roof had been partially destroyed and it was possible to see the sky.

'What is it?' I asked.

'A shell,' she answered in a sepulchral voice. 'A burned-out shell.'

'When was it burned?'

'Not very long ago.' And she added significantly: 'Since Napier came home.'

'What was it meant to be?'

'It was a little chapel in the woods . . . a beautiful little chapel and it was built in honour of Beaumont.'

'You mean as a sort of memorial?'

Her eyes lit up. 'How clever you are, Mrs Verlaine. It *was* a memorial, a memorial to Beau. After he was killed his father built this chapel so that he could come here . . . or any of us could . . . and be silent, shut away in the woods where we could think of Beaumont. It stood here for years and then –'

'It was burned down,' I added.

She came close to me and whispered: '*After* Napier came home.'

'How was it burned?'

Her eyes blazed suddenly. 'Mischief. No . . . not mischief . . . wickedness.'

'You mean someone did it purposely? Why should they? For what purpose?'

'Because they hated Beau. Because they couldn't bear that Beau was beautiful and good. That's why.'

'Are you suggesting that . . .' I hesitated and she said slyly: 'You should finish, Mrs Verlaine. Am I suggesting what?'

'That someone did it on purpose. I can't see that anyone would want to do that.'

'But there's a great deal you can't see, Mrs Verlaine. I'd like to tell you . . . to warn you.'

'Warn?'

Again that silly wise nod of hers.

'Napier burned this down when he came home because we liked to come here and think of Beaumont and he couldn't bear it. So he got rid of it . . . just as he got rid of Beaumont.'

'How can you be sure of that?' I asked almost angrily.

'I remember it well. One evening . . . it was just dark. I could smell the fire from my room. I was the first to discover it. I came out of the house and I couldn't tell at first where the smell was coming from. Then I saw . . . and I ran . . . I ran to the copse and there was the beautiful chapel . . . and the sparks flying out . . . It was terrible. I called everyone, but it was too late to save it. So now it's just a shell, nothing but a shell.'

'It must have been a very pleasant place,' I said.

'Pleasant! It was beautiful. Such a sense of peace and

calm. My beautiful Beau was *there*. He was. That was why Napier could not endure it. That was why he burned it down.'

'There is no evidence –' I began and stopped myself. I added rather hurriedly: 'I have some work to prepare so I suppose I should get on with it.'

She laughed. 'You seem as if you'd like to defend him. I told you you were beginning to take his side.'

I said coldly: 'It is not for me to take sides, Miss Stacy.'

She laughed again and said: 'But we often do things which it is not for us to do, don't we? You are a widow. In a sense I am too.' Her face looked older suddenly and mournful. 'I understand. And he . . . well, some people are attracted by wickedness.'

I said crisply: 'I really don't understand, Miss Stacy, and I do think I should be working. Thank you for showing me . . . the ruin.'

I turned and walked briskly away. I found her conversation not only distasteful but distinctly uncomfortable.

Two days later an even more disturbing event occurred.

I went along to the schoolroom in search of Edith and as I was about to open the door I heard her voice raised and distressed. I paused and as I did so she cried out: 'And if I don't, you'll tell. Oh . . . how can you.'

It was not only the implication of the words but the agonised tone in which they were spoken that shocked me.

I hesitated uncertain what to do. I had no wish to play the eavesdropper. I was a newcomer to this house and perhaps I was over-dramatising a situation. These girls all of them seemed little more than children to me.

That was a more important moment than I realised at the time. How I wished afterwards that I had been bold and walked into that room. Instead of which I went quietly and hastily away.

Edith was quarrelling with someone in the schoolroom, someone who was threatening her.

My excuse is that I thought of them as children.

It was half an hour later when I gave Edith her lesson. She played so badly that I thought she was making no progress whatsoever.

But of course she was distraught.

Chapter Four

I sat in the room next to Sir William's and played for
   him. I played first *Für Elise* and after that some Chopin
nocturnes. I believed that in that room I played my best,
because I was conscious of a sympathetic atmosphere there,
which may have suggested itself to me because I knew the
room had belonged to one who had loved music. Pietro
would have laughed at my fancies. An artist did not need
an atmosphere he would have told me.

Pietro's image faded from my mind as I thought of this
Isabella who had been Napier's mother and who had
loved music, who might have been a great pianist and
had given up her career for the sake of marriage. Oh yes,
we were in harmony. But she had had two sons and she
had lavished more love on one than the other – and when
her beloved son had died she had taken a gun and gone
into the woods . . .

When I had played for an hour I stopped and went to
the door. Mrs Lincroft, who was with Sir William, asked me
to come in and nodded for me to be seated. 'Sir William
would like to talk to you,' she said.

I sat down beside him and he turned slowly to me.

'Your performance is very moving,' he said.

Mrs Lincroft tiptoed from the room and left us together.

'It reminds me,' he went on, 'of my wife's playing. I am not sure though that she had quite your excellence.'

'Perhaps she had less practise.'

'Yes, no doubt. Her duties here . . .'

I said hastily: 'Yes, of course.'

'How do you find your pupils?'

'Mrs Stacy has some talent.'

'A flimsy talent, eh?'

'A pleasant talent. I think she will find great joy in the piano.'

'I see. And the others?'

'They could play . . . adequately.'

'And that is a good thing to do.'

'Very good.'

We were silent and I wondered whether he had fallen asleep and I ought to tiptoe away.

I was about to do so when he said: 'I trust you are comfortable here, Mrs Verlaine.'

I assured him that I was.

'If there is anything you need you must ask Mrs Lincroft. She manages everything.'

'Thank you.'

'You have made the acquaintance of my sister?'

'Yes.'

'And you have probably found her a little strange.'

I did not quite know what to answer but he went on: 'Poor Sybil, when she was young she had an unfortunate love affair. She was going to be married and something went wrong. She has never been the same since. We were relieved when she began to take an interest in family affairs, but Sybil could never do anything very reasonably. She becomes obsessed. She has probably talked to you about our family affairs. She does to everyone. You should not take what she says too seriously.'

'She has talked to me, yes.'

'I thought so. The loss of my son affected her deeply. As it did us all. But in her case . . .'

His voice trailed off. He was clearly thinking of that terrible day when Beaumont had died . . . and afterwards when his wife had taken the gun into the woods. A double tragedy. I was so sorry for him. I was even sorry for Napier.

Sir William was speaking of Napier and his voice was quite lacking in any emotion. 'Now that my son is married we shall be entertaining a little more than in the past. As you know, Mrs Verlaine, I should like you to entertain my guests.'

'I should be delighted. What would you suggest I play?'

'That shall be decided later. My wife used to play for our guests . . .'

'Yes,' I said gently.

'Well, now you will do the same, and it will be like . . .'

He seemed unaware that he had stopped speaking.

He leaned forward and touched a bell and Mrs Lincroft appeared so quickly that I felt she must have been outside the door listening.

I realised what was expected of me and left.

I was beginning to feel alive again – not exactly happy, but interested in what was going on around me. A fervent curiosity was growing up within me and at the heart of it was Napier Stacy, as in Paris Pietro had been the centre of everything. Then it had been love; now it was hate. No, that was too strong a word. Dislike. That was all, but of one thing I was certain and this was that my feelings for Napier

Stacy would never be mild. Dislike could easily flare into hatred. He had suffered because of that dreadful accident – and in my heart I refused to believe it was anything but an accident – but that was no reason why he should torment his poor little wife. He was a man who having been hurt himself, found satisfaction in hurting others and for this I despised him; I distrusted him; I disliked him; but at least I should be grateful to him for making me feel some emotion again. But perhaps no emotion was better than this violent dislike.

I had thought less of Pietro in the last weeks. There would be a lapse of hours when I did not give him one thought. I was shocked for I was, I told myself, being unfaithful to his memory.

One afternoon – during my off-duty period – I decided to take a long walk alone to think about the change in my attitude and my footsteps led me to the sea. It was a bright day and a fresh wind was blowing. I took pleasure in filling my lungs with that exhilarating air.

Whither was I going? I asked myself. I should not stay at Lovat Stacy forever. In fact my position there seemed most insecure. Three girls to whom I must teach music . . . and none of them, with the exception of Edith, musical. She was a married woman who might soon have a family. The idea struck me as incongruous. Napier a father . . . and the father of Edith's children! But they were married, so why not. And when she was a mother would she want music lessons? I was to play for Sir William's guests – but no one kept a pianist on the premises for the occasional musical evening. No, my post was a very insecure one and soon I should be dismissed. And then what? I was alone in the world. I had little money. I was no longer young. Should I not be planning my future? But how could anyone know what the future held. Once I had believed that Pietro and I would be together for the rest of our lives. There was no knowing, of course; but wise people planned for the years ahead so that they were not caught, like the foolish virgins, without oil in their lamps.

I had taken a winding path down to the sea and had come to a sandy shore. Above me rose the stark white cliff; overhead was Lovat Stacy but I could not see it, for the projecting cliff made a kind of shelf over my head.

The melancholy cry of a gull broke the peace and then I heard a voice calling me. 'Mrs Verlaine. Mrs Verlaine. Where are you going?'

I turned and there was Alice running towards me, her light brown hair streaming behind her.

She came running up to me, breathlessly, faintly flushed.

'I saw you coming down here,' she panted. 'And I came to get you. It's dangerous.'

I looked at her in disbelief.

'Oh yes,' she reiterated, 'it *is* dangerous. Look.' She waved her arms. 'We're in a little cove. The sea comes right in . . . and long before high tide you could get cut off. Then what would you do?'

She folded her arms behind her back and looked up at the overhanging cliff. 'You couldn't go that way, you see. You'd be quite cut off. You shouldn't come here – only at low tide.'

'Thanks for warning me.'

She said: 'It's all right now, but in ten minutes or so it won't be. Do come now, Mrs Verlaine.'

She led me back the way I had come and as I rounded a rock I saw how far the tide had come in. She was right; this part of the beach would be entirely cut off.

'You see,' she said.

'Yes, I do.'

'It can be dangerous. People have been drowned here.'

I said suddenly: 'I wonder if that was what happened to Ro . . . to the archæologist.'

'Why, I think that could be an explanation. You're very interested in her, aren't you?'

'It *is* interesting surely, when someone disappears.'

'Yes, of course.' She put out a hand to help me over the rock. 'It could be the answer,' she said. 'She came here and was drowned. Yes, I do think that could be the answer.'

I looked out at the water and imagined it creeping up. Roma was not a strong swimmer. She could have been carried out to sea.

'I should have thought her body would have been washed up.'

'Yes,' agreed Alice. 'But I suppose sometimes bodies *are* carried out to sea. I think people ought to be careful. Particularly those who are new to the place.'

I laughed. 'I will,' I said; and she seemed relieved, which was charming of her.

'Do you wish to continue your walk alone?' asked Alice.

'Do you mean that you will accompany me?'

'Only if you wanted me to.'

'But I should be glad of your company.'

Her smile was dazzling and I warmed to her. I wondered how keenly Allegra made her feel her position as housekeeper's daughter.

She walked sedately by my side and pointed out some of the flowers in the hedgerows.

'Isn't that blue lovely, Mrs Verlaine? It's germander speedwell and ground ivy. Mr Brown gives us lessons and brings us for walks so that we can see the flowers he talks about. Don't you think that's a good idea?'

'Excellent.'

'It's botany. Edith used to love it. I expect she misses it

now. Sometimes I think she'd like to go on taking lessons. But a married lady could hardly go to the vicarage for lessons, could she? Oh look, Mrs Verlaine, there's a swift. Do you see it? I like to come out at dusk. Then I might see a churn owl. Mr Brown told us about them. They sound like an old spinning wheel going round and round and they chase ghost-moths in the fields.'

'You seem to enjoy your botany lessons.'

'Oh yes, but not so much now that Edith doesn't come. I think Mr Brown enjoyed them more then.'

I felt again that uneasiness and remembered afresh my suspicions.

'The gulls are coming inland, Mrs Verlaine. That's a sign of stormy weather at sea. They come in by the hundreds and when I see them I think of the sailors at sea.' She began to sing in her high-pitched clear young voice:

"'Lord hear us when we cry to Thee
For those in peril on the sea.'"

She shivered. 'It must be terrible to drown, Mrs Verlaine. They say you re-live your life while you're drowning. Do you think that's true?'

'I don't know and I'd hate to put it to the test.'

'The trouble is,' she went on thoughtfully, 'that the people who have drowned can't tell us if it's true. If they came back . . . But they say only those who have died violently come back. They can't rest. Do you believe it?'

'No,' I said firmly.

'The servants think that Beaumont comes back.'

'Surely not.'

'Yes, they do. And they think he comes back more now that Mr Napier is back.'

'Oh, but why?'

'Because he's angry that Napier's back. Napier sent him away didn't he, and he wants Napier to be banished because of it.'

'I thought Beaumont was such a good character. It doesn't sound so if he wants to punish his brother for what was an accident.'

'No,' she said slowly, 'it doesn't, does it. But perhaps he has to. People who die like that may have to haunt people. Do you think that's so?'

'I think it's a pack of nonsense.'

'But what about the lights in the ruined chapel? They say it's haunted. And there *are* lights there. I've seen them.'

'You've imagined them.'

'I don't think so. My room is at the top of the house, above the schoolroom. I can see a long way, and I've seen the lights. Truly I have.'

I was silent and she went on earnestly: 'You don't believe me. You think I've imagined it. If I see it some time may I show it to you? But perhaps you don't *want* to see it.'

'If it existed I should,' I said.

'Then I *will*.'

I smiled. 'I'm rather surprised at you, Alice. I thought you were a very practical girl.'

'Oh, I am, Mrs Verlaine, but if something is there it wouldn't be very practical to pretend it wasn't, would it?'

'The practical thing would be to try to find out the cause.'

'The cause would be because Beaumont couldn't rest.'

'Or someone playing a trick. I'll wait and *see* the light first before I wonder what caused it.'

'*You* are certainly very practical, Mrs Verlaine,' said Alice.

I admitted to it and dismissing the subject talked of music and musicians all the way back to the house.

'I must say,' said Mrs Rendall, 'that I find this most inconvenient. After all we have done . . . I am surprised. As for the vicar . . .'

Her plump cheeks shook with indignation as I walked with her up the path to the vicarage door. I had come over to give Sylvia a piano lesson while Allegra and Alice were with the curate.

Mrs Rendall went on in this strain for some minutes before I discovered the cause of her indignation.

'He's such a good curate . . . and what he thinks he is going to do in that outlandish place I can't imagine. Sometimes there is more *useful* work to be done at home. I think it is time some of these earnest young men realised this.'

'Don't tell me that Mr Brown is going away.'

'That is precisely what he intends to do. What *we* are going to do, I can't imagine. He is going to some village in Africa, *if* you please, to teach heathens! A nice thing. I've told him that he will no doubt end up by being served for dinner.'

'I suppose he feels he has a vocation.'

'Vocation, fiddlesticks! He can have a vocation for working here at home. Why does he want to go to one of these far off places. I said to him "The heat will kill you, Mr Brown, if the cannibals don't." And I didn't mince my words. I told him straight out that I for one should consider it his own fault.'

I was thinking of the quiet young man . . . and Edith. And I wondered whether his decision to go right away had any connection with his feeling for her. I was sorry for them both; they seemed like two helpless children caught up in their emotions.

'I've told the vicar to *talk* to him. Good curates are hard to come by, and the vicar is overworked. In fact I have thought of telling the vicar that the Bishop might be able to help. If Mr Brown was told by the Bishop that it was his *duty* to stay . . .'

'Is Mr Brown very eager to go?' I asked.

'Eager! The young idiot is determined. Mind you, since he told the vicar of his decision he has been growing more and more mournful every day. I cannot imagine how he could have got such a foolish notion. Just when the vicar . . . and I . . . had taught him to make himself so useful.'

'And you can't persuade him?'

'I shall go on attempting to,' she answered firmly.

'And the vicar?'

'My dear Mrs Verlaine, if I can't persuade him, nobody can.'

What about Edith? I asked myself as I went into the house.

When I saw Edith that morning, I noticed how desolate she looked. She stumbled through the Schumann piece, not in time, playing several false notes.

Poor Edith – so young and so bitterly buffeted by life. I wished I could help her.

After I had played for Sir William, Mrs Lincroft came into the room and said that he wished to speak to me.

I took the chair beside him and he told me that he had fixed a date for the occasion when he wished me to play for his guests.

'You could play for about an hour, I thought, Mrs Verlaine, and I shall choose the music. I will let you know in good time so that you can run through it a few times if you feel that is necessary.'

'I should like to do that.'

He nodded. 'My wife used to be rather nervous on these occasions. Mind you, she enjoyed them . . . but that was afterwards. She would never have been able to perform in public. It was quite different in the family circle.'

'I think one is always a little nervous when one is going to perform before an audience. My husband was and he . . .'

'Ah, he was a genius.'

He closed his eyes, which was an indication for me to leave. Mrs Lincroft told me that he became tired suddenly and the doctor had warned her that when he showed the least signs of fatigue he needed absolute quiet.

So I rose and went away. Mrs Lincroft came in as I was leaving. She smiled her appreciative smile. I had the notion that she liked and approved of me, which was pleasant.

The musical evening was obviously a great event.

The girls were always talking of it.

Allegra said: 'It will be like old times . . . before I was born.'

'So,' Alice said gravely, 'we shall know what it was like before we were here.'

'No, we shan't,' contradicted Allegra, 'because it'll be quite different. Mrs Verlaine will be playing instead of Lady Stacy. And then nobody had been shot nor committed suicide, nor got the gipsy servant into trouble.'

I pretended not to hear.

They were excited though because although they would not be at the dinner party, they were to be allowed into the hall to hear my playing, which was to take place between nine and ten o'clock.

They were having new dresses for the occasion and they were very pleased about this.

I had decided to wear a dress which I had not worn since Pietro's death. I had worn it only once – on the night of his last concert. A special dress for a special occasion. It was of burgundy coloured velvet – a long flowing skirt, a tightly fitting bodice which fell slightly off the shoulders. On the front was an artificial flower – a mauve orchid – so delicately coloured, so beautifully made that it looked like a perfect bloom. Pietro had seen it in the window of one of the boutiques in the Rue St Honoré and had bought it for me.

I had thought never to wear that dress again. I had kept it in a box and never looked at it until now. I had told myself it would be too painful to look at it. Yet when I had known that I was to play before these people I had thought of this dress and I knew that it was just right for the occasion and that it would give me the confidence I needed.

I took the dress from its box, lifting it out from the layers of tissue paper and spread it on my bed. How it came back to me . . . Pietro . . . coming on to the platform, that almost arrogant bow; the quick searching for me, finding me and smiling, comforted because I was there, because he knew that I shared every triumph and that I cared as deeply for his success as he did himself, and at the same time he would be telling me: *You* could never have done this.

When I thought of that night I wanted to throw myself on to that soft velvet and weep for the past.

Put it away. Forget it. Wear something else.

But no. I was going to wear that dress and nothing must prevent me.

While I was looking at it the door of my room opened stealthily and Miss Stacy looked in.

'Oh, *there* you are.' She tripped to the bed. Her lips formed a round oh. 'It's lovely. Is it your dress?'

I nodded.

'I didn't know you had anything so grand.'

'I had it . . . long ago.'

'Ah, when your famous husband was alive.'

I nodded.

She peered up at me and said: 'Your eyes are very bright. Are you going to cry?'

'No,' I told her. And then to excuse my emotion, I added: 'I wore it at his last concert.'

She did her mandarin's nodding but I sensed her sympathy.

'I suffered too,' she said. 'It was the same . . . in a way. I understand.'

Then she went to the bed and stroked the velvet.

'Bows of the same velvet would look so pretty in your hair,' she said. 'I think I'll have a new velvet dress. Not this colour though . . . blue, powder blue. Don't you think that will be pretty?'

'Very,' I said.

She nodded and went out, thinking, I was sure, of the powder blue velvet dress she would have and the little bows to go with it.

A few days later Sir William had a bad turn and Mrs Lincroft was worried. For a whole day and night she scarcely left his room and when I did see her she told me he was a little better.

'We have to be very careful,' she explained. 'Another stroke could be fatal and of course he's vulnerable.'

She was clearly deeply moved and I thought how lucky he was to have such a good housekeeper who could at a moment's notice become a first-class nurse.

I mentioned this and she turned away slightly to hide her emotion, I imagined. 'I shall never forget,' she said, 'what he has done for Alice.'

Because she seemed so overcome by her feelings I sought

to change the subject briskly and said: 'I suppose this means the dinner party will be cancelled?'

'Oh no.' She was immediately in charge of herself. 'Sir William has actually said he doesn't want that. All arrangements are to go ahead. In fact he sent for Mr Napier and told him so.' She frowned. 'I was alarmed,' she went on, 'because Napier always upsets him. It's not his fault,' she went on quickly. 'It's merely the sight of him. He keeps away as much as possible. But on this occasion . . . it passed very well.'

'It's a pity . . .' I began.

'Family quarrels are the worst,' she said. 'Still, I think that in time . . .' Her voice faded away. 'I believe when there are children . . . Sir William is very anxious that there shall be children.'

There was a knock on my door and Alice came in. She smiled demurely and said: 'Mr Napier wishes to see you, Mrs Verlaine. He's in the library.'

'Now?' I asked.

'He said at your convenience.'

'Thank you, Alice.'

She lingered and I wished she would go because I wanted to comb my hair before I went down to the library and did not want Alice to see me do it. She was a very observant girl.

'Are you looking forward to playing before all those people, Mrs Verlaine?'

'Well . . . I suppose in a way I am.'

I was taking surreptitious glances at my hair. It was untidy. I wished that I had piled it higher on my head because that gave me height; it gave me a look of dignity too. I smoothed down my dress. I wished I was wearing the lavender with a faint white stripe on it. That was most becoming. I had bought it in one of the little shops near the Rue de Rivoli. Pietro had liked me to have beautiful clothes – when he had become famous of course – even before that I had always been able to get the most out of clothes . . . in contrast to Roma.

Now I looked down at my brown gaberdine dress. The cut was good, the dress serviceable, but it was not one of my best; and I wished that I had known this summons was coming.

I could obviously not change my dress but I could comb my hair. I did so while Alice still stood there.

'You look . . . pleased, Mrs Verlaine,' she commented.

'Pleased?'

'Well . . . more than that. Different in a way.'

I knew that I must have betrayed the excitement of going into battle, for that was what it was like . . . having an encounter with Napier Stacy.

I went past Alice and down to the library. I had been in this room only once before, when I had been struck by the character of the oak panelling. There was a design of arches divided by pilasters which was surmounted by a frieze and a cornice. The carved ceiling was the most intricate in the house, and the arms of the Stacy, Beaumont and Napier families were entwined up there to make an intricate pattern.

One wall was entirely covered by the most exquisite piece of tapestry which had interested me immediately not only because of the fine weaving of wool and silk on a linen warp but because of the subject – Julius Cæsar landing on these shores. Mrs Lincroft when she had shown me this room told me that it had been started soon after the house was built and that it had been put away – forgotten for more than a hundred years. Then a member of the family having committed some misdemeanour at Court for which she had been banished, discovered the unfinished work and to while away her exile had completed it. In a house of this kind one was always stumbling on little incidents of this kind – links with the past.

The three other walls were lined with books; some in leather binding with gilt lettering, behind glass. There were Persian rugs on the parquet floor, the usual seats in the window embrasures, and a heavy oak table in the centre of the room with several arm-chairs.

There was an air of solemnity about the library. I could not enter it without imagining all the serious family conferences which must have taken place in it over the centuries. Here, I had no doubt, Napier had been interrogated after the shooting of his brother.

Napier, who was seated at the table, rose as I entered.

'Ah,' he said, 'Mrs Verlaine!' Those lights seemed to shoot up in his eyes making them a more dazzling blue than ever; I called them mischievous – but they were more than that. He was looking forward to an amusing quarter of an hour which he was going to make as uncomfortable for me as possible. 'Please sit down.' His voice was silky. Dangerous, I thought.

'I suppose you've guessed that I want to talk to you about your performance. The tuners assure me that the grand piano on the hall dais is now in perfect condition, so everything should be satisfactory. I am sure you are going to delight us all.'

'Thank you.' So polite, I thought. Where is the sting?

'Have you ever played on the concert platform, Mrs Verlaine?'

'Not . . . seriously.'

'I see. Did you have no ambitions to do so?'

'Yes,' I said, 'great ambition.' He raised his eyebrows and I went on quickly. 'Not great enough apparently.'

'You mean that you failed to reach the standard demanded?'

'I mean just that.'

'So your ambition was not strong enough.'

I said as coolly as I could: 'I married.'

'But that is not the answer. There are married geniuses, I believe.'

'I have never said I was a genius.'

His eyes glinted. 'You gave up your career for the sake of marriage,' he said. 'But your husband was more fortunate. He did not have to give up his career.'

I was at a loss for words. I was afraid that if I spoke my voice would betray my emotion.

How I detested this man!

He went on talking. 'I have chosen the pieces which you will play for us. I am sure you will agree that my choice is a good one. Great favourites . . . and I know you will do justice to them.'

I did not answer. I was thinking of Pietro and so many scenes from the past. Pietro's egoism, my resentment, my sacrifice of which I had continually reminded him.

Why did this man have to bring it all back so vividly! I would not stay here to be tormented by him. I picked up the music he had laid on the table.

I said: 'Thank you, Mr Stacy.'

I glanced at the sheets in my hand. Hungarian dances. The Rhapsody No. 2. The music Pietro had played during that last concert!

I felt as though I were choking. I could not stay in that room.

I turned; the Julius Cæsar tapestry seemed to swim before my eyes. I groped for the handle of the door and I was outside.

He knows, I thought. He chose those pieces deliberately.

He wanted to play on my emotions; he wanted to taunt me, to trick me into betraying myself; he wanted to amuse himself as a boy does when he puts two spiders in a basin and watches their reaction to each other.

In such a way he taunted Edith. And now his attention was turned to me. I obviously interested him. Why? Could it be that he knew more about me than I had believed possible?

He had taken the trouble to find out what Pietro had played on that night. Perhaps it would have been mentioned in some of the papers of the time.

How much else did he know about me?

On the day preceding the dinner party Alice came to tell me that Edith was sick and I went along to her room to see her.

This was the apartment where Charles I had lodged during the Civil War. The actual room led out of the main chamber and was occupied by Napier, while Edith used the larger bedroom. In it was a huge bed over which was a dome upheld by four columns engraved with flowers. The bed head and tester were ornamented with gilt figures and the hangings were of blue velvet. It was a very elaborate bed – and I remembered that this was the bridal suite. The door leading to the next room – the chamber in which a king had lodged – looked less elaborate as far as I could see. The bed was a carved wooden fourposter and beside it were a pair of wooden steps used for stepping into the bed. That room doubtless looked as it had done in the days of the Civil War – but the furniture in this one was a later and more elegant period.

It was the first time I had been in the bridal suite and I felt embarrassed because I thought of Napier here with Edith and I wondered what their relationship could possibly have been like with so much fear on her side, so much contempt on his.

There was a consul table attached to one wall, over which was a tall mirror with a gilded frame; I noticed the secretaire-cabinet of satin wood and golden Honduras mahogany with fluted columns. This must be the most elegant room in the house – and that grim chamber leading from it made a strong contrast.

My quick survey of the room was over in a few seconds for it was Edith whom I had come to see.

She was sitting up in that ornate bed looking small and lost with her lovely golden hair in two plaits which hung over each shoulder.

'Oh, Mrs Verlaine, I feel . . . terrible.'

'What's wrong?' I asked.

She bit her lip. 'It's to-morrow night. I have to be hostess, and they'll be such terrifying people. I can't face them.'

'Why should they be terrifying? They're only guests.'

'But I shan't know what to say. I did wish I needn't go.' She looked at me hopefully, as though asking me to produce some reason for her absence.

I said: 'You'll get used to it. It's no use avoiding this one. You'll have to face up to the next. And I'm sure you'll find it's not so bad.'

'I thought you might . . . you might suggest that you . . . did it for me.'

'I!' I was astonished. 'But I am not even going to the dinner. I am merely coming down to play for the guests.'

'You would do it so much better than I would.'

'Thank you,' I said, 'but I am not the mistress of this house, I am merely employed here.'

'I thought you might speak to Napier.'

'And suggest that I take your place? Surely you must see how impossible that is.'

'Yes, I suppose so,' said Edith. 'Oh, I do hope I shall feel better. But he would listen to you.'

'If someone is to speak to your husband surely you would do that better than anyone else?'

'No,' said Edith, putting a hand momentarily over her eyes. Then she added: 'He does take notice of you, Mrs Verlaine . . . and he doesn't take notice of many people.'

I laughed, but a terrible uneasiness had come to me. He was interested in me. Why?

I said briskly: 'You should get up now and go for a long walk. Stop worrying. When it is over you will be asking yourself what there was to worry about.'

Edith lowered her hands and looked at me earnestly.

What a child she was. My words had made some impression on her.

'I'll try,' she said.

<hr>

How silent it was in the big hall! There was the piano on the dais. Banks of flowers would be brought in from the greenhouses. Tulips and carnations, I imagined. The seats were already there. It was like a concert hall . . . a unique one, with the suit of armour standing guard at the staircase . . . the weapons on the walls, the arms of the Stacys entwined with those of the Napiers and the Beaumonts.

I should be there – in my Burgundy velvet – looking as I had looked on that fateful night.

No, different. I should not be a member of the audience; this time I should be there on that dais.

I went to it. I sat at the piano. I must not think of Pietro. Pietro was dead. If he had been here in this audience I should have been afraid of faltering, of earning his contempt. I should have been conscious of him, his ears straining to catch the false note, the lack of sureness . . . and I should have known that while he trembled for me, yet he hoped that I should give a less perfect performance than his.

I played. I had not played these pieces since. I had told myself that I could not bear to. But I played now and I was caught up in the excitement which the master had felt when he composed them. It was there in all its glory, that inspiration which came from something not of this world. It was wonderful. And as I played I did not see Pietro's long hair flung back in the agitation of creative interpretation. To me the music meant what it had in those days before I knew Pietro. I was exalted as I played.

When I stopped it all came back so vividly; I could see him bowing to the audience. He had looked a little tired and strained and he never had looked like that after a performance . . . not immediately after. That came later after he had left the platform, when the flatterers and sycophants had left, when we were alone together. Then the effect of all that he had put into the evening would begin to show.

I saw him, lying back in the chair in the dressing-room . . . Pietro . . . who would never play again.

A low chuckle behind me. For a moment I thought he had come back, that he was there laughing at me. If anything could evoke the return of his spirit surely that music would.

Miss Stacy was sitting in one of the seats. She was wearing a dress of pale pink crepe material and little pink bows were in her hair.

'I crept in when you were in the middle,' she said. 'You play beautifully, Mrs Verlaine.'

I did not answer. And she went on: 'It reminds me of the old days so much. Isabella used to be so nervous. You're not. And afterwards she used to cry in her room. It was because she wasn't pleased with her performance and knew she could have done better if she'd gone on with her teachers. When I sat there listening I thought . . . I wouldn't be surprised if this brought the ghosts out. It's just like it used to be. Suppose Isabella couldn't rest. Suppose she came different back . . . Well, the hall would look just as it did on those nights when she played . . . all the same . . . only someone different at the piano. Isn't that exciting, Mrs Verlaine? Don't you think it would bring the ghosts out?'

'If they existed, yes. But I don't believe they do.'

'That's a dangerous thing to say. They might be listening.'

I didn't answer. Instead I closed the lid of the piano. And I was thinking: Yes, it would be an occasion for ghosts. And I wasn't thinking of the ghost of Isabella Stacy but that of Pietro.

The image that looked back at me from my mirror was reassuring – red velvet, and that orchid. It became me as no other dress ever had. Pietro had not said so, but his eyes had told me.

He had stood behind me and placed his hands on my shoulders, looking at us both in the mirror. That picture would be stamped on my memory for ever.

'You look worthy . . . of me,' he said, with typical Pietro candour; and I had laughed at him and said that if he thought that, I must look very well indeed.

We had gone to the concert hall together, and I had left him to take my place in the audience.

But what was the use of going over it. I must not think of him to-night. I smoothed one hand over the other, massaging my fingers. They were supple . . . adequate, I told myself. But I knew better. They had some magic in them to-night, and no one was going to rob them of it, not even the ghost of Pietro.

I was glad I had not been invited to dine with the party. Mrs Lincroft had said that she had thought it a little remiss of Napier not to suggest it, for she was sure it had been Sir William's intention. I replied that I preferred not to go.

'I understand,' she said, 'you want to be perfectly fresh for your performance.'

I wondered about the guests. Friends of Napier's or of Sir William? Scarcely Napier's for he had not been home long enough to make many. How did it feel, I wondered, to be exiled and then return? It would be a little like that for me to-night. I had been exiled in a way, and to-night I was to go on to that dais and people would listen to my playing. It would be an uncritical audience, I told myself, quite unlike the audiences Pietro had played to. There was nothing to fear.

At nine o'clock I went down to the great hall. Sir William was there in his chair. Mrs Lincroft in a long grey chiffon skirt with cornflower blue chiffon blouse wheeled him in. She was not of the company but like myself a kind of higher servant. I remembered thinking this as I saw her.

Sir William beckoned to me and he told me that he was sorry I had not joined the company for dinner. I replied that I preferred to be quiet before the performance and he bowed his head in understanding.

Napier came over to me, Edith was with him. She looked very pretty but highly nervous. I smiled reassuringly at her.

Then the company seated itself and I went to the dais.

I played the dances first as Pietro had done; and as my fingers touched the keys and those magical sounds came forth I forgot everything but the joy they gave me. As I went on playing, I saw pictures evoked by the music; and that wonderful mood of exultation came to me. I forgot that I was playing to strangers in a baronial hall; I even forgot that I had lost Pietro; there was nothing for me but the music.

The applause was spontaneous. I smiled at the audience who went on clapping. I scanned them lightly. I saw Sir William deeply affected; Napier sitting upright applauding with the rest; Edith beside him smiling almost happily; and somewhere at the back of the hall Allegra and Alice – Allegra bouncing up and down on her seat in her excitement and Alice gravely clapping. I sensed their pleasure – not so much in the music, but in my success.

The applause died down and I began the Rhapsody. This was Pietro's piece but I didn't care. To me it had always opened a world of colour and delight. I could undergo twenty different emotions while I played it and so had he. He had told me once that during one part of the Rhapsody he always imagined that he was sitting in a dentist's chair having a tooth removed which had made us both laugh at the time. 'It's pain,' he had cried. 'Sheer pain . . . and then that acute joy.'

I suffered; I rejoiced; and there was nothing for me but the music. And when I came to an end I knew that I had never played so well.

I stood up; the applause was deafening.

Napier was beside me. He said: 'My father wishes to speak to you.'

I followed him to Sir William's wheelchair. There were tears in the old man's eyes.

'I've no need to tell you, Mrs Verlaine,' he said. 'It was superb. Beyond . . . my expectations.'

'Thank you. Thank you.'

'We shall be requested to repeat this often, I believe. It – it reminded me . . .'

He did not continue and I said: 'I understand.'

'These people will be wanting to congratulate you.'

'I think I will go to my room now.'

'Ah yes. Exhausting. I know. Well, we understand that.'

Napier was looking at me and I could not read the expression in his eyes.

'Triumph,' he whispered.

'Thank you.'

'I trust you approve my choice of pieces.'

'They were magnificent.'

He bowed his head smiling and people began to approach to tell me how they had enjoyed my playing. I could not escape for a time. I was aware of Miss Stacy – lavender bows in her hair – looking excited and fey as though she were in touch with the ghosts she was sure would be visiting us that night; I saw Mrs Lincroft sending the girls to their rooms and I listened to compliments; several people mentioned my husband. Few of them had heard him play, but they knew his name.

It was some time before I could escape.

In my room I could not stop looking at my reflection. The faint colour under my skin, the luminosity of my eyes; my hair seemed darker and my skin gleamed magnolia colour against the rich burgundy velvet.

'I did it,' I whispered. 'Pietro, I did it.'

In a country house. To an uncritical audience. What do they know of music?

'They loved it!'

Pah! They would have been pleased with Essie Elgin. She could have done as well. Gymnastics, my dear Caro.

And I wanted nothing but to be with Pietro, to quarrel with him . . . anything, but to be with him.

My cheeks were burning; I felt that I was stifled in this

room and impulsively I left it and went down by means of a back staircase and out into the gardens.

The June night was warm, and it was a perfect night, for a near-full moon was high in the sky. I went to my walled garden and sat there, and I was filled with a longing to go back to those days when Pietro and I had sat outside the Paris cafés and talked. I should have had both Pietro and my music and how much better it would have been for us both if I had. I should have been closer to him; he would have respected me; I should have been better able to look after him; I should not have allowed him to subdue me; firmly I should have safeguarded his health.

I covered my face with my hands and wept for the past and longed to live it all again.

I sat there for some little time, my head buried in my hands; and then suddenly I gave a little cry of dismay for there was a movement beside me. Someone was sitting close to me on the seat.

'I hope I didn't startle you,' said Napier.

I drew away from him. He was the last person I wanted to see. I half rose but he took my wrist in a firm grip. 'Don't go,' he said.

'I . . . I didn't hear you come.'

'You were engrossed in your own thoughts,' he said.

I was horrified. I believed there might be a trace of tears on my face, and that he should see them was unendurable.

He seemed different, softer. That should warn me.

'I saw you come here and I wanted to speak to you,' he said.

'You . . . saw me?'

'Yes, I was a little bored with my father's guests.'

'I hope you did not tell them so.'

'Not in so many words.'

'You are . . .'

'Please go on. You know you need not choose your words with care as far as I'm concerned. I'd rather know exactly what you think.'

'Then I think that you are a little . . . uncivil.'

'What more can you expect, brought up as I was. But enough of me. You are far more interesting.'

'Surely you don't find anyone as interesting as yourself?'

'At the moment – much as it may surprise you – I do.' He turned to me suddenly and went on: 'Let's drop the banter. Let us talk seriously.'

'Please begin.'

'We have something in common you and I. You realise that.'

'I cannot think what.'

'Then you are not seriously thinking. Our pasts, of course. That's what we both have to put behind us. You to-night . . .' He put his hand up suddenly and with astonishing tenderness touched my cheek. 'You are grieving for your genius. It's no use. He's dead. You have to forget him. You have to begin again. When will you learn that?'

'And you?'

'I too have much to forget.'

'*You* make no attempt to forget.'

'Do you?'

'Yes. Yes.'

'To-night?'

'Those pieces I played.'

'I know, I chose them deliberately.'

'You knew.'

'I read it in one of the papers. The last he played.'

'How like you to remind me!'

'But you have taken a step away from your grief to-night. Did you know? You faced up to life. I'll swear you had never played those pieces since he died.'

'No, not till to-night.'

'Now you will play them often. It's a sign that you've moved on a bit.'

'And you chose them for my good?'

'You won't believe me if I say yes. If I say I chose them to discountenance you, you will, I suppose.'

'I believe,' I said, 'that I should believe what you told me to-night.'

He turned to me suddenly. I wanted to hold him off yet to draw him on. I could not understand what had happened to him . . . or to myself. He was different. I was different. I was unsure of myself. I felt I should not stay here with him. There was something evil about this night . . . this moon . . . this garden . . . and about him.

'Why . . . to-night?' he asked me.

'I think you will tell the truth . . . to-night.'

He lifted his hands; I thought he was going to touch me. But he refrained from doing so. Then he said: 'I chose those pieces deliberately. I wanted you to play them because it's better to face up to life and not turn away from it.'

'And you are doing that?'

He nodded.

'That is why you remind everyone that you shot your brother?'

'You see,' he said, 'it's true that we have something in common. We have to escape from the past.'

'Why should I want to escape?'

'Because you will go on grieving until you do. Because you have built up an ideal which grows rosier with every year and quite unlike what it was in reality.'

'How do you know what it was in reality?'

'I know a great deal about you.'

'What?'

'What you have told me.'

155

'You seem to be very interested in me.'

'I am. Didn't you realise that?'

'I thought I was beneath your notice.'

Then he laughed and it was the old laugh – mocking, taunting.

He said suddenly: 'You are fascinated by this place.'

I admitted it.

'And the people in it?'

'I always find people interesting.'

'But we are a little . . . unusual, aren't we?'

'It's usual for people to be unusual.'

'Have you ever known anyone else who killed his brother?'

'No.'

'Doesn't that make me unique?'

'Accidents can happen to anyone.'

'You're determined to dismiss the general view that it was not an accident?'

'I'm sure it was.'

'I should now take your hand . . . so . . . and raise it to my lips.' He did so. 'I should kiss it in gratitude . . .' His lips scorched my skin; the kiss was fervent, frightening.

I withdrew my hand as casually as I could.

'Should I?' he asked.

'Certainly not. There is nothing for which to be grateful. It seemed to me a perfectly logical explanation. An accident.'

'And you are always so logical, Mrs Verlaine?'

'I try to be.'

'Dispensing sympathy where it is deserved.'

'Isn't that where it should be dispensed?'

'You knew of course that I was sent to Australia . . . to a cousin of my father's. He couldn't bear the sight of me . . . my father, I mean . . . after the accident. My mother killed herself. They said it was because of my brother's death. Two deaths at my door. Well, you can understand it, can't you. I was such a reminder. So off I went to my father's cousin who was a grazier some eighty miles north of Melbourne. I thought I should stay there until the end of my life.'

'And you were content to do that.'

'Never. This was where I belonged, and when the opportunity came, I did not hesitate. I accepted my father's bargain.'

'Well, now you are back and all is well.'

'Is it, Mrs Verlaine?' He moved nearer to me. 'How strange it seems to be sitting in this moonlit garden and talking seriously to Mrs Verlaine. I know your name is Caroline. Caro, your genius called you.'

'How could you know that?'

'I read it. It was in the paper, you know. It said he spoke to you when you came into the dressing-room. All he could say was: "It's all right, Caro . . ."'

I felt my lips quiver. I burst out: 'You are deliberately trying to –'

'To hurt you? I want you to face it . . . Caro. I want you to face it and then you can turn your back on it. That's what we both have to do.'

There was a strange tremor in his voice and I turned to him. He put out his hands and it was as though he said: Help me. And I wanted to say: We'll help each other. Because oddly enough I believed him then. And I was glad . . . glad to be there with him in that moonlit garden which had a kind of magic which had driven away the evil.

He took my hands in his suddenly. And I did not withdraw them. We sat on the seat looking at each other and I knew that something had grown up between us which neither of us could deny.

And suddenly I was afraid, afraid of my emotions – and his.

I stood up.

I said: 'It's a little chilly. I think I should return to the house.'

He had changed; the arrogance had dropped from him. Or did I deceive myself? Was the moonlight playing tricks?

I was unsure of all but one thing: I only knew I had to get away from him.

Chapter Five

I had dined with Alice and her mother and had come to my room to prepare the next day's lesson. I had not seen Napier since the night of my performance and it was very hard for me to believe that I had not exaggerated in some way the scene in the moonlit garden. I had been overwrought on that night; and he, of course, had been aware of this. I must not forget that he was Edith's husband, and that he might well be a philanderer, for there was Allegra to bear that out. And how foolish had I been on that night? It was true I had not lingered in the garden but looking back I was sure I had been ready to delude myself. I wondered whether he remembered that scene with amusement.

I really must get the man out of my thoughts and concentrate on work.

There was a knock at my door. Alice stood there; she looked excited or frightened out of her usual gravity.

'You asked me to tell you, Mrs Verlaine. I – I've seen the light in the chapel. You said to tell you . . .'

'Where?' I said, moving towards the window.

'You can see it better from my room,' she said. 'Please come.'

She led the way to the schoolroom which was close to her mother's rooms and her own. We climbed a short spiral staircase and she took me into a neat little room with dainty curtains and a small bed covered with a chintz counterpane – a dainty room reflecting Alice's personality. She led me to the window and we stood side by side looking out across the grounds to the darkness of the copse.

'You could see from your room,' she explained. 'But here you can see it really *is* in the chapel.'

An almost full moon gave a cool steady light to the scene. There was no wind.

'What a calm, clear night,' I said.

'The sort of night when ghosts would walk,' whispered Alice.

I glanced at her; her grey eyes were wide; her little figure tense.

'You're not afraid?' I asked.

She shivered. 'I don't know. I think I should be if I saw . . . the ghost of Beau.'

'You won't,' I assured her. 'Don't be afraid, Alice.'

'But if he . . . walks.'

'The dead don't, I'm sure of it.'

'If they're angry, if they hate someone living . . . if someone had set fire to the sanctuary . . .'

'Alice,' I said, 'you are letting your imagination run riot.'

'But there *is* the light, Mrs Verlaine.'

'Perhaps you thought you saw a light.'

'I've seen it several times. There *is* a light in the chapel. That's not imagination.'

'It could be someone on the road.'

'It's too far away. Besides, it's right there in the chapel . . . You can see it from this window. It moves about in the chapel, and then it goes out. I've seen it more than once since Mr Napier came home.'

'There could be many explanations. People might meet there.'

'Lovers, you mean, Mrs Verlaine?'

'Anybody. Why shouldn't they?'

'It's an eerie place. Besides it's trespassing and if people were trespassing they wouldn't show lights to betray themselves, would they? Look! Look! There it is!'

She was right. I saw the light distinctly. It seemed as though it were held stationary against the window which I remembered seeing in the burned-out ruin.

I stared and could not entirely suppress a shiver. Who was there with the light? Who had gone to the ruin in the copse after dark for the purpose of haunting it? I was determined to find out.

Alice whispered: 'It's the ghost of Beau.'

'No, no . . . that's absurd. But it could be someone pretending to be.'

'But who would? Who would . . . dare.'

I did not answer her. I said: 'Would you like to come down there now with me?'

She shrank away from me. 'Oh . . . no, Mrs Verlaine. He – he might be angry. He might do something terrible to us. He might –'

'Who?'

'Beau.'

I said: 'I don't believe that. Beau is dead. And whoever is showing that light is very much alive. I want to know who it is. Don't you?'

She lowered her eyes and then lifted them to my face. 'Yes, I do, but something terrible could happen to us if we went down there.'

'What do you think would happen to us?'

'We might be turned to stone. He might change us into one of those figures on the altar. I always think they look as though they were once people.'

'Oh, Alice!' I scolded.

She gave a nervous laugh. 'I know I'm silly, but I should be so frightened.' She seemed to believe I was going myself for she caught my hand and cried: 'Mrs Verlaine, please don't go there. Please . . . *please*!'

I was gratified that she should be so concerned for me. I said gently: 'But, Alice, this is the sort of thing that should be investigated. No one should be allowed to play tricks like this.'

'Yes, but don't go now, Mrs Verlaine. Perhaps some of us could go with you. But not now . . . please.'

'All right. But Alice, I don't accept this idea of a ghost, you know. I am certain that we shall find a perfectly logical explanation if we look for it.'

'Do you really?'

'I most certainly do.'

'What a comfort.'

'Now, Alice, I think you should forget about this light.'

'Yes,' she sighed, 'otherwise I shall think about it in bed to-night and I shan't be able to sleep.'

'Have you a good book to read?'

She nodded. 'It's *Evelina*. It's fascinating, Mrs Verlaine. It's all about a young lady's adventures in society.'

'Why, Alice, I believe you would like to be a young lady in society.'

She smiled and I was pleased because I could see that the fear and the morbid imaginings engendered by the light in the chapel were already receding. 'Well,' she said, 'I can imagine it, Mrs Verlaine, though it could never happen to me. Allegra is always reminding me that although I live in a big house and enjoy some of the privileges of the family, I am only the housekeeper's daughter.'

'Never mind, Alice. It is really what you *are* that counts.'

'Do you think so?'

'I am sure of it. Now you get back to *Evelina* and don't give another thought to that mysterious light which I'm determined shan't be a mystery much longer.'

'You don't like mysteries, do you?'

'Who doesn't want to solve them?'

'A lot of people don't bother. Perhaps they're like me and imagine what happened. But you want to *know*. Like what happened to Miss Brandon.'

'I daresay a number of people want to know that.'

'But they never will now, I suppose.'

'One can never be sure what will be discovered.'

'No.' She was thoughtful. Then she said: 'That's what makes it all so exciting, doesn't it?'

I agreed and went back to my room.

I was not really as unconcerned about the mysterious light as I had led Alice to believe. There seemed no doubt that someone was playing tricks; it was someone who wanted to pretend the place was haunted, and keep alive the memory of Beaumont Stacy. As if that were necessary! No, that was hardly the answer. The haunting was meant to imply, I was sure, that the ghost of Beaumont was in revolt against Napier's return.

It was silly, childish, miserable and vengeful; and I was more angry than the situation warranted.

Napier undoubtedly had his enemies – and that did not surprise me.

Returning to my room I went to the window seat and looked out over the grounds. The moon had waned slightly since the night of my concert. I thought of the moonlit garden and of Napier who was trying to put the past behind him and I wondered who it was who was determined that he should not. Who would go to the copse and wave a light about in the hope that it would be believed his beautiful brother had returned because he was displeased. It was childish. And yet it was just the way to keep the story alive.

I looked across the lawns to the copse. Alice was right, it was not so easy to make out the ruin here as it was higher up. In fact I could not see the chapel – only the dark smudge of firs which was the copse.

The chapel had been destroyed by fire after Napier came back. Who had done that? Was it the same one who now 'haunted it' by waving a light about after dark?

I felt a desire to lay the ghost, to stop this childishness – and the reason was that I wanted to know what Napier would be like if he were no longer living in the shadow of the past. Much the same, was the answer to that. Just because of a few moments in that garden, when I was decidedly not my usual practical self, I was ready to endow him with all sorts of qualities which he undoubtedly did not possess.

'The maternal instinct, dear Caro,' Pietro would have said. He had mocked that in me on one occasion when I was anxious because he had walked through the streets for hours in the rain contemplating some cadenza which had failed to please him.

'Not that I want to discourage it, Caro. But it should be applied sparingly, and in secret. Worry about me, but don't let me know it. Be unobtrusive. Little attentions should be performed subtly so that they go unnoticed. I should turn in disgust from a fussy possessive female.'

Go away, Pietro. Leave me alone. Let me forget you. Let me escape.

I could hear his voice mocking over the years. 'Never, Caro. Never.'

Then momentarily I forgot Pietro for I saw a dark figure emerge from the shrubbery. For a few seconds that figure was in moonlight and I recognised Allegra.

She ran swiftly across the grass, keeping close to the hedge; then she disappeared into the house.

Allegra? I asked myself. Was she the ghost who was haunting the chapel in the copse?

I studied her closely while she stumbled painfully through the Czerny study.

'Really, Allegra!' I sighed.

She grinned at me and then frowned at the book, paused and proceeded.

When she came to the end of the piece she sighed and put her hands in her lap. I sighed too. Then she burst out laughing.

'I told you I'd never be a credit to you, Mrs Verlaine.'

'You don't concentrate. Is it because you can't or you won't?'

'I do try,' she said looking at me mischievously.

'Allegra,' I said, 'do you ever go to the ruin in the copse after dark?'

She looked startled and gave me a quick glance before she turned her head to stare down at the keyboard.

'Oh, Mrs Verlaine, I . . . I'd be scared. You know it's haunted, don't you?'

'I know someone shows a light there.'

'There is a light there sometimes. I've seen it.'

'Do you know who is playing the trick?'

'Oh . . . er . . . yes. I suppose so.'

'Who is it, Allegra?'

'They say it's the ghost of Uncle Beau.'

'They do? Who are they?'

'Oh . . . almost everybody.'

'But what do *you* say, Allegra?'

'What should I?'

'You might say it was someone playing a trick.'

'Oh no, Mrs Verlaine, I don't say that.'

'But you think it.'

She looked at me truly alarmed. 'I don't understand you.'

'There was a light in the chapel last night and Alice drew my attention to it. A little later I saw you coming into the house.'

She bit her lip and cast down her eyes.

'You do admit, Allegra, that you were out last evening.'

She nodded.

'Then . . .'

'You can't think that *I* –?'

'What I think is that if anyone is playing a silly trick Sir William would be glad to hear of it.'

She was alarmed. She said: 'Mrs Verlaine, I can tell you where I was. I borrowed Mrs Lincroft's scarf, then I left it at the vicarage and went back to get it. If Mrs Lincroft had missed it she would have told my grandfather. So I went out and got it.'

'Did you see the vicar or Mr Brown or Mrs Rendall when you called?'

'No, but I saw Sylvia.'

'Why didn't you leave it till the morning when you would be going over there?'

'Mrs Lincroft might have found out and she did say that if I borrowed anything else without asking she would tell my grandfather. It was scarlet,' she added ingratiatingly. 'I love scarlet.'

I turned over the leaves of Czerny's *Studies*.

'Let's try this,' I said. I had made up my mind that I didn't believe Allegra and I was going to watch her.

I lost no time in speaking to Sylvia, Sylvia was the girl of whom I necessarily saw least. She seemed to me a little sly. I wasn't quite sure what had given me this impression: perhaps it was because in her mother's presence she was so demure and seemed to change subtly when Mrs Rendall was not present. I was being unfair to her, I admonished myself. Poor child! Who would not be over-awed by the formidable Mrs Rendall, particularly one over whom she had as much control as her own daughter.

Sylvia was a painstaking pupil, and, I felt, did her best – a poor best, it was true, but all she was capable of.

'Did you see Allegra last night?' I asked when she had thumped out her scales.

'Allegra? Why . . .'

'Did she come to see you?' I persisted. 'Try to remember. I particularly want to know.'

Sylvia looked down at her nails which I saw were bitten. She seemed as though she were desperately trying to work out what she must answer.

'If you had seen her last night you would have remembered, wouldn't you?'

'Oh yes,' said Sylvia. 'She came to the vicarage.'

'Does she often come in the evening?'

'Er . . . no.'

'What did your parents say when she came?'

'They . . . they didn't know.'

'So it was a secret visit?'

'Well, it – it was the scarf. You see, Allegra had borrowed it. It was one of Mrs Lincroft's, and she was afraid Mrs Lincroft would find out and tell Sir William so she came over to get it and I let her in and no one knew she had come.'

So it was true. The story fitted, and if Allegra had been at the vicarage she could not possibly have been at the chapel at the time when the light was there.

I must look elsewhere for my practical joker.

I had dined with Mrs Lincroft and Alice, and the latter had left me with her mother.

'Don't go yet,' Mrs Lincroft had said. 'Stay and I'll make some coffee.'

I watched her making it. 'I like to make it myself,' she said. 'I'm rather particular about my tea and coffee.'

I watched her move about the room – an elegant woman in one of the long skirts which she favoured – grey this time – and the feminine chiffon blouse of the same colour with the tiny pink decorative buttons. She moved silently, and with grace; and I thought what a beautiful girl she must have been. She was not old but just a little past her youth; I was deeply conscious of that slightly faded air and fell to wondering what the late Mr Lincroft had been like.

When the coffee was ready she brought the brass tray to a little table and sat down near me.

'I trust this is to your liking, Mrs Verlaine. No doubt you know what good coffee is, having lived in France. What an exciting life you and your husband must have had.'

I admitted that that was so.

'And to be widowed so young!'

'*You* know what that means.'

'Ah yes . . .' I hoped for confidences but they were not forthcoming. Mrs Lincroft was one of the rare women who did not talk about herself. 'You have been with us now for some weeks,' she went on. 'I hope you are settling in.'

'I think so.'

'You begin to know something of the family now. By the way, how do you think Edith is looking?'

'I think she looks *well*.'

Mrs Lincroft nodded. 'There is a change in her. Have you noticed? But then . . . you did not see much of her before. I would say she is going to have a child.'

'Oh.'

'There are signs – I do hope so. This will make everyone so happy. If it's a boy . . . I do hope it's a boy . . . then Sir William will be reconciled.'

'I am sure it would be a very happy state of events.'

Mrs Lincroft smiled. 'It will change everything. The past will be forgotten.'

I nodded.

'I shall pray for a boy, and one who looks like Beaumont. I daresay Sir William would want the child called Beaumont. Why, if we had another Beaumont in the house the ghost would be completely laid.'

'It's a pity it was not laid long ago.'

'Ah, but he was such a beloved boy. If he had been a little less handsome, a little less charming, it would have been so much easier. The only way to forgetfulness is to replace him, and that can be done by a grandchild.'

'There is already Allegra.'

'Napier's natural daughter! But she only reminds Sir William of an unfortunate occurrence.'

'It is scarcely her fault.'

'No indeed. But her presence does nothing to make Sir William forget. In fact at one time I believe he was contemplating sending Allegra away.'

'He seems fond of sending people away,' I blurted out.

Mrs Lincroft looked at me coldly. I could see that she thought it presumptuous of me to criticise Sir William.

'You would understand that the presence of Allegra could be painful to him.'

'It is sad for the girl if he gives that impression.'

Again I appeared to be criticising Sir William and she said rather shortly: 'Allegra has always been a difficult child. Perhaps it would have been better if she had not been brought up here.'

'It must have been hard for her. A mother who deserted her, a father she did not know, and a grandfather who resents her.'

Mrs Lincroft shrugged her shoulders. 'I have done my best,' she said. 'It's not easy with a girl like Allegra. If she had been more like Alice . . .' She looked at me anxiously. 'You find Alice . . . obedient?'

'I find her a charming girl – intelligent and well mannered.'

Mrs Lincroft's good humour was restored. 'Ah,' she sighed, 'I wish Allegra were more like her. That child is a little light-fingered, I fear.' I thought immediately of the scarf. 'Oh, nothing criminal,' went on Mrs Lincroft quickly, 'but she is apt to think that other people's property can be borrowed without first asking permission as long as she puts it back afterwards.'

'She seems afraid of her grandfather.'

'She is naturally in awe of him. So is Edith. But then she is so meek. Not that that is a fault in itself, but she is so nervous, nervous of everything. Frightened of thunder and lightning . . . frightened of giving offence. It will do her the world of good to produce a child.'

I said: 'What in your opinion is at the bottom of this talk about a mysterious light in the chapel?'

She shrugged her shoulders. 'The servants are all discussing it. I think it's a trick played by someone who wants to keep the past alive.'

'But why?'

'Someone who has a grudge against Napier, perhaps. Or it might be just for mischief.'

'I suppose a ruin suggests a ghost.'

'The light was seen before the chapel was a ruin. As soon as Napier came back, in fact. And then one night there was the blaze and since then the light has appeared again.'

'What does Napier think about it?'

She looked at me intently. 'You, Mrs Verlaine, would probably know that as well as I.'

So this quiet enigmatical woman was aware that Napier was not indifferent to me – nor I to him. I was uneasy and changed the subject. I mentioned the gardens and she was very ready to talk of flowers – which were a passion with her. Then the conversation flowed easily until I left her.

It was just after dusk. I was suffering a painful session at the piano with Allegra when Alice came in.

'I thought I would be ready when my turn came,' she said.

She sat in the window seat while I finished the lesson with Allegra and suddenly she called out: 'There it is again. I saw it.'

Allegra got up from the piano and rushed to the window. I followed.

'It's the light again,' said Alice. 'I saw it clearly. Wait a minute. Look! There it is again.'

And sure enough the light was there. It flared up for a moment and remained steady like a light in a lighthouse and then all was dark.

'You saw it, Mrs Verlaine,' said Alice.

'Yes, I saw it.'

'No one could say it wasn't there, could they?'

I shook my head, my eyes fixed on the dark copse. Then

171

there it was again. It shone brightly through the darkness, lingered for a few seconds and was gone.

I was aware of Allegra breathing deeply beside me. I felt I owed her an apology for I had suspected her of playing the trick with the light; and now she was completely exonerated.

I had made up my mind that I was going to know the truth and one night at dusk I slipped out of the house and made my way across the lawns to the copse.

I hesitated on the borders of it and an almost irresistible impulse to turn back came to me; it was so eerie and however much one scorns ghostly happenings by daylight and in company one is inclined to be less bold alone in the dark. The idea of going to the chapel – which had been my first intention – and waiting there now seemed alarming. I stopped under one of the trees and peered into the gloom.

It would probably be a wasted effort, I told myself. Ghosts did not come to order. That was of course an excuse. Then I asked myself why I did not go back and suggest that Mrs Lincroft or Alice accompany me. They might think I was over eager to prove that someone was playing a trick. I could not forget Mrs Lincroft's remark about Napier. A sudden thought struck me. What if Roma had wandered into the chapel one night? What if she had seen something which was not meant to be seen. The thought sent a shiver through me. I could well imagine Roma's setting out sceptically determined to solve a mystery.

'Ghosts!' I could hear her rather strident voice saying. 'What utter nonsense!'

But she would have been trespassing had she come here for although she had Sir William's permission to dig on his estate that permission did not extend to his gardens. She was not, however, one to wait for permission if she wished to do something. But ghosts! As if she would worry about them! 'What,' I could hear her voice demanding, 'have lights in chapels to do with archæology?'

I started to make my way cautiously through the copse; and now I could see the dark shadow which was the ruin. I came close to it and put out my hand to touch the cold stone. I will just look in, I promised myself, and then go back. After all I might wait here all the evening. I would come back later with a companion. Allegra and Alice would no doubt like to share in a watch.

Then suddenly I heard the sibilant whisper. It was the breeze in the trees, I told myself. But there was no breeze. It was undoubtedly the sound of voices; they were coming from the chapel and they were making me shiver from head to foot.

My impulse was to run back the way I had come but if I did I should despise myself. I was on the verge of discovery and I must go on.

In an endeavour to calm myself I made my way to the opening where the door had been, all the time my ears strained.

Voices again – two voices, one high-pitched, one on a lower key . . . and they were whispering together.

Then the realisation came to me. These two had not come to haunt the chapel. They had chosen this place to snatch a few moments together.

Edith's voice: 'You *must* not go.'

And another voice which replied: 'My darling, it's the only way. When I've gone you will forget me. You must try to be happy . . .'

Not wishing to eavesdrop on this tender lovers' scene I moved away.

Edith had chosen to meet her lover in the ruined chapel; and this must surely be one of the last occasions when they would meet, for Jeremy Brown was leaving in a few days' time for Africa.

I went quietly through the copse thinking that this could well be the solution. The chapel was a lovers' rendezvous. Had they brandished the light to keep people away? I could scarcely imagine they would do that – but who would have believed that Edith was an unfaithful wife? When one probed below the surface one often found what one had least suspected.

A memory flashed into my mind of Alice standing before me gravely quoting:

> 'They are plotting and planning together
> To take me by surprise.'

I was almost at the edge of the copse but the trees were still thick about me when suddenly a figure loomed up behind me. I turned sharply and in that moment there came to me the absurd belief that I was about to come face to face with the ghost of Beaumont.

It was Napier, I saw almost immediately, and my relief was obvious.

'I'm sorry if I alarmed you.'

'I was temporarily startled, that was all.'

'You look as though you've been seeing ghosts. One is said to walk, you know, in this copse.'

'I don't believe that.'

'You did a moment ago. Confess it.'

'For a second.'

'I believe you are a little disappointed. You would have liked to come face to face with a ghost, wouldn't you . . . the ghost of my dead brother, for he is the one who is said to haunt this spot.'

'If I had come face to face with him I should have asked him most severely what good he thought he was doing here.'

He smiled. 'You are bold,' he said. 'Here you are . . . in the copse at night. Yet you defy the ghost. Would you dare to go to the ruin now and repeat what you have just said?'

'I should say there what I say here.'

'Then I challenge you.'

In the pale light of the moon I caught the gleam of his eyes and the cynical twist of his lips; and I thought of the lovers in the ruin and I wondered what his reaction would be if he found them there. I wanted very much to know the answer to this but I was absolutely certain that at all costs he must be prevented from going to the ruin now. I believed that Edith and Jeremy Brown were two innocent children who had been caught up in circumstances too strong for them; the very fact that Jeremy Brown was proposing to renounce her and go away proved that. I felt an urgent need to protect and preserve their secret, so I said: 'I don't accept that challenge.'

He smiled at me sardonically. Let him think me a coward. What did that matter as long as Edith was not exposed?

'But who knows what you might discover if you did?' he asked slyly.

'I am not afraid of ghosts.'

'Then why not come there with me . . . now.'

I turned away but as I moved towards the edge of the copse he came after me and laid a hand on my arm.

'You are afraid of something,' he said. 'Confess it.'

'There is a chill in the air.'

'Afraid of catching cold?'

My impulse was to leave him, but if I did so and he returned to the chapel and found the lovers . . . what would he do? I knew that I must try to stop that. So I did not move; nor did he; he stood beside me looking across the gardens to the house.

At last he spoke lightly. 'You shouldn't be afraid, you know. Nor should anyone else. I'm the one he comes back to haunt.'

'What nonsense.'

'On the contrary – once you accept the existence of ghosts it's perfectly logical. I banished him from this house. He resents my return. You follow the reasoning.'

'It is all of the past,' I said impatiently. 'It should be forgotten.'

'Can one forget at will? Can you?'

'It is not easy, but one can try.'

'You must set me a good example.'

'I?'

'You who have so much to forget . . . too.' He took a step nearer to me. 'Don't you see it gives us so much in common.'

'So much?' I said. 'I should have thought we had very little in common.'

'Would you . . . would you indeed. Do you know, Mrs Verlaine, I'm going to be very bold and contradict you.'

'I'm sure that does not need a great deal of courage.'

'And if I am going to prove myself right, you are going to need a certain amount of tolerance.'

'Why?'

'Because you will be forced to endure my company now and then to give me a chance to prove my case.'

'I can scarcely believe that you wish for much of my company.'

'There, Mrs Verlaine, I must again contradict you.'

I was alarmed. I drew a little away from him. 'I don't understand you,' I said.

'It's quite simple. You interest me.'

'How extraordinary.'

'Surely others have found you interesting. One person did at least. I am referring to your genius.'

I said hastily: 'Then I wish you would not refer to him in that way. He did have genius, and it's no use your sneering at that simply because –'

'Simply because I lack all the accomplishments that were his. That's what you mean. What a poor figure I must cut in comparison.'

'I never thought for one moment of comparing you.'

I was uneasy. What did he mean? Was this a kind of inverted flirtation? It was like a scene from a French farce Pietro and I once saw at the Comédie Française. His wife was with her lover in part of the wood; he was with me talking in this enigmatic way in another.

I should have walked across the lawns to the house and left him. But if he went back to the copse . . . Perhaps that was partly an excuse. Perhaps I wanted to stay. Perhaps I was only partly repelled – and a great deal fascinated.

These people's complicated affairs were not my concern, I kept reminding myself. Yet I *was* desperately sorry for Edith, and I knew that the worst thing that could happen to her was for her to be found in a compromising position with her lover. This man did not care for her; but what would his action be if he found himself cuckolded? And if Edith were going to have a child which he would disown . . . this house would see another tragedy.

'You should forgive me,' he was saying and his voice was suddenly soft and caressing, 'if I am too blunt. You see, I was seventeen when I shot my brother and when my mother killed herself because of it.' He almost relished the words, I thought, speaking slowly, savouring them. 'And then I went to the other side of the world. It was a different life . . . one

177

lived . . . rough. One did not enjoy the company of ladies such as yourself.'

'And your wife?' I said.

'Edith is a child,' he said dismissing her.

But I would not allow her to be dismissed. 'She is young yet. That is something which we have all been once and it is quickly remedied.'

'We have no interests in common.' The second time he had used that phrase. I thought with horror: He is comparing us. He is telling me he prefers me. I thought of Allegra's mother – the wild gipsy – what had his wooing of her been?

'Interests between married people are built up over the years,' I said primly.

'You take an idealised view of marriage, Mrs Verlaine. But then you enjoyed such a perfect one yourself, didn't you?'

'Yes,' I said fiercely. 'Yes.'

And again I felt that mockery.

'I should like to have met you . . . before . . .'

'Whatever for?'

'To see how it changed you. You were a music student, eager for fame. They all are, I believe. All the glories of the world are within the grasp. I'll swear you heard the applause of enraptured audiences as you sat at your piano.'

'And you . . . what did you experience before . . .'

I stopped and he finished for me. 'Before I fired the fatal shot. Oh, envy, malice, hatred, and all uncharitableness.'

'Why do you want me to think you are so wicked?'

'Because I would rather tell you myself than wait for other people to do so . . . Caroline.'

I drew away from him.

'Ah, I've offended you. I should not use your christian

178

name. "Mrs Verlaine, how do you do? What a nice day it is. It's going to rain." That's how I should talk to you. How dull. How inexpressibly dull. In Australia we never had conversation. There never seemed the time. I used to think of being home . . . gracious living as it would have been if Beau had lived. I could talk to him. He was witty, amusing; he knew how to enjoy life. That was why it was said that I was envious of him. Envy is the deadliest of the seven deadly sins, did you know?'

'It's over. For God's sake why can't you say it's over.'

'For the same reason that you can't forget the past. It's no use your telling me. You think of it all the time. You colour it up. It was a perfect idyll. So you believe, and you go on believing it. At least I try to see things as they are.'

'You had an accident . . .'

'Listen. Would they have believed those things of me if I had been different? No, I had shown my unpleasant character, my sullenness . . . my outbursts of temper . . . If Beau had shot me – believe me they would immediately have said it was an accident.'

'You are still envious of him,' I said.

'Am I? You see how it helps me to know myself . . . talking to you.'

'It could be so pleasant,' I said, 'if you put the past behind you. If you began again.'

'And you?' he asked.

'Myself too. I am trying to make a new life for myself.'

'You will,' he said. And then he added wistfully: 'Perhaps we both will.'

I could not meet his eyes. I was afraid of what I might discover there. At all costs I must get away now.

'Good night,' I said, and walked quickly across the grass and into the house. He fell into step beside me; and as the dark pile of stones loomed up before us I thought of Edith in the copse with her lover while I was here with her husband.

And I wondered too if anyone saw us out here together.

Chapter Six

When I next went to the vicarage I found Mrs Rendall in a state of great indignation. Jeremy Brown had gone and the vicar was more overworked than usual. She really did not see how he could manage to teach the girls *and* do justice to his parochial duties until he had a new curate to help him, and she wanted me to explain to Mrs Lincroft that until that time the vicar could not be expected to teach the girls.

I told her that I would speak to Mrs Lincroft without delay, and asked if she would like the girls to go back with me now so that the vicar could return at once to his church work. 'I could give them their music lesson at Lovat Stacy,' I said.

She was a little mollified. 'Come in and have a glass of my elderberry wine. I don't think we will disturb them this morning . . . as long as you will speak to Mrs Lincroft and some new arrangement is made without delay.'

I glanced at my watch. I was a little early and there was ten minutes to spare before the first piano lesson was due.

Mrs Rendall took me into her sitting-room, unlocked a

cabinet and brought out the wine bottle labelled in her neat handwriting.

'One of the best brews I have produced,' she said with satisfaction, 'though my sloe gin was superb . . . even better I think. However, perhaps you would prefer the elderberry.'

I said I would and she poured wine into two glasses and handed me one while she told me how she had always made her wines herself for one could not trust servants nowadays. A glass now and then was so good for the vicar and she often insisted on his taking it when he had one of his chests.

'Better than any doctors' medicine,' she said proudly, savouring the brew and watching me to see that I showed adequate appreciation, which I did.

'Yes,' she resumed satisfied, 'some other arrangement will have to be made . . . temporarily.'

'You mean they will have to employ a temporary governess?'

'I hardly think that's necessary. Governesses are so unsatisfactory nowadays. Mrs Lincroft was a governess at one time, I believe. She could I am sure manage until we get settled here.'

'Mrs Lincroft seems to be capable of doing anything.'

'A clever woman. Make no mistake about that. She ran that household . . . even when poor Lady Stacy was alive. There were some who said that Sir William was very fond of her . . . in fact more fond than he should have been.'

'No doubt he appreciated her talents.'

Mrs Rendall's laughter was explosive and unpleasant. 'Talents indeed! However, she went away for a while and came back with Alice, and she seemed to slip into her old place – running the house and being at hand for whatever was needed. And now of course she's almost the mistress of the house with Alice living there like one of the family.'

'One could hardly stress the difference in the girls' social standing.'

'And why not, pray? Alice *is* the daughter of the house-keeper, and I for one think it a little odd that she should mix with Edith – Allegra is different, I know, but she *is* Sir William's granddaughter. I have allowed Sylvia to be friendly with Alice. What else could I do?'

'You could do nothing else if you wish Sylvia to be educated with the others.'

'Exactly, but that does not alter the fact . . . By the way, how is Sylvia progressing with her lessons?'

'She has little talent for the piano, I fear.'

Mrs Rendall sighed. 'In my day, if people didn't show talent they were beaten till they did.'

'I'm afraid it is impossible to beat talent into a child where it does not exist.'

'I should punish her if I thought she was not working. And beating would not be necessary. A few days on bread and water, Mrs Verlaine, and that child would play the piano. I never saw such an appetite. She's always hungry.'

'She's growing.'

'I hope you will report to me when she does not do the work you set her.'

'She tries very hard,' I said quickly.

I glanced at the watch pinned to my blouse. 'It is really time for the first of the lessons.' I rose. 'I shall speak to Mrs Lincroft as soon as I return to Lovat Stacy.'

Mrs Lincroft rose admirably to the occasion. She would set the girls tasks and keep an eye on the schoolroom until a new curate could be found.

'If you could give me a hand I'd be grateful, Mrs Verlaine,' she said.

'I should be pleased to help,' I replied, but reminded her that I had not been trained as a teacher.

'Good gracious, Mrs Verlaine,' she replied, 'nor have I. How many governesses have been. They are usually impoverished gentlewomen forced to earn a living in some way. And I should say that you have had a better education than most. Wasn't your father a professor?'

'Oh yes . . . yes.'

'And I daresay you and your sisters and brothers were better educated than most.'

'I only had one sister.'

She was quick to notice I had spoken in the past tense. 'Had?' she queried.

'She is . . . no longer with us.'

'Oh dear, I'm so sorry. And now I remember your mentioning it. As I was saying it's obvious that you are well educated and if you can help me out just until the next curate arrives, I shall be so grateful.'

I said I would do my best.

Edith had not come for her lesson. I glanced at my watch. Five . . . ten minutes overdue.

Sylvia was in the schoolroom with Allegra and Alice.

I hesitated to go to Edith's room. Since my encounter with Napier that night near the chapel I had avoided him and I was reluctant to go to the room he shared with Edith; but when another five minutes passed I decided I must overcome my objections.

I knocked at the door and received a rather feeble request to enter.

Under the domelike canopy, her face pale, her eyes anxious, Edith was lying. 'Oh dear,' she cried when she saw me. 'My lesson! I'd forgotten.'

'Edith,' I said, 'what's wrong?'

'It was the same yesterday morning. I feel so ill.'

'Perhaps you should see a doctor.'

She stared at me miserably. 'I'm going to have a baby,' she said.

'That's a matter for rejoicing.'

'Oh Mrs Verlaine . . . you've been married, but you didn't ever have any babies.'

'No,' I said.

She looked at me earnestly and said: 'You seem sad about it.'

'I should have loved to have babies.'

'But it's terrible, Mrs Verlaine. I heard Cook talking about the time when her daughter was born. It was terrible.'

'You shouldn't listen to such tales. Why, women are having babies every day.'

She closed her eyes. 'I know,' she said.

'You should be so happy.'

She turned her face to the pillow and I saw from her heaving shoulders that she was crying.

'Edith,' I said. 'Edith, is anything wrong . . . apart from this?'

She turned her head sharply to look at me.

'What else could be wrong?' she asked.

'I wondered whether I could do anything to help.'

She was silent and I was thinking of those words I had overheard in the chapel. I was thinking too of something else I had overheard, a chance remark which had led me to believe that she was being blackmailed.

How could that be? She was an heiress, it was true, but I doubted whether she had control of her money. It might by now have passed into her husband's possession – an unpleasant reflection.

Poor little Edith, married for her money to Napier Stacy

when she was in love with Jeremy Brown, who had gone away to provide the only possible solution to their sad little love story.

But before he had gone had they consummated their love, and was the child she was now carrying the result? I suspected this might be the case for she was so young, so incapable of managing her life. I was filled with a great desire to protect her, and I wanted her to know this.

'Edith,' I said, 'if I could do anything to help . . . please let me . . . if you think that's possible.'

'I don't know what to say . . . what to do, Mrs Verlaine. I feel so . . . bewildered.'

I took her hand and pressed it; her fingers clung to mine and I was certain that she drew some comfort from my presence.

Then she seemed to come to a decision for she closed her eyes and murmured: 'I just want to rest for a while.'

I understood. She might confide in me some time but as yet she could not bring herself to do so.

'If you want to talk to me at any time . . .' I began.

She said, 'Thank you, Mrs Verlaine,' and closed her eyes.

I did not want to force confidences. I was sorry for her, because if ever I saw a frightened girl that girl was Edith.

❧

Sir William was jubilant. He sent for me to play for him and before I did so he asked me to sit beside him for a while.

'I'm sure you have heard the news,' he said. 'We are all delighted.'

He looked younger, I thought, and a great deal better than I had seen him yet.

'Your performance was such a success,' he went on, 'that we must have another. You are a very good pianist, Mrs Verlaine, I should say a great one.'

'Oh no. That is going too far,' I protested. 'But I'm delighted that I pleased you and your friends.'

'It is pleasant to have music in the house again. Mrs Stacy will continue practising now for a while yet, I daresay.'

'Perhaps she will not wish to continue with lessons after the child is born.'

'We shall have to ask you to teach him.'

I laughed and said a few years would have to elapse before then.

'Not so many . . . wasn't it Handel who was discovered playing the piano in an attic at the age of four? Music is in the family, Mrs Verlaine. The child's grandmother would have been a great pianist, I believe. She was, as you would say, very good.'

Yes, I thought, the atmosphere of this house was changing. He could refer to his wife without embarrassment. And this was all due to the child Edith was going to bear, a child which might not be this man's grandchild.

I had admitted the possibility of the doubts which had been niggling in my mind for some time. Poor Edith, what a dilemma for her. What if she confessed to her husband . . . My imagination was running away with me, and I could see a terrible tragedy looming up over Edith's head. I heard her voice raised in fear when she talked to a blackmailer. She looked so innocent on the surface, and she was innocent, I was sure of it. It was life that was cruel.

Sir William was silent for a while and I asked him if he would like me to play for him now.

He said he would and the pieces were on the piano for he had already selected them.

They were light, gay pieces; among them I remember were some of Mendelssohn's 'Songs without Words'. I remember in particular the 'Spring Song', gay light music, full of the promise of gay young life.

I had played for an hour when Mrs Lincroft appeared. She came into the room and quietly shut the door behind her.

'He's asleep,' she whispered. 'He is so contented.' She smiled as though Sir William's contentment was hers; and I thought of what Mrs Rendall had hinted about the relationship between them.

'It is really so satisfactory . . . so soon,' she went on speaking quietly. 'Personally I didn't think Edith was robust enough, but often those delicate looking girls are the ones who have the children. Then Napier . . . he has shown quite clearly that he . . . Well, what I mean is he could scarcely be called a devoted husband. But he knows that Sir William expects him to provide the heir. He was brought home for that.'

I said rather indignantly: 'Rather like a stud bull.'

Mrs Lincroft looked very shocked at my indelicacy and I was a little ashamed of it myself. There was no need for me to be so vehement. Napier had come home of his own free will, knowing what it involved.

'At least he must do his duty,' said Mrs Lincroft.

'And it seems he has.'

'This puts him on a firmer footing here.'

'But surely as Sir William's son, his only son . . .'

'Sir William would have left the house and a considerable portion of his income elsewhere if he had not come home. But he came . . . naturally he came. He was always ambitious; he always wanted to be first. That was why he was jealous of Beau. Well, that's all over now. He's accepted his father's terms and when the child is born Sir William will feel more kindly towards Napier, I am sure.'

'Sir William is a hard man.'

Mrs Lincroft looked pained. I had again forgotten my place. It was the influence of Napier. Why did I want to defend that man?

'Circumstances have made him so,' she said coldly, and there was a note in her voice which told me that I was showing poor taste in passing adverse opinions on my employer. She was a strange woman, but I was deeply impressed by her absolute devotion to two people – Alice and Sir William. She seemed to regret her coldness towards me for she went on in a different tone of voice: 'Sir William is delighted now with this news. Once the boy is born everything will start to go well in this house. I feel sure of it.'

'What if it should not be a boy?'

She looked a little startled. 'It's a trend in the family to have boys. Miss Sybil Stacy was the only daughter for several generations. Sir William will have the child named Beaumont – and then I think he will be quite contented.'

'What of the child's parents? They might have different ideas about naming the baby.'

'Edith will be very eager to give way to Sir William's wishes.'

'And Napier?'

'My dear Mrs Verlaine, he could raise no objection.'

'I don't see why. He might want to forget that . . . painful incident.'

'He would never go against Sir William's wishes. If he did it might mean that he were sent packing again.'

'You mean having done his duty in siring a child and bringing a Beaumont back to the family he might once more get his congé.'

'You are in a very strange mood to-day, Mrs Verlaine. It is unlike you.'

'I am becoming too interested in the family affairs I expect. Please forgive me.'

She inclined her head. Then she said: 'Napier's staying here depends on Sir William. I think he knows that.'

I looked at my watch. The old excuse of work to prepare was on my lips. I did not want to hear any more. I had thought of him as bold, frank – at least that. I did not like to think of him knuckling under to his father for the sake of his inheritance.

On my way back to my room I met Sybil Stacy. I had the idea that she had been hanging about waiting to intercept me.

'Hallo, Mrs Verlaine,' she said, 'how are you?'

'Very well, thank you, and you?'

She nodded. 'It's a long time since you've seen me, isn't it? But it's not a long time since I saw you. I saw you talking to Napier . . . In fact I've seen you several times. I saw you coming in one evening after dusk.'

I felt indignant. The woman was spying on me!

She seemed to sense this and be amused by it.

'You're very interested in the family, aren't you? Now I think that's very kind of you. I've discovered you are a very kind person, Mrs Verlaine. I have to observe you, don't I, if I am going to paint you.'

'Do you paint everyone who comes to work here?'

She shook her head. 'Not without reason. And only if they are interesting to paint. I believe you are going to be. Come along to my studio now. You said you would, didn't you. After all you didn't see very much when you came before.'

I hesitated, but she laid her hand on my arm with her little girl gesture. 'Oh please, *please* . . .'

Then she clasped her hands together and as she was standing so close I saw her face in the harsh daylight and thought once more how grotesque the blue bows were on that white hair, how pathetically the childish simpering was at odds with that wrinkled face.

But she fascinated me, as everyone in this house seemed to do and I allowed myself to be led to her studio.

The picture of the three girls was still on the easel. My eyes went to it immediately and she stood beside me wriggling a little in pleasure.

'It's a good likeness,' she said.

'It's very good.'

'But time hasn't drawn anything on their faces . . . yet.' She pouted as though she had a grievance against time. 'It makes it very difficult for the artist. You can't *read* anything in those faces, can you?'

I agreed. 'They look so young and innocent.'

'Yet we are all born in sin.'

'Some people manage to live good lives in spite of it.'

'Oh, you're one of those optimists, Mrs Verlaine. You always believe the best of everyone.'

'Isn't that better than believing the worst?'

'Not if the worst is there.' Her face puckered. 'I used to be like you. I believed . . . I believed in Harry. You look puzzled. You don't know who Harry is. Harry is the man I was going to marry. I'll show you a picture of him . . . two pictures of him, shall I? At the moment I am working on Edith.'

I looked at her steadily. She had tripped over to a pile of canvases; and I was aware that her footsteps were soundless. I pictured her silently watching the comings and goings of the people in this house . . . myself included. Why did she watch? Merely so that she could learn of our secret motives, so that she could come up to this room and record them on canvas. The thought made me uneasy; and she was aware of it and amused. Beneath the little girl attitude was a character she wished to hide.

'Edith!' she mused. 'You see her on the picture with the girls. How charming they look there. Now look at this one . . .' She whipped out a canvas and put it on the easel covering up the one of the trio.

There was a figure hardly recognisable. It was a picture of a heavily pregnant Edith, her face twisted in an expression of something between fear and cunning. It was horrible.

'You don't like it.'

'No,' I said. 'It's . . . unpleasant.'

'Do you know who it is?'

I shook my head.

'Oh Mrs Verlaine, I thought you were honest.'

'It has a look of Edith . . . but I am convinced she never looked like that.'

'She will though. She is very frightened now. And each day she will grow more frightened. She will never stop being frightened until the day she dies.'

'I hope no one has seen that picture.'

'No. I will show it later . . . perhaps.'

'Yet you have shown it to me.'

'That is because you are as interested as I am. You are an artist too. You hear music where others do not. Is that not so? You hear it in the sighing of the wind, in the trees and the rippling water of a stream. I find what I want in the faces of people. I never wanted to paint landscapes. I never cared for them. It was always people. When I was in the nursery I would take a pencil and sketch our governesses. William said it was uncanny. But I didn't have the same gift then. It was only after Harry . . .' Her face puckered and I thought she would burst into tears. 'I sometimes feel an urge to paint one person. I haven't that urge to paint you yet, Mrs Verlaine, but I know it will come . . . so I'm stalking you . . . like a lion stalks his prey. But lions never eat until they're hungry, do they?' She came close to me and laughed up into my face. 'I'm not hungry for you yet, but I'm in touch.' She lifted a hand and her face broke into a seraphic smile. 'I'm in touch . . . with . . . powers. People don't understand.' She touched her head. 'Do you know what they say in the village? People are three half-pence short – not all there. That's what they say of me. I know it. The servants say it. William says it, and so does that Mrs Lincroft of his. Let them. I'm far more here than they are because I'm in touch . . . in touch with powers they know nothing about.'

A feeling of claustrophobia came to me; she would keep grasping my arm, putting her grotesque little girl face close to mine . . . and I was in agreement with those who said she was not all there.

I glanced at my watch and said: 'The time . . . I'm forgetting . . .'

She had a little enamelled watch pinned to her frilly pink blouse and she looked at it and then shook her finger at me.

'You haven't to take Sylvia until half past. So you have twenty minutes.'

I was startled that she knew so much about my schedule.

'And,' she went on, 'you were all last afternoon preparing their lessons.'

I felt very uneasy.

'Now that there is no curate at the vicarage –' I began.

'They are all working on the tasks Mrs Lincroft has set them. What a clever woman she is.' She began to laugh. 'I know how clever. And getting her child brought up here too.

That would be one of her conditions. She thinks the world of Alice.'

'It's natural that she should think a great deal of her own daughter.'

'Oh, very very natural; and there we have Miss Alice brought up in Lovat Stacy, for all the world as though she were a daughter of the house.'

'She is a good child and works very hard.'

Sybil nodded gravely. 'But it is Edith I'm interested in now.'

'Well, I never expect to see her looking like that.'

'Shocked, shocked, shocked!' She pointed at me and chanted mischievously, the little girl again. Then her face stiffened. 'They will call the child Beaumont,' she went on. 'They think they can replace my Beau merely by calling a child by his name. They never will. Nothing will ever bring Beaumont back. My darling boy . . . he is lost to us.'

'Sir William is delighted at the prospect of having a grand-child.'

'A grandchild.' She began to titter. 'And to call him Beaumont!'

'Everyone is a little premature. The child is not born yet and it seems to be presumed that it will be a boy.'

'They can never replace Beaumont,' she said fiercely. 'What's done is done.'

'It's a pity it cannot be forgotten,' I said.

'Napier thinks that. And you take his view, of course,' she was accusing, mocking.

'I have been here such a short time, and as I am not connected with the family, it is not for me to take views.'

'But you take them all the same. Oh yes, I shall most certainly paint you, Mrs Verlaine. But not yet . . . I'll wait a while. Has anyone ever told you about Harry?'

'No.'

'You should know. You like to know everything about us, don't you? So of course you should know about Harry.'

'He was the man you were going to marry.'

She nodded and her face puckered. 'I thought he loved me . . . and he did. Everything would have been all right, but they stopped it. They took Harry away from me.'

'Who?'

She waved her arms vaguely. 'William stopped it. My brother. He was my guardian because our parents were dead. He said, "No. Wait. No wedding until you are twenty-one. You are too young." I was nineteen. Nineteen was not too young to be in love. You should have seen Harry, Mrs Verlaine. He was so handsome, so clever, so witty. He used to make me laugh with his quips. It was wonderful. He was very aristocratic, but he had no money and that was really why William said I was too young. William thinks too much about money. He thinks it is the most important thing in the world. He punished Napier through money, you know. Go away . . . you are banished. You shan't have my worldly goods. And then he wanted a grandson so Napier is summoned to return and meekly Napier comes. The bait is . . . money!'

'It might be something else.'

'Now what else could it be, Mrs Verlaine?'

'The desire to please a father, the desire to make amends, to forget old enmities.'

'You *are* sentimental. No one would believe it to look at you . . . except me of course. You look so coolly on the world . . . so it seems. But I could see that underneath it all you're as sentimental as – as – Edith.'

'There's no harm in sentiment.'

'As long as you don't smother the truth with it. It's like

pouring treacle over a suet pudding. You can't see anything but the treacle.'

'You were telling me about Harry.'

'Oh . . . Harry! He had debts. Blue blood doesn't pay debts, does it? But money does. I had the money. Perhaps William didn't want it to go out of the family. Did you think that was the reason? But you couldn't know that, could you? William said wait, and he wouldn't give his consent until I was twenty-one. Two years to wait. So we were betrothed. We had a dinner party to celebrate it. Isabella was there. She wasn't married to William then. There was an orchestra on the dais where the piano is now. We danced, Harry and I, and he said; "Two years will soon pass, my darling." It did pass and at the end of it I'd lost Harry because he'd met a girl with more money than I had, who could pay his debts without delay and it seemed the need was pressing. She wasn't as pretty as I was, but she had so much more money.'

'Perhaps then it was all for the best.'

'What do you mean . . . all for the best?'

'Since it was the money he wanted, he might not have been a good husband.'

'That's what they tried to tell me.' She stamped her foot. 'It's not true. I would have married him. He would have loved me most then. Harry just wanted life to be easy. He would have been happy with me if they'd let him marry me in the beginning. I'd have had my babies . . .' Her face puckered; she was like a child crying for a coveted toy. 'But no,' she cried fiercely, 'they stopped me. William stopped me. How dared he! Do you know what he said? "He's a fortune hunter. You're better without him." And he looked prim and virtuous, as though Harry was bad and he was so good. He – why, I could tell you . . .'

I was looking at her so sadly that she smiled and her

vehemence was stemmed. 'You have a kind heart, Mrs Verlaine,' she said, 'and you know what it means to lose a lover, don't you? You suffered too, didn't you? That's why I talk to you. I had a ring . . . a beautiful opal ring. But opals are unlucky, they say. Harry couldn't bring himself to tell me, and I was nearly twenty-one and I fixed the wedding day and the presents started to come in. And then . . . one day . . . I had the letter. He couldn't face me, he could only write it. He'd been married for months. I ought to have defied my brother and run away with him when he first asked me. William broke my heart, Mrs Verlaine. I hated him. I hated Harry too for a while. I took the opal ring and I threw it out to sea . . . and then I took my paints and painted Harry's face on the walls. Harry's face . . . horrible . . . horrible . . . horrible . . . but it comforted me.'

'I'm sorry,' was all I could say.

'You're truly so.' She smiled at me sadly. 'But don't you say things are forgotten. They are never forgotten. I shall never forget Harry. And I shall never forget Beaumont. My darling Beau . . . I felt happier when he was born. He took to me right away. He always wanted Auntie Sib. I let him use my paints and he liked that. He was always with me, he was sunny natured and so beautiful. Beau! We naturally called him that because his name was Beaumont. But it meant something too. It meant that he was beautiful.'

'So you had your consolation.'

'Until that day . . . the day he was murdered.'

'It was an accident. It could have happened to any two boys.'

She shook her head angrily. 'But this was Beau . . . my lovely, beautiful Beau.' She turned to me suddenly: 'There's something in this house . . . something *bad*. I know.'

'A *house* can't be bad,' I said.

'It can if the people who live there make it so. There are bad wicked people in this house. Be careful.'

I said I would and because I felt she was going to begin an attack on Napier and that if she did I should be forced to defend him, I said I must go.

She consulted her watch and nodded.

'Come again,' she said. 'Come and talk to me. I like talking to you. And don't forget . . . one day I have to paint a picture of you.'

Alice walked beside me in the gardens where I had come for a little exercise. It had been raining all the morning and now the sun had come out; the flowers smelt all the more delicious and the bees were already busy in the lavender bushes.

Alice was talking to me about the Chopin prelude which she was having some difficulty in mastering, and I was trying to explain to her that the effect of simplicity was often the hardest to obtain.

'How I should love to sit at the piano and play as you do, Mrs Verlaine. It always looks so easy for you.'

'It's due to years and years of practise,' I told her. 'You haven't been practising for years and years, and you have improved tremendously.'

'Does Sir William ever ask about our lessons?' she asked.

'Yes, he has done so.'

'Does he mention me?'

'He mentions you all.'

She was pink with pleasure. She said suddenly, her face grave: 'Edith was ill again this morning.'

'I believe it sometimes happens that expectant mothers are ill in the morning; as the time passes she will feel better.'

'What a good thing it is. Everyone is very happy about the baby. They say this is going to make everything right.'

'What is going to make everything right?' It was Allegra who had fallen into step beside me.

'We were talking about the baby,' Alice explained.

'Everybody is talking about the baby. Anyone would think no one had ever had a baby before. After all, they are married, aren't they? Why shouldn't they have a baby . . . People do. That's what they marry for . . . or part of it.'

Allegra was looking at me slyly as though to provoke me into some reproof.

'Have you done your practise?' I asked coolly.

'Not yet, Mrs Verlaine. I will though . . . later. Only it has been such a horrid morning and now the sun is out, and it's going to rain again soon. Look at those clouds.' She was smiling at me mischievously, but almost immediately her face darkened. 'I'm sick of hearing about this baby. My grandfather is a changed man. That's what one of the footmen told me this morning. He said: "Miss Allegra, this baby will make all the difference to your grandfather. It'll be like having Mr Beau back again!"'

'Yes, that's it,' said Alice. 'It will be like having Mr Beau back again. I wonder whether there'll be no more lights in the chapel then.'

'There's a perfectly logical explanation to the light in the chapel,' I said; and as they looked at me expectantly I added: 'I'm sure.'

Allegra stood still, expressing her exasperation by facial contortions. 'All this fuss. It nauseates me. Why should there be all this fuss about a baby? Perhaps it will be a girl and then serve them right. They seem to forget that I'm here. They never make this fuss about me. I'm Napier's daughter and Sir William is my grandfather. Yet he scarcely looks at me and when he does his face shows . . . distaste.'

'Oh no, Allegra,' I said.

'Oh *yes*, Mrs Verlaine. So what's the use of pretending. I used to think it was because Napier was my father and grandfather hated my father. But it's not that because this new baby will be Napier's, and they are all making such a fuss before it is born.'

She ran ahead of us and started pulling a rose to pieces.

'Allegra,' warned Alice, 'that's one of your grandfather's favourites.'

'I know,' spat out Allegra. 'That's why I'm doing it.'

'That's not the best way to relieve your feelings,' I said.

Allegra grinned at me. 'It's *one* way, Mrs Verlaine. The best available at the moment.'

Allegra had plucked another of the precious blooms and was bent on destruction.

I knew it was no use protesting and that once she had no audience she would stop, so I stepped off the path and started to walk across the lawn.

Some time before this Mrs Lincroft had suggested that I accompany the girls when they went out riding, and I had ordered a riding habit from London as I hated borrowing clothes and Edith's certainly did not fit me well. I admitted to myself that this was an extravagance but having acquired it I rode more frequently than I had previously.

My habit was in a becoming shade of dark blue – not quite navy; it was beautifully cut and as soon as I saw it I did not regret the money I had spent on it. The girls all assured me that I looked very elegant in it and they were constantly admiring it.

When she made the suggestion Mrs Lincroft went on: 'I can't tell you how pleased I am that you are here, Mrs Verlaine. It's a great help to us all now that we have this extra burden. I shall be very pleased when the new curate arrives. But then I suppose we shall have to wait until Mrs Rendall considers he is ready to help with the teaching.'

I said that I had contributed very little and in fact enjoyed what I had done, for what I dreaded most was to have too little to do.

I was in fact delighted with the turn of events because not only did it keep me fully occupied and make me feel I was earning my salary, but I was with the girls more often and was beginning to know them better . . . Allegra, Alice and Sylvia, that was. I saw less of Edith – she had given up riding now – though occasionally she would ask for a lesson at the piano; but even at such times she seemed to be shutting herself away from me as though she regretted the impulse which had almost made her confide in me.

One early afternoon when I was riding with the three younger girls, we saw Napier coming towards us.

He said: 'Hallo, enjoying a ride?'

I noticed how he avoided looking at Allegra – and she at him – and that her mouth formed into the sullen lines with which I was growing familiar. Why did he dislike her? Was he thinking of her mother, for whom he must have had some affection at some time? What had she been like? Exactly what had he felt for her? And what business was it of mine? Except of course that I was here to teach Allegra and I should have liked to help her if possible. A girl who bore so much resentment was storing up trouble for herself.

'It's a lovely day,' I said. And I thought, What a trite statement of the obvious that was! And I had said it as though I was just discovering it.

I was aware of three pairs of eyes watching Napier and me rather too intently for my comfort.

'I'll ride with you,' said Napier, and he turned his horse and we rode on, he a little ahead of us in the narrow road.

As I studied his straight back and the proud set of his head, I was thinking that Allegra would be aware of everything he said, every inflection of his voice. Poor Allegra! All she needed I thought was affection – and she had none at all. Sylvia's father would be tender and loving however much a martinet her mother might be, and there was no doubt of Mrs Lincroft's devotion to Alice; yes, poor Allegra was the unfortunate one. I must try to do something for her.

I turned to speak to her and saw that she was trying to push Sylvia out of her saddle.

'Allegra,' I said sharply, 'pray don't do that.'

'Sylvia was teasing me,' retorted Allegra.

Napier ignored the girls and said to me: 'I'm glad to see how you've taken to riding, Mrs Verlaine.' We had emerged from the narrow lane and he had brought his horse neck to neck with mine.

'I never thought I could enjoy outdoor exercise so much.'

'And everything you undertake you do well.' His eyes belied the respect in his voice.

'I wish I could be sure of that.'

'But you are sure. That is why you succeeded. You must have faith in yourself before you expect anyone else to . . . even horses. That horse knows he has a very determined rider on his back.'

'You make it sound very simple.'

'Theory always is. It's practise that is less so.'

'That sounds profound. Do you apply it to your mode of life?'

'Ah, now you have me, Mrs Verlaine, of course I don't. Like most people I'm very good at giving advice . . . to others. But it's true. You must admit it. I know what you're thinking. You dreamed of becoming the greatest pianist in the world, and here you are teaching music to four very indifferent pupils – that's so, I believe?'

'My little affairs are scarcely worthy of such a detailed analysis.'

'On the contrary they make a very good example.'

'Hardly of interest to you.'

'You are wilfully obtuse to-day, Mrs Verlaine.'

The impulse to fall back and wait for the girls seemed to me a wise move; but I had no intention of making it.

'You are fully aware,' he went on, glancing at me intently, 'that your . . . past is of the utmost interest to me?'

'I can't think why.'

'You are deceiving yourself but you don't deceive me.'

We were looking across the land to sea. The castle showed clearly its Tudor rose outline; below us was the shingle with the waves gently rising and falling over it with a low, almost contented murmur.

There was the row of houses looking from here as though they were almost falling into the sea. Fishing boats were drawn up on the shingle; the smell of fish was in the air, mingling with the odour of seaweed.

I said hastily: 'One would imagine that row of houses was actually in the sea.'

'The sea is encroaching . . . rapidly. In a hundred years they'll be washed away and that narrow street bounded on either side by houses will no longer be a narrow street, it will be open to the sea. The houses are continually being flooded. One could draw a parallel. You and I are like those houses; the past is like the sea . . . threatening to envelop us . . . and prevent our living free and full lives.'

'I had no idea that you would indulge in such fanciful observations.'

'Ah, but there is a great deal you don't know about me, Mrs Verlaine.'

'I never doubted it.'

'And you show no great curiosity to learn.'

'If you wished me to know you would no doubt tell me.'

'But that would deprive you of the pleasure of finding out. To revert to my poetic fancies. I was thinking that a strong sea wall now would save those houses.'

'Then why don't they build it?'

He shrugged his shoulders. 'It would cost a great deal; people don't like changes. It is so much easier to go on in the old way until something has to be done. I know that one day people will stand here looking on the town and they will no longer see that row of houses because the sea will have taken them. But a sea wall would have saved them. Mrs Verlaine, you and I have to build that sea wall . . . metaphorically, I mean. We have to protect ourselves against the encroaching sea of the past.'

I turned to him and said: 'How?'

'That is what we have to find out. We have to fight . . . we have to throw off those clinging hands . . . we have to snap the chains . . .'

'Your metaphors are becoming a little mixed,' I said, feeling the need to bring a little lightness into the conversation which I knew well was full of innuendos.

He laughed aloud.

'All right,' he said. 'All right. Plain straightforward . . . *frank* English. I think you and I could help each other to forget.'

Oh, I thought, how dare he! Did he think he could seduce me as he had Allegra's mother? A widow, I ruminated. Easy game. Could this possibly be his intention? Perhaps I should go away. I shuddered inwardly to contemplate returning to my room in Kensington, advertising for pupils. No, I was not an innocent young girl, I could take care of myself.

But I would have to show him that if he thought he could amuse himself with me he was mistaken.

I looked over my shoulder. The girls, with Allegra a little ahead were walking their horses, keeping a distance between Napier and me.

I pulled up and the girls came riding up. I sniffed the exhilarating air and gazed at the sea which was sending frothy frills against the glistening shingle.

'We were wondering what Julius Cæsar said when he first saw it,' said Allegra.

'Those poor ancient Britons!' whispered Alice. 'Imagine them.' Her eyes were round with horror and even the presence of Napier could not quell her. 'They would see the boats coming in, and they hurried to put on their woad and paint themselves blue to make themselves look frightening. They were the ones who were frightened. And the Romans came and saw and conquered.'

'And built houses here,' shouted Allegra, determined not to be left out. 'And if they hadn't Miss Brandon would never have come here and disappeared.'

'How that woman's memory is kept alive,' murmured Napier.

Alice went on as though hypnotised: 'And they built a town here and their villas and their baths.'

'Fortunately not under Lovat Stacy,' went on Allegra. 'Because if they had she would have wanted to pull our house down to find their remains.'

'I very much doubt whether that would have been permitted,' said Napier.

Sylvia, who had remained aloof murmured: 'Perhaps she wouldn't have asked permission. Those people don't, my mother says. Perhaps that was what she was trying to do when . . .'

Napier sighed as though he were bored and started to move on; we all followed and in a very short time he was beside me again.

'You're still thinking about the missing lady,' he accused me. 'You are very interested in her. Admit it.'

'The mystery intrigues me.'

'You like everything to be neatly rounded off with Finis written at the end.'

'If that were possible. But is it ever so?'

'Of course not. Nothing is ever finished. What happened a hundred years ago is still having its effect on to-day. Even if we built that sea wall we should still hear the sea thundering away behind it.'

'But without the power to creep into the houses and in time wash them away.'

'Ah, Mrs Verlaine . . . Caroline . . .'

I turned to look for the girls; they were still keeping their distance.

I said: 'The masts are clear to-day.'

'And,' he went on, 'there is another analogy for you. Perhaps better than the sea wall.'

'Pray spare me,' I said with a trace of his own mockery.

'To spare the rod they say is to spoil the child.'

'You are forgetting that I am not a child.'

'We are all children in some respects. Yes, this is much better than the sea wall. I am in fact trying to tell you that I am not such a Philistine as you imagine me. I have my flights of fancy. You and I are like those ships. We are caught in the shivering sands of the past. We shall never escape because we are held fast, held by our memories and other people's opinions of us.'

'This is *too* fanciful.'

'Do you look at them at night? Do you see the intermittent flash from the lightship, a warning to mariners. Keep off. Here are the shivering sands. Do not venture near . . .'

'Mr Stacy,' I said, 'I refuse to consider what has happened to me as having any connection with the Goodwin Sands.'

'Because you are an optimist, and those sands defeat optimism. They are malevolent . . . so golden and beautiful . . . so treacherous. Have you ever seen them close? You must let me take you out there one day.'

I shivered.

'It would be perfectly safe. I should make sure of that.'

'Thank you,' I said.

'Which means precisely "No thank you".' He laughed aloud. 'But perhaps I shall prevail on you to change your mind . . . about this and other things. Do you change your mind easily, Mrs Verlaine? I am sure you do. You are far too sensible to make up your mind and cling to an opinion in face of all arguments.'

'I hope that if I had made a wrong decision and was confronted by the truth, I should be eager to admit it.'

'I knew it.'

I said: 'I think we have ridden far enough. We should now make our way back.' I turned my horse and went to meet the girls.

'It's time we returned,' I said; and they obediently turned their horses and we rode along together for a while. Napier was silent; and in a short time the girls had dropped behind again and he was talking about the outlying estate which we had reached and which was the property of the Stacy family.

I quickly realised that this was something he cared about. How he must have longed for it when he was out of the country! I wondered how he had felt about it when he was young and knew that Beaumont would inherit. He must have been envious of his brother. Envy – the deadly sin which led to many of the others . . . perhaps murder.

'We're making improvements on the estate now,' he said. 'Until recently money was difficult.'

Until the marriage with Edith when the Cowan fortune

came into the possession of the Stacys, I thought. Poor Edith, perhaps if she had not been an heiress she might have married Jeremy Brown and been a parson's wife – and she would have been a good one in time – and lived happily ever after.

And now ... what sort of future would she have with Napier? What sort of future would any woman have with such a man? Some would be able to deal with it. Some might find it exhilarating in a repellent sort of way.

I shut off that line of thought promptly.

'Many of the cottages are in need of repair,' he went on. 'We are putting that to rights gradually. And about time too. I could show you, if you would care to ride round with me one day.'

'I am the music teacher.'

'That's no reason why you should not look at the estate, is it? You might find some budding genius tucked away in one of our farmhouses.'

'Is Mrs Stacy interested in the estate?'

His smile was a little sad. 'I have never been able to discover what she is interested in.'

'After all . . .' I was going to say that it was her fortune which was going to be used to improve the estate, but that seemed to be going too far. Perhaps I implied this, for he was frowning slightly and I summoned the girls again. I did not want them to think that I was taking a ride with Napier. We were a party and I wanted this stressed.

'Come on,' I called.

'Yes, Mrs Verlaine,' answered Alice and they came up with us.

'Aren't the wrecks clear?' she said, as though making polite conversation.

'Very,' I replied. I signed for Allegra to take her place beside Napier, but she hung back sullenly and I did not want to force it, so I turned my horse and we went on and in a short time we came to a cottage with a long front garden in which the weeds were growing.

I heard Sylvia's shrill voice: 'That's the Brancots. Their garden's a disgrace. The weeds blow to other people's and spoil their flowers and vegetables. There have been complaints.'

'Poor Mr Brancot,' said Alice gently. 'He's so old. How can he do his garden? It's not fair to expect it.'

'Still, it's a *rule* that tenants look after their gardens, my mother said.'

The only time Sylvia was bold was when she was quoting her mother.

We passed on and in a short time I noticed that the girls had fallen behind again. They were keeping their distance because they thought we wished them to, and what this implied made me uneasy.

A few days later an even more disturbing incident occurred.

As I came out of the house I found Mrs Lincroft with Alice about to get into the dog cart.

'We're just going to the little shop to get a few things,' she said. 'Is there anything you need?'

I thought awhile and remembered that I needed a reel of blue cotton.

'Why not come along with us?' she suggested. 'Then you can choose the exact colour you need.'

As we rode along I remembered the little shop which Roma and her friends had used and which I had once visited with my sister. It was in fact a house – little more than a cottage – and in the window of the parlour goods were displayed, the idea seeming to be to cram in as much as possible. Roma had said that the shop was a godsend and saved them going into Lovat Mill whenever they wanted any little thing. It was run by a large woman and all I remembered about her was that she talked a great deal and was shaped rather like a figure eight.

One stepped down into the interior of the shop, where bundles of firewood were stacked against a wall beside a great tin of paraffin oil, the smell of which permeated the gloom. There were biscuits, cheeses, fruit, cake and bread as well as haberdashery. I guessed it prospered largely because many of the people of the neighbourhood were saved, as Roma and her friends had been, from making the journey into Lovat Mill.

As soon as I entered memories came back to me of Roma and I thought of her standing there asking in that brisk voice of hers for glue or brushes or bread and cheeses.

Mrs Lincroft made her purchases and I asked for my cotton; and as the plump lady, whom Mrs Lincroft addressed as Mrs Bury, brought out her tray of cottons, she peered at me and said: 'Oh, you people are back then, are you?'

In dismay I understood at once. She recognised me.

Mrs Lincroft said: 'This is Mrs Verlaine, who teaches the girls music.'

'Oh . . .' A long drawn out sigh of astonishment. 'Well, fancy that. I could have sworn . . . I thought you were one of *them* . . . They were here for quite a time . . . always coming in for this and that.'

'Mrs Bury means the people who were working on the Roman remains,' explained Alice.

'That's right,' said Mrs Bury. 'Why, you're the spitting image of this one. I could have sworn . . . She didn't come in much . . . once or twice . . . but I'm not one to forget a face. I thought for a minute: Hallo, they're back. This is a nice blue. It depends of course –'

As she brought out a little brown paper bag and put in

the cotton I had selected, she was chuckling to herself. 'My word . . . For the minute I thought . . . I could have sworn you were one of them.'

She took my money and gave me my change.

'Mind you,' she said, 'I wouldn't be the one to say no if they wanted to come back and do some more. There's some that don't like it. But they were always in here. Some didn't like 'em cutting up the countryside but it's good for business, I say. Well, it takes all sorts to make a world. It was funny that one who disappeared. We never heard what became of her. I expect it was in the papers and I missed it. Though if it had been murder –'

'We shall never know now,' said Mrs Lincroft finalising the conversation. 'Thank you, Mrs Bury.'

'Thank you, I'm sure.' Her warm brown eyes followed me out; and I knew she was trying to cast back her mind to a certain afternoon when Roma had gone into her shop taking a companion with her.

'I had to cut her short,' said Mrs Lincroft as we climbed into the trap. 'Otherwise she'd go on for ever.'

I had been rather shaken by Mrs Bury's recognising me and I wondered what effect it would have on the Stacys if they discovered that I was Roma's sister. At best it seemed to make me appear rather sly. My only excuse would be that I thought her disappearance might be in some way connected with the house and its inhabitants, which could scarcely be expected to please them.

Perhaps I should do well to confess now. I could imagine myself telling Napier.

I wanted to be alone, away from the house to think of these things and what better solitude than riding through the country lanes.

I went to the stables and as I was about to ride out Napier came in. As he dismounted he threw a bag on to the ground where it fell with a clatter. I looked at it in some surprise and he said: 'It's only a spade and shovel and a few gardening things.'

'You've been working with them?'

'You look surprised. There are many things I can do. I turned my hands to all sorts of jobs on the Station.'

'I suppose so,' I said.

'Now you are putting on that "It's no concern of mine" look. Please don't. I like to think that what I do is a concern of yours.'

'That,' I said coolly, 'is more baffling than ever.'

'You say that but you know there is a perfectly simple explanation. I am eager for your approval, so I shall tell you what I've been doing.'

'It's not necessary and I'm sorry if I implied that I should like to know.'

'You implied it . . . most clearly. That's what I find so stimulating about you. You always want to know. There is one thing I cannot endure, and that is indifference. Now be prepared for a great surprise. I've been to the Brancots' helping with the garden. Ah, that has shaken you.'

'I – I think it's extremely kind of you.'

He bowed. 'It's pleasant to bask in the warmth of your approval.'

'You could of course have sent one of the gardeners.'

'So I could.'

'Your tenants will think you a most unusual landlord, working in their gardens.'

'One tenant – one garden – and I didn't do it as a land-lord.' He leaped back into the saddle. 'This is too good an opportunity to miss. We're going for a ride together.'

'I have only an hour to spare.'

He laughed again and as I could do nothing else but move away, he followed me out into the sunshine.

While we walked our horses through the narrow lanes he said seriously: 'About Brancots . . . yes, I could have sent one of the gardeners, but old Brancot didn't want that. There are some malicious people around here. So self-righteous they are. There's our dear vicar's wife for one. She believes in justice. No matter how uncomfortable everyone is, justice must be done. She would say that if old Brancot cannot manage the garden he should move to a cottage without one; but he's lived in that cottage all his life.'

'I understand.'

'And your opinion of me has improved a little?'

'Of course.'

He looked at me quizzically. 'Who is to say that I did it to win your approval and not for old Brancot.'

'I'm sure there is no question of it.'

'You do not know me. I have mean, ulterior motives. My ways are devious. You should beware of me.'

'That could very likely be true.'

'I'm so glad you realise it, because you will be much more interested in me for that very reason.'

I thought then: There is no doubt to what he is leading. I must show him quite clearly that he is making a mistake. I was not going to run away simply because the master of the house – well, he was not quite that while Sir William lived – but because he was trying to force his attentions on me. I would show him that he could make no headway with me, nor could he drive me away. For the first time the thought struck me that he might want to drive me away.

We had come to an open stretch of country and he broke into a gallop. I followed, and when he finally pulled up I was not far behind him.

I brought my horse to a standstill and we looked down on the sea together. Ahead lay Dover Castle, grey, impregnable and magnificent, standing like a sentinel guarding the white cliffs as it had for hundreds of years. Dubris – as Roma would have called it – the gateway to England; and there was the remains of the pharos – Roma again – which had so delighted her, on what was known as the Devil's Drop, built in green sandstone and Roman brick and cemented together by Roman mortar, which my sister had told me had stood up to the weather for nearly two thousand years. Away to the west was that wonderful formation known as Cæsar's Camp. Invisible now, but I remember my sister's taking me along this coast and gloating over the evidence of Roman occupation.

Napier's thoughts were clearly not with the Romans for he turned to me and said: 'Shouldn't we speak frankly?'

I was brought back to the present. 'It would depend on what that would entail.'

'Isn't frankness always desirable?'

'No, not always.'

'Your husband would not wish you to go on mourning him.'

'How can you know?' I fiercely demanded.

'If he did wish it, it should be easier for you to forget. That would show clearly that he was not worth remembering.'

I was angry – unfairly so perhaps, because he was making me look at what I did not want to see. Of course Pietro would want me to go on remembering him for the rest of my life.

I remembered something else then. There had been at the Paris *pension* a girl student who had been smitten with an incurable disease. She had had a lover and a sudden vision of their two melancholy faces came to me. They were in my

room in the *pension* and we drank coffee together and talked
of love and she quoted the poem which she said she had
given to her lover to read when she was dead if he should
remember her and be sad.

> 'No longer mourn for me when I am dead
> Than you shall hear the surly sullen bell
> Give warning to the world that I am fled . . .

And it went on:

> '. . . for I love you so,
> That I in your sweet thoughts would be forgot
> If thinking on me then should make you woe.'

My eyes filled with tears which I tried to blink away but
he had seen them.

'He was an extremely selfish man,' he said brutally.

'He was an artist.'

'Weren't you?'

'I lacked something. Otherwise I should never have been
deterred.'

He leaned towards me: 'Caro . . . no, not Caro . . . that
was his name for you. Caroline, you have forgotten sometimes . . . since you've been here.'

'No,' I said firmly. 'I never forget.'

'You are not telling the truth. You forget now and then,
and the times of forgetting grow more frequent.'

'No, no,' I insisted.

'Yes, Caroline, yes,' he went on. 'There is someone here
who makes you forget. Why were you not here when I came
back. Before . . .'

I looked at him coldly and prodding my horse, moved
away from him.

He was beside me.

'You are afraid,' he said accusingly.

'You are mistaken,' I replied. I was horrified to find that my hands were shaking. I should never ride alone with him again.

'You know I am not. What sense is there in pretending things are what they are not.'

'Sometimes it is necessary, to . . . accept.'

'I never would.' His voice rang out clearly. 'Nor should you, Caroline.'

He cut at some nearby bushes with his riding crop. 'There must be a way,' he said.

At that moment I heard a shout from the bushes and Allegra was calling to us. I turned and saw the three girls.

'We've come rather a long way,' said Alice almost apologetically. 'Then Allegra thought she saw you.'

'Shouldn't you have a groom with you?' I asked.

Alice looked at Allegra who said: 'I dared them.'

Napier had not spoken. He seemed scarcely aware of the girls.

'It's time we started back,' I said.

And we rode home, Napier and myself ahead; the girls keeping that discreet distance behind us which was so disturbing.

⁘

'It's a beautiful story,' said Alice. 'I felt I *knew* all the people . . . especially Jane.'

They had been reading *Jane Eyre* – a task set them by Mrs Lincroft and they had been commanded to write an essay commenting on the book and comparing it with others.

Mrs Lincroft had said to me: 'Sir William has had a bad night and he's a little fretful this morning. I feel I should hover over him. Could you go to the schoolroom for an hour or so?'

I had readily agreed, thankful to have something to do. I was disturbed by my conversation with Napier. He was very interested in me, I did not doubt that; what I did doubt was the depth of his emotion. I knew so little of him. But I had to admit that had he been free I might have been eager to discover more; that but for Edith I would have been willing to allow him to show me whether it was possible to forget the past.

'Have you completed your essays?' I asked.

Alice laid hers before me, three neat pages. Allegra had done half a page and Sylvia barely one.

'I shall leave these for Mrs Lincroft to see,' I said, 'since she set the lesson.'

'We were to discuss the book together and the characters,' Alice explained.

'I liked it,' said Allegra.

'Allegra liked the part about the fire, didn't you?' said Alice, and Allegra nodded, suddenly sullen.

'What else did you like?' I asked the girl.

She shrugged her shoulders and said: 'I did like the fire. It served them all right. He shouldn't have shut her up, should he . . . and he went blind.'

'Jane was very good,' said Alice. 'She ran away when she knew he was married.'

'He was very upset then,' said Sylvia, 'but it served him right, didn't it? He didn't tell her he was married to someone else.'

'I wonder whether she really knew and pretended not to,' suggested Allegra.

'The author would have told us if she had,' I pointed out.

'But *she* is the author,' put in Alice. 'Jane is writing the book. She says I . . . I . . . She might have wanted to pretend.'

'And she might not have told us,' added Sylvia triumphantly.

'Still, she did go away when it all came out that he had a mad wife.' Allegra's dark eyes were on my face.

'Which,' said Alice, 'was the right thing to do, wasn't it, Mrs Verlaine?'

Three pairs of eyes were fixed on my face. Questioningly? Accusingly? Warningly?

A few days later I was having dinner with Mrs Lincroft and Alice when the bell in Mrs Lincroft's sitting-room began to ring violently.

She looked startled. 'Oh dear, what can be wrong?' she said. She glanced at the clock on the mantelpiece. 'They should be halfway through dinner. Do go on, Mrs Verlaine. Omelettes should be eaten immediately.'

She left me with Alice, who continued to eat her food. I did the same.

'He doesn't usually send during dinner,' said Alice after a short pause. 'I wonder why he has to-day. Sometimes I wonder what he would do without my mother.'

'I am sure he relies on her.'

'Oh yes,' agreed Alice in her most old-fashioned manner. 'He would be quite lost without her.' She looked at me anxiously: 'Do you think he appreciates that, Mrs Verlaine?'

'I'm sure he does.'

'Yes, so am I.' She seemed satisfied and returned to her omelette.

After a while she said: 'And Sir William is very good to *me* too. He takes quite an interest. But although my mother is a good housekeeper, she is still only a housekeeper. Some people remember that. Mrs Rendall for one.'

'I shouldn't worry about it.'

'No, *you* wouldn't because you're wise and sensible.' She sighed. 'I think my mother is as much of a lady as Mrs Rendall. No, I think she is more.'

'I'm glad you appreciate her, Alice,' I said.

The door opened and Mrs Lincroft came in, looking distinctly worried.

'Have either of you seen Edith?'

Alice and I looked at each other blankly.

'She's late for dinner.' Mrs Lincroft glanced at the clock. 'Twenty minutes late. They've held up serving. It's so unlike her. Where could she be?'

'She's in her room, I expect,' said Alice. 'Shall I go and see, Mamma?'

'Someone has been there, child. She's not in her room. No one remembers seeing her since luncheon. One of the maids took tea up to her at four o'clock. She always has it at that time . . . and she wasn't there.'

Alice had risen. 'Shall I go and look for her, Mamma?'

'No, finish your dinner. Oh dear, this is alarming.'

'She's probably gone for a walk and forgotten the time,' I suggested.

'That must be the case,' agreed Mrs Lincroft. 'But I must say it is unlike her. Sir William is really annoyed. He so dislikes unpunctuality as Edith knows.'

'Your dinner is getting cold, Mamma,' said Alice anxiously.

'I know, but I must see if I can find her.'

'Perhaps she's taken the trap and gone visiting someone,' I suggested.

'Not alone,' said Alice. 'She was frightened of horses.'

We were startled, both Mrs Lincroft and I. It was the use of that word 'was.'

Mrs Lincroft said hastily: 'Yes, she *is* scared of the horses and always was. I wish I knew where to look for her.'

It seemed rather a fuss, I thought, just because she was

late for dinner. But it appeared she never had been before. But why shouldn't she have gone off visiting a friend and forgotten the time? I suggested.

'She doesn't go visiting friends. Whom would she visit? I expect she's gone out for a walk . . . sat down somewhere and dropped asleep. She's been acting a little absentmindedly lately. That's what it is. She'll turn up soon and be in such a state because she has offended Sir William.'

But she did not turn up, and it was borne home to us that Edith, like Roma, had disappeared.

Chapter Seven

I shall never forget the rising tension in the house as the hours passed and Edith did not appear. Napier was composed – the most calm of us all. He said that there must have been an accident and the sooner we discovered what the better.

He arranged a search party consisting of himself and five of the men servants and they went off in separate directions in three parties of two. We searched the house – the great cellars, the butteries, pantries, the outhouses which I had had no idea existed before. With Alice and Allegra I went through the attics; dusty cobwebs clung to our clothes and even our faces, while spiders scuttled out of sight alarmed and disturbed by the unexpected intrusion.

Alice held the candle high and her face thus illuminated had an ethereal quality; Allegra's dark eyes were enormous with excitement.

'Do you think she's hiding in one of the trunks?' suggested Alice.

'Hiding? From what?'

'From whom?' said Allegra on a note of hysteria.

We opened the trunks. The smell of mothballs; old-fashioned garments: gowns, shoes, hats; but no Edith.

From the top to the bottom of the house, down to the cellars where Sir William's wine was racked in order of its age and excellence. More cobwebs – an occasional cockroach scuttled across the stone flags, but still no Edith.

We were all gathered in the hall, a strange and silent company; the maids wide-eyed, their caps askew. Nothing like this could have happened since the day when they brought Lady Stacy in from the copse . . . and a short while before that when Beautiful Beau had lain dying by his brother's hand.

But no one was going to accept this as such a tragedy yet. Edith was lost – nothing more. She had, said Mrs Lincroft, gone for a walk, had tripped and hurt her ankle. She was lying somewhere. The searchers would find her.

But the search parties came back one by one, and none of them had found Edith.

All night we waited. The searchers went out again. I heard them calling her name; it sounded uncanny on the night air.

Mrs Lincroft had made some coffee which she insisted the searchers drink on their return before they went out once more to look. Practical as ever, she was determined to keep up our spirits. Edith would be found, she insisted; and she went on assuring us that this would be so.

'Shouldn't the girls go to bed?' I asked.

With a nod she directed my gaze in their direction. Alice and Allegra were sitting in a window seat, leaning against each other, fast asleep.

'Better not to disturb them,' she said.

So we left them and talked in whispers of what we could do next.

Sir William sat back in the chair which Mrs Lincroft had padded with cushions. She said to him: 'Do you think, Sir William, that we should inform the police?'

'Not yet. Not yet,' he said fiercely. 'They'll find her. They must.'

And we sat and waited; and when Napier came back without her I could not take my eyes from his face; but I could not read what was written there.

Edith had gone and no one knew where. It was the great mystery of Lovat Mill. Nothing else was talked of.

It was certain now that she was not in the neighbourhood for a thorough search had been made and there was no trace of her. Yet her personal maid had gone through her wardrobe, and nothing seemed to be missing but the clothes she had worn on that day.

As the next day wore on and there was no news of her Sir William agreed that the police must be informed. Police Constable Jack Withers, who lived next door to the small constabulary, came to see us. He asked questions such as when had we last seen her and had she been in the habit of taking lonely walks. When it was revealed that she was an expectant mother Jack looked very wise and said that ladies in such conditions often got odd notions into their heads. That was the answer to the mystery. Mrs Stacy would turn up, he was sure of it. She had merely got an odd notion into her head.

Sir William was inclined to favour this view, because – I felt sure – he wanted it to be so.

The next day he was less well and Mrs Lincroft was

occupied in looking after him. The doctor came and said that shocks like this were not good for a man in his state of health.

'If only Edith would come back,' fretted Mrs Lincroft, 'he would be better immediately.'

I walked out looking for Edith. I did not believe she had gone off on an odd fancy. I could only guess that she had gone for a walk and had had an accident.

How like this it must have been when Roma disappeared. And what an uncanny coincidence that two women should have disappeared in the same spot!

I was afraid, afraid of something shadowy and intangible, for fragments of thoughts kept coming and going in my mind.

My footsteps led me to the copse where in the ruined chapel Edith had gone to meet her lover. I stood here – those eerie walls about me; through that gap the light had shown. Had it been Edith's lover signalling to her? No. They were such a simple, uncomplicated pair. They should never have found themselves in such a position; they should have met in happier circumstances, fallen in love and married. Edith would have made a good clergyman's wife – gentle, kind; she would have listened sympathetically to the troubles of her husband's parishioners, but instead of that she had been forced into a tragedy which was too much for her.

'Edith!' I whispered. 'Roma! Where are you?'

Fearful thoughts came into my mind. Napier's face close to mine touched with passion. 'There must be a way,' he had said.

And Roma ... what of Roma? What had Roma to do with Edith?

Something, I insisted. It must be something. Two people could not disappear . . . in this very place. Napier could have had no interest in Roma.

There I had admitted it. Did I really believe that Napier knew something about the disappearance of Edith? It was absurd. Edith had had an accident. She was lying somewhere.

'Edith!' My voice sounded thin and weedy. 'Where are you, Edith?'

No answer . . . only the echo of my own voice.

I walked away from the copse. It was an evil place. Horrible thoughts had come to me in the copse. I walked across the gardens, out to the road to the Roman remains and the empty cottage where I had lived with Roma. What if Edith had gone there? Why not? Suppose Jeremy Brown had come to see her there? Suppose he had come back to see her before he left England, had said good-bye to her, and when he had gone she had fallen down the stairs and was lying there feebly calling for help? Those stairs were dangerous.

I was making up the tale to fit my wishes. Anything but that Napier . . .

I opened the door of the cottage. 'Edith . . . Edith, are you here?'

There was no answer. No crumpled body at the foot of the stairs. I ran up them. Through the little bedroom to the other. Empty!

On the way back to the house I passed the little shop. Mrs Bury was at the door.

She nodded a greeting.

'A terrible thing this,' she said. 'Mrs Stacy now . . .'

'Yes,' I said.

She was peering at me in a manner which made me feel uncomfortable.

'Where on earth can she have got to? They're saying she's had an accident and is lying somewhere.'

'It seems the most likely explanation.'

She nodded. 'Funny thing. It reminds me of that Miss er . . . what's 'er name.' She jerked her head in the direction of the Roman remains. 'I reckon it's a very funny thing. She walked out, didn't she . . . and we never heard where she got to. Now it's Mrs Stacy. Do you know what? I don't reckon it's right . . . disturbing things like that.' She jerked her head once more. 'I reckon it's asking for trouble.'

'Do you think so?'

'Mind you, it was good for business. Then there's the people who come down to look at it. We have more people here now than we did before. I reckon there's a real old to-do up there at Lovat Stacy.'

I nodded.

'Do you know, I could swear I've seen you before.'

'So you said.'

'And with her . . . too. Came in with her. You wouldn't forget *her* in a hurry. A bouncy type, you know. Full of herself. I'll have this and I'll have that . . . as though we all ought to go down on our bended knees because she'd come here to tell us we'd had Romans here.'

I smiled.

'Oh yes, I could have sworn it.'

'We all have doubles they say.'

'You have, my dear. You have.'

I started to move away and she said, 'Nice little thing, that Miss Edith. Always felt sorry for her, somehow. Hope she's all right.'

'I hope so.'

I felt her eyes on me as I went down the road.

As I passed under the gate house Sybil Stacy came towards me. She was wearing a big blue straw hat trimmed with marguerites and blue ribbons.

'Oh Mrs Verlaine,' she cried, 'what do you think of this?'

'I don't know what to think.'

She chuckled grimly. 'I do. I know.'

'You know?'

She nodded, like a little girl who has a secret which she knows she won't be able to keep.

'They thought they were going to replace Beau. As if anyone could ever replace him. He wouldn't have it.' Her face flushed pink; she stamped her feet as she placed them slightly apart and stood before me, bellicose for a moment. 'Of course we couldn't have that. They would have called the child Beaumont. There's only one Beau. He would see to that . . . and so would I.'

'So would you?'

She was pouting, the little girl again. 'They could have named him Beaumont but he would never have been Beau to me. I would have called him Nap. Nap. Nap. Nap.' Her face crumpled. 'It's never been the same since Beau went . . . and it never will.'

I felt too disturbed to listen to her and made as though to move towards the house, but she caught my arm. Her tiny hands were like claws; I felt them burning through the stuff of my sleeve.

'She won't come back,' she said. 'She's gone forever.'

I turned to her almost fiercely. 'How can you know?'

She looked at me slyly and brought her face closer to mine so that the wrinkles were more obvious, the simpering more sinister. 'Because I do know,' she said.

I drew a little away from her. 'If you know something you should tell the police or Sir William or –'

She shook her head. 'They wouldn't believe me.'

'Do you mean you really know where Edith is?'

She nodded smiling.

'Where? Please tell me . . . Where?'

'She's not here. She'll never be here. She's gone — forever.'

'You do know something!'

Again that wise nod, that sly smile. 'I know she's not here. I know she never will be. I know this because . . . I know such things. I feel it. Edith has gone. We shall never see her again.'

I felt impatient because I had temporarily believed she had some tangible information.

I murmured some excuse and went into the house.

Later that day there was a startling development. Mrs Rendall arrived at Lovat Stacy dragging Sylvia with her. The girl was tearful and obviously reluctant and alarmed; Mrs Rendall was her usual militant self.

I was with Mrs Lincroft in the hall and we were talking of Edith as everyone was at that time, and wondering what else could be done to solve the mystery. It was two days since her disappearance. Jack Withers had asked a great many questions of the household and was of the opinion that since he could discover nothing he should pass on the case to a higher authority, but Sir William was against it.

Mrs Lincroft was explaining this to me: 'He cannot bear the resultant publicity. The old case of Beau will be remembered and the story that there is a curse on the house will be revived. He believes Edith will come home sooner or later and he wants to give her the opportunity to do so quietly. The less fuss the sooner the whole affair will be forgotten . . . once she is back.'

It was then that Mrs Rendall burst in upon us, pushing Sylvia before her.

'A most distressing and alarming thing. I came over at once. I thought you should know without delay. Take me to Sir William immediately.'

'Sir William has been so upset by this affair, Mrs Rendall, that I have had to send for Dr Smithers,' Mrs Lincroft reminded her. 'Sir William is now sleeping under sedative, and Dr Smithers' orders are that his rest should not be disturbed at such times.'

Mrs Rendall pursed her lips and looked haughtily at Mrs Lincroft, who received this attitude with fortitude. I guessed she was used to it.

'Then I will wait,' said the vicar's wife. 'For this is of the utmost importance. It's about Mrs Edith Stacy.'

'Perhaps you should tell me in that case . . . or Jack Withers.'

'I wish to tell Sir William.'

Mrs Lincroft said: 'He is a sick man, Mrs Rendall, and if you will please tell me . . .'

'If it is of vital importance –' I began, but Mrs Rendall cut me short; she was not going to be dictated to by a housekeeper and a music teacher, her manner implied; yet at the same time she was longing to tell what she had discovered.

'Very well,' she said at length. 'Sylvia has come to me with a most shocking story. I must say I would never have believed it, not of her. But him . . . Of course he did leave the vicar in the lurch, and anyone who could do that – after all we've done for him – so I'm not surprised. But who would have thought we could have had such wickedness . . . such vice . . . in our midst.'

Mrs Lincroft said: 'You mean the curate, Mr Brown? What has he done?'

Mrs Rendall turned to her daughter and taking the girl by the arm shook her. 'You tell – you tell them what you told me.'

Sylvia swallowed and said: 'They used to meet, and she wished she was married to him.'

She paused and looked appealingly at her mother.

'Go on, go on, child.'

'They used to go and meet at night . . . and she was frightened when –'

Sylvia looked appealingly at her mother, who said: 'In all my years as wife to the vicar, in all the parishes in which I have served, I never heard of such wanton wickedness. And that it should have been a curate of ours! Mind you, I never liked him. I said to the vicar – and the vicar will tell you this is true – I said: "I don't trust him." And when he went off as he said . . . to teach the heathens he said . . . and all the time it was to go off with another man's wife! I wonder the heavens don't open. I wonder he's not struck dead.'

Mrs Lincroft had grown pale. She stammered: 'Do you mean that Edith and Mr Brown have run away together . . . eloped?'

'That's exactly what I do mean. And Sylvia knew . . .' Her eyes narrowed; she surveyed her daughter menacingly and I have never seen a girl so frightened as Sylvia. What did this woman do, I wondered fleetingly, to inspire such terror? 'Sylvia knew and she said nothing . . . nothing . . .'

'I didn't think I should,' cried Sylvia, clenching and unclenching her hands. She put her fingers to her lips and bit her nails.

'Stop that,' said Mrs Rendall firmly. 'You should have come to me at once.'

'I – I thought it was telling tales.' Sylvia was looking

230

appealingly at me, and I said quickly: 'I think you did what you thought was right, Sylvia. You didn't want to tell tales and now you have come and told what you knew. That was right.'

Mrs Rendall was regarding me with some astonishment: the music teacher taking the authority she had over her daughter out of her hands? But I was conscious of Sylvia's gratitude and I made up my mind that if I had an opportunity to help the girl, I would do so. Such a mother could warp a young person's character, I felt sure. Poor Sylvia! Her problem was no less acute than Allegra's.

Mrs Rendall cast her basilisk glare in my direction. 'You have not heard everything. Go on, Sylvia!'

'She was going to have a baby . . . and . . . she was frightened because . . .'

'Come along Sylvia, because what?'

'Because,' said Sylvia looking at me and then suddenly lowering her eyes. 'Because . . . It was Mr Brown's baby and everyone thought . . . it wasn't.'

'She told you this?' said Mrs Lincroft incredulously. Sylvia nodded. 'You? And not the other girls?'

Sylvia shook her head. 'It was the day before she ran away. Alice was writing an essay and Allegra was having her piano lesson, and we were alone, and suddenly she started crying and told me. She said she wasn't going to stay here. She was going to run away with . . .'

'With that scoundrel!' cried Mrs Rendall.

'So,' went on Mrs Lincroft, 'she just walked out of the house taking nothing with her. Where did she go? How did she get to the station?'

Sylvia swallowed hard and stared beyond us to the window. 'She said he was waiting for her. They were going right away and she didn't want them to look for her because she wasn't ever coming back. She said not to tell them. She made me swear not to tell anyone until two days and I swore on the Bible not to and I didn't, but the time is up and I couldn't keep it to myself any longer.'

She gabbled the last part of her speech expressionlessly almost as though she had learned it off by heart – which she probably had, for if this was true it must have been a strain for the poor girl to harbour such a secret in the face of all the questioning which had been going on.

I who had heard the lovers in the ruined temple, who had noticed their attitude together, readily accepted Sylvia's story. It was credible.

Mrs Lincroft seemed to think so too. Looking very worried she said: 'I will go to Sir William at once and see if he is awake. If so I do think he should see you and Sylvia immediately, Mrs Rendall.'

It was shocking; it was scandalous; but scandalous things had happened in the neighbourhood before.

Yet it was the most plausible explanation. Young married women did not walk out of their homes and simply disappear without leaving any trace. They had to be somewhere. And Edith had actually confessed to the vicar's daughter that she was planning to elope with her lover.

Who would have believed it! Young Mrs Stacy and the curate! The curate of all people. Well, these things were known to happen.

'The quiet ones are the worst,' said Mrs Bury to me. She had formed a habit of miraculously appearing at her door every time I passed; and almost on every occasion she would shake her head at me and tell me that I was the spitting image of one of those digger people. She never forgot a face.

'And married to *him*,' she said. 'I feel sorry for her. Nice little girl, Miss Edith was. No hoity-toity about her . . . not like Miss Allegra. There's one who wants a good spanking if ever anyone did. But Miss Edith and Miss Alice – always polite and well mannered, the both of them. I was sorry for her, marrying her off like that. It was the money. Well, money's not everything, is it? If she hadn't been a little heiress they wouldn't have married her off to that Mr Nap . . . and she could have fallen in love and married Mr Brown all nice and respectable.'

It was the view of the village. They were all sorry for poor little Edith, and Mr Brown had, they remembered, been such a nice young man, more approachable than the vicar and never prying into their affairs and giving them unwanted advice like Mrs Vicar.

Sir William was deeply affected by the news. I did not see him for I did not go to play for him during this period.

Mrs Lincroft confided in me: 'He's taken this badly. The thought of a grandchild did wonders for him, gave him a new interest, and now she's gone and it seems the grandchild might not have been his after all. It's changed him; he says he'll never have her in this house again. He doesn't want to find her and he doesn't want a lot more talk. He wants to forget about it. He wants it to be as though Edith was never here. He doesn't want her name mentioned and he wants inquiries stopped.'

'But,' I protested, 'it's not possible to behave as though something as important as that never happened. Napier is here and his purpose in coming was to marry Edith.'

'It is what Sir William wishes,' said Mrs Lincroft, as though that explained everything.

Sylvia's revelation brought a decided change. The matter in the minds of most people was neatly settled. Edith had done what others had done before her when trapped into an undesirable marriage; she had run away with her lover.

No one knew on what ship Mr Brown had left for Africa. 'I never questioned him,' declared Mrs Rendall. 'I wanted to have no part in his hare-brained schemes. And it seems that he must have left the church, for, my goodness, if we are going to let those sort of people stay in what are we coming to?'

Napier went to London and spent a week there trying to discover some news of Jeremy Brown's whereabouts; and after a week or so he came back with the news that a Mr and Mrs Brown had sailed for Africa on the S.S. *Cloverine*, but whether this was Jeremy and Edith was not certain. It might be possible to learn more when the ship arrived. Then they could discover through the Missionary Society whether Jeremy had arrived at his destination.

So Napier came back little wiser than he had gone and I avoided him and was relieved because he seemed to avoid me too. There were times when I thought the wisest thing for me to have done would have been to slip quietly away while he was in London and disappear as irrevocably as Edith and Roma appeared to have done.

Yet the very next minute I was reminding myself that I had come to solve the riddle of Roma's disappearance, and Edith's made me all the more determined to do so. I was in no danger from Napier Stacy, I assured myself – nor from any man. Of course if the reason for Edith's disappearance was her flight with a lover, it was in no way connected with Roma's; but it was still an odd coincidence that two women should have vanished in the same place.

The belief in the cause of the trouble was strengthened when Alice and Allegra made *their* confessions to Mrs Lincroft.

Allegra admitted that she had seen the lovers meeting on more than one occasion. She had said nothing to anyone because she thought it would have been telling tales. Alice admitted to once carrying a note from Edith to Mr Brown.

So Edith had gone. Everyone was ready to believe that she had gone off with her lover. But I was not altogether sure; I kept thinking of Roma.

Chapter Eight

During the following weeks when I continued to avoid Napier, it occurred to me that everyone was taking the explanation of Edith's disappearance too much for granted, and I was astonished at the attitude in the house. Mrs Lincroft was solely concerned with nursing Sir William. Perhaps it was Mrs Lincroft who jostled everyone into accepting the explanation because she wanted the matter put aside and forgotten – for Sir William's sake, of course. But the girls were always whispering about it. I would catch Edith's name often when I came upon them; then they would look a little embarrassed and talk of something else.

In the village they went on discussing the disappearance of Edith; but they were all convinced too that she had gone off with her lover. The story was embellished as the weeks passed.

I heard Mrs Bury whispering to one of her customers. 'They say she left a note telling them she couldn't live with that Nap any more. Poor thing!'

It was amazing how these rumours, which had no word of truth in them, could start.

'It was the curse on the house,' I heard Mrs Bury say on another occasion. 'You see, it should have been Master Beau's by rights. And Mr Nap came home and took his place. Oh, I know she went off with the curate. It's what they call predestination . . . part of the curse, you see.'

Whenever anyone from the house appeared it would set tongues wagging. Once I saw the three girls in Mrs Bury's shop and I guessed she was talking to them about the curse on Lovat Stacy and Edith's disappearance. There was an air of guilty conspiracy about them all.

I thought a great deal about Napier and that conversation when he had told me that he was not indifferent to me. I wondered how sincerely he meant those words. He had seemed genuine but this could be a method of approach. I was a woman and a widow, experienced of life. He was not free to make any honourable declaration – no more now than then. Yet he had made a declaration of a sort, and if I were wise I would stop thinking of him. But it was true that I was struggling out of my own slough of despondency as perhaps he was . . . If I could believe him . . . and it was partly due to him. Whatever I thought of him he had given me a new interest in life and because I was not thinking of Pietro every hour of the day it was rather like seeing a faint light at the end of a dark tunnel through which one had struggled for a long time – and being afraid of what one might find in the light.

I had promised myself that I would never be involved again. If I had visualised another life, marriage, children, a home of my own, I had seen my husband as a shadowy figure. I should be fond of him, but I would never give him the power to hurt me as Pietro had hurt me. Not only in dying and leaving me alone, but in our life together. Yes, I was admitting the hurts now, the carelessness, the lack of tenderness, the ruthless squandering of my career for his. This admission was new and – I must face it – it had come through my relationship with Napier. But children . . . I longed for children. With them I could build a new life. I might be freeing myself from my past but Napier was chained to his as surely as he had been when Edith was in the house.

Her memory was more vivid than she had been herself. Her clothes were still in the wardrobe and her room was just as she had left it. There were now Beau's room and Edith's room; but Edith's would not be a shrine as Beau's had been. I was sure that as soon as Mrs Lincroft had nursed Sir William back to health something would be done.

And then the new curate arrived and everyone had something else to talk about. Edith's 'elopment with the curate' was still a topic of conversation but not now of paramount importance. Mr Godfrey Wilmot had replaced her.

Mrs Rendall came over to Lovat Stacy to talk to Mrs Lincroft and me about Mr Wilmot. She was clearly delighted with him.

'What great good fortune! I am glad now that we rid ourselves of that – of that – well, no matter. Mr Wilmot is here now. The most charming man, and the vicar has taken such a fancy to him.'

Poor vicar, I thought, obviously he dare do nothing else.

'Oh yes,' continued Mrs Rendall, 'I have no doubt you will agree we have a find in Mr Wilmot. Such a charming young man!' She beamed on us both and whispered: 'He is thirty. Such good family. His uncle is Sir Laurence, the judge. Of course he will have a very good living in time. The reason he hasn't one already is because he made a late decision to come into the Church. We shan't keep him very long, I fear.' She smiled rather coyly. 'Though I shall do my best to make him so happy that he doesn't want to leave us. You must come to the vicarage to meet him. He is delighted, by the way, to help in the instruction of the girls.'

Mrs Lincroft said that she was eager to meet the new curate and it was most satisfactory that he should satisfy Mrs Rendall's requirements so completely.

'I believe,' said Mrs Rendall coyly, 'that Mr Brown's desertion is going to prove a blessing in disguise.'

The girls brought back glowing reports of Mr Wilmot from the vicarage.

'So handsome!' sighed Allegra. 'He'll never want to marry Sylvia.'

Sylvia flushed and looked angry.

I came to her rescue. 'Perhaps Sylvia wouldn't want to marry him.'

'She'd have no choice,' retorted Allegra. 'Nor will he if he stays. Mrs Rendall has quite made up her mind.'

'This is nonsense,' I said.

Alice and Allegra exchanged glances.

'Good Heavens,' I cried. 'The poor man has only just arrived.'

'Mrs Rendall thinks he's wonderful though,' murmured Alice.

'The arrival of a new personality at this place has turned everyone's head.'

It was true that people were talking of the new curate. 'Very different from that Mr Brown.' 'I hear his father's a lord or something.' 'He's very good looking . . . and such nice manners.'

These were the comments I heard throughout the village in the days before I met him and by this time I was looking forward to making the acquaintance of this paragon. At least his coming took the limelight from Edith's disappearance. Not that Edith was forgotten. When I saw the constable in the village I stopped and talked to him.

'The case is still open, Mrs Verlaine,' he said. 'Until it's definitely proved she's run off with this young man we'll keep our eyes open.'

I wondered what they were doing about the case, but when I asked him, he merely looked mysterious.

'Come into the drawing-room,' Mrs Rendall greeted us. 'Mr Wilmot is with the vicar in his study.'

We all followed her into the drawing-room where Sylvia was standing by the window.

'Pray sit down, Mrs Verlaine, and you too.' She signed to the girls. 'Sylvia, don't stand there so *awkwardly.*' Anxious maternal eyes surveyed Sylvia. 'How untidy you look! That hair ribbon is positively grubby. Go and change it at once.'

I saw Allegra and Alice exchange glances, and it occurred to me how observant – and critical – the young were.

'Don't slouch so,' said Mrs Rendall to the departing Sylvia who blushed uncomfortably. 'And put your shoulders back.' She added in exasperation: 'Girls!'

She talked desultorily of Sir William's health and the weather until Sylvia returned wearing a blue hair ribbon.

'H'm!' said her mother. 'Now go to the study and tell the vicar and Mr Wilmot that Mrs Verlaine is here.'

She watched her daughter speculatively, but perhaps I thought that because of the girls' comments. In a few moments the vicar entered the drawing-room accompanied by Mr Wilmot, who was indeed an extremely personable young man – a little more than medium height with a very charming and candid expression. He had perfect white teeth, which were very evident when he smiled, and his manners were easy. He was a contrast to the meek Mr Brown.

'Ah, Mr Wilmot!' I had never heard Mrs Rendall's tone so cooingly gentle. 'I want you to meet Mrs Verlaine. You will want to talk about lesson times with her. She is teaching the girls the piano.'

He came towards me. 'Mrs Verlaine,' he said. 'That's a very famous name.'

He took my hand; his warm brown eyes looked into mine.

'You are referring to my husband,' I said.

'Ah, Pietro Verlaine . . . what an artist!' His expression clouded. He would be remembering that I was a widow. It lightened suddenly. 'Why,' he went on, 'I knew your sister. It was here . . .'

I was unable to control my expression. I was exposed. It had been bound to happen sooner or later. Pietro was too well known; and in her circles so was Roma. Someone would one day be bound to link me up.

He must have noticed my expression of fear for he said quickly: 'Perhaps I am mistaken . . .'

'My sister . . . is dead,' I heard myself stammer.

Mrs Rendall said: 'How very sad!' She turned to Mr Wilmot. 'Mrs Verlaine's father was a professor. It is sad that her only sister died . . . not very long ago, I believe.'

Mr Wilmot came gallantly and magnificently to the rescue. 'Of course. I'm so sorry, Mrs Verlaine, for introducing a subject which must be painful.'

I did not speak, but I think my eyes must have expressed my gratitude.

'Mr Wilmot is very interested in our little village,' said Mrs Rendall archly.

'Oh yes,' said our new curate, 'I find the Roman remains quite fascinating.'

'They are, I believe, one of the reasons why you decided to come here.'

He smiled charmingly. 'They are just an added attraction.' He turned to me: 'I am an amateur archæologist, Mrs Verlaine.'

I swallowed and said: 'How very interesting.'

'At one time I intended to make it my profession. Then . . . rather later than usual . . . I decided to go into the church.'

'How very fortunate for us,' boomed Mrs Rendall. 'I do wish you could persuade Sylvia to show a little interest in our remains, Mr Wilmot.'

'I can try,' he said smiling.

The vicar said: 'Ah . . . very interesting!' And I could see he was pleased, for now that the curate showed an interest in the Roman remains Mrs Rendall had discovered how fascinating they were.

'I don't think our lessons are going to overlap,' I said, bringing the conversation to the subject we had come to discuss.

'I'm sure they won't.'

I was immediately conscious of his interest and I was not surprised. He must wonder why I was so anxious that he should not betray the fact that I was Roma's sister.

I had given Sylvia her music lesson and was crossing the vicarage garden on my way back to Lovat Stacy when I heard my name called, and there was Mr Wilmot running after me, smiling his engaging smile.

'I've set the girls some work,' he said. 'I had to speak to you.'

'About my sister?'

He nodded. 'I only met her once or twice. She mentioned you then. She was worried about you because of your marriage. She thought it wouldn't be good for your career.'

'Thank you for keeping silent,' I said.

His puzzled gaze met mine. 'They don't know of the relationship obviously.'

I shook my head. 'Let me explain. You know my sister . . . disappeared.'

'Yes. It's one of the reasons why I could not resist taking the opportunity – when it arose – of coming here. That . . . and the finds. And you?'

'I came here to teach the girls the piano and to try to find out what has become of my sister.'

'And decided to keep the relationship secret?'

'Perhaps it was silly of me, but I was afraid they wouldn't have me if they knew. Roma had come here though they didn't want her and her party. And then she brought unpleasant publicity here by disappearing. I wanted to find out what had happened to my sister . . . so I came here.'

He gave a deep sigh. 'How thankful I am that you stopped me in time. You know I might have mentioned it if I'd heard your name before meeting you.'

'Yes. It's difficult to remain anonymous after having been married to a famous man.'

He nodded. 'It's very . . . intriguing.'

'It's horribly mystifying. And now Edith has disappeared too.'

'Oh that unfortunate affair. She's run away from her husband, I hear.'

'I'm not sure. All I know is that she disappeared and Roma disappeared.'

He looked at me shrewdly. 'I understand your feelings. I wonder if there's anything I can do to help.'

'At least someone knows who I am . . .' I began.

'You can be sure no one else will learn through me.'

'I'm grateful.'

He smiled. 'I saw the panic in your face. We must have a talk about this. As an archæologist . . . strictly amateur . . . I might be of use. Incidentally I'm fond of music. I play the organ.'

I turned and saw the drawing-room lace curtain move slightly. We were being watched – by Mrs Rendall I guessed. She would be wondering why her attractive curate had come out of the house to speak to me.

In a very short time Godfrey Wilmot and I had become friends. It was inevitable. Our mutual love of music would have drawn us together in any case, but the fact that he knew who I was made an even greater bond. I was extremely grateful for the dexterous manner in which he had extricated me from an awkward situation.

We met at the remains and talked of Roma as we wandered around.

'She would have been one of our leading archæologists had she . . .'

'Lived,' I said tersely. 'I think I have faced the certainty that Roma is dead.'

'There could be other explanations.'

'I don't know of any. Roma would never have gone away without letting me know. I am sure of it.'

'Then what can have happened to her?'

'She's dead. I know it.'

'You feel there was an accident?'

'It seems the most likely explanation, for who would want to kill Roma?'

'That's what we have to find out.'

I warmed towards him when he said 'we' in that way. I said impulsively: 'It is good of you to make my problem yours.'

He laughed suddenly. He had the most infectious laughter.

'It's good of you to allow me to. I must say it's an intriguing situation. Could it have been an accident?'

'There is a possibility of course. But where is she? That's what I want to know. There should be some trace of her. Think of it. She was here in this place . . . packing up her things . . . She went for a walk and never came back. What *could* have happened?'

'She could have gone for a swim and been drowned.'

'Wouldn't there have been some evidence? Besides she had never swum very much. It was a cold day. And wouldn't there have been some evidence?'

He said: 'The alternative is that someone hid the evidence.'

'Why?'

'Because they did not wish it to be discovered.'

'But why . . . why, *why*? I sometimes think that someone *murdered* Roma. But why?'

'Some jealous archæologist. Someone who knew that she had discovered a secret which he – or she – wished to make his or her own discovery.'

'Oh, that *is* far fetched!'

'There is such a thing as professional jealousy. In this field as in others.'

'Oh, but it's not possible.'

'People who delve into the past are thought to be a little mad by lots of people.'

'Still, one should explore every avenue. She walked out of that cottage to . . . disappear. Let's think about it.'

We were silent for a while, then I said: 'And there's Edith.'

'The lady who ran away with her lover?'

'It's the general idea.'

He reminded me of Roma – that complete absorption, that sudden pause to examine a certain piece of paving which caught his notice. Then he would expound on it a little.

'Archæology has made such rapid strides in the last few years,' he explained to me. 'Before that it was little more than a treasure hunt. I remember when I attacked my first tumuli. It was in Dorset. I tremble now to think of how careless I was and what real treasure I might have destroyed.'

I told him about my parents and the atmosphere in which I had been brought up. It all sounded rather amusing when I related it to him and we laughed frequently.

Suddenly he said: 'There's a recurring motif in these mosaics. I wonder what it means. A pity they're so damaged. I wonder whether it's possible to clean them a little. I expect your sister and her party would have done that if it were possible. What a pity time destroys the colours. These stones must have been very vivid originally. Why are you smiling?'

'You remind me of Roma. You become completely . . . absorbed in all this.'

He smiled that frank and engaging smile. 'Don't forget,' he said, 'we are looking for clues.'

'Young widows,' said Allegra, 'are said to be very fascinating.'

The girls were in the schoolroom at Lovat Stacy and Sylvia

had come over for a piano lesson. I had walked in to remind Allegra that it was time for her lesson. She was never punctual. They were seated at the table and looked rather startled when I entered.

'We were talking about widows,' said Allegra saucily.

'You should've been thinking about your lesson. Have you done your practice?'

'No,' replied Allegra.

'And you Alice, and you Sylvia?'

'Yes, Mrs Verlaine.'

'They are the good girls,' mocked Allegra. 'They always do as they're told.'

'It's often wiser,' I put in. 'Now Allegra.'

Allegra wriggled in her chair. 'Do you like Mr Wilmot, Mrs Verlaine?'

'Like him? Of course I like him. I believe he is a very good curate.'

'I think he likes you.' She turned her withering gaze on Sylvia. 'And he does not like *you* one little bit. He thinks you're a silly little girl. Don't you agree, Mrs Verlaine? He's probably told *you* what he thinks of Sylvia.'

'I don't agree, and he has never mentioned Sylvia to me. I am sure he likes her very well. At least she tries with her lessons, which is more than some people do.'

Allegra burst out laughing, and Sylvia and Alice looked embarrassed.

'Of course he doesn't like silly girls. He likes widows.'

'I see you are trying to delay your lesson. It's quite useless. Now . . . come along.'

Allegra rose. 'All the same,' she said, 'widows *are* attractive. I'm sure of it. It's on account of having had a husband and lost him. I shall be very glad when I have had a husband.'

'What nonsense!'

I led the way to the music room conscious of three pairs of eyes studying me.

How often, I asked myself, did those three pairs of eyes watch me when I was unaware of it.

I came face to face with Napier on the wide staircase which led to the hall, 'I scarcely see you now – since Edith went.'

'No,' I answered.

'I want to talk to you.'

'What do you wish to say?'

'Nothing here. Not in this house.' His voice had sunk to a whisper. 'Ride out to Hunters Knoll this afternoon. I'll see you there at half past two.'

I was about to protest, but he said: 'I'll be waiting there,' and passed on.

I was aware of the silence of the house about us. And I wondered if anyone had seen us meet and exchange a few words on the stairs.

He was there waiting for me.

'So you have come,' were his first words.

'Did you think I wouldn't?'

'I wasn't certain. What have you been thinking these last weeks?'

'Wondering chiefly what has become of Edith.'

'She has gone off with her lover.' It was a cold statement of fact; he showed no rancour, no emotion.

'Do you believe that?'

'What else can I believe!'

'There could be other explanations.'

'This seems the most likely. There is something I want to say to you . . . I suppose because I don't want you to think

248

too badly of me. When I married her I believed we could make something of our marriage. I want you to know that I did try to do this. So did she, I believe. But it was just not possible.'

I was silent and he went on: 'I suspected that she was in love with the curate. I don't blame her. I am sure I was the one to blame. But I don't want you to think that I was callous . . . calculating . . . not completely so, anyway. She could not endure her life here. I understand that. So she went away. Let us take it from there.'

I was glad that he had said that because I believed him. He had not been unkind to her as I had at first thought. He had merely been struggling – clumsily perhaps – with an impossible situation.

'What did you wish to say to me?' I asked.

'That you should not avoid me as you have been doing.'

'Have I? I did not do so consciously. I've simply not seen you. I could say that *you* have been avoiding me.'

'If I've done so, you know the reason. But now we have this Mr Wilmot.'

'What of him?'

'He is by all accounts a very attractive young man.'

'Mrs Rendall seems to think so and she is not easily pleased.' I spoke lightly, but he did not enter into my mood.

'I've heard that you and he have quickly become good friends.'

'He is interested in music.'

'And you've both discovered a passion for archæology.'

'So has Mrs Rendall.'

He was determined that no lightness should enter the conversation.

'He is no doubt charming.'

'No doubt.'

'You would know.'

'We have known each other such a short time, but yes, I should say he would be a very charming companion.'

'I hope you will not do anything ... rash ... commit yourself ...'

'What do you mean?'

'I think you should not be impulsive, Caroline. Be patient.'

We both heard the sound of horses' hoofs together, and almost immediately three riders came into sight. Allegra, Alice and Sylvia.

I thought: They must have seen me leave and followed me.

Allegra confirmed this. She called out: 'We saw you leave, Mrs Verlaine, and we wanted to come with you. Do you mind?'

❦

Alice had stumbled through the Czerny study and looked at me expectantly.

'Not bad, but there's plenty of room for improvement.'

She nodded sadly.

'Well,' I went on consolingly, 'you do take pains and you are getting on.'

'Thank you, Mrs Verlaine.' She looked down at her hands and said: 'The lights have started again.'

'What?'

'The lights in the chapel. I saw them last night. It's the first time ... since Edith ... went.'

'Well, I shouldn't worry too much about it if I were you.'

'I don't worry, Mrs Verlaine. I just feel a little scared.'

'No harm will come to you.'

'But there really does seem to be a curse on the house, doesn't there?'

'Certainly not.'

'But there were all those deaths. It started when Mr Napier shot Beau. Do you think it's true that Beau has never forgiven him?'

'What nonsense. And I'm surprised at you, Alice. I thought you had more sense.'

Alice looked ashamed. 'It's what everyone says . . . that's all.'

'*Everyone?*' I repeated.

'The servants say it. They say it in the village. They see the light and say it. They say that there will never be any peace until Mr Napier goes away again. I think that's unkind, don't you? I mean it would make Mr Napier unhappy if he heard . . . and I think he has heard because he does look unhappy, doesn't he? But perhaps he's thinking of Edith.'

'Your head seems to be filled with a lot of silly gossip,' I said. 'No wonder you don't make progress with your music.'

'But you said I was making progress, Mrs Verlaine.'

'More progress,' I added.

'So you don't think it's Beau who is haunting the chapel?'

'Of course not.'

'I know what Mrs Verlaine thinks.' It was Allegra coming for her lesson, punctual for once. 'She thinks I do it. Don't you, Mrs Verlaine? You think I'm playing tricks.'

'I hope you would never do anything so foolish.'

'But you suspect me, don't you? Do you know what I am? I'm an object of suspicion.'

'I know it isn't Allegra,' said Alice. 'I've seen the light when Allegra has been with me.'

Allegra grimaced at me.

'We'll show you,' she said.

'And now,' I said, 'perhaps you will show me how well you have done your practice.'

The opportunity to 'show me' came a little too soon for my peace of mind. That very evening I was in my room when Allegra burst in. She was very excited. 'Now, Mrs Verlaine. Alice and I saw the light only a moment ago.'

Alice was at the door. 'May I come in, Mrs Verlaine?'

I gave permission and the two girls stood before me.

'A moment ago,' cried Allegra. 'We could see it from your window, but it's better from Alice's.'

I followed them up the stairs to Alice's bedroom; she lighted a candle and held it up to the window. She stood there for some moments until I said: 'Do put that candle down, Alice. You'll set the curtains on fire.'

Obediently she set it down and lighted another.

While she was doing so, Allegra caught the sleeve of my dress and whispered: 'Look. There it is.'

And there it was. The light flashing momentarily and then disappearing.

'I'm going to see who's there,' I said.

Alice caught my sleeve, her eyes agonised. 'Oh no, Mrs Verlaine.'

'Someone is playing tricks, I'm sure of it. Who'll volunteer to come with me?'

Alice looked at Allegra, her face visibly blanching. 'I'd be terrified,' she said.

'So would I,' replied Allegra.

'Until we discover who it is playing these tricks you will go on being terrified.'

I moved towards the door. I was not going to admit that I was uneasy myself. A sudden idea had come to me, and it startled me. What if there was something so mysterious going on in this house that I had no notion as to what it could be? In that moment I experienced what I can only call a premonition and it was as though Roma herself was warning me.

'Be careful. You know how impulsive you always were.'

She had said something like that to me on many occasions and I could distinctly hear her voice in my mind.

I had a friend now, an ally. Wouldn't it be wise to enlist the help of Godfrey Wilmot before trying to discover the reason for this strange phenomenon?

One of the candles suddenly went out; and it was immediately followed by the other; the room was almost in darkness.

Alice said shrilly: 'It's a sign, Mrs Verlaine. It's a warning, the two candles going out like that when there was no draught.'

'You blew them out.'

'I didn't, Mrs Verlaine.'

I turned to Allegra. 'She didn't either,' declared Alice. 'They went out of their own accord. Strange things happen in this house, you know. It's on account of all that happened all those years ago. It was a warning. We mustn't go to the ruin. Something awful would happen if we did.'

As she lighted the candles I saw that her hands were trembling.

'Alice,' I said, 'you are letting your imagination run riot again.'

She nodded gloomily. 'I can't help it, Mrs Verlaine. Ideas come to me. I wish they wouldn't . . . and then I think what could be and sometimes it's frightening.'

'You ought to live in some little house where nothing has ever happened,' said Allegra.

'No, no. I want to live here. I don't mind being frightened now and then as long as I can live here.'

She turned to the window and stood looking out. I went to stand beside her.

We were both watching the copse; but the light did not appear again.

The candles burned steadily and Alice turned to look at them with satisfaction.

'You see they're all right now. It was a warning. Oh, Mrs Verlaine, don't ever go to the ruin alone in the dark.'

I said: 'I should like to get to the bottom of the silly affair.'

I was relieved however that it was not Allegra; and it occurred to me then that it might be one of the menservants signalling to one of the women.

I had met Godfrey in the cottage near the site. Because of his interest in archæology he was frequently there and we had made the cottage a rendezvous.

I sat on the stairs and he perched himself on the table while we talked about Roma. I told him of her delight in this place because it was so close to the remains and how, when I had stayed here, I had tried to instil a little domestic comfort.

'Not,' I said, 'that one could cook much, but there was an oil stove which she kept in the little outhouse. It smelt abominably – but perhaps that was mainly the drum of paraffin oil she kept there. Oh, what a relief it is to talk of Roma!'

'What could have happened?' he asked. 'Let's think of all the possibilities. Let's explore them – one by one.'

'That's what I've been doing ever since I heard. I explore and reject. What was that?' I was sure the room had darkened suddenly. I had my back to the tiny window and so had Godfrey. It was so small that the cottage was always dark but in that moment it had become a degree darker.

'Someone was at the window,' I whispered.

In a second or two we were at the door, but there was no one in sight.

'Why,' said Godfrey, 'you're really scared.'

'It's the thought of being overlooked . . . when I'm not aware of it.'

'Well, whoever it is can't be far away.'

We hurried round the cottage, but found no trace of anyone.

'It must have been a cloud passing across the face of the sun,' said Godfrey.

I looked up at the sky. There was scarcely a cloud.

'No one could have got away in time,' he went on. 'Roma's disappearance has unnerved you naturally. It's made you jumpy.'

I was prepared to concede this. 'I shan't have a moment's real peace until I know where she is,' I said.

He nodded. 'Let's get out of this place. Let's have a walk round outside. We can talk as easily there.'

So we went outside and we talked; and after a while I said: 'We didn't look in the outhouse. Someone could have hidden there.'

'If we had we should probably only have found your old oil stove.'

'But I have a strange feeling . . .'

I didn't finish. I could see that he was thinking I had imagined the shadow at the window.

It was a few days later when the startling news was revealed. I had met Godfrey at the cottage, talked there for a while and then taken a walk round the site.

Godfrey was growing more and more certain that the answer to Roma's disappearance at any rate was to be found here. He enjoyed examining minutely the baths and the pavements, looking, he said, for clues. But I knew he delighted in studying them. I mentioned the light to him and told him that the idea had occurred to me that Roma might have gone there to investigate.

But Roma had disappeared during the afternoon. The light could not have been in evidence then. But had she? What if she had gone out in the afternoon, perhaps for a walk – and returned at dusk, saw the light, investigated.

'It was possible,' agreed Godfrey. 'We must go to the ruin one evening and wait for the kindler of the light to appear.'

I thought that might be a little compromising in view of the remarks the girls had made; and I believed that Mrs Rendall was eyeing me with attention and suspecting me of what she would call 'setting my cap' at the curate.

However I did not comment on this and when I said goodbye to Godfrey we were no nearer solving the mystery of Roma's death than we had ever been.

I came back to Lovat Stacy and as I entered the hall I heard footsteps behind me. I swung round and came face to face with Napier. He looked very tired and strained.

'I have just come back from London,' he said. 'There is news.'

'Of Edith?' I said.

'She is not with Jeremy Brown.'

'Not . . .' I stared at him.

'Jeremy Brown arrived in East Africa – alone.'

'But –'

'We have been quite wrong,' he said, 'to suspect that Edith went off with a lover. She did no such thing.'

'Then what?'

He looked at me blankly. 'Who can say?' he whispered.

But there were those who had much to say. The secret was soon out, and the village was gossiping about it. The vicar received a letter from Jeremy Brown to say that he had arrived safely and was becoming absorbed in his work. So this was further confirmation that he was alone. Edith had not gone with him. Then where was Edith?

Eyes were turned once more on Lovat Stacy. That house, that unlucky house which many said was cursed.

And why was it cursed? Because a man had killed his brother. They called it the curse of Cain. And because he had killed his brother his mother had died, and now his wife had disappeared. Where could she have gone? Who could say? But perhaps there was one who could.

When a wife met some misadventure, the first person open to suspicion was her husband.

I was aware of the mounting feeling against Napier, and it disturbed me deeply – more so, it appeared, than it disturbed him.

There was wild speculation everywhere. I noticed the way in which everyone was avoiding Napier. Mrs Lincroft's expression changed when she spoke of him; her lips tightened. I knew she was thinking of what Edith's disappearance had done to Sir William and was blaming him for it.

The girls were constantly discussing the affair together, although they did not talk to me very much about it. I wondered what construction they put on it.

Allegra did say on one occasion: 'If Sir William died and it was through the shock of Edith's going . . . that would be like history's repeating itself. You know, Beau died and then his mother . . .'

I retorted sharply: 'Who said Edith was dead?'

'No,' cried Alice vehemently. 'She'll come back.'

'I hope so,' I said fervently; and how I hoped it! I wanted Edith to come back more than I had wanted anything since Pietro had died. I tried to work out all sorts of reasons for her disappearance. Amnesia? Why not? She was wandering somewhere because she had lost her memory. What a joy that would be! I did not want Napier to be a murderer. And if Edith had been murdered . . .

I just would not accept that. But what of Roma?

The strangeness of this – the awful coincidence – struck me afresh. Two young women disappeared in exactly the same manner. They both walked out, saying nothing, taking nothing with them.

It was horribly, frighteningly sinister.

I was deeply concerned. One of those women was my sister; the other the wife of Napier.

I must know. If anything my determination was doubled; and at the same time I thought of them both – no two women could have been more unlike: poor Edith with her ineffectuality, poor frightened Edith; and Roma, the determined, the fearless, the woman who knew exactly where she was going . . . except perhaps on one occasion.

I don't care where it leads me, I told myself, I am going to find out.

'Have a care, Caro.' It was Roma's voice cautioning me. 'This could be murder.'

But I would not accept that it was murder even if others did. I could sense the wall of suspicion growing as fast as a jungle bamboo.

I wished that I had not heard that quarrel between Sir William and Napier. I had gone up to play for Sir William again because Mrs Lincroft had decided that my music soothed him. I did not go through Sir William's room but straight to the piano in the next, for Mrs Lincroft had said that he might be dozing and that he liked to wake and hear the music I was playing.

On this occasion as I entered the room I heard the sound of angry voices: Sir William's and Napier's.

'I wish to God,' Sir William was saying, 'that you'd stayed out there.'

'And I can assure you,' retorted Napier, 'that I have no intention of going back.'

'You'll go if I say, and let me tell you this, there'll be nothing for you.'

'You're wrong. I have a right to be here.'

'Listen to me. Where is she, eh? What's happened to her? Run off with a curate. I knew she'd never do that. Where is she? You tell me, eh?'

I should have slipped away. But I could not. I felt too involved. I had to stand there. I had to listen.

'Why should you think I know?'

'Because you didn't want her. You married her because there was no other way of coming back. The poor child!'

'You were the one who sacrificed her, weren't you? How like you, to insist on the marriage and blame me for it. I did my best to make the marriage succeed.'

'Marriage! I'm not talking of the marriage! I'm asking you what you have done with her.'

'You're mad. Are you suggesting . . . ?'

'Murderer . . .' cried Sir William. 'Beau . . . Your – your mother . . .'

'My God,' cried Napier. 'Don't think you're going to cheat me out of my inheritance with your lies.'

'Where is she? Where is she? They'll find her and then –'

I could not bear any more. I went to the door and sped silently away to my room.

I felt sick with fear.

Sir William believed his own son had murdered Edith.

'It's not true,' I whispered. 'I won't believe it.'

And in that moment I pledged myself to solve the mystery of Edith's disappearance just as I had that of Roma. It was of the utmost importance to me.

I couldn't bear the suspicion.

In the village they were whispering. 'It stands to reason. He married her. He wanted to be rid of her once he'd got her money. There's a curse on Lovat Stacy . . . and will be as long as that bad man is there.'

I saw Sybil now and then; the sly look of knowledge in her eyes and the general coyness were more grotesque than usual.

I wondered whether secret investigations were going on. It had been discovered that Edith was not with Jeremy Brown. What else would be found out?

Why should a husband rid himself of a wife? There were many reasons. Because he did not love her. Because he now had her money; because now that he was taken back into the family and had been reinstated as his father's heir . . . I paused there, remembering the quarrel I had overheard. Sir William hated Napier. Why should he harbour such an unnatural feeling? And now that Edith had disappeared they had quarrelled bitterly. Perhaps Sir William would disinherit his son, banish him as he had once before.

Why should this have happened?

Napier had not loved Edith. He had made no secret of that. And during the last weeks . . . I thought of the conversations we had had together and I was overcome with a feeling of horror. Had I mistaken his implications? Had he really been telling me that had he been free he would have proposed marriage to *me*?

It was an alarming situation. I thought of three pairs of youthful eyes studying me. How deeply enmeshed was I in this?

And at the same time I had a great desire to prove these people wrong about Napier. I wanted to shout: 'It's not true. He's being maligned now, as he was once before. Because of that accident in his youth is he to be blamed forever?'

What had happened to me? The most important thing in my life now was to prove Napier innocent.

Mrs Lincroft frowned across the table at me.

'This has upset Sir William terribly,' she said. 'I am very much worried about him. I do wish there could be some news of Edith.'

'What do you think has happened to her?' I asked earnestly.

'I dare not think.' She avoided my eyes. 'I'm very much afraid that he'll have another stroke. It would be better if Napier went away.'

'If he went away,' I pointed out, 'malicious people would say he was running away.'

She nodded; then she said: 'He may not have much choice in the matter. Sir William was talking of sending for the family solicitor. You can guess what that means.'

'He seems always to judge and blame without evidence. He was longing for a grandchild. And now . . .'

'Perhaps Edith will come back.'

'But where is she?'

I expounded my favourite amnesia theory.

'It is good of you to take such a deep interest in the

family's affairs, Mrs Verlaine, but don't become . . . too involved.'

'Involved!' I repeated.

She looked at me intently for a few seconds and her entire demeanour seemed to change in that brief spell of time. The gentle woman I had always imagined her to be receded and another personality, quite alien to everything I had known of her, took her place. Even her voice was different. 'It's sometimes not wise to interest oneself in other people's affairs. One becomes caught up.'

'But naturally I'm interested. A young wife . . . a pupil of mine . . . disappears. Surely you don't expect me to treat that as an everyday occurrence.'

'It could not be an everyday occurrence in anyone's point of view. But she has disappeared; we don't know where . . . yet. Perhaps we never shall. The authorities are trying to discover her whereabouts. Has it occurred to you, Mrs Verlaine, that if what some people suspect is the truth, your inquisitiveness could put you in danger?'

I was astonished. I had no idea I had betrayed my determination to discover the truth.

'Danger? What sort of danger?'

There was a pause. The change had taken place again. There was the Mrs Lincroft whom I had known since my arrival at Lovat Stacy, a little vague, remote. 'Who can say? But I should keep aloof if I were you.'

I thought: She is warning me. Does she mean that I must not become involved with a man who is suspected of being concerned in his wife's disappearance? Or is she telling me that by interfering I am putting my life in danger?

'As for danger,' she went on with a little laugh, 'I am being a bit too vehement, I expect. This matter will be cleared up sooner or later. Edith will come back.' She added with forced conviction: 'I feel sure of it.' I was about to speak but she hurried on: 'Sir William told me that he so much enjoyed the Schubert the other evening. Your playing sent him into a deep sleep which was just what he needed.'

She smiled at me gratefully. Anyone who could soothe Sir William was a friend of hers.

The disaster happened two days later. I went to the room next to Sir William's. Mrs Lincroft was there. She whispered to me: 'He's a little poorly to-day. He's dozing in his chair. How dark it is. There's been nothing but rain all day. I did think it showed signs of brightening a little, but now it's as bad as ever.'

The music was laid out for me . . . the pieces Sir William had chosen, I glanced at the top sheet, which was Beethoven's *Moonlight Sonata*.

'I think I'd better light the candles,' said Mrs Lincroft.

I agreed and when she had done so I sat down at the piano and she tiptoed out of the room.

As I played I was thinking of Napier and feeling increasing indignation at the way in which he was accused before anything had been proved against him.

I finished the sonata and to my surprise the next piece was Saint-Saëns' *Danse Macabre*, an unusual choice, I thought. I began to play. I thought of Pietro who had always brought something indescribably spine-chilling into the playing of this piece. He said that when he played it, he saw the musician as a kind of pied piper who, instead of luring children into the mountain side, brought people out of their graves to dance round the piper . . . in the dance of death.

It had grown darker outside and the light from the candles was scarcely adequate, but I did not really need to read the music.

And then suddenly I was not alone. I thought at first that my playing had indeed conjured up a ghost for the figure in the doorway looked like corpse.

'Go away . . . Go away . . .' cried Sir William. He was staring at me in a fixed, stony way. 'Why . . . did you . . . come . . . back.'

I stood up, and as I did so he cried out in horror; and the next thing I knew he was lying on the floor.

Frantically I called to Mrs Lincroft, who fortunately was not far off.

She stared at him in dismay.

'What . . . happened?'

'I was playing *Danse Macabre*,' I began . . .

I did not finish, for I thought she was going to faint.

Then she was her competent self again. 'We must send for the doctor,' she said.

Sir William was very ill indeed. He had had another stroke and there were several doctors with him. It was thought that he might not recover.

I told them that I had been playing and suddenly I had looked up and seen him in the doorway. As he could scarcely walk it must have been a great effort for him to do so, and that effort, said the doctors, could have been the cause of his collapse.

In a day or two it was believed that he was not going to die after all and Mrs Lincroft was greatly relieved.

She said to me: 'This will mean that Napier will stay after all. I'm sure Sir William doesn't remember what has happened to Edith. He's a little hazy about everything and keeps fancying he's back in the past.'

That July was a wet one; there was rain for several days and the skies were overcast.

Sybil Stacy came to my room to talk to me. I had to light the candles although it was only late afternoon. Sybil in deep mauve dress trimmed with black bows – and mauve bows in her hair – had chosen a colour which I had never seen her wear before.

'Mourning,' she whispered.

I started up from my little table at which I had been preparing lessons.

She wagged a finger coyly at me. 'For Edith,' she said.

'But how can you be sure?'

'I *am* sure. She would have come back if she wasn't dead. Besides, everything points to it. Don't you think?'

'I don't know what to think, but I prefer to believe that she is alive and one day she will walk in.' I turned to the door as though I expected her. Sybil turned too and watched it expectantly.

Then she shook her head. 'No, she can't come back. She's dead, poor child. I know it.'

'You can't be sure,' I repeated.

'Strange things are happening in this house,' she went on. 'Don't you feel it?'

I shook my head.

'You aren't telling the truth, Mrs Verlaine. You *do* feel it. You're sensitive. I know it. I shall put it in my picture when I paint it. Strange things *are* going on . . . and you know it.'

'I wish . . . oh, how I wish Edith would come back!'

'She would if she could. She was always so meek and would do what people wanted. You know what's happened, don't you . . . to William?'

'He's very ill, I'm afraid.'

'Yes, and all because he came to see who was playing.'

'He knew I was playing.'

'Oh no, he did not, Mrs Verlaine. That's where you're wrong. He thought it was someone else.'

'How could he? I play to him often.'

'He chooses the music for you, doesn't he?'

'Yes.'

'I know. He chooses the pieces he likes to hear, pieces which remind him of pleasant things. And now because of what happened Napier will stay. I believe Napier would have had to go but for what happened. So what is good for Napier is bad for Sir William. One man's meat, so they say, is another's poison. Oh how true! How true! Listen to the rain. It rained on St Swithin's Day. You know what that means, Mrs Verlaine. Forty days and forty nights it will rain now . . . and all because it rained on St Swithin's Day.'

She snuffed out the candles. 'I like the gloom,' she said. 'It fits everything doesn't it? Tell me what piece you were playing when Sir William came to the doorway.'

'*Danse Macabre.*'

She shivered. 'The Dance of Death. Well, it was nearly, wasn't it? For Sir William. It's an eerie piece of music. Did you think it was strange that he should have chosen it?'

'Yes, I did.'

'You would have thought it more strange if you had known it was the last thing Isabella played that day. She sat at the piano all the morning and she played it over and over again. And William said: "For God's sake stop playing that mournful thing!" And she stopped and she went out into the woods and shot herself. It's never been played in this house since . . . until you sat at the piano and played it.'

'It was in the music he set for me to play for him.'

'Yes, but he didn't put it there.'

'Oh! Then who did?'

'That's what would tell us a great deal. It was someone who wanted Sir William to hear it . . . to think that it was

Isabella come back to haunt him. It was someone who hoped he'd get up from that chair and see you playing there . . . because it was dark, wasn't it . . . as dark as it is now. It was someone who wanted him to fall down and hurt himself. It was someone who wanted to tell him that they knew.'

'Who could do such a thing? It was cruel.'

'Crueller things have been done in this house. Who do you think would do it? It might have been someone who was afraid of being sent away, and who wouldn't be if Sir William were dead – because he might have died, you know. Then on the other hand it might have been someone else.'

I was deeply disturbed. I wanted her to leave, that I might be alone with my thoughts.

She seemed to sense this. In any case she had said what she had come to say.

'How can we be sure, Mrs Verlaine?' she asked.

And shaking her head sadly she went to the door.

Sylvia came to her lessons with her two plaits wound round her head – a concession to growing up. Good Heavens, I thought, is her mother really trying to catch Godfrey Wilmot as a husband for her daughter? Poor Sylvia, she looked most self-conscious. In fact she almost always was. She gave me the impression that she had been sent to do something unpleasant and would know no peace until she had done her duty.

She was sixteen – another year before she reached that age which was the conventional one for putting up the hair.

She went through her lesson in a parrotlike way. What could I say? Only: 'Try to get a little more expression into it, Sylvia. Try to feel what the music is *saying*.'

She looked puzzled. 'But it doesn't *say* anything, Mrs Verlaine.'

I sighed. Really, I thought, now that Edith was gone my job was not worth doing. I could have made a competent pianist of Edith, someone to enchant the guests who came to her parties. I could have taught her to draw comfort and great pleasure from music – but Sylvia, Allegra and Alice . . .

Her hands were in her lap, those rather spatulate fingers with the nails painfully trying to grow. Even now she lifted her hand to her lips and dropped it hastily tasting in time the bitter aloes which her mother made her use.

'The trouble is, Sylvia, that you are too absentminded. You're not thinking of your music. You're thinking of something else.'

Her face lightened suddenly. 'I was thinking of a horrible story Alice wrote. You know she's always writing stories. Mr Wilmot says her essays show real talent. Alice says she wants to write stories like Wilkie Collins . . . the sort that make you shiver.'

'She must show me some of her stories. I'd like to see them.'

'She reads them to us sometimes. We have to sit by the light of one candle in her room and she does the actions. It's frightening. She could be an actress too. But she says what she wants most is to write about people.'

'What was this story?'

'It's about a girl who disappears. No one knows where she's gone. But just before she disappeared someone dug a hole in a copse which was near the house where she lived. There were some children who saw the hole in the copse. They nearly fell into it when they were playing and they came and watched and they saw a man. He saw them watching and he said that he was digging a trap to catch a man-eating lion because there were lions in this place. But they didn't believe him because people don't dig traps for lions, they shoot them. Of course he could only say that to the children but to pretend to the grown ups, he said he was going to help someone dig up his fields. But he murdered the girl and buried her in the copse and everyone thought she had run away with her lover.'

'It's not a very healthy sort of story,' I said.

'It makes your hair stand on end,' said Sylvia.

It was certainly making mine do so because I had suddenly remembered seeing Napier come into the stables with gardening tools. He had been helping Mr Brancot to dig his garden, he had said.

When I next rode out alone I turned my horse towards the Brancots' cottage. The garden looked neater than it had when I last saw it. I pulled up and stood looking at it.

I was fortunate, for while I was trying to think of an excuse for calling, old Mr Brancot came out of the house.

'Good afternoon,' I said.

'Good afternoon, Miss.'

'It's Mrs. Mrs Verlaine. I'm the music teacher up at Lovat Stacy.'

'Oh aye. I've heard of you. How are you liking this part of the country?'

'I find it very beautiful.'

He nodded, well pleased. 'Wouldn't want to leave it,' he said. 'Not if you paid me a hundred pounds for doing it.'

I replied that I had no intention of doing so either and added that his garden was looking in good shape.

'Oh yes,' he answered, 'it's looking fine now.'

'Much better than when I last saw it. It's been dug over since then.'

'Dug over and planted,' he said. 'Easy to keep in order now.'

'It must have been a big job. Did you do it all yourself?'

He grinned and whispered: 'Well, between you and me, I had a little help. You won't believe it but one afternoon Mr Napier came out and gave me a hand.'

I felt ridiculously happy. I was terrified that he had been going to say he had done it himself.

As I rode back the conversation with Sylvia kept recurring to me. The girls, naturally, were interested in everything that went on and because – being in that in-between stage, neither grown up nor children – they saw through immature eyes, they did not always interpret correctly. Why had Alice written such a story? How far did imagination feed on facts? Was it possible that she *had* seen someone digging a hole in the copse? Or had Alice imagined it? Perhaps she – or one of the girls – had seen Napier coming back to the house with the gardening tools. That would be enough to fire Alice's imagination; and because of the ruin in the copse and the light which had been seen there, the place had become one of mystery. Someone digging in the copse? Digging what? The imagination immediately supplied the answer: a grave.

Was this how Alice had worked it out? Did she feel she should make this known, and was she afraid to? She was, I believed, a timid child. I felt certain that her mother had impressed upon her the need for good behaviour that they both might keep their places at Lovat Stacy. Allegra was constantly reminding Alice of her inferior position as the housekeeper's daughter and of the necessity of not making herself troublesome. Unkind Allegra! And yet she, too, was unsure of her position, so I suppose one should not judge her too harshly.

I made up my mind that Alice had seen Napier with the

gardening tools, had felt it her duty to put this on record, but was afraid of giving offence, so she wrote a story which was largely imagination, but which did say something of what she felt should be said. Alice wanted to do the right thing which was to tell what she knew; but as it was only a suspicion she dared not mention it openly. That was the answer.

But suppose Edith *was* buried in the copse. And Roma? Where was Roma? They had to be somewhere.

If someone had dug a grave in the copse, wouldn't there be some sign of it? The grass would not be properly grown, so surely it should not be difficult to find a patch of newly disturbed earth.

This was becoming not only sinister but gruesome. I remembered Mrs Lincroft's somewhat oblique warning. Don't interfere. Interference could put *you* into danger.

Edith had been murdered, and if her murderer was aware of my determination to discover him, then *I* was in danger. But I could not help it. I must find the answer.

Having reached the copse I dismounted and tied my horse to a tree.

I looked about me. How still it was! How eerie! But was that because of its associations? Through the trees I could glimpse the grey ruin and instinctively I moved towards it.

The sun glinted through the trees throwing a shifting pattern on the ground. I thought once more: surely if the earth had been disturbed recently it would show.

I stared down at the grass which grew patchily.

If one wanted to dig a grave this would be an ideal place to dig it. Here one would be hidden among the trees and perhaps hear the footsteps of anyone approaching. And if one were seen with the spade in one's hand? 'Oh, I have just been digging for someone who is unable to dig for himself . . .'

'No!' I said and was surprised that I had spoken vehemently and aloud.

As I drew level with the ruins I put out a hand and gingerly touched those stone walls. One day I promised myself when the light shows I'll come down and see who is playing that little trick. I went through the gap in the stones where the door had been and stood there looking up at the sky through the damaged roof. My footsteps made a light noise on the broken tiled floor and the sound startled me. Yes, even by daylight I was a little frightened.

I felt as though those grey walls blackened by the fire were shutting me in; I turned quickly and went out into the copse.

If anyone had dug a hole, might he – or she – not have done so near those walls for since the place had the reputation of being haunted, people avoided it; perhaps it was just the spot in which to dig a victim's grave. And the light? Was that meant to keep people away from the spot? I felt I had to find a reason for all these strange happenings.

I studied the earth near the wall. There was one patch without grass. I went down on my hands and knees to examine it more closely. And then . . . the crackle of undergrowth; the shadow looming over me.

'Searching for something?'

I gasped and standing up looked into Napier's face. His voice was mocking but there was a deadly earnestness in his eyes and I knew he was angry.

'I . . . I didn't hear you until a second ago.'

'What on earth are you doing? Praying? Or have you dropped something?'

I said: 'My brooch . . .'

He touched the cameo at my throat. 'It's there . . . securely pinned.'

'Oh, I thought . . .'

I was making a bad job of it but I could not tell him that I – like everyone else – suspected him of murdering his wife. I didn't suspect him. I hastily corrected that. I wanted to prove that he was innocent in face of all the calumnies.

He stood, that sardonic smile on his face, not helping me out of my embarrassment at all.

'I saw you from the distance at the Brancots' cottage.'

'I didn't see you.'

'I know. Brancot told me you'd been complimenting him on the garden and that he'd told you I gave him a hand. You remember . . . seeing me come back with my spade?'

'I remember.'

He laughed. 'Well, it's brave of you to come to this place. It has such an evil reputation.'

'In broad daylight?' I said, recovering my calm.

'Well, if one is alone . . .'

'But I am not.'

'When you come to think of it, it is the fear of *not* being alone that makes people afraid.'

'You mean they're afraid of ghosts?'

'You looked very startled when I came on you kneeling here. Perhaps you are a little uneasy now.' He took my wrist and with a mocking smile put his finger on my pulse. 'A little too fast, I think,' he commented.

'I admit to being startled. You came on me so suddenly.'

'You weren't looking for the brooch, were you? The first place you would look is at your throat and it is there.' He put his hands on my brooch and came and stood very close to me. I caught my breath . . . as he meant me to. All friendliness seemed to have gone from him now. He knew what had been in my mind and I think he hated me for it.

'I'd like us to be frank,' he said reproachfully, dropping his hands.

'Of course.'

'But you haven't been, have you? Did you come because you think Edith is buried here . . . in this copse?'

'She must be somewhere.'

'And you think that someone . . . killed her and buried her here?'

'I don't think that can be the solution.'

'Have you an alternative solution?'

I said: 'I think it rather strange that two people disappeared in this neighbourhood.'

'Two?' he said.

'Have you forgotten the archæologist?'

'She disappeared too. Why, of course.' He took a pace backwards and leaned against the wall of the chapel. 'Do you think she's buried here, too And have you decided on the murderer?'

'How can I? But I believe we should all feel better if we knew the answer to those questions.'

'Except the murderer. Don't you think he would feel far worse?'

'I do not think he – or she – can be feeling very happy now.'

'Why not?'

'Could anyone take life and be happy?'

'If a man saw himself as all important and others of no account he would see no reason why he should not eliminate a person as he would a moth or a wasp.'

'I suppose there are such people.'

'I fear there are. I imagine our murderer is delighted with himself. He has won. He has gained what he set out to gain and the rest don't even know who he is. He has fooled them all. Let us walk through the copse together examining the earth for the graves of the victims. Would you care to do that?'

I said: 'I have work to do. I must get back to the house.'

He smiled as though he did not believe me, and we walked back to our horses. He held mine while I mounted; then leaping into the saddle he rode beside me to the house.

I went straight up to my room and looked at myself in the mirror. I hoped my emotions did not show on my face, for I was not even sure what they were.

I was terribly afraid and would not face the possibilities which were thrusting themselves into my mind. I would not believe them because I was determined not to.

Chapter Nine

G odfrey Wilmot was constantly seeking to be alone with me. This was not easy, for Mrs Rendall contrived to see that we did not have many opportunities.

Perhaps I should admit to a certain mischievous pleasure in teasing her, hoping it would help to lighten the heavy mood which had settled upon me. I was trying to thrust all thoughts of Napier from my mind and the company of Godfrey helped me to do this more than anything else. There was his knowledge of my identity; there was his love of music and his deep interest in that subject which had enthralled my sister and my parents and had in a way been responsible for their deaths. There was comfort, too, in feeling my friendship growing for a charming man who was open and frank and free of those complexes which while they seemed to cast some sort of spell upon me, could make me uneasy and extremely apprehensive.

Certainly I made no attempt to avoid Godfrey and we used to laugh together about Mrs Rendall's attitude and plan how to frustrate her endeavours to prevent our being alone together.

Sometimes we met in the church where Godfrey went to

practise the organ. I would slip in while he was playing and this was what I did on the day after my uncomfortable encounter with Napier in the copse.

The church was a beautiful example of fourteenth-century architecture with its grey stone tower and lichen covered walls. I stood at the door listening to the full tones of the organ and was deeply moved for Godfrey had a masterly touch. I did not want to disturb him so I stood very still while I gazed about me at the stained glass window – the one dedicated to Beau; the Stacy pew; the list of vicars engraved on the wall from the first in 1347 to Arthur Rendall in the year 1880. The musty damp smell of age was more apparent when the church was empty, and I imagined generations of Stacys coming here to worship. I thought of Beau and Napier being baptised at the font, of Sybil, dreaming of coming to this altar to her bridegroom. As the music came to its triumphant finale I went over to the organ.

'I'm glad you came,' he said. 'I was beginning to be a little worried about you.'

'Worried about me? Why?'

'The idea suddenly came to me. You could be putting yourself into danger.'

'What makes you say that?'

'It's the news about Mrs Stacy. When we thought she had gone off with her lover, looking for your sister seemed a reasonably safe project. But if these two disappearances are linked it appears that someone must be responsible for them. You can't make two people disappear very well without killing them. It struck me that we have a dangerous murderer in our midst. He wouldn't be very pleased with someone who probed into his affairs, would he? And it may be that when he isn't pleased with people he . . . eliminates them.'

'So you've marked me down for the next victim?'

'God forbid! But shouldn't you be careful?'

'I see what you mean. Have you anyone in mind?'

'Oh yes.'

'Who?'

'The husband, of course.'

'Isn't that too obvious?'

'Good heavens, this isn't a puzzle. It's real life. Who would want to be rid of Mrs Stacy except her husband?'

'There could be others.'

'Think of the reasons. I understand she was an heiress. He gets her money. And he wasn't very eager to marry her in the first place.'

'He had the money already so why bother to murder her?'

'He was heartily sick of her.'

'I don't like this conversation. It's . . . uncharitable. We have no right to continue with it.'

'But we must be practical.'

'If being practical means maligning innocent people . . .'

'But how do you know he is innocent?'

'Shouldn't one presume a man to be innocent until he is proved guilty?'

'You're talking about British justice. We're not judges . . . just amateur sleuths. We have to look at all possibilities.'

'In that case I might suggest that you are guilty, and you me.'

'I might. But where are the motives?'

'I daresay we could think of some. You might be a cousin in disguise who wants to inherit Lovat Stacy so you murder Edith and hope her husband will be accused of the crime and hanged, which will make you the heir.'

'Not bad,' he said. 'Not bad at all. And you want to

marry into the Stacy family so you murder Edith and leave the way clear for yourself.'

'You see,' I pointed out, 'you can make up a case against anyone.'

'But what of your sister? Where does she come into it?'

'That's what we have to find out.'

It was at this point that I felt certain we were being observed. I looked uneasily about me. Godfrey had noticed nothing. What was it? I couldn't say. Just an uncanny feeling – the extra sense one gets that somewhere, unseen, someone is watching . . . malignantly.

What was the matter with me? I could not explain this strange feeling to Godfrey. It sounded so absurd. I heard nothing. I saw nothing; I merely sensed it. And he had thought I was fanciful in the cottage.

'Be careful,' he said. 'Don't forget there may be a murderer among us.'

I looked over my shoulder and shivered.

'What's the matter?' he asked.

'Oh . . . nothing.'

'I've frightened you. Good! It's what I intended. You will have to be very careful in future.'

I kept thinking of Napier in the copse and my heart refused to accept the inference which my brain insisted on presenting to me.

'I'm determined to find out what happened to my sister,' I said fiercely.

'We both will,' he assured me, 'but we'll be cautious. We'll work together. Any little clue one of us discovers should be passed on to the other.'

I said nothing of Alice's story which had so disturbed me; I said nothing of my encounter with Napier in the copse.

He went on: 'I can't help feeling that the answer is somewhere on the dig. It's because of your sister. She was the first. I think we'll find the answer there.'

I let him expound on this – anything to stop him seeking to hang suspicion on Napier.

We were startled suddenly by a little cough behind us.

Sylvia was coming silently up the aisle towards the organ.

'Mamma sent me to look for you, Mr Wilmot. She says would you care to come to tea in the drawing-room.'

The girls had invited me to ride with them. I said I should be delighted and in due course we set out.

'There are gipsies in Meadow Three Acres,' Allegra told me. 'One of them spoke to me and said her name was Serena Smith. Mrs Lincroft was not very pleased when I told her.'

'She was not pleased because she knows Sir William will not be,' said Alice quickly in defence of her mother.

Allegra rode on a little way ahead and called over her shoulder: 'I'm going to see them.'

'My mother says they're a disgrace to the place,' said Sylvia.

'She would!' retorted Allegra. 'She hates anything that's . . . fun. I like gipsies. I'm half one myself.'

'Do they come here often?' I asked, remembering Mrs Lincroft's reaction to the news that they had arrived.

'I don't think so,' replied Alice. 'They roam the country never staying long in one place. Just fancy, Mrs Verlaine. That must be rather exciting, don't you think?'

'I'm sure I'd rather stay in one place.'

Her eyes grew dreamy and I wondered whether she would write a story about gipsies. I must see some of her stories one of these days. It could well be that if she had no talent for music she had for literature. She read a great deal; she was extremely industrious and she had undoubted imagination. Perhaps I should speak to Godfrey about her.

Allegra called to us not to dawdle and we broke into a canter. It was not long before we reached the encampment.

There were about four gaily coloured caravans in the field which was called Meadow Three Acres. But there was no sign of any gipsies.

'Don't go too close,' I cautioned Allegra.

'Why ever not, Mrs Verlaine? They won't hurt us.'

'They might not like to be stared at. You should respect their privacy.'

Allegra looked at me in astonishment. 'They haven't any privacy, Mrs Verlaine. People who live in caravans don't expect to have any.'

The sound of our voices may have carried over the air for as we stood there a woman came out of one of the caravans and towards us.

I could not say what it was but there was a vague air of familiarity about her. I felt I had seen her before, though I could not say where. She was plump and her red blouse was stretched to bursting point over her full breasts; her skirt was a little ragged about the hem, her legs and feet very brown and bare. Big gold-coloured Creole earrings dangled in her ears. Her laughter shattered the silence and while it was loud and raucous it suggested that she found life amusing. She had a bush of dark curly hair and was, in a robust and voluptuous way, beautiful.

'Hallo,' she called. 'Have you come to see the gipsies?'

'Yes,' said Allegra.

I saw a flash of white teeth. 'You have a fondness for the gipsies, you there with the black hair. Shall I tell you why? You're almost a gipsy yourself.'

'Who told you?'

'Ah . . . that would be telling. But I will tell you your name. A pretty one. It's Allegra.'

'Are you telling my fortune?'

'Past, present, and future.'

'I think,' I said, 'we should be going.'

The girls ignored me and so did the gipsy.

'Allegra from the big house. Deserted by her wicked mother. Never mind, my dear. There's a charming Prince and great fortune awaiting you.'

'Is there really?' said Allegra. 'What about . . . the others?'

'Let me see . . . there's the young lady from the parsonage and the other from the big house . . . though she doesn't exactly belong there. Give me your palm, dear.'

I said: 'We have no money.'

'Don't need money from some company, Madam. Let me see . . .' Alice held out her hand which looked very white and small in the gipsy's brown one.

'A . . .' said the gipsy. 'Alice. That's it.'

'You're wonderful,' breathed Allegra.

'Little Alice who lives in the big house and is not quite of it . . . but will be one day because someone very important is going to see that she is.'

'Oh,' cried Alice, 'it's wonderful.'

'I think we should be going back,' I said again.

The gipsy stood watching me; her hands on her hips.

'Introduce me to the lady,' she said insolently.

'She's the music teacher,' began Allegra.

'Oh, can't you tell . . . for her too?' cried Alice.

'The music teacher. Tra la la . . .' said the gipsy. 'Be careful, lady. Beware of a man with blue eyes . . .'

'And what about Sylvia?' cried Alice.

Sylvia's face puckered and she looked as though she were going to run away. 'She is the vicar's daughter and takes lessons with us,' Allegra explained.

'You don't have to tell,' reproached Alice. 'She knows.'

The bold gipsy turned on Sylvia. 'You'll always do what your mother tells you, won't you, ducky?'

Sylvia blushed and Allegra whispered: 'She knows . . . It's special powers. Gipsies have them.'

I said: 'It's all very interesting and now we must go.'

Allegra began to protest but I signed to Alice to turn her horse and obediently she did so.

'That's right,' said the gipsy, 'when in doubt, run away.'

Alice and I had started to walk our horses away from the encampment. Sylvia followed us but Allegra lingered.

I was thinking: Is it possible that that woman is Allegra's mother? The likeness was startling and if she were that would account for her knowing who the girls were.

Blowsy, voluptuous, sensuous as she now was, she must have been very attractive fifteen years ago when she was not much more than fifteen herself.

I shivered.

Do I really want to be involved in the affairs of Lovat Stacy, I asked myself as we rode back to the house.

Once again Mrs Rendall came to Lovat Stacy like a militant general, and Mrs Lincroft met her in the hall. I was with Mrs Lincroft at the time but Mrs Rendall took no notice of my presence.

'It is disgraceful,' she said. 'Gipsies here. I remember the last time they came. Making the lanes and fields untidy. They're everywhere with their baskets and clothes pegs . . . and cross your hand with silver. I said to the vicar, "Something must be done, and the sooner the better." It does happen to be Sir William's land and he is the one to give them their marching orders. That, Mrs Lincroft, is why I have come to see Sir William . . . so please tell him I am here, and take me to him as soon as possible.'

'I'm sorry Mrs Rendall, but Sir William is very ill. He is resting now.'

'Resting! At this hour. He'll want to know that the gipsies are here surely? He hates them on his land. I think he made that pretty clear.'

I rose to go but Mrs Lincroft signed for me to stay.

'I'm sorry, Mrs Rendall,' she said with the utmost firmness, 'but Sir William is really not well enough to be worried with these matters. I think you should see Mr Napier Stacy. He is managing everything now you know.'

'Mr Napier Stacy!' cried Mrs Rendall. 'Certainly not. I shall see Sir William and I'll thank you, Mrs Lincroft, to tell him I am here.'

'He would not thank me, Mrs Rendall. Nor would the doctor on whose orders Sir William is not to be disturbed.'

'The vicar and I are determined that something shall be done.'

'You should, then, speak to Mr Napier Stacy about the matter.'

Mrs Rendall cast venomous glances both at me and Mrs Lincroft and stalked out.

Two days later I found a sealed envelope in my room addressed to me. I opened it and read:

'DEAR C,
Will you come to the cottage at 6.30 to-night. I have something important to tell you.

G.W.'

Terse! I thought. And to the point. It was the first time I had received a letter from Godfrey and I guessed he had thought that six-thirty would be a convenient time, for it would enable us to have a quiet chat before we went back – he to the vicarage and I to Lovat Stacy – for dinner.

I slipped out of the house and arrived there a few minutes before the appointed time. It was very quiet and I didn't see anyone on the way there and it did occur to me even then that this was one of the quietest of times when the day was not yet over and the evening had not begun.

I went into the cottage and as Godfrey was not there I made my way to the upper rooms to watch for his arrival.

I stood at the little leaded paned window and looked out across the remains and thought of Roma, picturing a hundred scenes from our childhood, and I tried to imagine from all I knew of her what she could possibly have done on that day she disappeared.

Time passed slowly. It was five minutes after the half hour, and it was unlike Godfrey to be late, for I had discovered him to be the most punctual of people. I smiled, visualising him leaving the vicarage and being detained by Mrs Rendall.

The minutes were passing. Ten minutes late. How unlike him. I had no premonition of danger until I smelt that fearful acrid smell of burning. Even then I thought at first that it was something outside. I attempted to open the window but the bolt had grown rusty and I couldn't move it. Then I heard the crackle of flames and I knew that the fire was not outside but inside the cottage.

I went through to the communicating room and saw – though this did not strike me immediately – that the door to the stairs was shut, although I had left it open. I went to it and seized the handle, but I could not open the door.

Then the full horror of the situation came home to me. The door was locked. Someone had been in the cottage when

I entered it or followed me in, had crept up the stairs while I was looking out of the window, and locked me in . . . and then that person had set the cottage on fire.

I hammered on the door. 'Let me out!' I cried. 'Who's there?'

I ran to the window and desperately tried to open it. I could not but it would have been no use if I had. I could never have got through it. There was a broom propped up in a corner. I tried to break through those leaden panes but it was not easy to do so.

There was now a haze of smoke in the room and I began to cough and splutter. I could feel the heat below my feet. This was no accident. Someone had deliberately locked me in and set fire to the cottage.

Godfrey! I thought. But no . . . never, yet the note had come from Godfrey. I had been lured to this place to meet him. I couldn't believe it. Not Godfrey.

I picked up the broom and through the sheer force of horror smashed one of the little panes.

'Help!' I cried. 'Fire! . . . Fire!'

There was no response to my plea – only silence out there.

I went to the door . . . that heavy studded door which had so pleased Roma. I hammered on it. I turned the handle and shook it. But the horrible fact remained. I was locked in a burning cottage. Locked in!

I ran back to the window and shouted. I came back to the door and shook the handle. I could scarcely see now for the smoke was so thick that it was suffocating me.

Then my heart leaped with joy for I heard a shout from below.

I shouted out: 'Here. I'm up here.'

Then the smoke and the heat were too much for me . . . I felt the overpowering suffocation.

Suddenly it seemed I was not alone. Something was wrapped about my face. Urgent hands were pulling at me.

'Quick! Run! Run with me. I can't carry you.'

It was Alice's voice. Alice's hands . . . and I was being dragged through such heat that it was almost unbearable.

I was lying in the cool air and I heard voices.

'You're all right. You're all right.'

Then I was being lifted into a carriage I presumed, for I vaguely heard the distant clop clop of horses' hoofs.

'If it hadn't been for Alice, heaven knows what would have become of you,' said Mrs Lincroft.

I was in bed; the doctor had seen me, given me a sedative and Mrs Lincroft orders that I was to sleep.

Alice had seated herself by my bed, like my good angel, determined that having saved my life she would continue to protect it.

'All you have to do is rest,' went on her mother. 'You've had a nasty shock.'

So I obeyed and lay there thinking of Godfrey's note and of Roma walking out of the cottage and never coming back . . . and of my being lured there and locked in that I might die.

Godfrey! I thought, and I saw his face and it was Napier's face . . . and they were both standing over me, laughing at me. 'Trust no one,' said a voice in my mind. 'No one at all.'

Alice whispered, 'It's all right now, Mrs Verlaine. It's all over now. You're safe in bed.'

Alice was the heroine of the hour. She even looked exalted. But it was not only that; her eyebrows were a little singed and her left hand slightly burned where she had beaten out the flames which had caught my dress.

'She showed admirable presence of mind,' said Mrs Lincroft, her eyes full of tears. 'I'm so proud of my little girl.'

Alice said: 'I didn't do anything that anyone else wouldn't do. I was going over to the vicarage to get my history book which I'd left there. I wanted it to do my homework. What a blessing that I'd left it behind that morning. And I saw the cottage was on fire so I ran to look . . . and then I heard Mrs Verlaine shouting . . .'

John Downs, one of the gardeners at Lovat Stacy, had been in the neighbourhood too. He had heard Alice shout that there was a fire and he had run after her to the cottage, but he would have been too late to save me, although he helped when he saw Alice dragging me from the place.

'Just in time,' everyone was saying it.

'My word, that Mrs Verlaine has had a lucky escape. As for young Alice Lincroft, I reckon she deserves a medal.'

I was suffering from shock and kept in my bed for several days although otherwise I was not hurt. I had come through the fire miraculously. Alice had saved my life.

She sat by my bed during those days as though guarding me. I would awake from my troubled dozes to see her serene face at my bedside. She glowed; she was clearly delighted with the part she had played in my rescue. Who would not have been?

But there were other matters to consider.

People came to see me, among them Napier and Godfrey. Napier's eyes haunted me long after he left. He looked so fearful, and the memory was like a dose of healing medicine. Godfrey came too. Godfrey . . . He too was full of concern but I remembered when I saw him that it was due to his note that I had gone to that cottage.

He sat by my bed and I said to him: 'Why did you send the note?'

'What note?' he asked.

'The note asking me to meet you at the cottage.'

He looked helplessly about him.

'It's been a terrible shock to poor Mrs Verlaine,' said Mrs Lincroft. 'The doctor says she should rest for some days. She gets . . . nightmares. Anyone would.'

Godfrey looked bewildered and when I pressed about the note he changed the subject.

In less than a week I was recovered although I still dreamed of the cottage and as I slipped into unconsciousness I would often imagine I was in that upper room . . . locked in . . . while below a monster lurked waiting to destroy me. Sometimes I called out in these dreams and would awake in a cold sweat of fear.

The doctor said it was natural. I had had a terrible shock but my nightmares would diminish. In the meantime I should try not to think about my ordeal in the cottage.

I had looked for the note and could not find it but I asked Godfrey again for an explanation.

'I wrote no such note,' he declared.

'But I saw it. It was the reason I went to the cottage.'

He shook his head.

I went on in exasperation: 'It was addressed to me and it said as far as I remember: "Dear C. Will you come to the cottage at 6.30 to-night? I have something important to tell you. G.W."'

'I should never have written such a note.'

'Then who did?'

He stared at me in horror. 'Where is this note?' he asked.

'I don't know. I may have left it in my room. I may have put it into my pocket. But I can't find it now.'

'A pity,' he said. 'But you know my writing.'

'It's the first note you've ever written to me. But I've seen your writing of course, and it didn't occur to me that you hadn't written it.'

'Caroline, if someone forged my handwriting . . .'

'*If?*' I demanded. 'Are you suggesting that there was no note?'

'No . . . no . . . of course not.' He was a little embarrassed. 'But . . . if . . . I mean someone must have sent that note to get you to the cottage.'

'That inference is obvious.'

'What does it mean?'

'It could mean,' I said, 'that I am marked down as the next victim.'

'Caroline!'

'Well, I should have been, but for Alice.'

He nodded. 'But, my dear Caroline, it's . . . it's *frightening*!'

'I agree with you,' I said coolly, for I could not forgive him for merely hinting that I might have imagined that note. 'Roma . . . Edith . . . and now myself. Where is the connection? Is it because the person responsible for these two disappearances knows that I am trying to find the reason for them?'

'But *who* knows that you are doing this?' he asked. 'I am the only one who does. You don't think that I . . .'

I laughed and was almost immediately sober. 'But, Godfrey, someone is trying to kill me. What can I do?'

'You could go away from here.'

'Go away!' I visualised my lonely life, shut away from

Lovat Stacy, not knowing what was going on in that house which had become the background of my new existence. I knew that whatever happened I did not want that.

'I shall not go away,' I said vehemently. 'I'll take special care and the next time I receive a note suggesting a meeting place I shall insist on confirming it in the presence of witnesses.'

'For Heaven's sake do.'

'Godfrey, I do wonder how that note came to me . . .'

'And in my handwriting . . . at least with my initials.'

A cold sensation made me shiver uncontrollably. Where was the note? I was sure I had not destroyed it. I believed I had left it in my room. And there was the mystery of the locked door. Alice had said she had thought it was hard to open; she thought there was something strange about the handle.

'But,' she had said, 'I was so frightened that I didn't take much notice of it. I only knew I had to get Mrs Verlaine out. I just forced the door open. I can't remember it clearly. Once I got into the cottage I kept saying to myself: 'I've got to get Mrs Verlaine out . . .' and I don't even remember running up the stairs.'

Everyone said that was understandable in the circumstances, and that the door had become jammed possibly after all the rain we had, and finding it difficult to open I assumed it was locked which it obviously could not have been. I had panicked, was the general opinion, although no one said this. I had believed myself to be locked in a burning cottage; it was enough to make anyone get into a panic.

And the cause of the fire? Roma had used paraffin oil with which to cook and there was a drum in the outhouse which had obviously contained the remains of her supply. The theory was that a tramp had been sleeping in the cottage and left a pipe or cigarette smouldering somewhere. Fires could start easily enough.

'Tramps,' said Godfrey. 'It's the answer. And do you remember that day you thought you saw a shadow at the window? That could have been one of them and he hid himself in the outhouse when we came out.'

It was a plausible explanation, but somehow I did not believe it. I was certain the incident had been cleverly and diabolically planned.

If I mentioned this people would say I was letting my imagination run away with my common sense. Godfrey felt this, I was sure; and if he, who knew I was Roma's sister and had come here to investigate her disappearance thought that, how much more readily would others, who did not know that there was a special reason for my being here.

I knew that but for Alice I should have been burned to death – murdered as my sister and Edith, I was certain now, had been before me.

Chapter Ten

It took me some weeks to recover from the shock of my experience. Everyone was most concerned for me, which was flattering, but I just could not rid myself of the notion that one of these people who now inquired so solicitously after my health, had deliberately tried to kill me. But I kept my thoughts to myself; I pretended to accept the theory that a tramp's carelessness had started the fire, that it had probably been smouldering in the outhouse for hours and, by some trick of fate, had burst into a conflagration embracing the lower part of the cottage some five or ten minutes after I had entered the place and gone upstairs; and the door had not been locked, merely jammed. That was the comforting theory.

I avoided Napier. I could not bear to look into his face for fear I should read something there which I dreaded. I kept thinking of our meeting in the copse and it haunted my dreams.

Mrs Lincroft suggested that I take a little time off my duties.

'You will recover all the quicker,' she said. 'It was a horrible shock. And it won't hurt the girls to miss their music

lessons for a while. They can, in any case, do their practising.'

I myself found a great solace in the piano. I would sit by
the hour playing Chopin and Schumann and trying to stop
my thoughts going back over those nightmare moments when
I had realised I was trapped in the cottage. One day I heard
the girls discussing the fire. Allegra was leaning her elbows
on the table looking dreamily into space. While I sorted out
my music I listened to them.

'You'll write a story about the fire, I expect,' said Allegra.
'I'll read it to you when it's ready.'

'All about a gallant rescue,' said Sylvia. 'I wish I could
do a gallant rescue.'

'I know,' mocked Allegra. 'You'd like to rescue Mr Wilmot
from a burning cottage. You'd have to find another . . .
because that one's no good now.'

'It's odd,' mused Sylvia. 'Mamma was saying it was
odd . . .'

'Well,' mocked Allegra, 'it must be odd then.'

'. . . that there were two fires. The chapel in the copse
and the cottage. That's two, isn't it?'

'Your mathematics are improving,' said Allegra. 'Full
marks for a correct calculation. Two it is.'

'I'm only saying it's a coincidence and so it is. Two fires
and two disappearing ladies. I think that is very strange.'

'Two ladies?' queried Allegra.

'Don't say you've forgotten the archæologist,' said Alice.
Sylvia whispered: 'And there were nearly three.'

'But Mrs Verlaine didn't *disappear*,' pointed out Alice.

'Suppose no one had known she had gone to the cottage
and she had just been found there. There would have been
three ladies then.'

'But they would have found her . . . remains,' said
Alice.

A hush fell on them because they had become aware of me.

I was standing by the Stacy vault in the graveyard when Godfrey came to meet me. It was no use meeting in the church during his organ practice now; we had been discovered and Mrs Rendall was apt to send Sylvia either to call him or to sit and 'enjoy' the music.

'Sylvia has always *loved* organ music,' Mrs Rendall had said. 'I think it would be better if she studied the organ rather than the piano. She certainly doesn't seem to be making much progress in that direction, though she does work hard. Perhaps Sylvia is not at fault and if *people* are more interested in other things, it may not be surprising that their pupils suffer.'

Although since the fire, her attitude – like that of everyone else – had been gentler towards me, because of Godfrey's interest in me, she had added me to her many targets for attack, and because he and I were aware of this and knew the reason for it, the possibilities which could arise from our friendship were stressed.

As he came towards me, wending his way through the gravestones, the sun on his hair, I thought how good looking he was – not handsome, it was true, but there was great charm in his expression which came from the character within I was sure, and I thought how fortunate I was to have found such a friend. There was no doubt that friendship between us was growing at a great pace.

The incident of the fire had brought us even closer together and I found his concern for me most touching. He was particularly disturbed because I had gone to the cottage in response to a note which was supposed to have come from him. That, in my opinion, was the most alarming aspect of the affair. I had been *lured* to the cottage.

I had told no one but him about the note, and although his reaction when he had first heard of it was that I had had a shock and had imagined it, he was now perturbed. I persuaded him to say nothing; I thought it possible that the person who had written that note might betray knowledge of it in some way; but no one did. As for Godfrey he was constantly urging me to go away because it was clearly unsafe here. I could take a holiday, stay with his family. They would be delighted to have me.

'And what about Roma?' I demanded.

'Roma is dead, I feel sure of it. And if she is, nothing you can do will bring her back.'

'It's something I have to find out, no matter . . .'

He understood but he continued to be very uneasy. So was I. I had developed a habit of looking over my shoulder constantly whenever I was alone. I made sure that my door was locked every night. At least I was on my guard.

Now Godfrey was smiling as he saw me. 'I escaped the watch dog,' he said. 'It is believed that I have gone to play the organ. Little is it known that I'm skulking about the graveyard in the company of that teacher of music who has failed to turn Sylvia Rendall into Clara Schumann.'

'You're looking pleased with yourself this morning.'

'It's rather good news.'

'Can it be shared?'

'Certainly it can. I have had a living offered to me.'

'So you'll be leaving.'

'You look alarmed. How delightfully flattering. It's not for six months. Ah, now you look relieved. Equally flattering. A great deal can happen in six months.'

'Have you told the Rendalls?'

'Not yet. I fear when I do Mrs Vicar will bring up the

big guns. No one knows yet. I thought it appropriate to tell you first. Though of course I shall have to tell the vicar today. I must give him ample time to find a substitute. And, of course, if he does find someone before, I shall retire gracefully.'

'Mrs Rendall will never allow that.'

He smiled. 'You haven't asked for details.'

'I haven't had much opportunity yet. Please tell me.'

'The most delightful parish . . . in the country . . . not too far from London so that visits will be frequently possible. An ideal spot. I know it well. An uncle of mine held the living at one time before his bishopric. I spent quite a lot of my childhood there.'

'It certainly sounds ideal.'

'It is, I do assure you. I'd like you to see it.'

'And how long do you think you'll remain there before you become a bishop?'

He looked at me reproachfully. 'You make me sound like an ambitious man.'

I put my head on one side. 'Some are born to honours, some earn them, and others have them thrust upon them.'

'The quotation is not quite correct but the meaning is clear. Do you believe that some people are born as they say with a silver spoon in their mouths?'

'Perhaps. But it is possible to acquire a spoon even if one hasn't been born with one.'

'What a lot of effort is saved when it's already there. You think life is too easy for me.'

'I believe that life is what we make it . . . for us all.'

'Some of us are lucky though.' His eyes fell on the marble statue of an angel. 'We don't have to look very far. Poor Napier Stacy whose life went wrong through a dreadful accident which could have happened to any boy! He picked up a gun which happened to be loaded and he killed his brother. If that gun hadn't been loaded his life from then on would have been different. Fantastic, isn't it?'

'Fortunately chance is not always so cruel.'

'No. Poor Napier!'

It was like him to spare a thought for Napier in his present elation – for elated he was. He was looking to the future with eagerness and I didn't blame him. While at the moment he was content to dally here, to be amused by Mrs Rendall's scheming – how could she possibly think that Sylvia would be a suitable wife for such a man? – to talk with me, to become mildly involved in the mystery of two strange disappearances.

But it was more than that. He was thinking of me as earnestly as I was of him.

Good Heavens! I thought. I believe he is considering asking me to share this pleasant life of his. Not immediately, of course. Godfrey would never be impulsive. Perhaps that was the reason for his success. But it was there between us. At the moment an affectionate friendship existed, fostered by our common interests and our desire to solve the mystery. I was aware that life was offering me a chance to build something.

'I'd like you to see the place sometime,' he went on warmly. 'I'd like your opinion of it.'

'I do hope you'll show it to me . . . one day.'

'You can be sure I shall.'

I could see it clearly in my mind's eye, a gracious house with a beautiful garden. My home? My drawing-room would look on to the garden and there would be a grand piano. I should play frequently but not professionally; music would be my pleasure and my solace but I should not need to teach impossible musicians again.

I would have children. I could see them . . . beautiful children with placid happy faces – the boys looking like Godfrey, the girls like myself only young, innocent and unmarked by sorrow. I wanted children now as once I had wanted to startle the world with my music. The desire to win fame on the concert platform had gone. Now I wanted happiness, security, a home and a family.

And although Godfrey was not ready to make a declaration yet and I was not ready to give him an answer, it was as though I had really come to the end of that dark tunnel and I was looking at the sunny paths spread out before me.

When Mrs Rendall heard the news about Godfrey she was not unduly depressed. Six months was a long time and, as Godfrey said, a great deal could happen in that time. Sylvia must grow up; Sylvia must change from an ugly duckling into a swan. Therefore she must pay more attention to her appearance. Miss Clent, the seamstress of Lovat Mill was sent for and she made a new wardrobe for Sylvia. Mrs Rendall saw only one reason why her plans should go awry. A certain scheming adventuress, she believed, had her eyes on the prize.

I was put into the picture by the girls whose remarks, sometimes candid, sometimes oblique, made me aware of what was being attributed to me. Godfrey and I would laugh together over this and sometimes I felt that he considered it only natural that in due course he and I would slip into that relationship for which Mrs Rendall had convinced herself I was scheming.

Sometimes I would find Alice's grave eyes fixed on me.

She began embroidering a pillow case 'for a bottom drawer,' she told me.

'Yours?' I asked; and she shook her head and looked mysterious.

She was so industrious and whenever she had a spare moment she would bring out the needlework which she carried in a bag embroidered in wools – her own work, which her mother had taught her.

I knew the pillow case was for me because she was naïve enough to ask my opinion.

'Do you like this pattern, Mrs Verlaine? It would be easy to do another.'

'I like it very much, Alice.'

'Alice has had a great affection for you, since . . .' began Mrs Lincroft.

'Since the fire, yes.' I smiled. 'It's because she saved my life. I think she feels extremely gratified every time she looks at me.'

Mrs Lincroft turned aside to hide an uncharacteristic display of emotion. 'I'm so glad she was there, so . . . so proud . . .'

'I shall always be grateful to her,' I said gently.

The other girls had started to make pillow cases.

'It's very good,' said Alice looking at me almost maternally, 'to have a good supply of everything.'

Alice's work was neat and clean like herself – Allegra's was quickly grubby. In any case I did not think she would finish it. As for Sylvia, hers was not a success either. Poor Sylvia, I thought, forced to help furnish the bottom drawer for the prospective bride of the man her mother had chosen for *her*!

I watched them, their heads bent over their work, and I felt an affection for all of them; they had become so much a part of my life. I always found their conversation unexpected, often amusing and never dull.

Alice was exclaiming in dismay because Sylvia had pricked her fingers and had made a spot of blood on the pillow case.

'You would never earn *your* living by sewing,' she reproved.

'I wouldn't want to.'

'But you might have to,' put in Allegra. 'Suppose you were starving and the only way to earn your living was by sewing. What would you do?'

'Starve, I expect,' said Sylvia.

'I'd go off with the gipsies,' put in Allegra. 'They neither toil nor do they spin.'

'That was the lilies of the field,' explained Alice. 'Gipsies toil. They make baskets and clothes pegs.'

'That's not toiling. That's fun.'

'It's meant . . .' Alice paused and said with effort: 'figuratively.'

'Don't show off,' snapped Allegra. 'I wouldn't sew. I'd be a gipsy.'

'People who make shirts get very little money,' said Alice. 'They work by candle light all day and all night and they die of consumption because they don't get enough fresh air and food.'

'How horrible!'

'It's life. Thomas Hood wrote a wonderful poem about it.'

Alice began to quote in a deep sepulchral voice:

'Stitch, stitch, stitch,
In poverty hunger and dirt.
Stitching at once with a double thread
A shroud as well as a shirt.'

'Shroud,' screeched Allegra. 'These aren't shrouds; they're pillow cases.'

'Well,' said Alice coolly, 'they didn't think they were stitching shrouds. They thought they were shirts.'

301

I interrupted them and said what a ghoulish conversation. Wasn't it time Alice put her pillow case-cum-shroud away and came to the piano?

Neatly she folded her work, threw back her hair and rose obediently.

Lovat Stacy was indeed haunted – by the gipsy Serena Smith. I often saw her near the house, and once or twice strolling across the garden. She did not do this furtively but as if by right and I was becoming more and more convinced that she was Allegra's mother. That would account for her proprietory air and her insolence.

Coming into the house one day I heard her voice – shrill and carrying.

'You'd better, hadn't you?' she was saying. 'You wouldn't want to go against me, would you? Ha. There's people here that wouldn't like me telling things about them but you more than anyone, I reckon. That's the way I see it. So there'll be none of this talk about "Get the gipsies off." The gipsies are here to stay . . . see!'

There was silence and I thought sick at heart: Napier, oh Napier. What trouble you have brought on yourself. How could you become involved with a woman like this!

Then the voice again. 'Oh yes, Amy Lincroft . . . Amy *Lincroft*. I could let out some secrets about you and your precious daughter, couldn't I? And you wouldn't want that.'

'Amy Lincroft.' Not Napier!

I was about to turn away when Serena Smith came out. She was running and her face was flushed and her eyes sparkling. How like Allegra she looked – Allegra in a mischievous mood!

'Why,' she cried, 'if it's not the music lady! Ear to the

ground, eh lady . . . or to the keyhole?' She burst out laughing, and I could do nothing but walk into the hall.

No one was there and I wondered whether Mrs Lincroft had heard her remarks. She must have. But I expected she was too embarrassed to talk to me.

At dinner Mrs Lincroft was as cool and calm as ever. 'I hope you like the way I've cooked this beef, Mrs Verlaine. Alice, take this beef tea up to Sir William, will you? And when you come down I'll be ready to serve.'

Alice carried the dainty tray out of the room and I said what an obedient child she was.

'It's a great comfort to me that she should be so,' said Mrs Lincroft. My thoughts immediately went to the words of the gipsy; and I wondered once again whether there ever had been a Mr Lincroft or whether Alice was the result of a youthful indiscretion. This could be likely for I had never heard Mr Lincroft mentioned.

Mrs Lincroft seemed to read my thoughts for she said: 'I do wish Mrs Rendall would not interfere with the gipsies. They're doing no harm.'

'She certainly seems determined to drive them away.'

'If only she were as gentle and peace loving as her husband how much more comfortable life would be for us.'

'And for the vicar and Sylvia particularly.'

Mrs Lincroft nodded.

'I expect you've guessed who this Serena Smith is. You've heard some of the family history.'

'You mean she's Allegra's mother.'

Mrs Lincroft nodded. 'It's all so unfortunate. Why ever she was allowed to come here in the first place I can't imagine. She worked in the kitchen . . . though she did little work. And then of course she became embroiled with

Napier . . . and Allegra was the result. It all came out imme-diately after Beaumont's death when Napier was preparing to leave. She stayed here till the child was born and then she went.'

'Poor Allegra!'

'I came back and looked after her in time . . . It suited me well as I was able to bring Alice with me.'

'Yes,' I said sympathetically.

'And now here she is again . . . ready to make trouble unless we allow the gipsies to stay. That would be all right. They would never stay long. But that dreadful interfering woman has to try to make an issue of it. Do you know I believe she *likes* to make trouble.'

At that moment Mrs Lincroft really looked troubled; there was a frown between her eyes and she bit her lips, lowering her eyes as she did so.

Alice came back; she was a little flushed and her eyes were dancing.

'He's taking it, Mamma. He said it was very good and that no one knew how to make it just like you.'

'Then he is a little better.'

'And it is all thanks to you, Mamma,' said Alice.

'Come to the table, my dear,' said Mrs Lincroft, 'and I'll serve.'

I thought how pleasant it was to see the affection between those two.

Sir William was a little better, for the next day Mrs Lincroft joyfully told me that he had expressed a desire to hear me play. He had not been told about the fire. There was no need to upset him, said Mrs Lincroft and I agreed with her. Since that unfortunate occasion when I had played *Danse Macabre* I had not been to the room next to his. I could quite imagine why not. Any reminder of that day would be most distressing to him. However, it was clearly a good sign that he had asked for me to play.

'Something light and quiet that you have played before,' said Mrs Lincroft. 'He hasn't chosen. He's not really well enough. But you will know.'

'Schumann, I should think,' I said.

'I am sure you're right. And not too long . . .'

I was a little nervous remembering that other occasion; but as soon as I played I felt better. After half an hour I stopped playing and as I turned from the piano I was startled to see someone in the room – a woman with her back to me wearing a hat of black lace trimmed with pink roses. She was looking up at the picture of Beau and for a moment I thought that this was indeed the dead Isabella. Then there was a laugh and Sybil turned to face me.

'I startled you,' she whispered.

I admitted it. 'If Sir William had seen you,' I said, 'he might have . . .'

She shook her head. 'He couldn't leave his chair. And it was *your* playing that shocked him.'

'I played only what was put out for me.'

'Oh, I know. I know. I'm not blaming you, Mrs Verlaine.' She laughed. 'So you thought you really had lured my sister-in-law from the grave by your playing? Confess it.'

'You intended me to think that, did you?'

'No, of course not. I wouldn't want to frighten *you*. I just didn't think of it. I put on my hat because I thought of going into the garden. And I came in here instead. You didn't hear me. You were so absorbed in your music. You are all right now. I don't frighten you, do I? You are very calm, you know, even now after what happened in that cottage. You're like Mrs Lincroft. She has to be cool, doesn't she, for fear of betraying herself. Do you have to be calm for the same reason?'

'I don't quite understand what you mean.'

'Don't you? William is asleep now, so he is perfectly safe. Your music soothed him. 'Music hath charms to soothe the savage breast.' He's not savage now, but he has been. Come up to my studio. I want to show you something. I've started on my portrait of you.'

'That's very kind of you.'

'Kind. I'm not kind. I'm not doing it for kindness. It's because you're becoming involved . . . part of the house. I've watched.'

'I came here to play for Sir William.'

'But he's asleep. Go and look.'

I went to the door and looked into his room. She was right. He was fast asleep.

'You might wake him if you played on.'

She laid her hand on my arm . . . that little hand with the long tapering artist's fingers which had once worn the ring she had thrown into the sea.

'Come on,' she coaxed. So I went.

In the studio I at once recognised the picture as a portrait of myself, although it shocked me a little. Did I really look as cool and worldly as she had depicted me? The features were mine – the slightly tiptilted nose, the large eyes and the heavy dark hair. There was even a touch in the eyes of that romanticism on account of which Pietro had teased me. But I felt that a veneer of sophistication was there which I did not believe I possessed.

She watched my vague discomfiture with a faintly malicious delight.

'You recognise it,' she accused me.

'Oh, yes, of course. There can be no doubt who it is.'

She put her head on one side and regarded me shrewdly.

'You know,' she said, 'you are beginning to change. The house is doing that to you. It does something to everyone. A house is a living thing, don't you agree Mrs Verlaine?'

I said that as it was made of bricks and mortar I did not see how it could be.

'You are being deliberately obtuse, I know. Houses are *alive*. Think what they've seen. Joys, tragedies . . .' Her face crumpled. 'These walls have seen me weep and weep until I had no tears left . . . and then they saw me rise like the phœnix and find a reason to be happy again with my painting. That's what happens to great artists sometimes, Mrs Verlaine. And I'm an artist . . . not only in paint. Sybil! That's what my parents christened me. Did you know it meant a wise woman?'

I said I did.

'Well, I watch and learn . . . so I grow wise. That Mrs Rendall . . . I should paint her, I suppose. But she's too obvious, isn't she? Everyone can see what she is like. They don't need to be told. Other people are less obvious. Amy Lincroft for instance. Ah, there's a deep one. And she's worried now . . . I sense it. She thinks I don't. But she betrays it in her hands. They pick up things and put them down. She's practised keeping her face in order . . . she's practised very hard at that. But everyone has some special thing which betrays them. With Amy Lincroft it's her hands. She's afraid. She lives in fear. She has a secret . . . a black black secret, and she's a frightened woman. But she's lived with fear and thinks she knows how to hold it in check. But I wasn't called Sybil for nothing, so I know it.'

'Poor Mrs Lincroft. I'm sure she's a very good woman.'

'*You* see what's on the surface. You're not a painter. You're only a musician. But we didn't come here to talk about Mrs Lincroft, did we? *Lincroft!* Ha! Ha! We came to talk about *you*. Do you like this picture?'

'I'm sure it has great merit.'

She laughed again. 'You amuse me, Mrs Verlaine. Now you know I didn't ask you whether it had merit. I said: "Do you like it?"'

'I . . . I'm not sure.'

'It's perhaps not you to-day . . . but you to-morrow.'

'How do you mean?'

'I'm painting you as you're becoming, Mrs Verlaine. Very sure of yourself . . . very much the lady of the vicarage . . . who is learning to be the Bishop's wife. Very successful . . . she will help the Bishop in every way possible and everyone will say: "The dear Bishop is so fortunate. What a lot he owes to that efficient wife of his."'

'I think you must have been taking a few lessons from the gipsies.'

'"Clever conversationalist! Never at a loss! That's such an asset to the dear Bishop, you know."' She pouted. 'I don't much like the Bishop's wife, Mrs Verlaine. But that won't matter because I shan't have to see her, shall I? I can see her at the breakfast table smiling across the napery at her husband. Oh, this is years and years ahead and she is saying: "And what was the name of that place where we met? Lovat Something? Such odd people! I wonder what became of them all." And the Bishop will wrinkle his brow and try to recall and he won't be able to. But she will. She will go to her bedroom alone and think and think and there'll be a pain because . . . because . . . But you don't want me to go on.'

She laughed aloud and whipped the canvas from the easel exposing that of the three girls.

'Poor poor Edith! What does she look like now, I wonder. But it is nice to remember them as they were together. One moment. I have another picture of you.'

'Of me? What a quick worker you are.'

'Only when my hands are guided.'

'Who guides them?'

'If I told you I was guided by Inspiration, Intuitiveness, and Genius you wouldn't believe me, would you? So I won't mention it. But here you are again. There.'

She had put a picture on the easel which was recognisable as myself though it was quite different from the one it had replaced. My hair was flowing loose; there was an expression of rapture on the painted face; my shoulders rose bare from a sea green smock. It was beautiful. I gasped and could not take my eyes from it.

She crowed with delight and pressing her palms together stood on one foot like a child.

'You like it?'

'It's a wonderful picture. But I don't look like that.'

'You don't look like the woman in the other . . . *yet*.'

I looked from one picture to the other and she whispered: 'I told you . . . I told you . . .' Then she went on: 'This woman is happy and she is sad . . . and she lives. The other is calm and grows more and more contented as the years pass by. Cows are contented chewing the cud. Did you know that, Mrs Verlaine? They put their heads down and see the rich verdant grass. It is all they ask because they do not see anything else.'

'Well, which is myself? They can't both be.'

'But none of us is one person. I could have been a wife and mother if Harry had not deceived me and if he had not met a richer girl he would still have deceived me but I should not have known it, should I? It isn't so much what we know as what we believe. I wonder if you agree with me. If you don't know, you will some day. Two paths are opening for you, Mrs Verlaine. You will choose. You chose once before. Oh Mrs Verlaine, you are not as wise as you pretend to be. Once you had a big decision to make . . . and you didn't choose your music. Were you right . . . or wrong? Only you can say because it is what you believe to be right which will be right for you. Perhaps you believe you have been unwise once. You are lucky. Second chances are not given to us all. This time you must make the right choice. I never had a second chance . . .' Her face puckered. 'I wept and wept . . .' She came close to me. 'I think you'll choose safety this time, Mrs Verlaine. Yes, I think you will.'

She disturbed me. I was sure she was mad, and yet . . . She seemed to have an uncanny gift for reading my thoughts for she said: 'Of course I'm mad, Mrs Verlaine. My misfortunes drove me mad, but there are always compensations. Blind people find them. They become philosophical. So why shouldn't the mad find them? Some are given special powers, special insight. They sometimes see what others fail to. That's a pleasant thought, isn't it, Mrs Verlaine? There are always compensations.'

'I think it's a comforting philosophy.'

She laughed aloud. 'So diplomatic. Yes, I think it will be the Bishop's wife. But it shows you have changed, doesn't it? The Bishop's wife would have chosen music.'

Her expression changed again; it became sly, malevolent.

'But,' she said, 'it may be that you won't be either if you meddle. You *are* a meddler.' She was her childish self again, lifting an admonishing finger. 'Admit it. You know what happens to those who try to find out too much when there are wicked people about.' She laughed. 'You ought to know. It nearly happened to you, didn't it?'

She stood in the centre of the room nodding like a mandarin, an incongruous figure, her flowery, feminine hat shading her wrinkled face, a shrewd wisdom looking out of her mad eyes.

I pictured her writing that note, creeping into my room with it, hiding herself in the outhouse, waiting, sprin-

kling the floor with the paraffin oil that was left in the
drum.

But why?

How could I know what secrets this old house was hiding,
and how each member of this household was concerned in
them?

Roma, I thought, what did *you* discover?

Sybil had disturbed me more than I cared to admit.

Everyone seemed to have decided that an understanding
was growing between myself and Godfrey Wilmot, and in
a way it was true. I could dream if I wanted to of a peaceful
future and I did; but when I dreamed of it, it was not Godfrey
I saw but my children. It's natural, I told myself. Every
woman wants children; and when she is of a mature age
and never expected to have them, then the prospect is very
desirable indeed. Yet . . . But why should there be any doubts?
I was lucky, as Sybil said. I had a second chance. Or I could
have – if I took care not to meddle.

When I was with Godfrey the time passed quickly and
pleasantly but there were occasions when I did not want
his company. I liked to be alone with my thoughts and
one of my favourite spots was the little walled garden.
Perhaps because she was such an observant little person
Alice knew this. She came into the walled garden on this
afternoon and asked in a demure voice whether she was
disturbing me.

'Of course not, Alice,' I said. 'Have you done your practice?'

'Yes, Mrs Verlaine, and I came to talk to you.'

'That was nice of you. Sit down for a moment. It's very
pleasant in this garden.'

'You love it, don't you, Mrs Verlaine? I've often seen you

here. So quiet and peaceful, isn't it? I expect you will make a garden like this in your new home.'

'My new home?'

'When you're married.'

'My dear Alice, I have been married once and I am not engaged to do so again.'

'But you will be soon.' She brought her face closer to mine and I could see the freckles across the bridge of her nose. 'I think you'll be very happy.'

'Thank you, Alice.'

'I think Mr Wilmot is a charming man. I'm sure he'll make a good husband.'

'How is it that you can judge a good husband?'

'But it's easy to tell in this case. He's handsome and rich I think . . . otherwise Mrs Rendall wouldn't want him for Sylvia. And he's kind and he wouldn't be cruel to you as some husbands are.'

'Your knowledge astounds me, Alice.'

'Oh well,' she said modestly, 'I have lived here with Edith and Napier. He was unkind to her. You see I have an example close at hand.'

'How can you be sure that he was unkind to her?'

'She used to cry a lot. She said he was cruel to her.'

'She told you that?'

'Yes. She used to confide in me a lot. It was because we were both little girls together.'

'You haven't a notion why she . . . went away?'

'It was to get away from him. I think she's gone to London to be a governess.'

'What gave you that idea? You thought she had run away with Mr Brown, remember.'

'So did everybody. But that was silly. She couldn't run away with him, could she? Any more than a married woman could run away with Mr Wilmot, because he is a curate and curates don't run away with people whom they can't marry.'

'So you think she has gone off on her own. Oh Alice, as if she would! You remember Edith. She would never be able to stand on her two feet.'

'Do you know, Mrs Verlaine, that if a tiger came into this garden you and I would run as we never had run before. We'd have special reserves of strength. Our bodies would provide them. Isn't that interesting? And it's true, I read it somewhere. It's Nature's provision. That's what it is. Well Edith, had to get away so Nature gave her the strength to do so.'

'What a little wiseacre you are.'

'Wiseacre,' she repeated. 'I haven't heard that word before. I like it. Wiseacre. It makes me sound like a clever piece of land.'

'If you know anything about Edith you should tell it, Alice.'

'I only know that she's run away. I don't think she'll ever be found because she won't want to be. I wonder what she's doing now. Teaching some children their lessons I expect . . . in a house like Lovat Stacy. Isn't that strange, Mrs Verlaine?'

'Too strange to be believed,' I said. 'I'm sure Edith would do no such thing. It would be wrong and wicked.'

'But while he has a wife, Napier won't be able to marry anyone else. I've written a story about it, Mrs Verlaine. There's a woman who is married to a bad man and she cannot escape from him, so she runs away and hides herself. You see, she has no husband and he has no wife and while she is hidden he can't take another wife. It's her big sacrifice. She remains hidden away until she is an old woman. And then she is lonely because she has no grandchildren. But that was her sacrifice.'

'You must let me see some of your stories, Alice.'

'Oh, they're not very good. I have to improve a lot. Shall I tell you a secret, Mrs Verlaine? It will probably shock you.'

'I'm not easily shocked.'

'Mr Lincroft was not my father.'

'What?'

'Sir William is my father. Oh, it's true. I heard them talking – my mother and Sir William. That's why I'm here . . . living in the house. I'm what is called a love child. I think that's rather a nice thing to be . . . in a way. Love child. It's like Allegra. She's one too. Isn't it strange, Mrs Verlaine, that there should be two of us. Two love children . . . in the same house, brought up together.'

'Alice, you are romancing again.'

'No, I'm not. After I heard them talking I asked my mother and she admitted it. She loved Sir William and he loved her . . . and she went away because she thought it was wrong to stay here. And she had me and she married Mr Lincroft . . . to give me a name. That's why I'm Alice Lincroft but really I'm Alice Stacy. Sir William is very fond of me. I think that one day he will make me legitimate. You can do it, you know. I'm going to write a lovely story about a girl whose father makes her legitimate, but I'm saving that one. It's going to be the best I've ever done.'

As I looked at the earnest little face beside me I could well believe this would be so.

The skein of circumstances grew more and more tangled with every new circumstance.

It had been raining heavily all day long. The girls had come back from their morning at the vicarage wet through and Mrs Lincroft insisted that they take off all their clothes and put on dry ones.

As I saw her efficiently taking charge I thought what a strong sense of duty she had and I believed that she was trying to expiate her misdemeanour. I pictured her coming to the house, a companion for Isabella – a lovely creature she must have been with that quiet grace and beauty. What bitter tensions there must have been, with Sir William falling in love with her and she with him, and Isabella ... poor and tragic Isabella, suddenly growing aware of it.

No wonder I sensed the sadness in her room.

And when Mrs Lincroft was going to have a child she went away and then, but perhaps that was later – married Mr Lincroft for the sake of the child. I wondered about Mr Lincroft who had conveniently died so that his wife could come back to Lovat Stacy after the death of Isabella.

I always had the impression that she was living in the past; there was an aura of 'days gone by' about her. It was in those chiffon blouses and the long sweeping skirts which she favoured – the greys, the misty blues ... they were hazy, indefinite ... ghostly, I thought and laughed at the word.

After tea I gave the girls a music lesson.

'Poor Sylvia! She's missing hers,' said Alice.

'A fact for which she'll be truly grateful to the rain,' declared Allegra. 'Listen to it ... pouring. All the gipsies will be in their caravans making pegs and baskets as fast as they can. That's one thing I wouldn't be a gipsy for. I'd hate to make baskets.'

'You hate to work anyway. All you want to do is lie in the sun.

> '"Who doth ambition shun
> And love to lie i' the sun",'

sang Alice. 'The answer is Allegra. But do you shun ambition? I don't think you do really. What is your ambition? I know what Mrs Verlaine's is.'

'What?' I asked.

'To live in a lovely house far away from here . . . with a handsome husband and ten children.'

'It's not such an unusual ambition.'

'I think it's mine too, in a way, always to live in a house like this. Only I'm not sure about the husband. I don't know what I think about them. I'm too young yet.'

'Ha!' laughed Allegra. 'She's pretending.'

'I'm not,' said Alice. 'Listen to the rain. Nobody would be out in weather like this. Not even ghosts.'

'It's just the time they would come out,' contradicted Allegra. 'Don't you agree, Mrs Verlaine?'

'I don't agree that they come at all.'

'The ghost will be in the chapel to-night, you see,' said Allegra.

Alice shivered.

'I shall watch,' declared Allegra.

'You can't watch all night,' Alice reminded her.

'No, but I shall keep looking. It'll be easy to see the light flash because it's so dark.'

'Now let's discuss something sensible,' I suggested. 'Alice, I'd like to hear you play that minuet again. You weren't at all bad last time. Of course there's plenty of room for improvement.'

Alice arose with alacrity and sat at the piano. As I watched those painstaking fingers picking out the melody, I thought that the two girls were good for each other because they were so different. Alice was a great help in curbing Allegra's wildness; and Allegra put a curb on Alice's primness. The two little love children.

The next morning the showers were intermittent and brighter weather was obviously on the way. In the morning I set out with the girls to walk to the vicarage.

'I was right, Mrs Verlaine,' Allegra said as we left the house and went along Church Path. 'We saw the light last night, didn't we, Alice?'

She nodded. 'Very bright it was, Mrs Verlaine, because of the darkness.'

'Alice wanted to come and tell you but we didn't because you don't believe in it.'

'It was a trap or something on the road most likely,' I said.

'Oh no, Mrs Verlaine. The road doesn't go that way.'

'Then whoever played tricks on a night like that must be in his dotage.'

'Or dead. The rain wouldn't worry the dead, would it?'

'Well, we have a lot of work to get through this morning. I think I'll take Sylvia first.'

We had arrived at the vicarage and as we went up the path Mrs Rendall appeared at the door, her arms folded, in a not unusual attitude.

'Sylvia,' she answered, looking through me, 'will not be available for lessons to-day. She is not well. In fact, I have sent for the doctor.'

'I'm sorry to hear that,' I said. 'I do hope she will soon be well.'

'I can't understand what's wrong. Shivering and sneezing . . . it's a thorough chill.' She turned and we followed her into the vicarage. 'Ah!' her tone softened because Godfrey was coming down the stairs. 'The pupils are here,' she added. 'I was just explaining that dear Sylvia is having a few days in bed.'

'Doctor's orders?' asked Godfrey.

'Mine. The child would go out yesterday to take some

soup to poor Mrs Cory. I said it was too wet but the dear girl insisted and said that it did not matter if she had a soaking and that what was important was that Mrs Cory should have her soup.'

'What a little saint she is!' said Godfrey lightly and Mrs Rendall smiled warmly

'She has been brought up to think of others. So many people nowadays . . .' She threw a baleful glance at me, and I wanted to burst out laughing and I could see that Godfrey did the same.

I said that as Sylvia would be unavailable for her music lesson there was no point in my staying. I could give Allegra and Alice theirs at Lovat Stacy. This arrangement seemed to please Mrs Rendall mightily and she smiled almost graciously at me.

On the way home I thought of poor Sylvia and I wondered if she had caught her cold by going into the copse to shine a light in the ruined walls.

She would never have the courage. But would she? She was a strange girl – the one I knew least about.

Godfrey was leaning against the Stacy vault. It was afternoon of the same day and my walk had led me there. We had fallen into a habit of being there at certain times of the day in case the other should turn up. The grass grew long between the gravestones and there were trees which gave a certain privacy.

'How's the invalid?' I asked.

'Poor Sylvia! Not very well. The doctor says her temperature is too high and she's to stay in bed for a few days.'

'Do you think it might be the result of getting wet in the rain?'

'She's had a cold for several days. She often has colds, poor child.'

'What do you think of Sylvia?'

'I don't think of her.'

'Shame on you after all her mother's efforts. I'm sorry for her and I wonder what effect it's having on her.'

'It?' he said. 'Do you mean her Mamma?'

'I do. Sylvia always seems so cowed. Do you think that someone who's treated as she is might want to assert herself in some way?'

'I'm sure she would like to assert herself if she could.'

'What about going to the ruin and waving a lantern about?'

'As the ghost, do you mean? But ghosts are so anonymous. So where's the glory?'

'In knowing that people are afraid to go there because of her. In knowing that she is the one who is making them all uneasy.'

He shrugged his shoulders. 'I can't quite see where the glory comes in.'

I felt a little impatient with him. 'Of course you don't. You've never had to make people notice you. You're so ... so normal.'

He burst out laughing. 'You sound as though there's something rather disreputable about that.'

'No, too reputable. But I want to understand Sylvia.'

'That's easy. She's just a mouse of a girl with a great big tom cat of a mother always waiting at the mouse-hole to catch her.'

I laughed. 'More like a bulldog than a tom cat. And I'm sure we're both wrong to change her sex. The female of the species is always more deadly than the male.'

'Do you believe that?'

'In the case of the vicar and his wife ... yes. But I want

to think of Sylvia. Do you know it wouldn't surprise me if she's the one who is doing the haunting. Frustrated mouse . . . seeking self expression . . . seeking to form her own personality . . . seeking a chance of gaining power. That's it: Power. She who is made uncomfortable so often now has the opportunity of discomfiting others. It fits. Besides, how did she become ill? By going out in the rain when she already had a cold.'

'Wait a minute,' said Godfrey thoughtfully. 'When I came in last night after going to visit Mrs Cory . . .'

'The same who had previously received soup through Sylvia's bounty?'

'The same. When I returned from visiting her and hung up my clothes in the cloakroom I saw that Sylvia's boots were there also . . . saturated.'

'So she had been out, too. Could she have done so without her parents knowing?'

'Yes, if she had retired to bed early as she might have done – having a cold – and slipped out afterwards.'

'We're beginning to get somewhere,' I said. 'So it's Sylvia asserting herself, not someone trying to drive Napier away. The very next chance I get I'm going to catch that girl.'

'Mr Wilmot. Mr Wilmot . . .' It was Mrs Rendall's voice, cooing sweetly yet somehow invincible.

'You'd better go and take tea with her,' I said. 'For if you don't she will search until she finds you.'

He grinned and went off.

I stood for some time looking at the memorial to Beau, thinking that I should be glad if it did prove to be Sylvia asserting herself.

As I moved through the long grass a voice cried: 'Hallo!' And the gipsy seemed to materialise before me. She had in fact been lying in the long grass and I wondered if she had overheard my conversation with Godfrey.

She grinned at me.

'Where did you come from?' I asked.

She waved a hand. 'I've a right, ain't I? This place is free to the dead and the living alike . . . music teachers and gipsies.'

'You appeared so suddenly.'

'I was wanting to have a talk with you.'

'With me?'

'You look surprised. Why not? I like to know what's going on up there.' She jerked her head in the direction of Lovat Stacy. 'How do you like working there? I worked in the kitchens once. The cook they had . . . ran me off my feet, she did . . . or tried to. I was always missing when there was taters to peel. I never could abide peeling taters. Lazy good-for-nothing, that old cook used to call me.' She winked at me. 'But I found something better to do than peel taters.'

'I am sure you did,' I said coldly and turned away.

'Hey. Not so fast. Don't you want to talk to me about them up there . . . about Nap, for a start?'

'I can't believe you would be able to tell me anything I want to know.'

She burst out laughing. 'Do you know,' she said, 'I like you . . . in a way. You remind me of myself. Oh, that makes you sit up and listen, don't it. How can a high class lady music teacher be like a gipsy? Don't ask me. Ask Nap.'

'If you'll excuse me I have work to do . . .'

'But I won't excuse you. Don't you know it's rude to push a lady off when she wants to talk with you? Tell me about Allegra. She's a little beauty, wouldn't you say? A bit different from that Alice. I wouldn't change Allegra for Alice not for a mint of money. I've got four of them now . . . girls . . . all girls. Now that's a funny thing. Some has girls and can't get boys. That's me. I've seen it in the cards every time. "It'll be a girl again" I say and so it is. But Allegra . . . she plays the piano lovely, does she? Do you know she's the image of what I was at her age. Only I had me wits about me more than she has. Had to. I was a woman at her age. Why it was then I came to work in the kitchens? . . . What made me do that? Wouldn't you like to know? Oh, wouldn't you like to know! But I reckon you can guess . . . though you might guess wrong.'

I had no desire to continue this conversation so I assumed a look of indifference and glanced at my watch.

She came closer to me and said: 'I saw you with me lord from the vicarage just now. Very nice and friendly. I've heard talk too the way the wind blows there. Good luck I says. Why don't you take that luck, eh, and get out while you can? You've been warned, you know. Can't you take a hint?'

'What are you talking about?'

'You should know after being nearly snuffed out in that old cottage. And would have been but for Miss Alice. I reckon Amy Lincroft was very proud of her daughter on that day.' She laughed aloud. 'Oh, very proud.'

'If you know anything I should be glad if you told me.'

'Gipsies! They're an ignorant lot. Don't know anything, but they can warn you. Ever heard of the Gipsy's Warning?'

'What do you know about the fire at the cottage?'

'I wasn't there. How could I know? But I'll tell you this much. People are not what they seem. There's Amy Lincroft for one. Why don't you get away from here. Why don't you marry his lordship and go. You won't though, will you. Not yet. Mettlesome, that's you. You've got to *know*. But tell me about Allegra.'

I thought: She is talking as gipsies will talk, feigning some second sight which is denied to the rest of us – and I suppose a woman who has had a narrow escape from death seems a good subject.

In fact she was really a mother eager for news of her child.

'Allegra is a very intelligent girl but she's rather lazy and won't concentrate. If she did I think she would do very well indeed.'

She nodded and then went on: 'In the house there you see the way things are. Sir William, is he fond of her? Is he going to find a husband for her?'

'She is young yet.'

'Young! Why, at her age . . . but no matter. Is he fond of her?'

'Sir William has been ill since I've been in the house. I haven't seen him and Allegra together.'

She was fierce suddenly. 'He'll have to remember her. After all she's his granddaughter.'

'I'm sure he does not forget it.'

'Wrong side of the blanket,' she said. 'It counts. But she's the granddaughter for all that . . . no getting away from it. I tell you what I'm afraid of. That Amy Lincroft. She's a cunning one, she is. She'll try to push her Alice in and my Allegra out.' She narrowed her eyes and looked wicked. 'If she does, I'll . . . I'll . . . I'll make her sorry she was ever born and Alice was ever born too.'

'I'm sure Mrs Lincroft couldn't be kinder to Allegra.'

'Kind! When she's trying to get her pushed aside for her Alice! She'd better not.'

'I don't think anyone's being pushed aside. I'm sure both Alice and Allegra will be provided for.'

I moved impatiently, asking myself what I was doing standing in a graveyard arguing with a gipsy.

'But suppose Nap was to get pushed out again.'

'Pushed out?'

'Well, he was before. Sent away. Sir William couldn't bear the sight of him. There was talk then that he'd disinherit him because he'd shot Beau. Well, then who'd inherit? If Nap's pushed out? He has a granddaughter, my Allegra. So . . .'

'I really must be going.'

'Listen!' Her eyes were pleading and she was suddenly beautiful. I could see in that moment why Napier had fallen into temptation. 'Keep your eye on Allegra, will you? Tell me if anyone tries to hurt her.'

'I shall certainly do my best to see that she is not harmed. And now I must go.'

She smiled at me, nodding slowly.

'I'll be on the watch,' she said. 'No one's going to drive me away. They daren't. I've told them so. Neither Nap – and he'd be glad to see me go – nor Amy Lincroft. I've told them both and they know I mean it.'

'Good day,' I said firmly and walked towards the lych gate and the road.

❧

That evening I saw the light again. Alice had come to my room to bring me the first of the pillow cases she had been embroidering.

'I wanted to see whether you like this kind of flower. It's pansies. Pansies are for thoughts, they say. But you could have another flower. I wonder whether it would be nice to have all your pillow cases with different flowers.'

'Why, Alice,' I said, 'you've worked it beautifully.'

She smiled with pleasure. 'I'm so glad you like it, Mrs Verlaine. You've been so kind to me and to Mamma. Mamma was only saying the other day how glad she was that you had come here.'

'And you,' I said, 'saved my life. That's something one never forgets, Alice.'

She turned pink and replied: 'But I just happened to be there. It would have been the same with anyone who had been on the spot. They would have done the same.'

'It was very brave to go into a burning house.'

'I didn't think of it. I only thought that you were in there and how awful it would be . . . But my mother says we shouldn't talk of it. It's better for you not to think of it . . . if you can help it. Allegra's pillow case is coming along very nicely now. She does try, you know – but I think sometimes she feels she has to be naughty. It's on account of her unfortunate birth. Mine was unfortunate, too, in a way. It would have been so much more respectable of Mamma and Sir William to have waited . . . and then married. But you see, he never married her. It was because she gave in first, but you mustn't think badly of her for that. It was because she loved him. May I sit in your window seat? I love window seats. There are lots in this house. What a lovely view you have across the copse.'

'Yes, it is a beautiful view. I have to be grateful to your mother for . . . giving me this room.'

'All the rooms are beautiful but naturally Mamma would want you to have one of the best. Poor Sylvia! I do hope she is better. She looked ill when we saw her. She could hardly speak to us and the doctor says she's to have at least three days in bed. I'm going to collect some books to take over for her to-morrow.'

'Does she enjoy reading?' I asked dubiously.

'No. But that's all the more reason I should take her books, isn't it? Then she will learn to like it and improve her mind.' Alice caught her breath. I took a step to the window and saw the light flash.

'There!' she cried. 'It's there again.' She stood up. 'Would you like to come to my room, Mrs Verlaine?'

'No thank you, Alice,' I said.

She nodded gravely and went to the door.

'I'm glad you saw it to-night,' she said, 'because I believe you thought it was Sylvia doing it. And now you know she's in bed . . . so it couldn't be her, could it?'

I said: 'It's someone on the road somewhere.'

'But the road doesn't . . .' She paused and smiled at me a little sadly. 'I want to go up to see if it flashes again. I always think I may see something else.'

'Then you go,' I said; and she went.

As soon as she had gone I put on a cloak and went swiftly down the great staircase, through the hall to the gardens.

I might just be in time. It wasn't Sylvia then, so who was it? Someone who wanted to keep the legend of the ghost alive and so the story of the unfortunate shooting accident. Someone who was hoping to drive Napier away.

The ground was a little spongy underfoot on account of the recent rain and when I reached the copse the grass was very wet. My footsteps made a squelching sound which I feared would betray me. The important thing was speed. I must reach the ruin before whoever was haunting it had time to disappear.

There was no moon but the sky was clear of cloud and there was enought starlight to show me the way. I confess to a sudden panic as I caught sight of the grey bricks of the chapel.

I hurried on wishing I had changed my footwear for I was only wearing house shoes and I could already feel the damp seeping through them. I put out a hand to touch the wall and with my heart leaping uncomfortably went inside the ruin. It was a little darker than outside for some of the roof remained, but glancing up I could see a patch of starlight, which was comforting.

There was nothing there. No sign of anyone.

'Who's there?' I whispered.

No answer. But I had heard a faint sound which could be that of feet on wet grass?

I felt a great urge to get outside, to escape from those walls, and as I stepped out and looked up at the sky I was suddenly caught from behind and held firmly in a vice-like grip.

I had not been so terrified since my adventure in the cottage and I immediately thought what a fool I had been to come. I had been warned – as both the gipsy and Sybil Stacy had pointed out to me. I could not expect to be so fortunate again.

'Well,' said a voice, 'you always wanted to meet the ghost of Beaumont Stacy.'

'Napier!' I gasped, and tried to wriggle free but he would not release me.

'You came here to meet Beaumont, didn't you?' He let me go but as I turned he caught me by the shoulders. 'What are you doing here?'

'You terrified me.'

'You haven't by any chance been displaying lights?'

'I came to see who was.'

'Good God, haven't you learned your lesson?'

'My lesson?'

He looked at me quizzically; and I thought of his bringing the spade into the stables, of his meeting me here in the copse when he discovered that I was looking for a grave. And shortly afterwards I had been trapped in the cottage – and he was asking me if I had not learned my lesson! And I was here in the copse with him. It was dark and no one knew I had come.

I heard myself stammer: 'I . . . I saw the light. I was with Alice. I said I would come and investigate . . .'

'All alone?' His voice mocked me. 'You are a very brave woman. Only recently . . .' His voice sounded suddenly harsh; his grip tightened on my shoulders. 'You were up there . . . and couldn't get down. For God's sake, take care.'

'It is the sort of thing which happens once in a lifetime.'

'Some people are accident prone.'

'You mean without a reason?'

'Perhaps the reason is an unseen one.'

'This sounds very mysterious.' I was recovering after that terrible fear. I could not help it but when I was in his presence I could feel an elation which banished all my fear. I said: 'Did you come down here to discover the source of the light?'

'Yes,' he said.

'And found nothing?'

'The "ghost" was too quick for me. Every time I am too late.'

'And have you a suspicion as to who it might be?'

'Only that it is someone who is trying to drive me away.'

'How could they?'

'By making things so uncomfortable here that I preferred to be elsewhere.'

'I should scarcely have thought you were the sort of man to be driven away because you were uncomfortable.'

'You're right. All the same it revives the old story. It keeps it alive in my father's mind. He could be the one to decide that I went away. He was before. I'm not really very popular here, Mrs Verlaine.'

'It's a pity.'

'Oh, don't be sorry for me. I'm used to it. It doesn't bother me.'

I felt a great surge of emotion then because he was lying. Of course it did bother him.

I said: 'Do you think we should talk? We might frighten the ghost away.'

'Don't you think he – or she – has done his – or her – haunting for the night?'

'I don't know how he or she works. Let's wait awhile . . . quietly.'

He took my arm and we went into the shelter of the ruined walls. An almost unbearable excitement had taken possession of me. I leaned against the cold damp wall and looked up at his profile. It appeared stern, sharply defined in the half light – tortured and sad; and my emotion was so mixed that I could not altogether understand it. I only knew that I would never forget his face as I saw it on this night and that the longing to help him was something as intense as my love for Pietro had been. Perhaps there was something of the same nature in my feelings – the longing to care for, to protect against the world.

I wanted so much for the person who was playing the tricks to come into that enclosure; I wanted us to lay hands on that person, to expose him as the ghost, to put an end to this attempt to keep open an old wound.

I wanted to see Napier settled in Lovat Stacy, doing work which was so suited to him. I wanted to see him happy.

He looked down at me suddenly and said in a whisper: 'I believe you *are* sorry for me.'

I could not answer him because my emotion threatened to choke me.

'Why?' he whispered. 'Why?'

'Hush,' I said. 'The ghost will hear and keep away. Don't forget we want to catch him.'

'I want to know why you're sorry for me even more than to discover the ghost.'

'It was so unfair,' I said. 'Everything was unfair. One accident, and your life . . . shattered.'

'You put it too strongly,' he said.

'No,' I answered firmly. 'They were so cruel to blame you . . . to send you away from your home.'

'Everyone is not as tender-hearted as you are.'

I laughed. I had stopped thinking of catching the ghost. It seemed to me too that it was more important that we should understand each other.

'You were so young.'

'Seventeen is not young really. I was old enough to kill . . . therefore old enough to be dealt with accordingly.'

'Please don't talk of it if it upsets you.'

'Why shouldn't I be upset? I ended his life didn't I? There he was . . . magnificently alive and then . . . dead. And here am I alive and having had thirteen years of life which has been denied him. And you say I shouldn't be upset.'

'It was an accident. Can't you get that into your head? Can't anyone?'

'How vehement you are. The counsel for the defence!'

'How flippant *you* are. But you don't deceive me. It's because you feel it so deeply now.'

'I am very happy to have you speak so vehemently in my defence. So some good comes out of evil.'

We were standing side by side and suddenly he took my hand.

'Thank you,' he said.

'I wish I could deserve your thanks.'

'I should not have given them if I had not considered them deserved.'

'I don't see what I have done.'

His face was close to mine and he said: 'You are here.'

I said uneasily: 'Perhaps we should go in. The ghosts won't come back having heard us talking.'

'It's rarely now that I have an opportunity of talking to you.'

'Yes . . . it has changed since Edith . . . went.'

'So much. You are full of doubts. How could it be otherwise? But at least they are doubts. You do not stand in judgment. Nor will you until you have proved your suspicions to be true.'

'Don't think that of me. I loathe people who judge others. How can they know every little detail which led up to disaster . . . and it is the details which are often of so much importance.'

'I think of you often,' he said. 'In fact . . . all the time.'

I was silent and he went on: 'There is so much between us. You know, don't you, that it is believed by many people that I disposed of Edith. I'm not surprised. I soon realised how hopeless it was – and so did she. I knew of course that she was in love with the curate and I suppose I despised her for allowing herself to be forced into marriage with me – as I despised myself. But I tried to make something of our marriage – quite wrongly of course. I tried to make her into the sort of woman I could admire. Her meekness irritated me . . . her timidity, her fears. There is no excuse. My conduct was despicable. But you know what kind of man I am. Not very admirable, I fear. Why am I trying to explain?'

'I understand.'

'And do you understand too that I don't want you to be involved . . . now?'

'How could I be?' I asked sharply.

'People tarnish with their thoughts . . . their evil whisperings. I have to prove to you, don't I – and to the world – that I had nothing to do with Edith's disappearance . . . at least directly.'

'You mean that indirectly you may be responsible?'

'I fear that's obvious. The poor child – for that was what she was – was afraid of me. Everyone was aware of this. So . . . I am branded Edith's murderer.'

'Don't say things like that.'

'Why not, when they're true? I thought you would be the first to agree with me that it is never wrong to speak the truth. I am telling you why you should spare your pity on my account. You can ask the advice of a number of people and they will all give you the same answer. They will assure you that you waste your pity. And more than that. They will warn you. Think of the case against me. Are you wise to linger in a haunted chapel with me?'

'Please be serious. This is a serious matter.'

'I'm deadly serious. You are in danger. You, my beautiful, poised widow are in acute danger.'

'How and from whom?'

'Do you really want to know?'

'Of course I do.'

His answer was to turn to me and with a swift movement put his arms about me. He held me tightly against him so that I could feel the beating of his heart and I knew he could feel mine. He put his face against my head. I thought he was going to kiss me, but he did not. He just stood very still holding me, and I remained in his arms, without protest because my one desire was to stay there and it was too strong to be resisted.

At length I said: 'This is . . . unwise.'

Then he laughed bitterly and answered: 'That is what I told you. Most unwise. You wanted to know why you are in danger. I told you.'

'And you wish to preserve me from that danger?'

'Oh no. I want to lead you right into it. But I am perverse. I want you to walk straight into it . . . knowing the danger . . . seeing the danger . . . I want you to choose it.'

'Are you talking in riddles?'

'Riddles to which we both know the answer.'

'You could call it that. I will state my intentions which can scarcely be called honourable. Let's look at the facts. I murdered my brother.'

'I insist on the truth,' I said. 'You shot your brother accidentally.'

'. . . when I was seventeen. My mother killed herself because of it. So there were two deaths at my door.'

'I don't agree. You can't be blamed for that.'

'Sweet counsel,' he said. 'Sweet vehement counsel for the defence. While I was in Australia I longed to come home . . . but when I arrived I discovered that what I had longed for was no longer there. I had dreamed of my home before the accident. How different it was! I was married. It was after all for this I had come home. My wife was a child . . . a frightened child who was afraid of me and I don't blame her. She was in love with someone else. What could I do with such a marriage? No sooner had I made it than I began to wonder whether it would have been better for us all if I had remained on the Station.'

'But you love Lovat Stacy!'

He nodded.

'It's your home . . . where your roots are.'

'And it's not easy for some to uproot themselves. Why, I am taking over your job . . . defending myself, and that's exactly what I must not do. There is no defence. I shot my brother. It is something I shall never forget.'

'But you must . . . you must.'

'Please don't be so determined. You unnerve me. No one has ever tried to make a hero of me before.'

'I . . . make a hero of you! I assure you I am not doing that. I merely want you to face facts as they are . . . to realise that it is a mistake to brood on tragedies of the past . . . particularly when they are accidents which could happen to any of us.'

'Oh no,' he said. 'Could this happen to your friend Godfrey Wilmot for instance?'

I was dismayed and he was aware of it. How deeply conscious we were of each other!

'Anyone could have such an accident,' I said sternly.

'Did you ever hear of anyone who did but me?'

'No, but . . .'

'Of course you didn't. And there is Godfrey Wilmot, that eligible young man, who can offer so much. Perhaps he has already offered and been accepted.'

'I fear a great many people have been jumping to conclusions.'

'At which I infer there has been no formal betrothal.'

'It is embarrassing when one is friendly with a young man and everyone attempts to marry one off to him.'

'People like to imagine they are prophets.'

'Then I wish they would leave me out of their prophecies.'

'You have not thought of marrying again? It is because you still think of your late husband. But you've changed,' he added softly. 'I've noticed the change. Did you know you laugh more frequently? You seem to have found a new reason for living. Lovat Stacy has done that for you.'

I was silent and he went on: 'Could you have cared so much for him if you can forget him so quickly?'

'Forget him!' I said vehemently. 'I shall never forget Pietro.'

'But you are ready now to build a new life. Is he going to be there always . . . the shadowy third? He will grow more perfect every year. He will never grow old. How could anyone compete with him?'

I shivered and said: 'The night air is cool. I can feel that my feet are damp.'

He stooped and taking my foot removed my shoe. He held my foot in his hand and said: 'You should have put on something heavier than this flimsy thing.'

'There wasn't time. I wanted to catch the ghost.'

'You wanted to know who was so determined that my brother's death should not be forgotten.'

'Yes, that's true.'

'You are a very inquisitive young woman.'

'I fear so.'

'And an impulsive one!'

'That's true.'

'You were impulsive once. Perhaps you will be so again.' He put on my shoe. 'You are shivering a little. Is it the night air? There is a question I want to ask you. Once you made a decision. From a worldly point of view it was a very stupid decision. You threw away your career . . . for a man. You must have experienced a great deal of soul-searching when you did that. Did you?'

'No.'

'There was no great wrestling with yourself?'

'No.'

'As usual you were impulsive and you believed that decision the right one . . . the only one?'

'Yes.'

'And you regret it now.'

'I regret nothing.'

'You made a bold decision once.' He spoke almost wistfully. 'I wonder if you would ever do it again.'

'Perhaps I have not changed very much.'

'Perhaps we shall discover how much. I am glad you don't regret. People who do are often sorry for themselves and self pity is such an unattractive quality. I try to avoid it.'

'You do . . . very successfully.'

'But I fear I am often sorry for myself. Constantly I say to myself:

'How different it might have been if . . .' And I have said that more frequently since you came here. You know why.

There is so much between you and me,' he said. 'Edith. Poor Edith . . . so much more effective in death than in life.'

'Death?' I said sharply.

'I think of her as dead. Ah, how suspicious you are. You doubt me. And yet a little while ago . . . Oh yes, you doubted me, and in a way I wanted you to. I want to say to myself . . . in spite of her doubts . . . You see then it would be the same sort of blindness which affected you before. No consideration for anything.'

I interrupted quickly: 'I must tell you that I overheard your quarrel with your father . . . some of it at least. I heard him telling you that he would send you away.'

'And you heard me refusing to go.'

'And shortly afterwards I played that piece of music which someone put with the sheets he had chosen for me.'

'And you think I put it there.'

'Not unless you tell me you did.'

'Then I will tell you I did not. And you will believe me?'

'Yes,' I said, 'I believe you.'

He took my hand and kissed it.

'Please,' I said, 'always tell me the truth. If I am going to be of any use I must know the truth.'

'You make me very happy,' he said; and I was deeply moved because I had never heard his voice so low, so tender.

'It is what I want,' I replied impulsively. Then I added quickly: 'I must return to the house.'

I started to move away. He was beside me and he said suddenly: 'There was always a link between us. We were both being smothered by the past. I killed my brother; and you loved not wisely but too well.'

'I do not believe it is ever unwise to love and one cannot love too well.'

'So you defy the poet?'

'I do. I am sure one cannot love too much . . . give too

much ... for the greatest joy in life is surely loving and giving.'

'More than loving and receiving?'

'I am sure of it.'

'Then you must have been very happy.'

'I was.'

We were crossing the lawns and the garden loomed before us.

'So,' I said, 'we did not find the ghost.'

'No,' he answered, 'but perhaps we discovered something more important.'

'Good night,' I said. I left him standing outside and went into the house.

Chapter Eleven

I looked in at Mrs Lincroft's sitting-room to tell her that
I was not going to the vicarage that morning and that
Sylvia would be returning with the girls for her music lesson
now that she had recovered from her spell in bed.

The door was slightly ajar and I knocked lightly. There
was no answer so I called Mrs Lincroft softly and pushing
open the door, looked in.

To my astonishment she was there, seated at the table, a
newspaper spread out before her. She had not heard me,
which was strange.

'Mrs Lincroft,' I said, 'are you all right?'

She looked up then, and I saw how pale she was and that
there was a strange glazed look in her eyes which could have
been unshed tears.

Almost immediately her expression changed, and she was
her serene self.

'Oh, Mrs Verlaine, do come in.'

'Are you feeling well?' I asked as I entered.

'Oh . . . er . . . yes. I feel rather sleepy actually. I didn't
sleep well last night.'

'Oh dear, I'm so sorry. Is that unusual with you?'

She shrugged her shoulders. 'I haven't had a good night's sleep for years.'

'That's very bad. You're not worried about something, I hope.'

She looked at me in some alarm and taken off her guard she laid a hand on the paper as though to hide it from me.

'Worried? Oh . . . no, certainly not.'

A little vehement? I wondered.

She laughed but her laughter sounded high-pitched. 'Since I came back here I've had a very comfortable existence. Nothing to worry about. I can't tell you what a relief it is, when one has a child.'

'I can imagine it. It's difficult for a woman to bring up a child on her own.'

A faint colour came back into her cheeks and I went on: 'And you have made an admirable job of it.'

'Dear Alice. I didn't want her when she was on the way but when she arrived . . .' She said suddenly: 'Alice told you whose child she is, I know. She confessed it to me. She's apt to boast of it, I believe. Perhaps I can't blame her. It's unfortunate in a way that she knew, but it's hard to keep these things secret . . . especially with a girl like Alice. She seemed to sense the truth.'

'I think she is proud of her birth, which surely is better than that she should be ashamed.'

'Little to be proud of,' said Mrs Lincroft. She spread her hands over the newspaper. 'You're a woman of the world, Mrs Verlaine. You've lived abroad and you've travelled about, and I daresay you understand better than most how these things come about. I wouldn't like you to judge me . . . or Sir William too harshly. He wasn't enjoying a happy marriage, and I was able to comfort him. I don't know how it happened, but I suppose one falls into these situations.'

'Of course,' I said. She seemed as though she had to go on and could not stop herself.

'My mother used to say that there was a slippery stone on all doorsteps. She was Scottish and it's a saying they have up there. It means of course that any of us can slip up if we're a bit careless . . . and it's true to some extent.'

'I'm sure it is.'

'When I came here I was very young. I had been a governess for a few months and then I came as companion to Lady Stacy. My duties were to sit with her, to read to her, to do her hair. It was a comfortable enough position for she was very gentle, very sweet, which somehow makes it worse. She reminded me a little of Edith. Perhaps that's why Sir William was so fond of Edith.'

As she talked I saw the picture clearly; the beautiful young woman, for she must have been beautiful before she had grown so sad and faded. How appealing she must have been, with her slender willowy figure and beautiful features and those deepset blue-grey eyes. And Isabella Stacy . . . the mother of two boys, the adored Beau, and Napier who could never quite compare with his brother. I saw the picture clearly. Isabella who was perhaps a little resentful because she had given up her career for marriage, a woman who had not succeeded in holding her husband's affections completely. And then this beautiful creature appeared on the scene and Sir William fell in love with his wife's hand-maiden.

She went on: 'I was there when the accident happened. I shall never forget the day.'

'How was Napier then? The accident must have changed him considerably.'

'He was just an ordinary boy. But for the fact that he must be constantly compared with his elder brother one would scarcely have noticed Nap. We called him Nap then.

He was a little wild . . . as boys will be. I believe he had gone through most of the scrapes that boys do. He had just managed to get through his examination at school, whereas Beau was brilliant. Beau was a social and an academic success; his charm was irresistible. No one could describe Beau. He had to be seen and known to be believed. He had a sunny nature; nothing perturbed him; I never saw him lose his temper, whereas Nap was inclined to be moody. Jealous perhaps . . . always trying to equal Beau but never succeeding. I think that was why he was so bitterly blamed. Sir William never quite believed that it was entirely an accident.'

'That's unfair.'

'Life is unfair. I was there at the time when the gipsy girl disclosed the fact that she was pregnant and that Nap was responsible. It had already been decided that he should go.'

'So the gipsy's condition was discovered before he went.'

She nodded. 'I left too because I thought I should. The position was becoming intolerable. Lady Stacy was stricken with grief. I did not wish to add to that so I went away. I discovered that I was going to have a child. I was fortunate. I had an old friend who knew the position and he married me. I thought I would settle down to a quiet life, make a home for my child and never let her know that my husband was not her father. Then Lady Stacy killed herself.'

'What a dreadful tragedy!'

'It was like a series of explosions. In a way each tragedy was connected with the others. Alice was born and I lost my husband. I was desperate. I had no money and a child to think of. So I wrote to Sir William and told him of my predicament. His suggestion was that I return in the capacity I now hold and it was my great good fortune to do so. I was lucky. There are few positions where one can work and bring up a child at the same time.'

I nodded.

'So I was able to care for Alice, and since Allegra was born and deserted by her mother I looked after them both. Then Edith joined the household and I know that I have been of some use. It's a comfort really for all the sins of the past. You understand that, Mrs Verlaine.'

'I can't imagine what they would all have done without you.'

'I can't imagine why I'm boring you with all this.'

'It is far from boring.'

'But then you're so interested in people, aren't you? I've noticed that often. You are intensely interested . . . as few people are.'

'I suppose it's true.'

'So I don't have to apologise for talking so much. I'm sure it's not a failing of mine in the ordinary way. Let me give you some coffee.'

'That would be very nice,' I said.

She went away to prepare it and my natural curiosity urged me to look at the paper for I had a notion that something she had read in it may have disturbed her.

There had been a vote of censure on the government. That occupied most of the space; two trains had collided on the Brighton line; a Mrs Brindell had been caught teaching her daughter of seventeen to shoplift; one man had escaped from a prison and another from a mental home; a whole family had been burned to death in a fire; a Mrs Linton, aged seventy, had married a Mr Grey aged seventy-five. Linton! I thought; it was not unlike Lincroft.

No, I thought, the paper had nothing to do with it. I just caught her in an unusually communicative mood after a bad night.

By the time we were drinking her delicious coffee she had completely recovered her equilibrium.

When I left I asked if I might borrow the newspaper.

'Please do,' she said. 'There's very little interesting news in it, though.'

Alice sat at the schoolroom table reading aloud from the newspaper. It was the same one which I had picked up in her mother's room. Allegra was listening idly, drawing horses on a pad of paper. Sylvia, who had come over for a music lesson, was leaning her elbows on the table biting her nails and looking dreamily into space. I had come in to collect my music and give Sylvia her session at the piano.

Alice looked up and smiled at me and then went on reading the paper.

'"Mrs Linton and Mr Grey had known each other for sixty years. They were childhood sweethearts and the course of true love did not run smoothly and they each married someone else. Now Romance has come . . ."'

'Fancy being married at seventy-five,' said Allegra. 'That's the time to be dead.'

'Does anyone ever really believe it's the time for them to be dead?' asked Sylvia.

'No, but perhaps other people *know* it,' added Alice.

'Who's to say it's the time?' asked Allegra.

'If they die it's obviously the time,' retorted Alice. 'Listen to this: "Harry – inverted commas Gentleman – Terrall has escaped once more from Broadmoor where he has been for the last eighteen years. 'Gentleman' Terrall is a homicidal maniac."'

'What's that?' asked Allegra.

'It means he kills people.'

'And he's escaped?'

'He's at large. That's what it says at the top. 'Gentleman Terrall is highly dangerous because he behaves normally and with great charm. He is very attractive, particularly to women who become his victims. He has escaped twice before and during one of his bouts of freedom murdered Miss Anna Hassock. He is a man now in his mid-forties with charming manners which have earned him his name.'"

'Gentleman Terrall,' breathed Allegra. 'I wonder if he'll come here?'

'We shall know him if he does,' put in Allegra. 'If we see a man with good manners . . .'

'Like Mr Wilmot,' added Alice.

'Do you think Mr Wilmot . . .' began Sylvia, awestruck.

'Silly!' snorted Allegra. 'This man's only just escaped and Mr Wilmot's been here ages. Besides we know who Mr Wilmot is. He's related to a knight and a bishop.'

'Sounds like a game of chess,' said Alice. 'But this Gentleman must look rather like Mr Wilmot except that he's older. Like Mr Wilmot's father then, if he has a father . . . which of course he has. But it's exciting. Imagine this Gentleman prowling about looking for victims.'

'Suppose Edith was one,' suggested Allegra.

There was an immediate silence round the table.

'And,' added Sylvia, 'what about that Miss . . . er . . . Brandon. Perhaps she was, too.'

'Then he must have been here . . .' whispered Allegra, looking over her shoulder.

'But what did he do with the bodies?' cried Alice triumphantly.

'That's easy. He buried them.'

'Where?'

'In the copse. Don't you remember we saw . . .'

I said: 'This conversation is becoming too gruesome. And it's all froth and bubble.'

'Froth and bubble,' Allegra giggled.

'It's all grown out of a paragraph in the newspaper and you have all been talking utter nonsense.'

'I think you rather liked it, Mrs Verlaine,' said Alice demurely, 'because you didn't try to stop us till we talked of the copse.'

Alice and Allegra were poring over a book at the school-room table.

I went closer and saw that it was a fashion book and that it was open at the page of young girls' dresses.

'I like this,' cried Allegra.

'It's too fussy.'

'You like things too plain.'

Alice smiled up at me. 'We're going to have new dresses and we're choosing our patterns. Mamma said we might. Then we shall go up to London and pick the material. We go once a year.'

'I think I'll have this red,' announced Allegra. 'I suppose you'll have the blue.'

I sat down with them and studied the dresses and we talked of the kind of material which would suit them best.

I met Godfrey in the graveyard by the Stacy tomb. I had never felt quite the same sense of privacy here since the gipsy woman had risen out of the grass and ever after had always had a special feeling of being overlooked in this place. In fact, since the fire I had had many uneasy moments when I was in isolated places. It was a natural reaction in view of my doubts and suspicions.

Godfrey was coming towards me. He was certainly pleasant to look at and I immediately thought of Gentleman Terrall. How absurd! That frivolous conversation of the girls had made me picture the escaped homicidal maniac as Godfrey.

He now seemed a little thoughtful.

'Hallo,' I said. 'Has anything happened?'

'Happened? What do you think?'

'It is just that you seem unusually pensive.'

'I've been down to the site. Those mosaics are very interesting . . . that pattern running through. I can't make out what it is, though.'

'But just a pattern!'

'Well, one never knows. It might lead to some fresh light on the Romans.'

'I see.'

'Don't sound so disappointed. It is interesting . . . really. Do go and look at it. Of course the stone is so discoloured that you can't see the pattern, but I can make out the similarity all over the pavement and in the baths.'

'I haven't been there since . . .'

'No. Naturally you'd feel reluctant. But I was thinking of Roma.'

'In what way?'

'Suppose she'd found something there . . . some glimmer of a notion and she told it to someone who wanted to develop an idea . . .'

'You *are* still harping on the theory of the jealous archæologist.'

'Surely one should never discard a theory until it's proved wrong.'

'But it wouldn't explain Edith's disappearance.'

'You've linked the two disappearances firmly in your mind. It may be you're wrong there.'

'But the coincidence!'

'Coincidences do occur now and then.'

'I wonder if Roma ever came here . . . to this graveyard,' I said irrelevantly.

'Why should she? There's nothing of archæological interest here.'

I looked over my shoulder.

'You're nervous to-day. Why?'

'I just have an uneasy feeling of being watched.'

'There's no one here but the dead.' He took my hand and held it firmly. 'There's nothing to be afraid of, Caroline.' And his smile meant: There never will be while I'm here to take care of our lives. And I thought how right he was; and I saw clearly that future of which I had thought now and then: the peace, the security, which I was not sure that I wanted.

Perhaps he was not completely sure either. He would never be impulsive. He would give our friendship a chance to develop; he would never force anything. That was why when he made his decision it would be the right one . . . from his point of view.

I said: 'I'll go along some time and look at the motifs.'

'Yes, do.'

We came through the graveyard towards the lych gate and as we did so Mrs Rendall was standing there. She looked baleful like the avenging angel until she smiled sweetly at Godfrey. She ignored me.

I left them together.

I walked beside the baths and it seemed as though Roma was beside me for I was seeing her so clearly. How excited she had been when she had shown me these!

I did not want to look in the direction of the burned-out

cottage but I could not prevent my eyes straying there. How eerie it looked – a blackened shell like the chapel in the copse.

Roma seemed very close to me that day. I almost felt that she was trying to tell me something. Danger was very close to me. I could sense it all about me. I tried to shrug off the feeling, but I had been foolish to come here. It was too close to the scene of my terrifying experience. The place was too lonely and there were too many ghosts from the past.

Pull yourself together, I scolded myself. Don't be so absurdly fanciful. Look at the mosaics and see if you can pick out this pattern.

The colour was dingy. Centuries of grime had made it so. Dear Roma, how she had tried to give me an interest in life when Pietro had died and because she had believed that archæology could provide the panacea for all troubles she had set me fetching and carrying for those who were piecing the mosaic together. Of course the picture on the mosaic would be part of the pattern about which Godfrey was so interested.

I felt as though Roma were applauding me. I had helped work on that mosaic. I must tell Godfrey about this at the earliest possible moment.

I went straight back to the vicarage.

I had to find some way of letting him know I was there and by good luck one of the frightened little maids was polishing the brass knocker so I did not have to knock.

'Mrs Rendall is in the still room,' she volunteered.

'It's all right, Jane,' I said, 'I just want to go up to the schoolroom. I've left some music.'

I went upstairs, where Godfrey was giving a lesson in Latin. He was alert as soon as he saw me.

The girls looked at me in surprise. I knew they missed very little.

'I've left some music, I think,' I said, and went across the room to the drawer where I kept a book of elementary studies.

'Can I help you?' Godfrey was beside me, his back to the girls.

I fumbled with the book and taking a pencil wrote on it: 'Graveyard in ten minutes.'

'Is that what you're looking for?' asked Godfrey.

'Yes, I'm sorry to have interrupted the lesson. Only I did need this.'

I went out of the schoolroom, aware of three pairs of eyes following me. Down through the hall, quickly, lest Mrs Rendall emerge from the still room, and out to the grave-yard to wait.

In less than ten minutes Godfrey was with me.

'Perhaps I'm being overdramatic,' I said, 'but I've remembered something. When I came here and stayed a few days with Roma, they were piecing the mosaic together. It was too precious to move, Roma said, and she had some of her people working on it. I was supposed to be helping . . . doing nothing important, of course, but it was to give me an interest.'

'Yes, yes,' he said, dispelling all my doubts that what I was telling him was important.

'Well, that mosaic was a part of this pattern, I believe. In fact I'm almost sure of it.'

'We'll have to look at it,' he said.

'Where is it?'

'If any piecing together was successful it would be in the British Museum. We must take the first opportunity of looking at it.'

'When can you go?'

'There'd be comment if I took a day off at the moment. What about you? You've been here some time and haven't had a day off, have you?'

'No, but . . .'

'I shan't rest until one of us goes.'

'I believe Mrs Lincroft is taking the girls to London to buy dress material some time soon.'

'There's your opportunity. You go up with them and while they buy material you go into the Museum and see if you can find that mosaic.'

'All right,' I said. 'If I get the opportunity before you do, I'll go.'

'We're getting somewhere,' said Godfrey, his eyes gleaming with excitement. He returned to the schoolroom and I hurried back to Lovat Stacy where I met Mrs Lincroft in the hall. She said: 'You're later than usual.'

'Yes. I had to go back for this.' I flourished the book and it slipped from my fingers. She picked it up for me and I was aware of 'Graveyard in ten minutes' written on the cover. I wondered if she had seen it.

* * *

The girls were excited as we travelled up on the train.

'What a pity,' said Alice, 'that Sylvia couldn't come.'

'She would never be allowed to choose her own material,' put in Allegra.

'Poor Sylvia! I feel quite sorry for her,' said Mrs Lincroft; and she sighed. I knew she was thinking of the births of Alice and Allegra – highly dramatic and unorthodox both of them; and yet she had managed to give them a happier home than Sylvia's conventional one. I thought of her remark about the slippery stone and I thought: That woman has done everything she can to make up for her lapse.

'Poor Mrs Verlaine,' went on Alice. 'She isn't going to buy material for a new dress.'

'Perhaps she is,' said Mrs Lincroft.

'She is going to the British Museum,' added Allegra, eyeing me with speculation. I felt vaguely uncomfortable because I had not told them I was going to the British Museum. 'I heard you say so to Mr Wilmot, Mrs Verlaine,' added Allegra.

'Oh,' I stammered, caught off my guard. 'I thought I'd look in there. I used to live near and go in quite a lot.'

'Because your father was a professor,' went on Alice. 'I expect he made you work very hard which is why you are so good at the piano.' She looked at Allegra who said: 'I should like to go to the British Museum. Let's all go.'

I was so dismayed that I could find nothing to say for a few seconds. Then I said: 'I thought you were all eager to choose your new materials.'

'There's always plenty of time, isn't there, Mamma?' put in Alice eagerly, 'sometimes we go into the Park. But I'd rather go to the British Museum.'

Mrs Lincroft said: 'I don't see why you shouldn't have an hour or so there. When did you propose to go, Mrs Verlaine?'

'Oh please, I don't want to force this on you.'

'It can scarcely be said to be forced,' she replied with a smile. 'I tell you what we'll do. We'll go straight to the Museum and then we'll have luncheon at Brown's Hotel and afterwards choose the material and catch the four-thirty train home.'

Thus was my frustration complete but there was worse to come. While I sat back in my seat watching the fields and hedges skim by I was trying to think of some way of diverting their desires from the British Museum, but I dared not seem too disturbed. How had Allegra overheard my talk with Godfrey? We must have been careless.

At length I realised that there was nothing to be done but take them along with me to the Museum, where I must try to lose them and find my way to the Roman section alone.

Luck was against me that day. We had alighted from the cab which took us from the Station to the Museum when a voice called me by name.

'Why . . . surely . . . yes it is . . . Mrs Verlaine.'

Fortunately I was a little ahead of my companions so I moved quickly towards the speaker whom I recognised immediately as a colleague of my father's.

'A bad business that of your sister,' he said, shaking his head. 'What was it all about?'

'We . . . we never discovered.'

'A great loss,' he said. 'We always used to say that Roma Brandon would go even farther than your parents. Poor Roma . . .'

How resonant was his voice. Mrs Lincroft was near enough to have heard every word, but the children did not seem to be listening. Alice was standing with her back towards me pointing out something on the road to Allegra. But Mrs Lincroft must have heard.

'You must look us up sometime. Same address.'

'Thanks,' I said. 'Thanks.'

He had lifted his hat, bowed and moved off.

Mrs Lincroft said: 'I've never been in this place before. We don't take advantage of our museum, do we?'

My heart was beating fast. Perhaps she had not heard. Perhaps I had imagined that his voice was unusually resonant. She had not been so close as I thought her and her mind was on the material for the girls' dresses.

'No,' I said and there was a nervous laugh in my voice. 'We don't really.'

'We are taking advantage now.' Alice had come up with Allegra. 'How solemn it all is! How *important*!'

They walked beside me exclaiming as they went. I thought of the old days when I had come here so frequently, when my parents had believed that the greatest treat any child could enjoy was within these walls.

I had escaped them. I had left them all poring over an illuminated manuscript dating back to the twelfth century while I sped silently over those stone floors and here I was where I had been so many times with Roma.

I asked one of the guides where I could find any of the Roman relics from the Lovat Stacy site and I was directed immediately.

To my great joy it was there among other relics. The very mosaic which was so like that broken and battered one Godfrey and I had examined with such care. There was more than one. I had not known of this. Roma had only mentioned one, but perhaps she was so successful with it that she had attempted some sort of restoration of others. In the case with the mosaics was a printed notice describing them and the process used in the reconditioning. The first of them showed a figure – probably a man – who appeared to be without feet, for he stood on a pair of stumps which I realised were meant to be legs. His arms were stretched out as though he were attempting to catch at something which was not there. I looked at the second mosaic. The pictures were less vivid on this one and there were gaps in the scene which had been filled in with some sort of cement; but this was a picture of a man whose legs were cut off to the knee. I realised then that he was standing in something; and in the final one only the man's head was visible and he had clearly been buried alive.

I could not take my eyes from them.

'Why, they're ours,' said a voice at my elbow. I turned. Allegra and Alice were standing on either side of me.

'Yes,' I said, 'they were discovered on the site near Lovat Stacy.'

'Oh, but that makes them so very interesting, doesn't it?' said Alice.

Mrs Lincroft was coming towards us.

'Look, Mamma,' said Alice. 'Look what Mrs Verlaine has found.'

Mrs Lincroft studied the mosaics with what appeared to be a cursory interest. 'Very nice,' she said.

'But you haven't looked,' protested Allegra. 'They're ours.'

'What?' Mrs Lincroft looked closely. 'Well, fancy that!' She smiled at me apologetically. 'Now I really do think we must think about getting luncheon.'

I agreed. My mission was accomplished, though I was not sure how successfully. But I should have a great deal to tell Godfrey.

We made our way from the Museum and took a cab to Brown's while the girls chattered about what they would eat and what material they would choose.

When we came out the newsboys were shouting excitedly. 'Gentleman Terrall captured. Madman safe.'

'That's our Gentleman Terrall,' said Alice.

'What do you mean ... ours?' asked Mrs Lincroft sharply.

'We were talking about him, Mamma. We said he must be a little like Mr Wilmot.'

'Whatever made you say that?'

'Because he was a *gentleman*. We thought he'd look exactly like Mr Wilmot, didn't we, Allegra?'

Allegra nodded.

'You shouldn't think about such things.' Mrs Lincroft sounded quite cross and Alice was subdued.

No one mentioned the mosaics. More comforting still, none of them showed that they had overheard that conversation outside the Museum. My confidence began to return and by the time we had bought the material and we were ready to return home I was convinced that my identity was still a secret.

Godfrey was excited about my discovery in the Museum.

'I'm certain it means something,' he declared.

We had walked along beside the three baths and he stooped to peer at the mosaic as though he felt that if he looked long enough he would discover some meaning there.

'Don't you think they would have found out if it did?' I asked.

'Who, the archæologists? It may not have occurred to them. But I've a notion that there's something behind it.'

'Well, what do you propose to do? Go to the British Museum and lay this information before the powers that be?'

'They'd probably laugh at me.'

'You mean because they didn't discover it. Here is another version of the jealous-archæologist theory. It's fascinating, but it hasn't brought the solution of Roma's disappearance any nearer.'

I heard a little warning cough and turning saw the three girls coming towards us.

'We've come to see the mosaics,' announced Alice. 'We saw them in the Museum, you know. Mrs Verlaine showed us.'

'I liked the one with just the head showing,' said Allegra.

'It looked as if they'd chopped off his head and put it on the ground. It was gruesome, that one.'

'It made me feel sick,' commented Alice.

Godfrey straightened up and gazed towards the sea.

I guessed he wanted to change the subject for he said: 'How clear it is. They say that means rain.'

'It does,' agreed Allegra. 'When you can see the masts on the Goodwins it often means rain.'

Godfrey caught his breath; he seemed to have forgotten the presence of the girls. 'It's just struck me,' he said. 'These mosaics . . . they're meant to portray someone being buried alive.'

'You mean sinking in quicksand?'

Godfrey looked inspired. 'It was a sort of warning probably. As a punishment they took people out to the Goodwins so that they could gradually sink.'

'That wouldn't be possible, would it?' I asked.

He looked disappointed. 'Hardly. There might have been other sands.'

'Where?'

'Somewhere.' He waved his hand vaguely. 'But I'm sure that's what it means.'

'I think that's . . . horrible,' said Sylvia with a shudder. 'Fancy being . . .'

Godfrey stood rocking on his heels, entranced. I don't think I had ever seen him really excited before.

'Don't be a baby, Sylvia,' chided Allegra.

'We mustn't keep Miss Clent waiting,' said Alice. Then to me: 'Miss Clent is going to fit our dresses this morning.'

'Oh dear,' sighed Allegra. 'I wish I hadn't chosen that crushed strawberry. The burgundy red would have been so much better.'

'I did tell you,' said Alice mildly reproachful. 'In any case we can't keep Miss Clent waiting.'

So they left us to discuss the possibility of Godfrey's theory regarding the mosaic.

∽◈∼

'Alice has written a story about the mosaic,' Allegra announced. 'It's really a good one.'

'That's very creditable,' I said. 'You must show me this one, Alice.'

'I want to wait until I'm really satisfied.'

'But you showed Allegra and Sylvia.'

'I just see the effect on them. Besides, they're only children . . . well, they aren't much more. Grown ups would be more critical, wouldn't they?'

'I don't see why they should be.'

'Oh yes, of course they would. They are experienced of the world, whereas we have so much to learn.'

'So you won't show me this story?'

'I will one day . . . when I've perfected it.'

'It's about the man in the quicksand,' said Allegra.

Alice sighed and looked at Allegra who shrugged her shoulders sullenly.

'I thought you were proud of it,' she said.

Alice ignored her and turned to me. 'It's about the Romans,' she said, 'If anyone did anything wrong they used to put them in this quicksand and it very slowly swallowed them right up. It was slow. That was why they used it. Some quicksands swallow things up quickly . . . that's why they call them quicksands. But these were slow sands . . . it makes it last longer and is more of a punishment. They move and grip . . . you see . . . and the victim can't get away. So the Romans put their criminals into these sands. It was a good punishment. And there was a man in my story who had to make a mosaic of the sands and himself being swallowed up in them . . . before it happened to him. You see that was what was called refined torture. It was worse than just putting him in and letting him go down . . . because all the time he was making the mosaic he knew what was going to happen to him. And because he felt all that he made a wonderful mosaic . . . better than anyone could if they hadn't been so personally involved.'

'Alice, what ideas you get!'

'You think it's a good thing, don't you?' she asked anxiously.

'It is, provided you don't let your imagination run riot. You should let it dwell on *pleasant* things.'

'Oh,' said Alice, 'I see. But one has to be truthful, doesn't one, Mrs Verlaine. I mean one mustn't shut one's eyes to truth.'

'No, certainly not, but . . .'

'I was only thinking that why did they make those pictures on the mosaic if they were thinking of pleasant things? I can't believe it's very pleasant being caught in the shivering sands. That's what I'm calling my story. The Shivering Sands. It made me shiver when I wrote it. And the girls did, too, when I read it to them. But I will try to let my imagination work on pleasant things.'

When I came out of my room I ran straight into Sybil who seemed to have been lurking outside waiting for me.

'Ah, Mrs Verlaine,' she said, as though I was the last person she expected to see coming out of my own room. 'How nice to see you! It seems a long time since I last did. But then you have been so busy.'

'There are the lessons,' I replied vaguely.

'Oh, I didn't mean that.' She was looking into my room with excited prying eyes. 'I'd like to talk to you.'

'Would you care to come into my room?'

'That would be nice.'

She tiptoed in as though we were partners in a conspiracy and looked all round the room. 'Pleasant,' she commented. 'Very pleasant. I think you've been quite happy here, Mrs Verlaine,' she said. 'You'd be sorry to go.'

'Yes I should . . . if I were going.'

'I saw you with the curate. I suppose some would say he was a very handsome young man.'

'I suppose some would.'

'And you, Mrs Verlaine?' Her archness made me feel uncomfortable.

'Yes, yes, I suppose so.'

'I hear he'll soon be going to a very fine living. Well, it was to be expected. He has the right connections. He'll get on. A suitable wife is just what he needs.'

A flicker of irritation crossed my face and she may have noticed it for she said: 'I've taken a fancy to you. I shouldn't want you to go away. You seem to have become part of the place.'

'Thank you.'

'Of course everyone here is part of the place. Even people like Edith – who hadn't much personality, poor girl – she had her effect, didn't she? And a big one too. Poor child!'

I wished that I had not asked her in. I could have made my escape easily from the corridor.

'And of course,' she went on, 'it was your playing that startled William and made him so ill.'

I said with some exasperation: 'I've already told you that I was only playing what I was given to play.'

Her eyes brightened suddenly – glinting points of blue light embedded in the wrinkles.

'Oh yes . . . but who gave you that particular piece do you think, Mrs Verlaine?'

I said: 'I wish I knew.'

She had become so alert that I knew she was about to disclose what she had come to tell me.

'I remember the day she died . . .'

'Who?' I asked.

'Isabella. She played all the day. It was a new piece. She had just found the piano arrangement of it. *Danse Macabre.*' She began to hum it off-key which made the melody sound supernatural. 'The Dance of Death . . .' she mused. 'And all the time she was playing it she was thinking of death. Then she took the gun and went into the woods. That was why he couldn't bear to hear it played. *He* would never have put that piece in for you to play, would he?'

'Someone did.'

'I wonder who?'

She began to laugh and I said: 'Do you know?'

She did her mandarin's nod. 'Oh yes, Mrs Verlaine, I know.'

'It was someone who wanted to upset Sir William . . . to shock him. And he a sick man!'

'Why not?' she said. 'Why should he pretend to be so virtuous? He wasn't. I can tell you that. So why shouldn't he be shocked?'

'But it might have killed him. He's not to be upset.'

'You thought it was Napier. They quarrelled and he threatened Napier that he'd send him off again. Imagine it. There'd be no excitement here then. Why should Napier have to go? Why should Sir William pretend to be so good? There was a time . . .'

'Miss Stacy,' I said, 'did you put that piece of music among the selection I was to play?'

She hunched her shoulders like a child and nodded.

'So, you see,' she said, 'you shouldn't think too badly of Napier, should you?'

She was mad, I thought, dangerously mad. But I was glad then that she had come to my room. At least he was not guilty of that.

The mosaic was constantly in my mind and I could not rid myself of the idea that we had discovered something of importance. I went back again to the remains, and wandered about thinking of Roma, trying to remember what she had told me. One morning I met Napier there.

'You've started coming here again,' he said. 'I guessed I'd meet you some time.'

'You have seen me then?'

'Often.'

'When I was unaware of it? It is a little alarming to be watched when one is not conscious of it.'

'It shouldn't be,' he countered, 'if you have nothing to hide.'

'How many of us are as virtuous as that?'

'It's not necessarily a matter of virtue. For instance one might be engaged on a very creditable undertaking which required . . . anonymity. In which case it would be alarming to be secretly observed.'

'Such as . . .'

'Such as coming to a place incognito to solve the mysterious disappearance of a sister.'

I caught my breath and said: 'You know!'

'It was not so difficult to discover.'

'How long have you known?'

'Very soon after you came.'

'But . . .'

He laughed. 'As I said it was very easy. I wanted to know so much about you, and as you had a famous husband that simplified matters considerably. A famous husband, a sister who was well known in certain circles. Oh come, you must admit it was not a very difficult proposition.'

'Why didn't you tell me?'

'It would have made you uneasy, and I would rather you had told me who you were.'

'But I should never have been allowed to come had I told.'

'Told me,' he said. 'Not others.'

'Well, what are you going to do about it?'

'Precisely what I have been doing.'

'You are annoyed with me?'

'Why should I be so suddenly when I have known all along?'

'Are you laughing at me?'

'I'm admiring you.'

'For what?'

'For coming down here . . . for caring enough for your sister to put yourself in danger.'

'Danger! What danger should I be in?'

'People who try to discover what became of one who was possibly a murderer's victim often are.'

'Who said she was murdered?'

'I said "possibly". You can't say that she was not.'

'Roma was the last person anyone would want to murder.'

'Most murderers' victims are believed to be that. But how do you know what secrets she had? You could not know everything in her life.'

'In fact I knew very little.'

'So there you are. You may have rushed boldly into danger, and that is what I admire you for . . . and other things as well, of course.'

He had taken a step closer to me, gazing at me with an intense longing, and I felt excited and eager to comfort him.

'It has occurred to you,' he went on, 'that there are two

disappearances . . . and two is one too many for this to be accidental.'

'It's an obvious conclusion,' I said, 'so it did occur to me.'

'What do you think happened to your sister?'

'I don't know, except that she would never have gone away without saying where.'

'And Edith?'

'Edith too.'

'And you feel the two are connected?'

'It seems likely.'

'Has it occurred to you that Edith discovered something . . . some clue that might have thrown light on your sister's death? If this were so . . . what of you yourself who are boldly attempting to do the same thing? Shouldn't you be careful? You should not hunt alone . . . ah, but then Godfrey Wilmot hunts with you, doesn't he?'

'You can hardly call it that.'

'But he knows who you are.'

I nodded.

'You told him although you kept the secret from the rest of us.'

I shook my head. 'He knew who I was as soon as he saw me.'

'And confessed it? Of course he is frank and open . . . unlike some.'

'It was all so spontaneous. He knew me at once, and I was grateful that he did not betray me.'

'I have kept the knowledge to myself. Are you grateful to me?'

'Thank you.'

'You know,' he said looking intently at me, 'that I would do anything to help you.' I did not answer and he insisted: 'You do believe that?'

'Yes.'

'I'm glad. If we could solve our mysteries there is a great deal I could say to you. You know that too? So that it is as important to me . . . perhaps more so . . . to find the answers to these riddles.'

I was afraid suddenly of what he might say next and I was perhaps afraid of my own response. When I was with him I was fascinated by him; it was only when he was not there that I could view him coolly and dispassionately.

He seemed to understand this for he did not pursue it and went on: 'I saw your sister once or twice. She was passionately dedicated. She lived in that cottage all alone.'

'I came and stayed with her for a few nights.'

'How strange! You were so close and we did not meet.'

'It was hardly strange. I daresay there were many people on the dig whom you didn't see.'

'I was not thinking of many people . . . but of you. And you have come no nearer to discovering what happened to her than you were when you arrived?'

'Godfrey Wilmot thinks she may have made some fantastic archæological discovery of which some other archæologist was jealous. *I* think that is extremely far fetched.'

He looked at me earnestly. 'You must tell me if you discover anything that you think is leading you to the solution. You must let me help you. You must remember that if these two disappearances are connected it is of vital importance to *me* to discover the connection.'

'Nothing would please me more than to find the truth.'

'Then I can hope that we shall be together . . . in this?'

'Yes,' I said, 'let us be together in this.'

He reached out as though to touch me, but I turned away, pretending not to notice, and said I must return to the house.

Sybil had worked herself into a passion about the gipsies. She could talk of nothing else and seemed even to have forgotten her painting. She stalked about the house murmuring to herself of their shortcomings.

Sir William's health had improved during the last weeks. I expected a fresh outbreak of that quarrel between himself and Napier, but I heard nothing, and it occurred to me that Sir William realised how useful Napier was on the estate and had decided to make the best of the state of affairs as it stood. Not a very desirable set of circumstances but better than violent quarrelling.

My walled garden was a favourite spot of Sir William's and for that reason I now avoided it. His usual practice was to sit there for an hour every morning. Mrs Lincroft would bring him out and wrap him about with rugs and precisely an hour later would come out to bring him back into the house.

The first time I discovered him there Sybil was with him. I heard her voice as she talked to him.

'You've got to clear them off the land,' she was shouting. 'They bode no good. Look at the last time you let them stay. That girl came to work in the kitchens and look where that led us.'

'Sybil, be quiet,' said Sir William. 'Don't raise your voice so.'

'You always said you wouldn't have them here. What are you going to do about it?'

'Sybil . . . be quiet. Be quiet.'

I turned away and as I did so I came face to face with Mrs Lincroft. She gave me a hasty glance and ran into the walled garden.

'Miss Stacy,' she said, 'please don't worry Sir William. He is not well enough.'

'And who are you?' cried Sybil. 'Don't tell me. I know.

It's disgraceful. You regard yourself as mistress of this house, don't you? But let me tell you this, you may be his mistress but you are not the mistress of this house. You are encouraging those gipsies to stay. Why? Because that girl Serena knows too much, that's why.'

I walked away thinking: She is mad. Why did I ever listen to her nonsense? I have foolishly allowed her to influence me, when all the time she is living in a fantastic world of her own.

A few minutes later I saw Mrs Lincroft wheeling Sir William into the house, her face flushed, her eyes downcast.

But Sir William did listen to his sister. He declared that he would not have the gipsies encamping on his land and to Sybil's delight issued orders that they were to go.

Napier had joined his voice to Mrs Lincroft's and there had been a noisy scene which I heard the girls discussing.

'They will go.' Allegra had said, 'because Grandfather has said they will. He is the master here. My father and Mrs Lincroft are both against it.'

'My mother thinks they should go.' said Sylvia. 'She says it's a disgrace to the neighbourhood. They spoil the countryside and steal chickens, and they ought to go.'

'Well, *I* think it's a shame,' declared Allegra.

Alice shrugged her shoulders philosophically and said that the gipsies could find another pleasant place to have their camp and it would be better for everyone if they went.

Later when I was alone with Sylvia she looked slyly over her shoulders and whispered to me: 'My mother said that the only two who want the gipsies here are Mrs Lincroft and Mr Napier and the reason is the gipsy woman is blackmailing them.'

'I shouldn't spread a rumour like that, Sylvia, if I were you,' I said quickly.

'I wouldn't spread it. I'm just telling you, Mrs Verlaine. But that's what my mother says. Napier was that woman's lover once and she is Allegra's mother. My mother thinks that's very regrettable and that things like that shouldn't be allowed to happen. As for Mrs Lincroft . . . my mother says she's a mystery and she doesn't believe there ever was a Mr Lincroft.'

'I should keep that to yourself too, Sylvia,' I said; and I thought that she was the least attractive of the girls. 'Come along, we're forgetting your practice.'

The battle with the gipsies continued and Sir William had now committed himself to the attack. Mrs Lincroft was very uneasy; so was Napier; and I was beginning to believe that the gipsy woman had threatened them with exposure if they did not fight her tribe's battle for shelter on the Lovat Stacy land.

Then came that morning of revelation.

I was in the walled garden when Mrs Lincroft wheeled in Sir William. I was about to leave when he detained me and suggested that I remain and talk to him for a while. He wanted me to talk about music.

So I sat beside him and Mrs Lincroft remained while we conversed. He wanted to assure me how he enjoyed my performances on the late Lady Stacy's piano. He was often asleep when I finished, he knew; but that meant I had soothed him and that he had found my performance deeply satisfying.

We were talking thus peacefully when I was suddenly aware – one split second before the others – that someone had come into the courtyard. It was Serena, the gipsy.

Then Mrs Lincroft saw her. She started up with a little cry and said: 'What are you doing here?'

'I've come to see Sir William. How d'you do, Sir William. It's not easy to get to see you, but you can't help that, can you?'

'What does the woman want?' asked Sir William.

'You know who she is?' whispered Mrs Lincroft.

I rose and started to move away but the gipsy cried: 'No, you're to stay, M'am. I want you to hear this, too. I've got my reasons.'

I looked askance at Mrs Lincroft who nodded and I sat down again. The colour in Sir William's face had deepened to an alarming purple.

'Now, are you going to stop ordering us off your land, sir?'

'No, I am not,' retorted Sir William. 'You'll be gone by tomorrow night or I'll have the police on you.'

'I don't think you will,' said Serena insolently. She was standing with her hands on her hips, her legs slightly apart, her head thrown back. 'You'll be sorry if you don't stop that order right away and that's a fact.'

'Sorry!' he demanded. 'Is this blackmail?'

'You! To talk of blackmail, you old rogue! I reckon you're no better than the rest of us.'

Mrs Lincroft rose. 'I can't have Sir William upset.'

'You can't? And you can't have yourself upset either. But you've got to do what I want or you will. Oh, I know I'm poor. I know I don't live in this mansion here, but I've got a right to live where I want, same as anyone else . . . and if you try to stop me you're going to be sorry . . . both of you.'

Mrs Lincroft looked at me. 'I'll take Sir William in now,' she said.

I rose but the gipsy waved us both back.

'So you won't take off your ban?' she asked.

'No, I won't,' declared Sir William. 'You're going before the week's out. I've sworn I won't have gipsies on my land and I mean it.'

'I'll give you one more chance.'

'Be off with you.'

'All right. You've asked for it. I'm going to tell you one or two things you won't like. There's my girl Allegra, your granddaughter . . .'

'That's unfortunately so,' said Sir William. 'We have looked after the child. She has had her home here. There our duty ends.'

'Oh yes . . . and Napier is said to be her father. That suits you, don't it? But what if I tell you he's not, eh? That's what I'm telling you, and you won't like it. One of your sons was the father of my child but it wasn't Nap. Oh no, it was your precious Beau . . . him you build temples to.'

'I don't believe it,' cried Sir William.

'I thought you wouldn't. But I ought to know who the father of my own child is.'

'It's lies,' said Sir William. 'All lies.'

'Don't listen to the woman,' said Mrs Lincroft, rising and putting her hands on the wheelchair.

'Listen to that woman instead!' jeered the gipsy. 'She'll tell you all you want to know. She'll say yes, yes, yes . . . like she always has.' Serena thrust her face forward and leered. 'Right from the beginning, eh . . . even when poor Lady Stacy was alive. And why did she kill herself, do you think? Because her son was accidentally shot by his brother? Because she'd lost her boy? That perhaps, but mostly because she hadn't a husband to comfort her and help her over her loss. She'd discovered that he was far more interested in comforting the pretty companion.'

'Stop it,' cried Mrs Lincroft. 'Stop . . . at once.'

'Stop it! Stop it!' echoed the gipsy. She turned to me.

'Some people don't like to hear the truth. And can you blame them? I don't. Because the truth ain't very nice. Poor old Nap! He was the scapegoat. He'd shot his brother so it was easy to blame him for everything. If I'd said Beau was the father of the child I was going to have I'd have been sent packing. No one would have believed me. So I said it was Nap. Then they believed me all right and accepted their responsibility and I did it for the child's sake. So I lied ... because I knew it was the only way to get a home for her ... and when Lady Stacy killed herself and left a note saying why ... not only because she'd lost her beautiful boy but because her husband was unfaithful to her right under her own roof ... they blamed Nap for that too and sent him away. That made it all very simple. One villain instead of three.'

'You're upsetting Sir William,' said Mrs Lincroft.

'Let him be upset. Let him come out from behind Nap. Let him stop kidding himself that he's not responsible for his wife's suicide. And don't forget ... if the gipsies are moved on everyone will know this, not just Madam Music here.'

Mrs Lincroft looked appealingly at me. 'I must get Sir William into the house,' she said. 'I think we should call the doctor. Would you see about that please, Mrs Verlaine.'

I went down to the stables because I knew that Napier would be coming in at that hour. When he arrived I said: 'There is something I must tell you. We can't talk here.'

'Where?' he asked.

'In the copse. I'll go there now and wait.'

He nodded; he could see by my expression that this was something important.

I walked across the gardens to the copse. I had to talk

to him about what I had heard in the enclosed garden; and even as I walked across the lawns on that bright and sunny day I felt that eyes were watching me. I could not rid myself now of the notion that everything I did was being observed, that someone was waiting for the chance to strike at me. It would not be death by fire this time. But there were other alternatives. And the one who was watching me, planning my destruction was, I felt in my bones, the one responsible for the deaths of Edith and Roma.

I was not safe, but I was learning rapidly; and what I had heard this morning – if it were true – was knowledge that made me joyous. And I could not wait to tell Napier what I knew.

I waited in the copse, near the ruin. Destroyed by fire . . . like the cottage. The first of the fires. I leaned against the walls and listened. A footfall in the woods. How foolish I was to come here alone. What could happen to me in this copse, this haunted copse to which people did not come frequently because they were afraid of ghosts.

But Napier would be here soon.

I looked over my shoulder uneasily. The crackle of under-growth had startled me. I had a notion that somewhere . . . among those trees . . . some alien eyes regarded me. Someone was asking himself – or herself – what is she doing here? Is this the time?

Panic seized me. I called out: 'Is that you, Napier?'

There was no answer. Only a rustle of leaves . . . and again that crackle of undergrowth which might have been a footstep.

And then Napier was coming towards me.

'I'm so pleased to see you.'

I held out my hands and he grasped them warmly.

'I have discovered the truth about Allegra,' I said. 'Her

mother has just confronted Sir William and told him. I had to see you. I had to . . .'

He repeated: 'The truth about . . . Allegra?'

'That Beau was her father.'

'She told him that?'

'Yes. In the courtyard a short while ago. He was threatening to evict the gipsies and she came to see him and told him that his precious Beau was Allegra's father and that she had blamed you because they would have said she was lying and turned her away if she had accused Beau.'

He was silent and I said: 'And you let them believe it.'

'I'd killed him,' he said. 'I thought it was a way of making amends. He would have hated them knowing about the gipsy. He had always cared so much for their good opinion.'

He was still grasping my hands and I looked up into his face, smiling.

'I was going away,' he went on. 'It didn't seem to matter. One more misdemeanour . . . when there had been so many.'

'And your mother . . . she killed herself because she discovered that your father and Mrs Lincroft were lovers. It was not only because she had lost Beau.'

'It's all in the past,' he said.

'It is not,' I cried passionately, 'when it continues to affect the present and the future.'

'As you know very well.'

I lowered my eyes. Pietro had never seemed so far away as he was at this moment.

'You are a fool, Napier,' I said.

'Has it taken you so long to discover that?'

'We are all foolish. But you have allowed them to *blame* you.'

'I killed him,' he said. 'If you could have seen him . . . like everyone else you would have loved him.'

'He was clearly not perfect.'

'He was young, virile . . . full of life.'

'So he seduced the gipsy girl.'

'He was so full of vitality, and if he had lived he would never have disclaimed responsibility. He would have set her up somewhere, looked after her – and kept it from them. On the day I shot him I wished fervently . . . and most sincerely . . . that he had been the one to fire first. Then it would have been less of a tragedy. They would have forgiven him.'

'Were you jealous of him?'

'Of course not. I admired him. I wished I were like him. I tried to imitate him because I thought he was wonderful. I followed him and tried to be as much like him as possible. But I didn't envy him. I was as fond of him as the others were . . . perhaps more. I thought him perfect.'

'So you took his blame on your shoulders.'

'It was the least I could do after taking his life.'

'If you had killed him deliberately you could not have paid much more fully.'

'So?'

'The affair is finished. You must banish it from your mind.'

'Do you think I can ever do that?'

'Yes, I do. And you shall.'

'Perhaps there is one person who could force me to do that . . . one person in the world. And you . . . have you forgotten your past?'

'Perhaps there is one person who could make *me* do so.'

'And you are not sure . . .'

'I am becoming more certain of it every day.'

We stood hands clasped but apart, for Edith still stood between us.

But I vowed I would not rest until I had discovered what had happened to Edith. It was imperative that I did. He was cleared of seduction of the gipsy, of causing his mother to kill herself, but he must be cleared of Edith's disappearance ... or death ... before either of us could move into that future which was beginning to be so desirable to us both.

Chapter Twelve

*I*t was afternoon . . . the time of quiet. Sir William had
been ordered to rest by the doctor, and Mrs Lincroft
was lying down. She felt very distressed, she told me; and I
saw the guilt in her eyes for she could scarcely bear to look
at me.

I wanted to think about everything. I wanted to go over
minute by minute that interview with Napier. I had to think
about him and Godfrey.

But in my heart I did not need to make a decision. I
knew . . . just as I had known when I had pretended to
consider whether to give up my career for marriage with
Pietro, that I would always follow my heart's direction. If
Roma were here now she would say I was mad to throw
aside marriage with Godfrey for the sake of Napier. Godfrey
offered security . . . the comfortable, easy life. And Napier?
I was not sure what life would be like with him. I did not
believe the shadow of Beaumont's death had receded
suddenly. I could not hope to eliminate it so easily. It would
appear at unexpected moments; it would be a shadow across
Napier's life for many years to come. And what of Pietro?
Should I ever forget?

On this sunny afternoon with an hour or so to spare I would go to the walled garden to think.

I made my way there and was surprised when I arrived to find Alice sitting there demurely, her hands folded in her lap.

'I thought you'd come here, Mrs Verlaine,' she said.

'Did you want to see me?'

'Yes, I did. I want to tell you something ... show you something I've found and I don't really want to talk about it here.'

'Why ever not?'

'Because I think it may be very important.' She stood up. 'Could we go for a little walk?'

'But certainly.'

As she walked away from the house, she kept looking over her shoulder.

'What's the matter, Alice?' I asked.

'I was making sure that no one was following us.'

'Did you think they were?'

'I always think they are – after the fire.' I shivered, and she went on: 'And so do you, Mrs Verlaine, don't you?'

I confessed that I often felt uneasy. 'Of course,' said Alice, 'anyone might get trapped in a burning cottage. But I felt ever since, that I had to look after you rather specially.'

'That is sweet of you, Alice. And I certainly feel very cherished.'

'It's how I want you to feel.'

'It's comforting to have a guardian angel.'

'Yes, it must be. Well, you have one now, dear Mrs Verlaine.'

'Where are we going and what are you going to show me?'

'We're turning off here and going down to the shore.'

'Is it down there then?'

'Yes, and I do really think it may be very important.'

'You're keeping me in suspense.'

'Not really, Mrs Verlaine. But I don't know how to describe it. But I think it may be of archæological significance.'

'Good Heavens, Alice, don't you think we ought to . . .'

'To tell someone else? Oh no, not yet. Let us be the ones to discover it.'

'You are being mysterious.'

'You'll soon know.' She looked over her shoulder.

'What's the matter?'

'I just had a feeling that we were being followed.'

'I can see no one.'

'They could be hidden by those bushes.'

'I don't think so. In any case there are two of us. We mustn't be so nervous.'

Alice led the way down the winding cliff path to the sands. Halfway down she paused and said: 'Listen.'

We stood still listening. 'You can hear footsteps clearly here . . . even if people are a long way away.'

'All's well,' I said. 'I came this way before.'

'Yes, and I warned you to be sure you didn't get cut off by the tide. Remember? Perhaps I saved your life then.' The thought pleased her. 'It seems to be my mission in life.'

We had reached the sands and a little way ahead of us was that little cove with the overhanging rock where she had told me previously it was so easy to get cut off by the tide.

Purposefully, now and then looking uneasily about her, she led the way.

'Here, Mrs Verlaine.' She had disappeared in an opening in the rocks.

'What is this, Alice?'

'It's a sort of cave. Come in.'

I entered and she said: 'This part is just a cave. But I think

377

I've found some drawings in an inner cave. They're very crude . . . the sort that people did hundreds of years ago. The Stone Age probably. Mr Wilmot was telling us about that. Or perhaps the Bronze Age.'

I thought of Roma. Drawings in a cave! Had Godfrey been right? Had she made some startling discovery and had she been murdered because of it?

'I believe it's of very great importance,' went on Alice.

'But where . . .' I looked about the dim cave and could see nothing.

She laughed almost indulgently. 'If it had been easy to see it would have been discovered long ago. Look.' She advanced into the cave. 'There's a great boulder here. You have to roll it away . . . and I suppose nobody thought of doing that . . . until I did. Oh, Mrs Verlaine, it's really *my* discovery. I could be famous, I suppose.'

'It depends what you've found, Alice.'

'Something wonderful. And I'm going to show you.'

She had succeeded in rolling away the boulder and beyond it a cavern yawned. 'Look,' she said. 'You have to squeeze through here . . . It's not easy. I'll go first and you follow.'

'Alice. Is it safe?'

'Oh yes . . . it's only caves. I've already explored. You don't think I'd let you come if it wasn't safe, do you? Come on.' She had disappeared and I could just see the white of her dress. I followed it and stepped through into another cave.

Alice produced a candle from her pocket and striking a match lighted it. 'There!' There was now a faint glow in the cave and I exclaimed with wonder for as my eyes grew accustomed to the dim light I saw that here was a wealth of stalagmite and stalactite formation and its beauty was unearthly. All kinds of shapes had been formed and even in this light I could see that the colours were wonderful – copper had produced that green, iron the brown and red, manganese that delightful pink. It was like stepping into a world of fantasy.

'Alice!' I cried. 'But it's a wonderful discovery . . .'

She laughed gleefully. 'I thought you'd say that. I was longing to show it to you.'

'But we must get back. We must tell of this. It's like the caves of Cheddar. Fancy all this time . . . it was here . . . and no one knew.'

'You are excited, Mrs Verlaine.'

'It's a great discovery.'

'There's something else I want to show you though . . . this isn't all. Give me your hand, you have to go carefully.' She took my hand and almost immediately I nearly stumbled. She was alarmed 'Oh, Mrs Verlaine, do be careful. It would be awful if you fell here . . .'

'I'll be careful, Alice. But let's get someone else. Mr Wilmot will be delighted. He'll be mad with joy.'

'First I want to show *you*, Mrs Verlaine. Oh *please*, let me show you first.'

I laughed. Then I said: 'Listen! I can hear the sound of running water.'

'Yes. The next cave is far more exciting. Do come and look at it now. I can't wait to show you. It's a sort of water-fall. It's an underground stream I think, and it goes through the caves and out into the sea somewhere. There are the drawings on the walls . . . that's what I think is most interesting, Mrs Verlaine.'

I said: 'The sand here is quite damp.'

'It's the stream and the waterfall.' She produced another candle. 'One each,' she said. 'I thought you'd like to have one. Isn't this exciting? I call it my cave. It's on the Stacy land, you know, and all the foreshore belongs to Sir William and his heirs.'

I could not take my eyes from those marvellous formations; the shapes were quite fantastic and when I thought that they had been slowly forming through the centuries I was so overawed that I could only stand and stare.

But Alice was impatient to disclose further wonders. I followed her through a gap in the rock and we were in a third cave. I could hear the water clearly now and I saw it freely trickling over the rocks. I peered forward.

Alice said; 'The drawings on the walls are like those we saw in the British Museum.'

'Alice!' I cried. 'But this is wonderful.' I was sure now that it was what Roma had discovered. Was it possible that Godfrey's theory of the jealous archæologist had some truth in it after all?

'You can see for yourself,' said Alice. 'Over there.'

As I advanced my feet sank into the damp sand and it was difficult walking. I went forward holding the candle high, my eyes on the walls of the cave. Alice stood watching me.

'It's quite . . . miraculous!' I began; and then suddenly I knew.

I turned to Alice. 'Alice,' I cried, 'stay where you are.'

She was standing at the mouth of the cave, the candle held high over her head.

'Yes, Mrs Verlaine,' she said meekly.

'Alice . . . I . . . can't . . . move . . . my feet. Alice . . . Alice . . . I'm sinking.'

She said: 'They're *slow* quicksands, Mrs Verlaine. It takes a long time for you to disappear altogether.'

'Alice!' I shrieked. But she just stood there smiling at me.

'You!' I cried.

'Yes,' she replied. 'Why not? Because I'm young. I'm clever, Mrs Verlaine. I'm cleverer than the rest of you. These are my caves. These are my sands . . . and I shall never let anyone take them from me.'

'No,' I murmured, my thoughts confused. I could not believe this. It was a nightmare, a fantastic dream. I should wake in a moment.

She stood watching me, holding the candle above her head – and she was the more evil because she looked so meek, so docile. My candle slipped from my fingers; I stared at it as it lay on the sand for a second or so before it was sucked under.

Alice had moved; I saw her turn away and then she was holding up a rope . . . the thick kind which I had seen tethering boats on the shore.

She was going to save me. She had been teasing me. Oh, what a dangerous and cruel trick to play!

'If I threw this to you, Mrs Verlaine, I might be able to pull you in . . . but I might not . . . the sands are strong. They look so soft . . . but they grip so tightly and they don't like letting their victims go. Just little particles of sand! Isn't it fascinating, Mrs Verlaine? But then nature *is* fascinating. The vicar always says so.'

'Alice, throw me the rope.'

She shook her head.

'It's what is called exquisite torture, Mrs Verlaine. All the time you think I may throw you the rope and that makes it all the harder. You see if you give up hope you're resigned . . . and you let yourself slip away . . . Don't struggle. That makes you go down more quickly. Unless you want to go quickly, of course. I shall stay here . . . until you've gone.'

'Alice . . . you *fiend*.'

'Yes, I am. But you must admit I'm a clever one.'

'You deliberately brought me here.'

'Yes, deliberately,' she said. 'You and the others.'

'No!'

'But yes. This place belongs to me. I'm Sir William's daughter. It should be mine. Napier is his son but Napier

killed Beau and Sir William hates him. He hated Napier's
mother and he loves mine. He will leave me the place when
Napier is sent away. That's what I want. And when anyone
bothers me I shall bring them down to my cave. You bothered me, Mrs Verlaine. You came here to look for your sister.
She bothered me because she almost discovered my cave.
She came looking for it. She came down here so I showed
her what I had found . . . just as I showed you.'

The sand was about my ankles now. She watched me with
the eye of a connoisseur. 'The deeper you sink the quicker
it swallows you,' she told me. 'But you are tall and these
are slow quicksands.'

'Help me, Alice,' I pleaded. 'What have I ever done to
harm you?'

'You are too inquisitive, and you came here to find out,
didn't you? That was very sly to pretend it was only to teach
us music when all the time you were *her* sister. I knew that
as soon as Mr Wilmot came. He gave it away, didn't he? I
used to follow you and hear you talking. I knew I'd have
to kill you, but another disappearance seemed too many so
I lured you to the cottage and that would have been an end
of you but for that old gardener.'

She was smiling – diabolically, so delighted with her
cleverness, so anxious that I should realise how skilful she
was.

'He saw me and I thought I might be suspected so I saved
you instead. I saved your life . . . well, now I'm taking it
away. I'm a goddess with power over life and death.'

'You're mad,' I said.

'Don't say that,' she cried angrily.

'Alice, what has happened to you?'

'Nothing. It's all very easy to understand. You should
have become engaged to Mr Wilmot and stopped thinking
about *us*. But you wouldn't, would you? You wanted to

marry Napier and it would have been the same as Edith. She had to go away because she was going to have a baby and I wasn't going to let there be another heir. So I brought her here and she went where you're going now. I will drive Napier away because Sir William loved Beau and Napier killed him and Beau will haunt the house until Napier goes away. I shall see to that. Then Sir William will recognise his own daughter and all this will be mine. You always thought I was a *good* little girl, didn't you? You didn't know me really, although I told you when you came here that we should take you by surprise. You had a hint and you didn't take it. Now you're caught. You meddled. You found the pattern in the mosaic, didn't you, and you went to the British Museum. There was a man there who knew you – but I knew already who you were. But after that it had to happen quickly because you'd found out about a pattern . . . and that pattern was my shivering sands.'

'Help me,' I said and my voice echoed in the cave.

'No one can hear and the deeper you sink the greater the grip it gets on you.'

I thought: This is the end. Oh Roma, what did you feel in those moments before the sands swallowed you? Poor Roma! The discovery of the paintings in the cave would have been the greatest adventure of her life – and she had died here as they were revealed to her.

And Edith. What had Edith felt?

'Alice,' I cried. 'You're mad . . . mad . . .'

'Don't say that. Don't dare say it.'

I felt numb with fear. This was the second time in a very short period that I had faced horrible death. I could feel the cold sand above my ankles now and in vain did I try to extricate my feet. I tried not to see that demure, diabolical figure standing there on the edge of the quicksand holding the candle high above her head. I tried to think what I could do.

'Help me! Help me!' I sobbed.

And I could feel the implacable sand drawing me slowly and surely down.

⸙

There was someone else in the cave. I heard a voice cry: 'Good God!' And it was Godfrey's voice. 'Caroline! Caroline!'

'Don't come near,' I shouted. 'I'm sinking . . . sinking in the sand.'

Alice said coldly: 'Please go away. This is my cave.'

Godfrey stepped forward. I screamed: 'No. Don't set foot on the sand. Stay . . . stay where she is . . .'

'We need a rope.' He turned to Alice. 'Go and get one . . . quickly.'

She stood there not speaking. I cried out: 'She has a rope there. It's for . . . exquisite torture. She's a murderess. She murdered Roma . . . and Edith.'

Then Napier was there and in his hands he was holding the rope.

⸙

The nightmare of that cave lives with me still. The drawings on the walls, the pictures, the knowledge that hundreds of years ago men had been brought there to die . . . And Alice . . . strange Alice . . . had brought her enemies to die in the same way. Roma . . . Edith . . . myself.

I caught at the rope. They were shouting to me to tie it about my waist. They would save me . . . these two men together who both loved me.

I heard Alice's voice – strange, mad, chanting, 'Hurry, my shivering sands. Take her . . . take her as you took the others.'

I kept my eyes on those two men.

'We'll do it,' I heard Napier say.

And I knew they would.

I lay in bed, nightmare haunted. I kept starting out of my unconsciousness to feel the soft implacable grip about my knees. It was only the bed clothes. I was haunted by the memory of a nightmare figure holding a candle . . . a face revealed to me in all its horror which was even greater because of the guileless mask with which I had become familiar.

Napier was at my bedside; so was Godfrey.

'Try to rest,' said Napier; and the pressure of his hand on my wrist reassured me. It shut out the nightmare and brought me back to reality.

'Everything is all right now,' said Godfrey.

Then I was able to sleep.

I had been fortunate on that day. What luck for me that Godfrey should have been coming over to Lovat Stacy to show me pictures of Roman mosaics in a book he had found in a second-hand bookshop in Dover.

He had seen me descending the cliff with Alice. She had been right to fear that we were being followed.

As for Napier, he believed that I would marry Godfrey and in a jealous mood, believing that Godfrey was going to meet me, he had followed him. A set of circumstances which had brought them both into the cave when the strength of two men was needed for my rescue.

Yes, I was undoubtedly fortunate on that day.

I lay in bed thinking of it and I kept telling myself: the barriers are down now. The way ahead is clear for us.

And Alice? Why had this strange girl behaved as she had? What canker had eaten into her soul?

The girls were questioned . . . they who had lived so much closer to her than any of us and who knew so much of her.

Allegra said: 'She made us do what she wanted. It started long ago. She used to find out things we'd done and make us do what she commanded . . . to show she had power over us. We had to pretend that she was a sort of goddess and we were ordinary mortals. At first it was little things like making a face at Miss Elgin when her back was turned or breaking the handle off a cup or picking roses in the garden when we weren't supposed to, or going to Beau's room and making fun of his picture. Then it was bigger things. We had to haunt the chapel. Sometimes with candles, sometimes with a lantern. It was to pretend Beau didn't want Napier here and was haunting it. And one day I set fire to the altar cloth and it all blazed up. I ran away and the fire started. After that I had to do everything she said because if I didn't she would have told what I'd done. I was afraid Grandfather would send me away. So we haunted the chapel in turns . . . and when Mrs Verlaine suspected one of us the other had to do it, while Mrs Verlaine was with the one she had suspected. And then when she thought that Napier was getting too fond of Mrs Verlaine we pretended we had seen him digging a hole in the copse . . .'

Sylvia said: 'I had to do the haunting, too. I was always hungry and used to take things from the pantry at home. She said she would tell my mother that I was a thief. And she knew that Edith was meeting Jeremy Brown and so Edith had to do what she was told. Then Jeremy went away and Edith said she wouldn't do anything more and that she was going to stop Alice's blackmailing . . . which was what she called it. And so . . . she disappeared.'

It was small wonder that we asked what canker of madness was working in that youthful mind.

And what should be done with Alice?

When she had been brought back from the caves she had resumed her docile demeanour. I was deeply sorry for Mrs Lincroft who had become like a woman who walked in her sleep.

Strangely enough it was to me that she told her story. I was in my room, for the doctor had said I should rest for the whole of that day and the next for I had sustained a great shock, and it was when I was lying in my room that this strange woman glided in and sat by my bed.

'Mrs Verlaine,' she said, 'what can I say to you? My daughter tried to kill you . . . twice.'

I said: 'Don't distress yourself, Mrs Lincroft. I'm safe now.'

'But I am to blame,' she insisted. 'I only am to blame. What will they do with my little Alice? They will not punish her. It is not her fault. I and I only am the one to blame.'

She walked about my room – a strange shadowy figure in her long grey skirts and her chiffon blouse with the loose bishop's sleeves caught in at the wrists.

'I am the murderess. I . . . Mrs Verlaine . . . not Alice.'

I said: 'Mrs Lincroft, try not to distress yourself. This is a terrible thing. But the doctors will know what to do with Alice. Where is she now?'

'She is sleeping. She looked so strange when they brought her back. She behaved as though nothing had happened. She was so gentle . . . so sweet . . . as she always was.'

'There is something terrible wrong with Alice.'

'I know,' she said. Then: 'I know what is wrong with my daughter.'

'You know?'

'She cared so much that she should live here; it was important to her that she should be Sir William's daughter . . . she wanted to own this place . . .'

'But how could she?'

'She would never accept defeat. Even now . . . she does not. She behaves as though nothing has happened, as though . . . in time she will convince us of this.'

Mrs Lincroft was silent for a moment and then she went on: 'I shall have to tell the truth now. There is no holding back. Perhaps I should have told it years ago. But I kept my secret. I kept it well and no one knew. No one at all . . . least of all Alice. I felt it was important that no one should know . . . not only for my sake but mainly for hers. But you are supposed to be resting. Perhaps I shouldn't tell you. It will only disturb you. Anyone would be disturbed by such a story.'

'Tell me, please, Mrs Lincroft. I want to know.'

'You already know that Sir William was my lover and that I came here as a penniless girl to be a companion to his wife. You know of the position between us; you know of the death of Beau and how Lady Stacy shot herself soon afterwards. The gipsy spoke the truth. It was because of us . . . Sir William and myself. There was a scene when she found us together and that, added to her grief over Beau's death, was more than she could endure. I went away when she died. We thought it best for a while. I was very unhappy. I did not think Sir William would want me back, and I was terribly shocked by the tragedy for which we were responsible . . . and I could only remind him of it. During the years he has tried to convince himself that she killed herself because of her grief over Beau – but in his heart he knew that that wasn't true. It was her grief over his infidelity. But for that, he could have helped her over the tragedy. But Sir William tried to force himself to believe that it was due to Beau's death. He blamed Napier;

388

and every time he saw his son he was reminded of what he had done. And so . . . he could not bear the sight of Napier. He blamed Napier for everything so that he could stop blaming himself. People often hate those to whom they are unjust.'

'I know this is true,' I replied. 'Poor Napier.'

'Napier knew this. But he could not get over the fact that he had killed his beloved brother, and he seemed to *want* to be blamed. You see he took the responsibility for Allegra's existence on his own shoulders.'

'People's motives are so mixed . . . so difficult to fathom.'

She nodded and went on: 'I was frightened when I left here. I knew I had to find another job. First though I took a little holiday.' She shivered and it was evident that she found it a great effort to go on. 'I met a man. He was charming, attentive . . . and I was greatly attracted to him . . . and he to me. He talked of marriage and all in the space of a fortnight we became lovers. He left me at the boarding house where we were staying and said he would go back to his home in London and in a week or so send for me. We were to be married there. He was arrested and I learned that my lover was a homicidal maniac who had already murdered three women. He had escaped from Broadmoor and in his lucid moments appeared to be perfectly normal. I believe that had he not been arrested he would have murdered me in time. Perhaps it would have been better if he had. I was completely shattered when this was discovered. I hastily left the boarding house and tried to lose myself in London. And then I discovered that I was to have a child: "Gentleman" Terrall's child.'

I caught my breath. Now I understood why she had been upset when she had seen the announcement of this man's escape, how relieved by his recapture. This man . . . Alice's father!

'I was desperate!' she said. 'What would you have done,

Mrs Verlaine? What could anyone have done? Tell me that. I was alone in the world . . . about to have a madman's child. What could I do? I made a plan. I wrote to Sir William. I told him I was going to have a child . . . *his* child. It was easy to delude him by making Alice six months older than she actually is. He sent me money . . . enough to enable me to get comfortably through my difficult time. And when Alice was two years old I came back as Mrs Lincroft, a widow with one child, and that is where I have been ever since.'

'Oh, Mrs Lincroft, how sorry I am for you.'

She rocked herself gently to and fro. 'What tragedies we hide behind our masks,' she murmured. 'And one builds a little refuge and one feels one is safe but there is the slippery step . . . at everybody's door.'

'And now?' I asked.

'Who knows?' she answered. 'I expect they will take her away from me now. I must tell them the truth. My poor child . . . She was so like him . . . I used to watch for the signs. He had her gentleness. He wanted to be good, I am sure.'

I could only murmur my sympathy. I could offer her nothing else.

'What will become of us?' she murmured. 'What will become of us now?'

Alice herself decided what should be done.

The day after we had come back from the caves she was missing. Her little room was as neat as ever, the bed made, the coverlet smooth; everything neatly folded in her drawers.

But there was no Alice.

I knew where she was. She had heard that she was not Sir William's daughter, that she would have to go away. This was something she had vowed she would never do. She had determined she would stay at Lovat Stacy forever. She would not accept the fact that it was not her home.

She would always think of the dramatic effect. Beside the shifting sands she had dropped a handkerchief with 'A' neatly embroidered in the corner.

I pictured her standing there, holding her candle in her hand. Now she would be buried forever in the land which she had determined should be her own.

Nothing would be the same again. Between the new and the old life was a great chasm which could never be crossed. The past was dead and the future was vital and living. For one thing Death had taught me when it had come close to me and all but taken me by the hand was that I wanted to live. I wanted desperately to live. I wanted to build up a new life over the ruins which should be so completely hidden that it would be as though they had never existed.

There were two men waiting for me. One was cool and charming, so certain of his place in the world; and the other was scarred by life. Godfrey was so sure, Napier so unsure.

They had both been at hand when I needed them; they had both been watchful since the fire; in their different ways they loved me. Godfrey tenderly, kindly, gently and perhaps dispassionately; perhaps he had chosen me because I would make a suitable wife. And Napier fiercely, possessively, desperately.

'Marry Godfrey,' my head told me. 'Go right away from here and forget your nightmares. Live graciously . . . bring up a family in ideal surroundings . . . comfortable and easy.'

'But,' said my heart, 'this is where you belong.' Nightmares, perhaps. Memories. Devils to fight, his and your own. Pietro to mock you for having once more followed the call of the heart.

And when Napier came to me and took my hands in his, different now, Napier the free man, he said: 'Now I suppose you think you should marry Godfrey and settle down in your country vicarage while you await your bishopric. But you're not going to.' And he laughed and I laughed with him. 'You're going to be a fool. Caroline. Everyone will tell you you're a fool.'

'Not everyone,' I said.

And I was confident. My heart would always win.

The Time of the Hunter's Moon

Victoria Holt

Said to be a time of mystical significance...

During the last weeks of her stay in an exclusive finishing school in Switzerland, Cordelia Grant, in the company of three friends, has a strange experience in a nearby forest. It occurs at the time of the Hunter's Moon and the attractive man whom the girls encounter seems to them to be a mysterious figure conjured up out of local legend.

Returning to England, Cordelia takes a post in a girls' school, situated among the ancient ruins of a Devon abbey. There she becomes disturbed by Sir Jason Verringer, the local landowner. His reputation is sinister and yet Cordelia cannot help but be drawn to him...

Tension mounts at the time of the Midsummer Moon when a pageant is staged by the school among the abbey ruins; and when Cordelia has news from the girls who had shared her forest adventure, she begins to realise that her past is becoming dangerously entwined with the present...

'For a good escapist read Victoria Holt never disappoints.'
Annabel

ISBN-13 978 0 00 723552 0
ISBN-10 0 00 723552 6

Mistress of Mellyn

Victoria Holt

Martha Leigh's arrival at Mount Mellyn, an eerie mansion set high on the Cornish cliffs, leaves her with a sense of deep foreboding. She is dreading her new life as a governess, particularly when she meets her arrogant employer, Con TreMellyn and his precocious young daughter Alvean.

Martha quickly realizes why three governesses before her had left that cold and brooding house. Even stranger, the sinister air that surrounds the place is encouraged by the neighbours and servants, who seem eager to give hints and fuel rumours about haunted rooms, strange accidents and past infidelities.

When Martha's resolve to stay on however, is quickened by her growing fondness for Alvean and an unwilling attraction towards Con TreMellyn, she becomes determined to unravel the mysteries that surround the family, a decision that ultimately threatens her own life.

Mistress of Mellyn is a novel of considerable power and beauty written in the great romantic tradition, a work of unforgettable suspense.

ISBN-13 978 0 00 723551 3
ISBN-10 0 00 723551 8

ENJOYED THIS BOOK? WHY NOT TRY OTHER GREAT HARPERCOLLINS TITLES – AT 10% OFF!

Buy great books direct from HarperCollins
at **10%** off recommended retail price.
FREE postage and packing in the UK.

☐	**The Time of the Hunter's Moon**	Victoria Holt	0-00-723552-6 £6.99
☐	**The Shadow of the Lynx**	Victoria Holt	0-00-723553-4 £6.99
☐	**Mistress of Mellyn**	Victoria Holt	0-00-723551-8 £6.99
☐	**Much Ado About You**	Eloisa James	0-00-722948-8 £6.99
☐	**The Constant Princess**	Philippa Gregory	0-00-719031-X £6.99
☐	**The Borgia Bride**	Jeanne Kalogridis	0-00-714883-6 £6.99
☐	**Seeds of Yesterday**	Virginia Andrews	0-00-724030-9 £6.99
☐	**Garden of Shadows**	Virginia Andrews	0-00-720431-7 £6.99
☐	**The Hour Before Dawn**	Sara MacDonald	0-00-719429-3 £6.99
☐	**The Villa in Italy**	Elizabeth Edmondson	0-00-722377-3 £6.99

Total cost _____

10% discount _____

Final total _____

To purchase by Visa/Mastercard/Switch simply call
08707 871724 or fax on **08707 871725**

To pay by cheque, send a copy of this form with a cheque made payable to
'HarperCollins Publishers' to: Mail Order Dept. (Ref: BOB4),
HarperCollins Publishers, Westerhill Road, Bishopbriggs, G64 2QT,
making sure to include your full name, postal address and phone number.

From time to time HarperCollins may wish to use your personal data
to send you details of other HarperCollins publications and offers.
If you wish to receive information on other HarperCollins publications
and offers please tick this box ☐

Do not send cash or currency. Prices correct at time of press.
Prices and availability are subject to change without notice.
Delivery overseas and to Ireland incurs a £2 per book postage and packing charge.